COME IN
F R O M T H E
COLD

Charlotte Milne

Published 2019 by Charlotte Milne Books
Copyright © Charlotte Milne 2019

The moral right of the author has been asserted.

This novel is a work of fiction. The names and characters are of
the author's imagination. Any resemblance to actual persons,
living or dead, is entirely coincidental. Any references to
historical events or real places are used fictitiously.

ISBN: 978-1-9162785-0-9
E-book ISBN: 978-1-9162785-1-6

Cover Design by Jane Dixon Smith of J D Smith Design
Map of Loch Ewe by Alex Gray of Wordworks Ltd, Gairloch

Printed and bound in Great Britain by Ingram Spark

charlotte@charlottemilne.com

To all who sailed
The Road to Russia

1941 – 1945

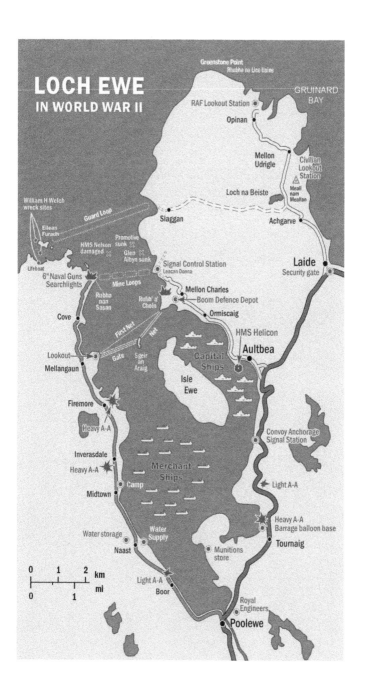

LOCH EWE
IN WORLD WAR II

Greenstone Point
Rhubha na Lice Uaine

GRUINARD BAY

RAF Lookout Station

Opinan

Mellon Udrigle

Civilian Lookout Station

Loch na Beiste

Meall nam Mealfan

William H Welch wreck sites

Eilean Furadh

Guard Loop

Promotive sunk

Slaggan

Achgarve

HMS Nelson damaged

Glen Albyn sunk

Signal Control Station
Leacan Donna

Laide
Security gate

Lifeboat

6" Naval Guns
Searchlights

Mine Loops

Rubha nan Sasan

Mellon Charles

Boom Defence Depot

Rubh' a' Choin

Ormiscaig

Cove

First Net

Net

HMS Helicon

Lookout

Gate

Sgeir an Araig

Capital Ships

Aultbea

Mellangaun

Isle Ewe

Firemore

Heavy A-A

Convoy Anchorage
Signal Station

Inverasdale

Heavy A-A

Merchant Ships

Camp

Midtown

Light A-A

Water storage

Water Supply

Heavy A-A
Barrage balloon base

Naast

Munitions store

Tournaig

Light A-A

Boor

Royal Engineers

Poolewe

0   1   2   km
0   1   mi

1

November 2011

At her age, Annie thought crossly as she hefted two suitcases into the spacious spare bedroom, she shouldn't be moving back in with her parents, however comfortable it was. Charlotte, her mother, closed the thick curtains, shutting out the vista of wet and leafless trees in Holland Park, and pulled the embroidered silk bedcover to one side. She leant up against the pillows in preparation for a session of mother/daughter bonding and Annie shifted an old leather suitcase to one side to make room for hers. This room was becoming more of a storeroom.

'Heavens, Mum! What on earth have you got in here? It weighs a ton!'

Charlotte made a face. 'I know. I must do something about it. It was my mother's and I never got round to it after she died because it was locked and I never found the key.' She sounded guilty, as if procrastinating were her personal sin.

'Well, why don't we burgle it and do it together? It's a foul day, you've done your practicing and I'm in decluttering mode.' Her recent departure from the marital mansion had brought on a tornado of disposal to charity shops, eBay and recycling centres, and a huge effort to keep herself busy and not think about her husband. Ex-husband.

Charlotte laughed. 'You're so good for me. I'd think about it and find some excuse not to, but it would be less depressing to do it together. How will we get into it?'

'A screwdriver would do the trick.' Annie peered at the case. 'No, we'll need a hammer too.'

'And a waste bin probably. I hope it's not full of un-washed clothes.'

When Annie had unpacked, Charlotte fetched the tools and they hammered the latches open. It was full to the brim with envelopes, loose letters, diaries, notebooks and a few photos. Charlotte heaved a sigh and picked out a notebook.

'Oh! My goodness! Her petty cash books. She wrote down every penny she spent and if the cash book didn't balance, she went into a tailspin thinking she was bank-rupt. Look, 1950, bread 4d, a pint of milk 3d. And six eggs 8d.' Charlotte dropped the notebook in the bin and picked up another. 'I wonder if they have a historical value?'

Annie shook her head firmly. 'I doubt it. Let's sort everything into separate heaps.' The chaotic contents gradually became orderly, if still unknown, piles. Picking up a crumpled folded sheet, Annie opened up a child's wax crayon scribble. Meandering blue lines, singed edges. There was a spidery adult scrawl in the corner. 'Peter Aug 15'.

A jolt passed through her—an electric frisson similar to the prickle induced by a creepy story.

'Mum? Take a look at this.'

Her mother put down the notebook she held and took the paper from Annie's hand. She became very still. 'Peter. It must be my brother. He died when he was three.' She seemed stupefied. 'How is it possible for this to have survived? The house was bombed!' Her voice was a whisper and Annie saw tears in her eyes. Her own eyes went blurry, something that occurred rather too frequently these days.

'I knew your brothers died in the war, but I didn't know what happened.'

Charlotte took a breath and folded her hands in her lap. 'I don't know what happened either. Mummy hated talking about the war, even before she got ill. They lived in Portsmouth and the house was bombed. The two boys,' she blinked, 'my brothers, were killed, along with my grandmother. I don't know how or why my mother survived. I think it was 1944, but I don't know the date—that paper says August 15, but was that the date of the bomb, or when she made the note?' She looked down at the scribbles again. 'Isn't that the most heart-rending thing you've ever seen? A little boy—two little boys. Before their lives had even begun.' She put a hand to her mouth. 'They were never quite real before.' She stared down, a thumb stroking over the faint waxy marks. 'How did she keep her sanity?' She paused. 'I'm not sure that she really did.'

The front door opened and closed with its habitual thunk, and Charlotte's sombre face lit up with the smile that Annie had always adored. Whenever Will appeared, Charlotte was happy.

'Hello, darling. We're in here.' She got up and met him with a hug and a kiss.

'Heavens—what are you doing?' he said, dropping a kiss on Annie's forehead as she lifted her head to him. 'Are you bringing us more clutter?'

'No—it's Granny's suitcase. We've broken into it. Look, Daddy.' She gave him the charred paper and pointed to the notation. 'We think it must have been Mum's brother Peter, and this somehow survived the bomb.'

Her father peered at it. 'She kept it all those years. I expect it was all she had. How very sad.' He looked at the various piles of paper. 'Have you been through the letters yet?'

'No. It's a bit daunting—but tantalising too,' Annie said. 'Perhaps we'll discover a bit more about what happened.'

Will glanced at Charlotte. 'It's probably time it was gone through. You've always put it off since she died.'

Charlotte sighed. 'I know. But it's difficult to head-hop from my concerts to Annie's… difficulties, to sorting out my mother's stuff.'

Familiar self-reproach rose in Annie's throat, like sickness. 'I'm sorry. This whole mess has been such a pain for you.'

Will shook his head and put the backs of his fingers against her cheekbone. The comfort of it made her want to cry.

Charlotte was brisker. 'You're the last person who needs to be sorry. But now the worst is over for you and you're out of that house and away from wretched Justin. Dealing with Mum's papers is a bit daunting as I don't feel I have either the time or the energy to do it, but it has given me an idea.' She looked at Annie hopefully. 'Perhaps you might think about doing the research I always wanted to do, but never had time for? I've always wanted to find out about my father, John Elliott, and why my mother was so reluctant to tell me about him. I think he was a teacher before the war—before the navy—and I've wondered what happened to him, and when and how and where he died. And the bomb that killed my brothers—it was in Portsmouth, I suppose, but I'm not sure.' She lifted her shoulders helplessly. 'I feel rather sad, not knowing anything, but I wouldn't know where to start, and these days everything happens online—'

Annie laughed. 'And online is not a place you want to be.'

Will grinned. 'My darling dinosaur. You can barely use a phone, and email is pretty tricky. You'd better leave the online bit to Annie.'

Over drinks, they discussed Will and Charlotte's forthcoming trip to South Africa, and Charlotte was at her most persuasive. 'Darling, do come with us. After this ghastly year, you really do need to unwind, put it all behind you—well, as much as you can anyway—and get some warmth into you. We'll have a wonderful Christmas together here, just the three of us—' She cast a glance at Will, standing with his back to the elegant false coal fire, who nodded in the indulgent agreement born of advance warning. '—and then we'll leave the cold and the wet, the dark and the dreary far behind us and go get us some gorgeous tans, and for God's sake, meet some nice men.'

She meant, of course, that Annie should meet some nice men. She, Charlotte, already had one. Annie glanced at the photograph on the mantelpiece behind Will's shoulder. Will and Becky and Charlotte, all together, all smiling, all young, all such close friends. How blessed Charlotte was to have Will, and how cursed she had been to have had Justin.

She still smarted from the judgements of Justin's family. As if anyone could believe that she was barren by design. But it was an old, old family with an old title, and so far, no eldest son had failed to marry and produce an heir, most of them with several spares. Justin wasn't going to break the tradition if he could possibly help it. Annie wanted, like a dog, to go and lick her wounds and wrap up her very public humiliation in private.

Annie hugged him. 'Darling Daddy—you are so generous. What a splendid idea to have your miserable daughter round your neck for your entire holiday, weeping into the cocktails.'

He returned the hug. 'Yes, come and dilute the drinks. You need a break. And if you can't bear a whole month with your parents, then come for some of it.'

Charlotte opened her mouth as if to extend the persuasion, but Will was firm. 'Leave it now, Char. Let's have dinner. I have a nice bottle of claret.'

Annie knew that her parents had discussed this invitation, and they both meant it, even though this yearly retreat to South Africa was almost the only opportunity they got to be together for any length of time. They both hopped all over the globe, Charlotte as a concert pianist, and Will in his capacity as advisor to various financial institutions. But this year the trip to South Africa was different. Necessary. Charlotte needed winter warmth and the little bottles—some of them quite large bottles—no longer kept the pain or the stiffness at bay. At first, it had been just health supplements, innocuous fish oils, herbal concoctions, but as time went on prescribed medicines made an appearance. Annie had noticed, even in the middle of her own misery, that Charlotte subconsciously rubbed and stroked her fingers to ease the joints, now becoming slightly thickened, and her practice sessions were sometimes laced with unladylike curses.

Arthritis wasn't a killer, but it could kill a career as a pianist. Charlotte had reminded Annie that her career as a pianist had lasted a long time already.

'I'm sixty-six, my darling. I've long since told my agents I want to start winding down, with less travel. I'm going to be doing far fewer concerts this coming year. I love the music, not the travel.' She eyed Annie's face and laughed. 'Don't look so unbelieving. It's true.'

Annie was uncertain about going to South Africa. The suggestion that she do some research about Charlotte's father had already begun to intrigue her. It seemed extraordinary that not only was John Elliott's background unknown, but his personality, his genetic influence, was unknown too. She looked at Will and thought how devastating it would be not to have known him, not to have experienced his intellect and humour and love for them both. In any case, for her to be interested in something other than her own troubles was a good antidote to self-pity and introverted guilt.

'How old was your father when he was killed, Mum?'

'Born 1911, died 1945. Um—' she never had been good at mental arithmetic.

'Thirty-four,' Annie said. 'So young. What a waste.' She twisted her wine glass so that the candlelight flickered through it. 'He was musical, too, wasn't he?'

'Oh, I wish I really knew. Mummy was always so negative and unforthcoming. He played the violin, but she never said whether he played seriously or well. I wished that we'd had his violin, and if it had been a good instrument then Becky could have played it when we performed together. It would have been rather a special connection, my best friend playing my father's violin with me on piano.' Her tone was light, and she smiled at Will, but Annie knew that the sadness of Becky's death was always there for them both. Annie thought of Becky's violin, snug in its case, in Charlotte's music room. Could a violin be sad not to be played?

'My guess is that he was musical,' Will said, 'because Elspeth certainly wasn't, and there has to be some genetic inheritance, I think.'

'I guess that's true,' Charlotte said. 'Towards the end, she often talked about John's violin, how it had never been returned to her with the rest of his personal belongings. She talked about his "betrayal".'

'Betrayal?' Annie queried.

'I always thought "betrayal" was an extraordinarily strong word. Why was she so resentful? He was a naval officer, with wartime postings. Did she perceive he'd abandoned her? Or did betrayal mean something else? Another woman? I can't believe he was a spy.' All three of them cogitated over the possibilities.

'Is that little case all you have of them?' How wretched that the remnants of two people's lives could be stuffed into one small case.

'There were bits of his uniform and some clothes sent back, but I think she disposed of virtually everything,' Charlotte said sadly. 'But she really did seem to mind about his violin. I wish I knew more about him.' Her left hand was doing arpeggios on the dining-room table. 'But there was no one to ask, except her. He had several siblings who all died young—I think an older brother was killed in the first war and another early in the last war. Your grandmother was an only child, and because both my brothers were killed, I was an only child too. And now you are—an only, I mean.' Annie knew that she regretted that her career had come before family life until it was too late to have children. She knew Charlotte was even sadder knowing that Annie wouldn't have a child at all. The family would come to an end with her. The familiar surge of misery threatened to engulf her again. As usual, Will knew what she was thinking and put a hand on hers.

'Don't,' he said, and she smiled a watery smile at him.

'Wouldn't have had it any other way, Mum,' Annie said. 'Otherwise I'd have had to share you and Dad.'

After they had all gone to bed, she listened to the rain pattering on the bedroom window and knew it wasn't true. She would have loved a sibling; she would have wanted to share Will and Charlotte. If only Justin had known how much she had wanted a child. How much she had wanted her parents to have a grandchild.

* * *

Putting away her Christmas shopping, Annie sat on the bed and contemplated Elspeth's brown leather case. The contents had been somewhat reduced by their initial explorations and roughly sorted into plastic bags. Curiosity, combined with a strong disinclination to deal with lawyers' letters, divorce procedures and somewhere to live, got the better of her and she cleared a table before opening the case.

A large manilla envelope with 'HMS *Helicon*' scrawled across it contained many smaller documents. She put them in date order where possible and began to read.

A three-line letter from the Admiralty to Lieutenant John Elliott informed him, with regret, that his house in Portsmouth had been hit and demolished by a V1 flying bomb on 15th August 1944 with the loss of his two sons and his wife's mother. He was granted two weeks leave to rehouse his wife and return to duty. She sat and reread it, over and over again. The dry official typing, faint and faulty letters, unadorned by any handwritten note of commiseration, initialled by an unknown clerical officer. How appalling, she thought. Even in wartime, surely that must rank as brutal thoughtlessness towards a serving officer? What can his reaction have been on reading that? And where and when did he read it? Her imagination boggled. She thought of the dates again: their two sons killed in August 1944 and John himself killed in January 1945. With a shudder she thought of Elspeth, losing her children and her mother and her husband within five months. No wonder she had been so reluctant to talk about the war. No wonder she had been a depressive for the rest of her life. Annie regretted that she had never really known Elspeth or understood her.

The other papers in the manilla envelope were official notes about postings, transport vouchers, and housing subsidies. There were ration books, and several letters from friends commiserating with Elspeth on the death of her mother and boys, and later, on John's death. Her lever arch file began to fill up with transparent document holders.

Sitting at her laptop, she searched HMS *Helicon* and found that it was not a ship, but a naval shore base on Loch Ewe in Scotland, departure point of the wartime Arctic convoys that delivered supplies to Russia. Could this have been John Elliott's naval posting? A sense of anticipation, excitement, tingled through her. She was going to do something for Charlotte instead of wallowing in her own gloom.

2

November 1941

'Please come.' He was pleading now, like a little boy. 'We can make it work. I can make it work. I'll find somewhere for you and the children. It will be much safer in the country than here.' He indicated the blackout curtains behind him, and more largely, the battered, bruised town of Portsmouth and its dockyards. 'I can't bear being away during these air raids and me not here to help you. And if you were on a farm or somewhere in the country, you'd get better rations, well, there'd be extra eggs and milk and butter which might come your way, and God knows, the boys could do with it.'

He knew these tactics would have far more effect on her than any need of his. He would keep that last urgent need until they were warm under the covers.

'But you won't be there.' She sounded desperate. 'I won't know where you are, and I wouldn't know anyone.' Elspeth had lived her whole life in Portsmouth and John knew that the thought of being anywhere else, even during the bombing, left her rudderless. Her huge eyes had dark circles under them from worry and weariness of the hungry wakefulness of a seven-month-old baby. Getting three-year-old Richard and a baby down three flights of stairs, across the garden and into the Anderson shelter as the air raid warnings shrieked must be a nightly horror, and she would never know, when the all-clear sounded, whether they would have a house to go back to. He now understood that Elspeth's gentle nature hid a life-threatening stubbornness and it infuriated him. She refused to leave her parents, and they both knew that her parents would not, could not, move. It was beyond her view of the possible.

'I don't know' was all she could say, her hands tugging at the neckline of her dress, and his thoughts jangled and reverberated with the discussions they had already had during his leave. She argued that she couldn't think of anyone she knew well outside Portsmouth, that she had no good friends, and no relatives of John's that she knew, much less liked.

'This war has already lasted longer than you said it would and now everything is worse than ever. Here at least I'm on home ground and can get clothes for the children from friends and neighbours. And Mother and Father's rations help a bit.'

John thought that his in-laws were the most selfish people he'd ever met and doubted that much of their rations were passed on. He guessed that Elspeth's breast milk was thin and too meagre to assuage little Peter's hunger.

And as if in answer to the thought, Peter started whimpering, and within seconds the whimper had changed to an all-out bawl.

John went to lift the screaming baby, the sharp ammonia smell of the sodden nappy flaring his nostrils, and in sudden irritation at Elspeth's indecision, put him unceremoniously in her lap. He had never quite understood her helplessness, but initially it had attracted him, being the strong male in counterpart to her adoring weakness. She had ridden on his optimism and encouragement without providing any herself. But his optimism for a speedy victory, for the greatness of the navy, for the new planes, for the troops—it seemed he had been wrong, and if he was wrong about all that, why should he be right about anything else? But now her stubborn indecisiveness threatened his innate kindness and consideration and made him angry. Surely the marriage vows were clear? You left and you cleft. Husband and children came before parents, and Elspeth's parents were, to his mind, particularly unlovable. Nevertheless, he could not bring himself to force her to obey. She had seemed so depressed after the birth of this child.

'Elspeth,' he said brusquely. 'You haven't long to make up your mind. I can't make arrangements without knowing whether you'll go or not, and I only have three days before I go back to Liverpool. And go I must. By tomorrow morning you must decide. No more discussion.'

She was weeping—long agonised breathless sobs. The baby seemed to sense her pain; he arched his back, rejecting the nipple, screaming in incoherent and uncomprehending misery. Unutterably weary, John looked at his wife and son, unable to speak or act to alleviate the distress. Unhooking his greatcoat from the peg at the door, he went out into the lightless streets, swept with gusts of sobbing wind and the heavy tears of rain.

3

December 2011

The hired car slithered in the wet snow, pushed and shoved across the potholed tarmac by the paws of the wind. It was not even five in the afternoon, but it could have been midnight, so deep was the northern darkness, crushed downwards by the gale and the low black clouds carrying the snow.

Annie's research on John Elliott had revealed his naval postings in the 1940s and she had used research as her excuse for coming here, although if she was honest with herself, it had as much to do with needing to keep her mind occupied; to keep it off Justin, keep it off her own shortcomings, keep it off school problems, keep it off the fact that here she was, aged thirty, sacked from her job, with a failed marriage behind her and no children. London had seemed as pointless and unattractive as South Africa. Loch Ewe in Wester Ross had at least the merit of isolation and the possibility of doing something special for her mother.

But now, lost in a snowstorm before she'd even arrived, she was afraid.

Her fear was made up of two components: the last two garages at Kinlochewe and Gairloch had both been closed. Not just closed: lightless, brooding. The little yellow petrol warning light had come on before Achnasheen, making her heart jump in her chest, and the digital countdown of miles left in the tank had gone to zero before Gairloch. All that remained thereafter was a red message. 'Refuel at the earliest opportunity'. She cursed the hire car company who had given her a half empty tank and herself for not checking.

Secondly, she was lost. Her phone had run out of battery at the airport, but surely a satnav should be essential for a hire car? Every time she consulted the small-scale map she had to stop, which was petrol being used but the car going nowhere. Now, as she slithered up this single-track road, the few houses she had passed had been dark and lightless too. Had she taken a wrong turning? Soon, if the car didn't run out of petrol first, she would hit the end of this road, where the north-western end of Loch Ewe met the sea. And nobody lived up here—why would they?—in this godforsaken maelstrom of wind and snow. She would die of cold when the fuel ran out and the car stopped and cooled, and to try to walk back—how many miles? Five, eight?—to the doubtful civilization of Poolewe in this weather, was unthinkable. No way.

'Shut up, Annie. Stop panicking. You've got thick sweaters and a warm coat. And the house must be here—somewhere.'

Talking aloud put half a lid on the panic. The little car pottered on gamely. Then up ahead she saw a track running down to the right, towards the sea—not that she could see the water, it was more of a sensation. Please, *please* let it be here. For the umpteenth time she slowed to look for a house name, and there it was, a battered wooden sign, the snow beginning to stick to it, but underneath an indistinct 'Mackenzie', a clear 'Inveruidh'. She gulped in relief and had to wipe her watering eyes as she made a cautious turn on to the snow-covered track.

The house was in a little hollow; whitish, the windows

blank, black and unwelcoming. The headlights pinpointed a wooden gate, standing ajar between the house and an outbuilding, and she guessed the house door would be through the gate. Putting on the interior light, she reached for her handbag and the house key which had arrived in the post. A quiver of unease swept through her as she looked at the passenger seat. A mess of maps, sweet wrappings and sandwich boxes, but no handbag. No bag on the floor or under the seat. She took a deep breath, opened the door and got out into a freezing wind and wet, sleety snow. No bag in the boot, no bag amongst the box of foodstuffs she had bought in Kinlochewe, nor tangled in her coat, nor on the floor in the rear. She got back into the driving seat, slamming the door, hugging the warmth. She searched the passenger seat again with no success.

How brilliant. What a splendid end to a splendid day. She put her head back against the headrest, then turned off the ignition and the lights while she tried to think. No point in having a flat battery as well as no petrol. Where on earth was her handbag? The last time she had used it was at Kinlochewe, to buy her stores. She remembered her phone was in her bag. Her wallet, cards. The correspondence about the cottage. More specifically, the key to the cottage. If her bag wasn't in the car, it must be at Kinlochewe, thirty miles behind her. The darkness outside was not just alien, it was terrifying and primitive. There was no darkness in London. She couldn't remember experiencing real darkness before.

The house would have to be broken into, as a conveniently open window seemed unlikely in this weather. The landline would work, broken windows could be mended, petrol could be sent, banks had emergency numbers. Annie suddenly laughed aloud. One day this adventure would make a good dinner party anecdote. She struggled into her coat, turned on the headlights again and embarked on breaking into a cottage on the edge of a world transforming from grey slush to white snow.

The headlights naturally did not reach around the corner. She fumbled her way to a door of thick solid wood. The huge iron doorknob had a crust of frozen snow on it and slipped in her cold fingers. No breaking in there. How about the windows. The cottage might look old, but the windows most certainly were not. They were modern and double-glazed. She needed a hard, strong implement and went searching in the wet snow for something suitable. Jammed under the gate was the perfect weapon: a stone rounded at one end which fitted her palm nicely, tapering to a flat point like a wedge, which was exactly what it had been used for, to prevent the gate swinging in the wind. It was as heavy as a bag of sugar and must surely be more than a match for a pane of glass. Triumphantly she returned to the window.

Her first attempt had no effect, except to jar her arm up to the shoulder. Desperation lent her strength, and this time there was a crushing noise and a small crazed area appeared at the point of impact. How could glass be so bloody strong? This was going to be one tough break-in, but break in she must.

The headlights turned themselves off and she was left in the dark, the wind roaring in her ears and the snow slapping wetly into her face. Switching the headlights on again, she returned to the window, but as she raised the stone for a third effort her wrist was caught in a crushing grip, and the stone fell to the ground behind her. Overbalancing on the slippery surface, she screamed as she fell backwards on to her bottom.

Shock and fright held her speechless. Her assailant seized an arm and jerked her painfully to her feet.

'What the hell do you think you're doing, you little thug?' Without waiting for an answer, she was whipped round to face the headlights and her hood was torn back. As her long hair blew sideways across her face a stunned male voice said, 'My God! A girl!'

There was what seemed like a long silence, except for the howling wind. Annie gasped with shock, quite unable to put into three words what might take half an hour to explain.

'What on earth are you doing, and why, and who are you?' He sounded utterly bewildered. Annie took a deep breath to try to steady herself, but her voice shook, the wind tearing it away to a thread.

'I'm so sorry. I really am. I didn't know you were here.'

'Obviously not. Do I need to call the police? Are you some kind of inept burglar?'

She shook her head frantically. 'No! No, of course I'm not. I lost the key, and I didn't know how to get in.'

'You lost the *key*? What were you doing with a key in the first place? What the hell is all this?'

Annie took another deep breath. 'I think I may have mistaken the house in the dark. I really am so sorry. I'll pay for the window. I thought it was my cottage—I rented for a month—but the snow—and I've no petrol, and I can't find the key—I must have made a mistake.' Cold and shock had her shaking like a jelly.

'I think you must have.' The irony was obvious. 'You'd better come in while we sort you out.' Putting a forceful hand on her shoulder, he propelled her through the gate and then through the solid wooden door by the simple expedient of turning the door handle. Clammily cold, she was temporarily blinded by a flood of bright light. They were in a boot room, lino on the floor, coat pegs on the walls, a pair of enormous wellingtons standing beside the outer door, which he slammed shut.

Well, it might all sound odd, but there's no need to be so chippy, she thought, recovering slightly from the shock of being manhandled.

'It's winter—why would you want to rent a house here now, for heaven's sake? And instead of breaking and entering through my expensive glazing, why not try the door—it's not locked.'

It would help to have an outside light in order to see a door. How was I to know you were here? Shock was beginning to give way to infuriation.

'I did. I couldn't turn the handle and I didn't expect it to be unlocked—she sent me a key. There were no lights.' She hesitated, bewildered. 'It was the right name, in the right place—I don't know, I mean, is there another house?'

'No, there is not.' He was looking as confused as she felt.

The whole scenario was beyond her comprehension. 'But I had emails—a letter. Confirmation. *The key*.' She saw his frown of disbelief.

'Let's see these emails and letters if the key has mysteriously disappeared. Then we'll try to sort out the fact that you're a hundred miles off course for a house with a similar name on the Black Isle or Mull.'

'I can't.' She was going to have to admit that she was an idiot. 'They're all in my handbag. Which I've lost.'

'Of course you have.' He rolled his eyes. 'Go through.' She preceded the ripped and faded jeans through a half-built kitchen into what might in better times be a sitting room but was now obscured by a vast dust sheet covered with machinery, a great deal of sawdust and wood in a myriad of shapes and sizes. This was not a cottage in a rentable state, but at least the room was warm.

She tripped on the edge of the dust sheet and a strong hand caught and steadied her and then dropped away. Picking up a notepad and pen, he sat at a table without inviting her to sit down. How rude was that? She took a closer look at him. Tall and heavy-boned, but with a sense of muscular fitness. His sweater had more holes than wool over a check shirt with a worn collar, but he didn't give the impression of the average workman. In his early forties perhaps, with crinkly lines round eyes which at this moment were not smiling.

'What's your name?'

'Anne. Devereux.'

'Devero?'

She saw him glance at her wedding ring as she spelt it. He seemed to have calmed down, but the fact that she couldn't provide any evidence of rental arrangements, nor was there anyone who could verify her story, didn't seem to make him less sceptical. The disbelief and lack of apology exasperated her and extinguished any remaining contrition about cracking his window. He had a solidity which would have been quite attractive in better circumstances. But it was a most unsatisfactory interview.

'You don't believe me,' she said, by now thoroughly annoyed, 'but how can I possibly be anyone other than who I say I am?' She wanted to add 'You stupid man' but just managed not to.

'Even if you are,' he said tartly, 'I have no information about you or about the house being let. Winter lettings just don't happen. I'm renovating during winter to rent in the summer, and frankly, it isn't habitable.'

'Well, I can see that.' She was equally tart. 'But as I need some sort of accommodation, perhaps you could suggest somewhere I could go—and even be so kind as to allow me to make a phone call, seeing as my mobile is in my handbag as well.'

The man had the cheek to be amused. 'No network here anyway. I'll ring the Poolewe Hotel. They don't normally take guests in winter, but maybe they'll make an exception.'

His description of 'a lady who made a silly mistake thinking it was tourist season in Scotland' was about the last straw in a very unpleasant and traumatic day. Patronising bastard. Waiting only until he confirmed they would give her a room, she turned on her heel and with a cold 'thank you' left him to his sawdust. It was only when she got back into the car that she remembered she had no petrol. Wonderful. Do I eat humble pie and crawl back to beg him to drive me the five miles, chatting away like the pathetic little idiot he thinks I am? Or do I put up an urgent prayer that the car will both start, and get me there? She decided she was not crawling anywhere.

* * *

He never expected to see compensation for his damaged window, or indeed to see the woman ever again. He returned to cutting and fitting the kitchen counter tops, having lost almost an hour of work, and when the landline rang he swore under his breath.

A hesitant west coast voice, a woman's, said, 'Would it be possible to speak to a lady Deverex? Is she there, I am wondering?'

'No. Nobody of that name is here.' It took a moment to penetrate. 'Not at present. May I ask why?'

There was a moment's hesitation. 'Well, you see, I'm at the stores in Kinlochewe and at closing I found a lady's handbag on the potatoes by the till.' He closed his eyes briefly and pulled a chair under him. 'And I've had to look inside to find out whose it is, do you see?'

'I do,' he said resignedly.

'Well, a lady is lost without her handbag, is she not? But she's never come back to get it, see, and I'm closing up now, so I am, in this weather and all, and there was only one stranger, do you see? So I'm afraid I've had to be very, very nosy, do you see? And there's an envelope and a key and papers with this number on it and today's date, so I wondered, do you see, that she might have gone there?'

He did see. 'I know the lady,' he said, 'and yes, she's lost

21

her handbag.' At the back of his mind he was concocting a minor apology. 'Could you read out to me the details on the paper?'

'Do you think I should do that?'

He took a heroic pull at his memory bank. 'It's Mrs Graham, is it not, at Kinlochewe? This is David Mackenzie, of Mackenzie and Sons at Poolewe. I think it would help the lady get her bag back if I had the details on the paper—it's a booking form, is it?'

There was an audible sigh of relief down the line. 'Oh! Mr Mackenzie! Is it you then? Oh, well, it will be all right then.' He was relieved that the family still had a decent reputation. 'Let me see now—the lady was worried, you see, she had not enough petrol in the tank, she said, and Donald had closed up the station yesterday—the weather, and the holiday you see—' He could hear the crackling of paper. 'The dates are for 27th December to 24th January and the signature is "Kate".'

The minor apology was becoming more major. He breathed in through his nose, made arrangements to have the bag collected and then rang the Poolewe Hotel.

The lady had not arrived. The lady should have arrived some time ago. The lady had slithered off the road into the loch and drowned. The lady really had run out of petrol and was now freezing to death somewhere on the road to Poolewe. Remorse seized him.

Contemplating the non-existent kitchen and the chaos in the sitting room, he conceded he wasn't going to be working on it any more tonight. He went out to the shed to start the car and realised that the cottage did indeed look lifeless and dark—the interior shutters, plus the curtains, prevented any chink of light from showing.

He closed up and locked the house, kicked the stone back under the gate and reversed the by-now warm car out of the shed. Secretary Kate should be sacked for having made such a monumental cock-up, but it would have to wait as she was on her honeymoon.

Two miles down the road he found the locked car, but no sign of the lady. With the light from his torch, he could see her belongings were still in it. Faint footprints in the snow led more or less down the middle of the road towards Poolewe, and after a mile or so became less faint, and then they stopped because Mrs Devereux was standing firmly in the centre of the road, as determined as the angel before the Garden of Eden, waving him down.

He stopped in front of her, the headlights throwing her shadow far down the road, leant across and opened the passenger door.

4

March 1942

Mhairi saw him first from Aultbea post office window. He moved like an old man, but then all the seamen came back looking like old men. She noticed him because as well as his kit bag he was carrying an old, scuffed violin case. It was cold March, but for once it was a day to rejoice in, blue sea, blue sky, with high, thin cloud, rippled like the sand on the beach.

Later, when they stood in line for their mail, he handed her his ID. He was slightly bent at the waist. She smiled at him and remarked, 'That fiddle will cheer us all up, I'm hoping, Mr Elliott.'

'I hope so too, ma'am. But we'll eat and sleep before dancing, I think.'

She liked his voice, cultured and calm, though very soft. He was good-looking under the stubbly beard, although he looked grey and ill. You would, after nearly five weeks of convoy hell. Taking the mail she handed him from the E-F pigeonhole, he glanced at the envelopes and put them in his pocket before smiling at her and going out. A little rush of anticipation caught at her chest as she thought of the opportunity she had just engineered.

Mrs Reid was sharp-tongued and sharp-eyed. 'Mhairi. Stop dreaming and get on.'

Mhairi liked working at the post office. There were plenty of girls who would jump at the chance of it and there was a sense of purpose, a sense that this little post office and shop was necessary and important. That Aultbea village was important. Glamorous it was not.

She turned back to her job of sorting telegrams, but watched the officer with the violin case out of the corner of her eye. Trailing in the wake of the others towards the naval base captain's office in a chilly Nissen hut, he looked unsteady and she saw him put out a hand to a pile of boxes to balance himself.

'That Mr Elliott looks unwell, Mrs Reid. Do you think we should see if he's all right? He almost fell then.'

'No.' Mrs Reid was firm. 'You've got a job to do, and the navy will look after him. There's more telegrams come in, so you get on with them and the cables.'

These days Aultbea rang to the echoes of ships' tannoys and the rattle of anchor chains interspersed with air raid sirens and the vibrations from the heavy AA guns around the loch. Small boats moved in restless traffic between ships and shore, and amidst the concrete gun emplacements and the detritus of the naval base, it was the low, white village houses that looked incongruous, as if they'd been dropped there quite by mistake.

Mhairi saw her friend Rhionna come down the road carrying a bag. She poked her head in the door and hissed at Mhairi.

'Are you staying tonight, or do you want a cabbage to take home?'

'I'm going home, and a cabbage would be dandy.' She could feel Mrs Reid's frosty eye and avoided it. Taking the bag, she winked and blew a kiss to Rhionna.

A whole cabbage! She thought of the starving Russians and the motley ships massed in Loch Ewe. The ships were huge storage vaults that carried the inconceivably vast tonnage of armaments, aircraft and food for the Russians. It made you count your blessings to have a whole cabbage when there were some in Russia who, it was said, were at present eating rats if they were lucky. Whenever she was hungry, which as a healthy nineteen-year-old was often, she would think of those Russians who counted a dead rat as a blessing. She thought of her father in his prisoner-of-war camp and wondered whether he was starving too.

When the post office closed Mhairi slipped the letter she had kept back into her pocket and walked along the road towards the officers' mess. There was considerable noise from inside and she banged hard on the door to make herself heard.

A young officer grinned with pleasure at the sight of her, and at her request went away in search of John Elliott. After some minutes, he came to the door, bent over and holding his side.

He looked awful, grey-faced and sweating. 'Mr Elliott, whatever is the matter? Have you been wounded?'

'No. It's just a pain in the stomach. You were in the post office, weren't you?' His voice was even quieter than before as if it hurt to speak.

'There's another letter for you. It got overlooked this afternoon,' she said untruthfully as she handed it over. 'Have the medics seen you? You look really done in.'

He shook his head. 'Thanks for bringing it. Beyond the call of duty, isn't it?' He turned away and she watched him limp away with concern.

Mhairi knew virtually everyone in Aultbea and on the base, and she went in search of Ben Bradley, one of the senior Naval Sick Berth Attendants. She had to hunt for him amongst the metalled tracks, dumps of chain, and empty stores boxes, at last finding him bandaging the foot of a young soldier who had dropped an ammunition box on it.

Returning to the officers' mess with him, she was relieved to see John Elliott escorted out after some minutes to be taken to the hospital in Gairloch, rather than the sick bay. Ben put her bicycle in the back of the old ambulance, alongside the young officer who had curled up on the mattress and was now groaning quietly at intervals. Mhairi climbed in beside Ben.

'What's wrong with him, Ben?'

'Dunno, but something is. His belly is like a rock and he's got a high fever. Infection, gall bladder, appendix, poisoning—could be anything for all I know. The hospital will sort him.' He glanced across at her. 'Angel of mercy today, aren't we? Do you want to come into Gairloch? I can put your bike down at the Poolewe Hotel and you can get a lift back on a Tillie if I can't bring you back. Don't know how you do that ride from Inverasdale and back every day. It must be more than ten miles each way.'

She grinned at him. 'Well, to tell you the truth, I almost always get a lift at least part of the way. That bike gets carried as much as the wheels turn. And no, I'll not come on to Gairloch, thank you, because I know those fancy military nurses won't let me anywhere near him. If you'll put me down at Poolewe, you'll have saved me half my journey.'

He shrugged regretfully.

'Not going out with Archie tonight?' he asked, his voice deceptively light.

'Not tonight. He's busy. Tomorrow we're going to the film and on Friday there's a dance at the NAAFI.'

'Can I book a dance on Friday or will Archie be jealous?' He said it jokingly, but she heard the irritation and smiled sideways at him. 'No booking necessary.' She didn't bother to deny Archie's jealousy.

As the ambulance rattled up the hill, she looked down on the currently calm but filthy waters of Loch Ewe. The hundreds of ships and trawlers, tugs and barges, launches and cranes blackened the water, hull on hull, held and swinging in perfect unison as the tides rose and fell, the continual dance of arms, men, and supplies to the merchant vessels and the naval warships.

'That convoy must be leaving soon, surely?' she said. 'There isn't room for another ship on the water.'

Ben grunted. 'You'd think so. Poor bastards.' He indicated the back of the ambulance. 'They leave young and come back old.' He crunched into third gear. 'If they come back.'

He lifted out the bicycle at Poolewe and shut the door quickly so that his moaning passenger would not be exposed to the bitter wind. As she wrapped her coat round her Ben said quietly, 'Archie's a bad one, Mhairi. Be careful, girl,' before climbing back into the cab and roaring off. The tail-lights disappeared round the bend and she shivered in the deepening twilight before mounting her bike for the last five miles. Rhionna's father, Mr MacRae, had also warned her about consorting with Archie. She wondered if the kirk elders had put him up to it.

As she bicycled home, she found herself thinking of the groaning Mr Elliott and that shabby violin case. Not much opportunity for jolly *ceilidhs* on board a ship dodging U-boats and torpedo bombers on the road to Russia. He had a nice smile. Undoubtedly nicer and kinder than Archie Mackinnon's. But he had letters—several—from a woman today. She didn't know how she knew they were from a woman, she just did. And he was older, in his thirties she guessed—though as Ben had said, men returning from the convoys always looked older than when they'd left—and those letters were, in all likelihood, from his wife. So what was the point of Mhairi Mackenzie, nineteen years old, who had never been further afield than Achnasheen, dreaming of a kind, good-looking man with a nice smile, with his educated voice and eyes that had seen far too much? What was the point of scheming to get to know him by withholding a letter? She might dream and scheme, but he was not for the likes of her. Ben Bradley had said Archie was a bad one, but with his hard eyes and cold smile, his money and his aura of danger, Archie was a bit of a thrill, there was no denying it. Although he made her nervous with his gifts of nylons and lipsticks, fabric and food, and the bottles of whisky and rum, it made life much more interesting to be known as the girlfriend of Archie Mackinnon.

5

December 2011

'Betrayal,' Elspeth had said to Charlotte. It was an oddly personal word, Annie thought as she logged on to the surprisingly decent Wi-Fi at the Poolewe Hotel. Had Elspeth felt that somehow he could have avoided dying on her? Had he left her for another woman? Difficult, if he was on the convoys. Perhaps it wasn't personal but had something to do with the war. Treason? There wasn't much point in thinking that he couldn't possibly have been a closet Nazi sympathiser. Some people had been. Could he have had knowledge of naval missions which he passed on via secret radio to German U-boat commanders? Fanciful; unlikely. But possible.

She googled 'British Navy, Treason. 2nd World War', followed various links, and found nothing. She tried to think of what to search for next, but her thoughts kept drifting back over the last eventful twenty-four hours.

David Mackenzie—he had introduced himself in his car the previous night—had bought her some necessary alcohol after collecting her luggage from the car and installing her at the Poolewe Hotel. Just as well he'd had a crisis of conscience, otherwise she might have been lying in a ditch, frozen to death. He had apologised, rather half-heartedly, but with a faintly redeeming grin, and obviously thought she was an idiot to have left her handbag in Kinlochewe, to have run out of petrol and to have tried breaking through a double-glazed window.

This morning he had appeared while she was having breakfast.

'Your adventures have given you an appetite,' he said, eyeing her plate of full Scottish with amusement. 'I've brought a can of petrol so that we can retrieve your car and my sister Louise will collect your handbag from Kinlochewe on her way here from Inverness this evening.' She noted the 'we' and felt strangely safeguarded. She had had a different reaction when Justin arranged things without reference to her.

He ordered himself a coffee and sat down at her table without asking. He moved confidently, at ease in his big work-boots and shabby jeans.

'I'm sorry about yesterday. This morning I checked the rental book and there you were. We'll reimburse your advance payment on the cottage.'

'Thank you.' At least he was man enough to apologise. 'Your secretary didn't mention anything about renovations.'

He shrugged a little, strong shoulders lifting his sweater. 'She didn't know. She got married just before Christmas and I guess had too many things on her mind to remember to tell me about your booking.' He smiled faintly. 'If I complain about that, she'll give me a thick ear for not telling her I was going to do the kitchen.'

Annie laughed. 'Well, it's a relief the fiasco was not entirely of my own making. What is Kate the secretary of? Is your business in property?'

'No, we're an engineering firm, with various specialities. From marine engineering to building. We can fix most things.' He poured himself a coffee. 'Kate is hideously efficient and makes us keep appointments and demands money from customers and files everything.'

But he admired her, she thought. Perhaps he had fancied Kate before she married someone else. That might account for the faint aura of grumpiness about him. He looked weary in a melancholy sort of way. For a man she guessed was only in his mid-thirties it seemed a little odd.

Later in the morning she walked up the River Ewe to Loch Maree, in the occasional light drift of snow. When the thin sun disappeared behind overcasting clouds, she returned to the warmth of the hotel and her research.

Just after six, David's sister Louise arrived. Annie was so pleased to see her handbag again, she almost kissed her, a total stranger.

Louise was accompanied by a younger brother, Patrick, less solid and an open flirt. They all had a drink at the bar and Patrick noticed she wore a wedding ring and asked where her husband was, straight out. Much less tactful than brother David, who had also noticed but had not asked.

'Away,' Annie said, in the tone of voice she used to squash sassy teenagers at school. Irritatingly, he recovered form like a foam sponge.

'Away on business, or away for good?'

She gave him a charming but cold smile. 'On business, but not yours.' That ought to freeze him out, impertinent puppy.

His mouth quirked in acknowledgement and Louise glanced at her uncomfortably.

After they had left, Annie had a dinner of steak, cooked to *saignant* perfection, and half a bottle of red wine. A good way to end a better day. There was a leaflet on her table advertising a New Year *ceilidh* in the village hall and Annie considered whether to go or not. Mrs Mackenzie (another Mackenzie) who ran the hotel with her husband, (another Mr Mackenzie), assured her she would not have to dance or recite poetry if she didn't want to, but she would have fun and good music. Talking of music, Annie asked, rather shyly, if Mrs Mackenzie would mind if she played the piano in the lounge as there were no other residents beside herself. Would it disturb the drinkers in the bar? Mrs Mackenzie didn't mind and didn't think the drinkers would mind either.

She had hardly thought of Justin, or of buying a flat, or of unborn children or of being unemployed and, she supposed, unemployable, but she pondered on the word 'betrayal' once more. Had she betrayed Justin by not conceiving? Had Justin betrayed her by casting her off? Quite unbidden, David, that big, attractive, grumpy man with a smile that crinkled up his sad eyes, came briefly to mind, and then she slept dreamless, full of red wine, Christmas carols and cold air.

6

March 1942

He woke up slowly. Vaguely astonished in a soft, uncaring sort of way. A hospital ward. QA nurses in their crisp white headgear and red capes. John didn't remember being wounded. He didn't remember anything.

Later he woke up again. The nurses were still there, and he remembered something: a pretty black-haired girl telling him that his violin would cheer them all up. All who? He'd been shot in the stomach. One of the nurses made him swallow some liquid.

Later again, a doctor. No, not wounded, he said. A burst appendix on arrival at Aultbea. Not a good idea, and just as nasty as being shot. John had to agree.

Later—several weeks later—after convalescence at the Loch Maree Hotel, he hobbled into the Aultbea post office to collect his mail, and there was the black-haired girl again, trim as a grass blade.

'Well, Mr Elliott,' she remarked with a wide smile. 'It's good to see you on your feet. You gave us all quite a turn, to be sure. We don't have many burst appendixes.'

He was mystified. 'How did you know?'

She laughed. A crisp, fresh sound. 'I dropped in a couple of times to the hospital, but you were sleeping like a baby and I left you to it. You almost pegged it and they weren't taking any bets, I can tell you.' She handed him his letters.

He grinned weakly. 'I'm tougher than you think. I've got to report to the base, but I can't go back to my ship as I'm on sick leave for another two weeks. The officers' mess is pretty full and pretty horrible, so I'd like to find a billet locally. I wondered if I could put a card on your board?'

She looked at him appraisingly. 'I agree I can't see you climbing in and out of boats, or up and down ladders just yet, so I don't think you'd be much use on your ship. Write your card and we'll put it on the board.' Her eyes were laughing, but he resisted the inclination to laugh, too, and confined himself to another weak grin.

'It's rather an unromantic complaint. I wonder if they'll give me leave to see my family.'

'I doubt it, Mr Elliott. Where are they?'

'Portsmouth,' he said with a grimace.

She shook her head, her expression revealing her thoughts. What a place to leave your family, with the Germans dropping bombs daily.

'I doubt it, Mr Elliott. Health, time, distance, transport.' She handed him a card and a pen and pinned it on the board when he'd written it. 'Come back at the end of the day and see if there's a billet available.'

On his return, she said, 'A billet has been allocated and you get a transport allocation, too, Mr Elliott. Very helpful.'

'I'm not allowed to drive yet.' He was anxious. 'Is it far?'

'Not a problem, Mr Elliott. You have a driver.' A driver? For a humble lieutenant? He was puzzled by Mhairi's grin and on leaving the post office with her was surprised by the information that he was billeted in her croft at Inverasdale and that she was the driver.

'How did you manage that?' he asked, nervous and animated at the same time. Mhairi was so unlike his wife and the shy girls of his acquaintance, and her neat, smart persona, in the scrabbling mess of Aultbea, was enough to fill him with a frisson of adventure. She had taken the wheel of a rattly car provided by the base transport office.

'I waited till Mrs Reid wasn't looking, took the card down and gave you a billet in my croft.'

He loved it instantly, from the warmth of the kitchen range to the immaculate privy down the garden, ventilated by a myriad of knotholes which blew the newspaper squares into merry fluttering. Standing at the kitchen window he looked far out across the loch towards Aultbea, drifting into grey anonymity under blackout regulations.

'It's lovely, Miss Mackenzie. So peaceful.'

'We'll not get far with Miss Mackenzie and Mr Elliott, will we now? I'm thinking we'll start off as Mhairi and John.'

Her name was strange to him, and needing to sit down, he turned to the table, plain rough wood, but polished by years of hard use. 'Varri is an unusual name. Does it mean something in Gaelic?'

She looked round from peeling potatoes and smiled. 'Oh, all sorts. It would be Mary in English, and the spelling is MHAIRI. It means mountain wind, or north star of the sea, whatever you choose.'

He smiled too. 'I'll choose north star of the sea, seeing as I'm a navy man and will be sailing north.'

'But not yet,' she said, looking over what he knew was a thin and rather frail shadow of his normal self. 'You'll be sleeping and eating and not much else for a while yet. Sleep is the great healer and there will be no disturbance here while I'm away at the post office.'

She sounded firm, if not bossy, and he thought that sleep would be the most desirable thing in the world, although he felt awkward about their sleeping arrangements.

'I feel bad taking your bed and you having to climb up to the rafters to sleep.' He thought of the narrow-runged ladder set diagonally up the wall of the bedroom.

She laughed, her black hair swinging across the pale translucent skin of her cheek. 'Don't feel bad. I've slept there most of my life, and it's my cosy wee space. My father floored over the beams and I'm queen of all the house up there.' The potatoes began to ring in the pan, and the smell of her stew seeped into the air. 'I came down to the box bed when father left for war, and I'll be back up the ladder when he comes home. If he comes home.' She came and sat opposite him, tucking a black strand behind her ear. 'Your ship is the *Countess of Minto*. Is that a navy ship?'

He shook his head. 'No such luck. She's an anti-submarine trawler. And very uncomfortable.'

'Are you the captain?'

'No, thank God. I'm a gunner and in charge of the ASDIC.'

She tilted her head. 'ASDIC?'

'Anti-submarine detection. Sonar.' He smiled. 'A somewhat inexact science.'

Her interest warmed him, the dark eyes intent. 'And are you a navy man when there's no war to go to?'

Going to war. He hadn't thought of it that way. 'No, I was a teacher at a boys' school in England.'

Her eyebrows rose. 'Are girls not worth educating then?' There was the faintest disapproval in the challenge, and he grinned apologetically.

'Often boys and girls are educated separately in England. Otherwise the boys would become too despondent when the girls outshine them.' She gave him a glancing sideways look, black eyes glinting, enjoying the fact they had both been teasing.

'And what do you teach them? Fiddle playing?'

'Music, yes. And everything else. English, arithmetic, science, French, cricket, swimming.' He remembered the pleasure of those sunny summers on a cricket pitch now trenched with cabbages, potatoes and turnips.

She was watching his face, eyes solemn. 'You liked being a teacher, didn't you?'

He put his elbows on the rough table, fingers laced under his chin. 'I loved it. They are like thirsty plants, soaking up knowledge.'

'Only if you know how to give the knowledge to them,' she said. 'Sphagnum moss absorbs more than twenty times its dry weight in water, but if you give knowledge the wrong way, it runs off, like water droplets on moss. Will you go back to teaching after the war?'

'Oh yes.' He was firm. And in the silence. 'If I survive.'

He blinked away the thought. 'Are you not lonely living out here with your father away?'

She shook her head. 'I don't always come back here. On bad nights I stay with my friend Rhionna in Aultbea. But no, I don't find it lonely. I have the sheep and cows and the gulls, and the peewits and oyster catchers and otters and the mice. I like the silence and the house wraps its arms around me, and it still smells a bit of my father's tobacco.' She got up to drain the potatoes, and John saw she poured the water into a broth pot at the back of the range. No wastage here.

'While I'm here, I'd like to help if I can. Perhaps not too much carrying peats quite yet. Will you tell me what I can do?'

She turned to smile at him, swinging from the waist. 'That's kind thinking, and yes, I'll keep you occupied, even if it's just sleeping at first. There are tatties to peel, and knives to sharpen, pots to polish, and songs to be sung.'

She put dishes of stew and potatoes and another of a brown shiny vegetable on the table.

'What's that?' He was curious.

'I'll tell you after our tea.' She was laughing, and the laugh was truly infectious. He put a hand to his stomach to prevent his own laugh getting out. He really liked Mhairi Mackenzie.

Kelp! he thought later, as he lay in the warm curtain-enclosed alcove, sleep ensnaring his mind. I'd never have thought I'd eat seaweed and quite like it. Or was it because Mhairi had gathered it, cooked it with her herbs and put it on the table? Maybe kelp would not be quite so acceptable from other hands.

7

29th December 2011

David laid his hand flat on the kitchen door, preparing himself to be cheerful. Normal. The previous night, unloading Louise's Mercedes, full of New Year treats for their mother Fiona, and assorted musical instruments and luggage, David knew from his sister's tight embrace how aware she was of his continuing loneliness. He wasn't normal. They were gathering as a family, but the missing members, Christopher, Seamus, and above all, Shona, shouted their absence. In the middle of his warm and loving clan, there was aching isolation. Into his mind came another lonely figure, Annie Devereux. In spite of her feistiness he sensed she had a pain and lostness too. He had nearly gone to meet his siblings at the hotel in order to see her again and was angry at himself for even thinking of it. Taking a deeper breath, he pushed the kitchen door open and found his mother turning a vast tin of roast potatoes. His father, Jem, was clearing the table of the day's accumulations.

'Inveruidh is more or less finished,' David said, knowing that his father would be relieved. 'Just the clearing up and the painting to do.' He started to lay the big table. 'How many are we? Ten?'

'Eleven.' Fiona put her hands on her ample hips and

stretched her back. 'Your grandmother says she wants to go and see what's happening up at the cottage.'

Jem looked alarmed. 'Don't you let her—not till it's finished. She'll throw a complete tantrum. And that new window has to go in yet.'

'Why do you need a new window?' Fiona said, puzzled, as Patrick joined them in the kitchen.

'The lady burglar put a stone through it. That'll take a day's work. And cost a pretty penny.' Jem snorted in annoyance.

Fiona looked up in amazement and threw a questioning glance at David. 'You never told me that. She put a *stone* through it? My, she must have a strong arm. Desperate, she must have been! I saw Jan today. It seems she asked to play the piano and it was so nice that Jan opened the lounge door a crack and all the lads in the bar began singing Christmas carols. Not very Highland, that.' She closed the oven door on the tin of potatoes. 'Go get your grandmother, David. I'm ready for the moment.'

He went through to the annexe, relishing the few moments of silence. His grandmother didn't break it as he walked her back to the main house, her grip strong and bony on his arm. There was never any need for dissimulation with Mhairi.

Jem said, 'Hello, Mother. Are you in a better temper with the boy?' David handed her a glass of whisky.

'Not yet. I want to see what he's messing with.' She eyed David with mock disapproval, and he looked back in mock terror.

'But there's an awful mess, and no kitchen, and no bathroom either—and a would-be burglar has broken a window, so there's a hole in the wall. And no heating, and no electricity.'

'I may be ninety, but I'm not a fool, David. You can't work without electricity.' Mhairi glared at him with the adoration of a doting grandmother. 'What burglar and what window? Have they stolen anything?'

'No. All is safe and well. I'll tell you the story over dinner. And you're not ninety for three weeks yet, Granny, and I'm not going to risk you having a heart attack before the due date.' He took his own whisky from his father as the big sitting room filled up with his brothers Mark and Hugh, Hugh's wife Catherine and their two little girls. Everyone greeted everyone else and kissed Mhairi and the girls disappeared upstairs on some prearranged ploy.

'Where's Edward?' Mhairi demanded. Her fourth grandson had a Derby-based haulage company.

'He can't come. It's a long way and there are always problems with drivers at New Year. He's going to come for your birthday.' David knew she had been told this before, but thought she chose to forget things she didn't want to remember.

'Are there not enough of us, then, that you're missing Eddie?' said Mark laughing.

'Six of you, there are, and just two of you married.' Everyone else remembered that Shona was dead even if Mhairi chose not to, and the sweep of anger and loss churned in his chest. 'Jean Macleod has only three children,' Mhairi went on, 'and they've given her nine grandchildren and eighteen great-grandchildren.' She sounded cross. 'I wish the rest of you would get on with it, else I'll have to be here at a hundred. Which I don't wish to be.'

'Well, Granny,' said Mark, 'we'll do our best, but there are not many girls that come up to your exacting standards, and we can't marry without your approval, now can we?'

'And Jean Macleod is ninety-eight, and has lost her marbles,' Patrick added irreverently. 'Which would you rather, four with your marbles, or eighteen without them?'

A reluctant smile crossed her face. 'Marbles are important,' she admitted.

Over dinner, the conversation returned to the burglar.

'She's not Mrs Devereux, she's The Lady Anne J Devereux,' Patrick announced.

'Really? How do you know that?' Fiona asked, pushing mustard and horseradish up the table.

'He went through her handbag,' Louise said disapprovingly. 'Is that a surprise?' There was a chorus of reproach which Patrick cheerfully ignored. David frowned, remembering Mrs Graham's, 'Is there a lady Deverex there?' He had mistaken her meaning.

'It was all over the place, credit cards, driving licence, and she's rented Inveruidh for a month. In January!' Patrick rolled his eyes. 'She must be off her head. According to her driving licence she's thirty. The Lady Devereux was expecting a nice cosy cottage, and David has torn its innards out. What are you going to do about that? Put her up at the hotel for a month?'

'It's got new innards now,' David said. 'It just needs cleaning up. The painting can wait and Mrs—Lady—Devereux can do what she likes.' That sounded petulant. 'I mean, she can choose to stay in the hotel if she wants or go to Inveruidh.' He wondered why that tall, striking girl, somehow confident in a worldly way, but hesitant in personality, should be here at all.

Patrick voiced David's question. 'She's got a wedding ring. I asked where the husband was, and she said, 'Away' in a none-of-your-business sort of voice. Funny place to come in the middle of winter, but she wouldn't say why.'

The conversation about Annie and the cottage went on, but he didn't really hear it as he absently turned his own wedding ring. Shona had been buried with hers, loose on a finger that was just skin-covered bone. He became aware of his grandmother's direct, thoughtful gaze and tried to pull himself back to the present, feeling the familiar restlessness pour through him. He wanted to get up from the table, to distance himself from the family, but he made himself sit there with them. Made himself listen and take part. Christopher and Seamus were in Edinburgh for a week with Shona's parents, but he wished they were here now, with their inconsequential chatter, allowing him to be silent.

As they ate his mother's delicious dinner, he reflected that Shona had been a natural cook, too, experimenting with herbs and spices, able to rustle up appetizing meals from whatever she might have had in the fridge. She should be here, he thought, baking her delectable cakes, letting the boys explore textures and flavours as they added chilli powder to chocolate butter icing, and tried to add frog spawn to the soup. Even Shona had drawn the line there. The sadness metamorphosed into anger. She should be here, not lying in an icy graveyard in Edinburgh.

He thought of her just over a year ago, implacably dying, getting smaller by the day, and he and the boys helplessly watching it happen.

The stem of his wineglass cracked in his fingers.

8

31st December 2011

'So, what are you doing in Poolewe in mid-winter?' David asked. 'It's a curious destination.'

They were sitting between band numbers at a village hall table. The paper tablecloths were printed with holly and red bows and little plastic dishes filled with holly and escallonia sat in the middle of each table.

Annie had almost chickened out of the New Year *ceilidh*, knowing no one, and still shy and uncomfortable as a single after eight years of marriage. She had a terror of alcohol-fuelled men trying to kiss her, and of New Year jollity she was not feeling, but in the end she had allowed Mrs Mackenzie to persuade her. She drank the cheap white wine for Dutch courage and reminded herself that she could always go back after half an hour. However, between numbers, David Mackenzie had put down his accordion and taken the trouble to leave the stage to talk to her. It had made her feel much more at ease. Like the rest of the musicians, he was wearing a kilt and his solid body looked entirely at home in it. Patrick and Louise played drums and piano respectively.

'I want to do some research on my mother's father who died on one of the Arctic convoys.' She didn't feel it necessary to tell him about any of her personal demons. 'I haven't discovered much yet, as the last thing I want is to run out of petrol again.'

'We can solve the petrol—there's a pump down at the yard.' The band was beginning to reassemble. The singer, a pretty, petite girl with short, dark hair and the voice of an angel, glanced towards them. David had his back to the stage, but Annie clearly saw the girl's combative, hostile stare directed at her. A jealous lover? In former times she would have been entertained by such obvious and unnecessary resentment, but now she didn't find it amusing. She chided herself for being over-sensitive.

'What do you know about your grandfather?' David said. 'Was he an officer or a sailor?'

'He was a lieutenant in the RNVR,' she said, noticing the fiddle player glancing their way. 'My mother doesn't know much about him, nor about his naval history and she really would like to discover what he did and what happened to him. He was killed before she was born in 1945 and I want to help her find out about him.' The glance had become an impatient summons. 'I think you are needed!'

He looked up to the stage with a grin and drained his glass. 'That's my father.' The band was quite a family affair, she thought, intrigued. 'So he was based at Loch Ewe during the war?'

'I think so. Part of the time anyway. That's what I've come here to find out.'

'And you, Lady Devereux? What's your job that you can take a whole month off to do research?' His smile robbed the question of any offence, but she looked at him sharply. At no point had she been anything other than Anne Devereux.

'How do you know that?'

His mouth twisted apologetically. 'I'm sorry. I'm afraid Patrick looked in your handbag.'

'He shouldn't have done that.' Anger burned in her

46

chest. It was a violation—as if someone had entered her house uninvited. They had discussed her, just as London had discussed her.

He nodded in agreement. 'He should not have. And I apologise for him.'

She felt cool and sounded it. 'Perhaps he should apologise to me himself.'

'Indeed he should.' He rose, looking uncomfortable, before rejoining the musicians on the stage.

She sat sipping her glass of wine. It was one thing for the shopkeeper at Kinlochewe to have looked in her bag in order to return it, but it was quite another for a strange man to do so, quite unnecessarily. She relaxed her hands from the tension that had built up in them. All this was because she was going through an identity crisis. She and Justin were no longer married, and at some point, there would be a new Lady Devereux, hopefully a childbearing one. She had omitted to ask the lawyer how she would be addressed. Anne, Lady Devereux? She had no desire to announce to the world her status as a divorcée. Would it be easier to revert to her maiden name? Miss Meredith? Mrs Meredith? She'd have to bite the bullet and sort it out, as all her credit cards and accounts would have to be changed.

She looked at her left hand. Perhaps she ought not to wear her wedding ring as she was no longer married, but it was a form of protection, and taking it off might give all the wrong signals to predatory males. Like nosy Patrick Mackenzie, with his flirty innuendos, graceless questions and bad manners. David Mackenzie wasn't predatory, though; his mind was somewhere else. She didn't know what had brought him to talk to her. Just kindness perhaps. Loneliness?

The band introduced a reel, and an older man asked her if she would like to dance. Mr Mackenzie Senior called the steps and she was surprised by how much she enjoyed the dancing. Her partner brought her a soft drink and the entertainment became more general with various people offering or being pushed, to contribute items. Unexpectedly, she heard her name over the microphone. Patrick, announcing that they had a pianist; come on, Annie, come and play a little something. How did he know she was a pianist? She flushed with embarrassment and annoyance and shook her head, but he wouldn't let it go until everyone in the hall was turning her way. Abruptly her temper flared. She got up, unsmiling, and took Louise's place at the piano, the father giving her a serious, considering look as she passed him, and David frowning at his brother. She played 'The Marino Waltz' and was gratified to see, after the first few bars, that virtually everybody got up to dance. Mr Mackenzie Senior picked up his violin and accompanied her. The violin was a good one, with sweet tones, and he played with feeling, never overtaking the piano, but enhancing it. As they finished, they smiled at each other, Annie's temper soothed, and the older man acknowledging the lovely piece. There was applause, but then there was applause after every item. She drank the rest of her wine, trying to put Patrick's disrespect out of her mind. An urgent desire for solitude came over her and she slipped out of a side door into the silence of the night. It was too cold to stand around, but she had no desire to return to the noisy hall and walked the few hundred yards back to the hotel.

She sat at the window of her room, looking out over the loch sliding silvery in the slight wind. What on earth was she doing, six hundred miles from home, trying to chase the faint traces of a man who had died nearly seventy years ago? Charlotte's face, wistful and rather tired, flitted through her memory. Then another memory; that crumpled, stained and singed paper, with blue wax scribbles and Elspeth Elliott's scrawled writing. 'Peter. Aug 15th.' She had a sudden sense of all humanity's briefness. The passing of the generations. What was it the bible said? Something about the grass, springing up in a day, then withering. She was irritated not to remember and looked it up on Google.

The life of mortals is like grass,
they flourish like a flower of the field;
the wind blows over it and it is gone,
and its place remembers it no more.

What were her little traumas of work and divorce and barrenness compared with her mother's losses? The loss of her father, brothers and best friend? The loss of a baby? Charlotte's losses were so much greater than hers, and Charlotte's love and sacrifice for her was the answer to what on earth she was doing six hundred miles from home, chasing John Elliott's memory.

The wind won't blow over you, John Elliott, and your place will be remembered.

A new year was coming. New opportunities, new challenges; past mistakes to be learnt from, and new experiences to be revealed. David Mackenzie's behaviour at the cottage and Patrick Mackenzie's intrusion must be shrugged off. David Mackenzie, however, had made amends and had been kind tonight. She went to bed, oddly peaceful, long before the witching midnight hour of the old year, and the exuberant excesses of the new.

9

August 1942

When the *Countess of Minto* arrived back in Loch Ewe, John's pleasure at seeing Mhairi and her unabashed welcome lifted his spirits. While the next convoy gathered, and ships loaded their supplies, water and fuel, that dreamtime August was a blessed oasis of normality, peace and happiness. Even the malevolent presence in Aultbea of Archie Mackinnon, who seemed to have a presumed ownership of Mhairi, could not spoil his contentment.

Today there was a bright cloudless sky and a wind off the sea took the edge off the blazing sun. The combination ensured there was not a midge to be seen. They lay side by side on the short turf below the croft after their swim, and she lazily brushed the drying sand from her arm, the white skin now golden from the summer sun. The long, raised scar down his abdomen was mostly hidden by his bathing suit, but it was still a livid red and he hated the ugliness. His eyes traced the blue vein down her inner arm to the wrist, and he was seized by her perfection. The moment is perfect. The day is perfect.

'I'll remember this all my life,' he said, almost to himself, although she heard it and turned her head to face him straight on, her smile engulfing him. 'It won't matter if

I live to be a hundred, or whether I die next month, I'll remember this and be happy.'

'You won't die next month. You'll come back safe. I know these things. I have the Highland sight.' Her eyes were closed, the mouth lax in the soft warmth of the sun, her voice utterly sure. The desire to trace her lips with his finger was almost overwhelming.

How he loved that Gaelic lilt to her voice. He pushed away the thread of Elspeth and the children, just for this moment. There was a faint reverberation in the air and his mind automatically evaluated engines, aircraft, submarines. He pushed away that thought too.

'I believe you,' he said, almost too relaxed to tease her. 'Mystic Mhairi, mysterious mistress of the myriad mountains of wisdom—misdom—misdemeanours, cables, telegrams, letters.' She was giggling.

'You're a teacher. You shouldn't be running out of M words.' Suddenly there was a change in her, a tensing of mind and body, and he shifted his gaze to her now wide eyes. She was looking beyond him, over his shoulder to the low dunes which hid the cottage.

'What's the matter?' he said, turning over to look the same way. The horizon was empty. She seemed to relax, but it was forced, a false resumption.

'Nothing,' she said. 'A sheep.'

That faint reverberation again and a faint unease in them both. The magic thread was broken.

'Tell me how the *Countess* is improved,' she said. 'Tell me what luxuries lie in store for you.'

He grinned in easy fabrication. 'Well, in my five months absence they've replaced the cracked steering column, given us new this, and second-hand that, the crew are faster to action stations and haven't dropped any shells since Liverpool and sea trials have been completed. We are ready to take on the might of German U-boats and torpedo bombers.'

And I am a coward. I want to escape with Mhairi to some mountain fastness far from the long arm of naval discipline, German wolf packs, bombed-out Portsmouth and a dreadful mother-in-law. I am afraid of what is to come.

He thought of Elspeth's depressing letters and his brief leave with the family in July. Her parents' house had been hit, and her overbearing father had had a fatal heart attack on emerging from the shelter to find it demolished. Her mother, who John had always found difficult, had moved into the flat with Elspeth and the children and refused to move, air raids and incendiary bombs notwithstanding. She slept in their bed, while Elspeth occupied the old sofa in the sitting room and in the tiny room next door the little boys slept in their cots, restless and hungry. His anger and frustration at having to lodge with a friend had caused him to be discourteous to his mother-in-law and to quarrel with Elspeth, all of which made him despondent. She was not managing well, though he ensured she was not short of money, and she allowed her mother to tyrannise the household. He was anxious about leaving them there, in the shattered city, but Elspeth stubbornly refused to leave Portsmouth despite his efforts. In contrast to the untidy, dirty flat, Mhairi cheerfully kept the croft clean and neat, even though she worked in the Aultbea post office every day. He knew that his infrequent and minor contributions in the garden and helping with the sheep relieved her workload and brought in a few more rations. Her sharp intelligence fascinated him. Elspeth was by no means stupid, but she had little curiosity about the world around her, especially since the boys had been born. Mhairi wanted to know everything; an unashamed greed for knowledge, a humble recognition of her inexperience. A rush of shame washed over him at his disloyalty. Elspeth was his wife. Mhairi was just a friend. That was all there was to it.

She must have felt his thoughts darken.

'Don't be sad. You will come back safely, I promise.' As if to endorse the guarantee, her hand traced over his cheekbone, the finger coming to rest at the corner of his mouth, at the dark line of his moustache. Her touch was a charge of energy, a lift of happiness, extraordinary pleasure. Elspeth rarely touched him spontaneously these days.

All too soon the convoy departure date came. He went to the post office and handed Mhairi his final letter to Elspeth for posting. She took the envelope and lifted her hand in farewell without a word. She looked as if she might cry if she said anything, and he longed to embrace her. To comfort and be comforted. She did not come to the quayside, but he saw Archie Mackinnon standing in the shadow of the officers' mess watching the embarkation. Was he watching him in particular? The man seemed very still, with the poised concentration of a predator. A spear of concern stabbed him, not for the first time. His instinct told him that Archie was dangerous, and his possessiveness and aggression towards Mhairi made him more than anxious for her. He had seldom met such an unpleasant man, and every time he came across him his muscles contracted with dislike.

As the convoy left the oily waters of Loch Ewe and slid, one ship at a time, through the boom at the mouth of the loch and into the Minch, John looked to his left towards Inverasdale. He fingered the hunk of sheep's wool that Mhairi had cut from the inner pelt of one of her ewes. For good luck, she had said. Bring it back. It was white and soft and smelt of lanolin. Goodbye, little grey croft. Goodbye, silly conversations while we peeled turnips or lifted potatoes. That manic laughter as we fled from the cold sea pursued by clouds of midges. I do not want to leave.

Seagulls screamed overhead, and the *Countess of Minto*'s crew were subdued. He suspected that he was not the only man to wonder if this passage would be as bad as the previous convoy, if any of the rumours were true, and whether Wester Ross would be their last sight of land this side of eternity. He'd come back safely before, against the odds. Perhaps the Almighty had heard their prayers.

* * *

Three months later, Mhairi rebilleted John at Inveruidh. The remnants of the fleet had limped back into Loch Ewe, the men exhausted but strung up with elation at being home, and alive. Almost without exception, their first port of call had been to the messes for their first decent meal in weeks. It may have been wartime rationing, John said, but to those who had been living on a diet of tinned corned beef and dry bread, it was a banquet. And the food was hot.

She lay above him in her little bed in the rafters as he twisted and shouted and sweated through his nightmares: the fogs and icebergs, the 'tin fishes' which seemed to hunt them down like malevolent sharks, and the U-boats, sneaking through the escorts and wreaking havoc through the mangled columns of ships, the unreliable depth charges which exploded too soon or too late, the pathetic guns with which to fight the JU88s and the waves of torpedo bombers.

'They hit the US ammunition ship *Mary Luckenbach*. She blew into fragments, along with all the crew. The noise literally deafened us. Thirteen merchant ships were lost. There must have been hundreds of men killed.' He couldn't begin to describe the horror. There were no words which could express the awfulness, the waste, the fear.

The *Countess of Minto* was an anti-submarine trawler, but her crew had also pulled many survivors out of the sea or off sinking ships. John had seen so many burnt and drowned and blown-up seamen that his sleep ran with bodies, red with blood and black with crude oil, and their eventual arrival in Archangel had been equally distressing. The Russians were surly and barbaric, hospital provision so basic that many more men died than was necessary.

'There were no cranes. All those ships had to be unloaded by hand,' he said, his hands wrapped round a hot mug of tea as if the Arctic cold still permeated his bones. 'That's why we had to wait all those weeks. Often the water tenders didn't come, and we all ran low on fuel so there was no heating in the ships. We couldn't go ashore—there was nothing there anyway—and we weren't allowed to use our own boats if we were anchored. We ran out of food and there was nothing to replace it with, no shops, no supplies.'

'But the ships were crammed with food supplies!' Mhairi said, horrified. 'Why couldn't you use them?'

'They weren't for us.' His lips tightened angrily on the memory. 'We saw sacks of rice and beans thrown on to the docks, sprouting stalks and going black and rotten. If the paperwork wasn't correct, nobody could touch it. The people didn't dare, even though they were starving; they'd have been shot.' He shook his head as if trying to dislodge the memories. 'All those supplies that had cost so much to get there.' Mhairi took his mug and refilled it as if the hot tea could melt his memories away. He couldn't stop the flow of his thoughts and gripped her hands as if she were the one stable structure in his universe.

'The RAF were there, but they couldn't fly. We had brought the spare parts, but they were either stolen or abandoned or the Russians wouldn't release them to repair the planes. It's unbelievable. Heart-breaking. The waste of good men, good ships, supplies that we ourselves badly need. I don't understand how they can be an ally when they hate and distrust us so much. They are a terrible nation.' He squeezed his eyes shut in an effort to blank it all out.

Sometimes he woke from the nightmares to find Mhairi, barefoot and anguished, holding and comforting him like a child as he cried, but she never slid under the blankets, and nor did he ask her to, however much he longed for it.

10

January 2nd 2012

David had welcomed his drive to Inverness, alone, with no interruptions, just the CD playing under his thoughts. Looking forward to seeing the boys, hoping that Tom and Tilly, his in-laws, had enjoyed having them to themselves, hoping they had seen Shona's sideways look in Christopher's cheeky grin, and her gentle touch in Seamus's confiding hand-hold. He suppressed the underlying anxiety about them travelling on the train from Edinburgh to Inverness, albeit chaperoned by an acquaintance of Tom and Tilly's, which had dogged him ever since the arrangement had been made. He knew his inclination to drive down and collect them was over-protective. Still, he'd be more than relieved to see them on the platform.

The first anniversary of her death had passed in September. They had taken flowers to her grave, a stormy day of driven rain, finding the headstone pale and clear and unsullied by twelve months' exposure to the elements. Did her parents go weekly and polish it? He didn't ask. He hadn't wanted her buried in the north, reminding him and the boys of what they missed. The physical breath-stopping pain of her absence had passed, replaced by a dull ache underneath the busyness he cultivated. The moments when the boys called for her in mental or physical need had become fewer and sometimes he passed hours without thinking of her. He knew she wouldn't have wanted this irrational guilt—she would have wanted them to start again. Sometime.

He wondered about Annie Devereux, and how her oddly beautiful face had somehow conveyed a sadness that he recognised. Had she, too, been through some tragedy? A death? A lost child? Divorce? It was not something you could ask. It had to come out naturally, in the course of getting to know someone. But he wasn't ready to get to know anybody yet. He turned away from thoughts of Annie Devereux, purposefully, and thought instead about the new term beginning on Monday, the new school clothes that Louise had bought, and the two new pairs of shoes that were on the seat beside him ready to be tried on and changed at the shop if they didn't fit. Louise had done what Shona would have done and he was infinitely grateful. He hadn't quite got to grips with the shopping and cooking and clothing, changing sheets and helping with homework.

Yet again he chewed at his concerns over the school. It was—not exactly a problem—but not quite as good as he had hoped. The teachers were delightful and encouraging and the boys loved them, but he was troubled by the lack of constructive criticism. The comments were all congratulatory, encouraging; smiley faces and exclamation marks, the spellings not corrected, the homework not checked, the extraordinary methodology of their arithmetic, the emphasis on football and non-emphasis on music. He sighed. He ought perhaps to offer some music teaching, but he was no teacher, being, he knew, impatient and critical. Both boys were intelligent, and so they should be given that Shona had a First in English and he himself a First in Engineering, but they weren't being extended in any way.

He remembered the conversation he'd had with his mother the previous evening.

'Am I expecting too much? Of the boys? Of the teachers?' He had fired irritable questions at her. 'I remember the thrill of getting eight out of ten when it was usually six or seven. Now they get 'Well done!' for everything, good, bad or indifferent. There's no competition, nothing well-earned, no incentive to do better.' He raked his fingers through his hair. 'You're a school governor! Am I wrong? Is constructive criticism so damaging?'

Fiona pursed her lips. 'That's how teachers are trained these days. Your boys will do well whatever their education because both you and Shona were a clever pair, but I agree they are not being stretched.'

'And Christopher—' he hesitated, uncomfortable with his thoughts.

'Yes. Christopher. I see the signs, just as you do. He's doing less well, he's getting lazy, he's getting cheeky.'

'Is it losing Shona?'

She shook her head. 'I'm no expert, but I don't think so. I think you've already put your finger on it. He's not challenged, and he needs to be. I think his problem is boredom.'

She took a batch of cakes out of the Aga. 'Maybe you need to think more seriously about your own future. I've no desire to see you leave here, but you, too, need to be stretched, to find a job which challenges you. And you need to find a better school for the boys.'

She put the oven gloves on the rail and sat down opposite him. 'I think you need to consider moving on, David, and I think Shona would want you to.'

Her words had provoked a shaft of dread that alarmed him. Where was his natural decisiveness, the old certainty about the future, his ability to take charge of his family's life?

They erupted from the train trailing coats and cases and a vast IKEA bag stuffed with Christmas presents and rubber boots. The carrier bags, established as carrying only crumpled foil and apple cores from Tilly's picnic, were disposed of in a bin, the smiling chaperone thanked, effusively by David, less enthusiastically by the boys. Louise's school shoes were pronounced OK, if only to prevent a detour to the shop, and they joined the exodus on to the Kessock bridge. The initial inability to tell him what they'd done in Edinburgh gradually gave way to a stream of information from both at once, on quite different subjects. David smiled and occasionally got a question in. It had obviously been a good week. When they got round to asking him what he had been doing, he told them about the new kitchen and bathroom at Inveruidh and about Louise and Patrick's New Year visit and the *ceilidh* at the hall.

'Do you want to come to Inveruidh tomorrow afternoon with Gee Gee and Grandpa, and a lady called Annie who might want to stay there?' There were yips of enthusiasm. They loved the cottage. He would normally not have encouraged them to call a strange adult by their first name, but it seemed ridiculous to refer to her as 'Lady Devereux', and in any case, she had been cross that Patrick had discovered it.

'Can't we go in the morning and have lunch there, Dad?'

He shook his head. 'Granny Fiona is doing a slap-up back-to-school humungous gigantic roast beef, with Yorkshire pudding and pints of gravy closely followed by certain favourite puddings, probably followed by large slabs of chocolate to fill up any remaining hollow places. So there's not enough time between church and that.' He put out a hand and ruffled Christopher's mop of hair. 'So not in the morning. We'll go after lunch.'

11

3rd January 2012

The snow had long since gone except on the mountain slopes, and the bright sun reflected from the wind-scoured rock faces, from the snow itself, and from the turbulent blue-grey of the sea, foaming as if it, too, was white-tipped with snow. Although Annie had passed this way once in daylight since that dreadful first night, the little house was in fact almost hidden from the road by a low mound and she had not driven down to it, unwilling to be seen casing the joint, as it were. It was a world away from her first arrival, and there were no awkward questions to answer. David's enormous car took the six of them with ease and the boys didn't seem to find it odd that she wanted to stay in the cottage in midwinter and asked no questions about a husband or children. Soothing. Her enquiries determined that Christopher was eight and Seamus six. David's grandmother was clearly pleased that her great-grandsons loved the cottage.

'Tell us about the wind that blew away the privy, Gee Gee.'

David grinned. 'It'll make Annie count her blessings when she discovers there's a bathroom!'

'Well now,' Mrs Gillespie began, and her voice was different, Annie thought. A storytelling voice, rather slow; deliberate and very Gaelic. 'Let me see now. It must have been towards the end of the war, 1944 perhaps, and cold. And windy. Very, very windy. So windy I was nearly knocked down on my way to the privy. Down the garden it was, you see, on the edge of the moor. Well, inside it was very cosy compared to the outside, and one could read the newspaper on the string, very peaceful, you see—'

'They had newspaper squares instead of loo paper in those days,' Seamus interposed informatively for Annie.

'So there I was,' Mrs Gillespie went on, paying no attention to the interruption, 'reading old news—which is just as interesting as new news, so it is, when suddenly—' the 'suddenly' was drawn out into three separate words, 'there came a tremendous gust, and the sound of rending, and cracking and squeaking, and before I had a notion of what was happening, the privy door sprang open, and the whole wee hoosie bent over sideways like a drunkard, and then—poof—up it lifted and away over the moor, leaving me all alone and perched on my wee bench with one square of newspaper in my hand.' The boys were in hysterics on the seat beside Annie and she caught a glimpse of David's face in the mirror, amused by his sons' amusement, tolerant, the story evidently a perennial family favourite. He has a lovely smile, she thought, and his eyes crinkle with affection when he looks at his children. Where was his wife? Surely she couldn't have left him for someone else? Justin had been immensely good-looking in a polished, high-boned aristocratic way, but he hadn't been *attractive* as this man was attractive. David's eyes in the mirror caught hers in a brief conspiracy of merriment.

As David helped his grandmother out of the car, Annie considered the cottage in its little hollow, hunkered down before the winds, gazing across the heathery rocks sticking out of the sheep-nibbled turf. She could see down to the huge white beach where the tide was already halfway back, and across the great expanse of Loch Ewe, past the flat teardrop of the Isle of Ewe to the snow-covered dragons' teeth mountains beyond.

Her gaze shortened focus to the window next to the gate. There was a crazed area the size of a man's fist about six inches from the bottom left-hand corner. She knew she blushed and saw David suppressing a grin.

'There you are, Granny,' he said, indicating the offending patch. 'That's where housebreaker Annie tried to get in.'

She looked from Annie to the window. 'Not very effective. What did you use? Your elbow?'

'No, a stone.' Her blush was hotter.

'The gate stone,' David said. 'I put it back.'

'The gate stone.' The old lady turned to stare at the gate and the stone under it. Annie distinctly heard a little intake of breath; a tension which held for some seconds. Then Mrs Gillespie turned away and began her deliberate walk towards the door. 'You should have aimed for the middle,' she said.

'Possibly,' he glanced in Annie's direction, 'but even a blacksmith with an anvil would have a tough time getting through one of these.' Annie saw his amusement and ducked her head in embarrassment. 'This place is like Fort Knox—when all the doors are locked. Anyway, the replacement window's coming tomorrow, I hope, and then there'll be nothing to show for it. If Annie wants to rent the cottage for her last three weeks, she knows no one can get in without an invitation.'

She gave him a brief stare. What did that last remark mean? If anything.

The interior bore no resemblance to her last visit. Gone was the wilderness of sawn wood, cardboard boxes and gutted cupboards. The kitchen was a gleaming expanse of pale granite counters and cream-coloured Shaker-style cupboards, a double Belfast sink, a Rangemaster oven and hob and Miele equipment, with a large table and chairs in the centre of a faux plank floor. The two boys experimented with soft-close drawers and cupboards and said 'Wow!' in awed voices. The sitting room was tidy, clean and comfortable; flat screen TV, Wi-Fi, plenty of sockets, work and coffee tables, magazines and information leaflets. David shepherded his temporarily speechless grandmother to an armchair and smiled at Annie.

'Go and have a look round and see if it's what you want. I'll show Granny the bathrooms in a while when she's finished being horrified about her kitchen, and then she'll haul me over the coals about them, too, so you've got plenty of time.'

'It's lovely!' Annie exclaimed. 'I do hope you like it, Mrs Gillespie. Only, of course, I don't know what it was like before, and change is rather shocking, isn't it?'

'It's certainly changed.' The old lady was acerbic. 'There was nothing wrong with my kitchen, young David, and it seems to me you've thrown good money away for no reason.'

The boys clattered upstairs, and Annie followed through the kitchen where their grandfather was exploring the fuse boxes and other technical-looking switches.

'How's he doing explaining himself to my mother?' he enquired with a rueful smile.

Annie laughed. 'Not much progress yet, I don't think, but he doesn't look terribly worried.'

Mr Mackenzie shook his head. 'It really had to be done. She had hardly changed a thing since the seventies, and much though we loved it, it was becoming hard to maintain, and not many people want to rent a remote cottage with practically no mod cons at all.' His face took on a comical expression. 'Except you, apparently. I understand you're researching a wartime grandfather?'

Annie nodded. 'He was an RNVR officer, but my mother knows hardly anything about him. This cottage was near to Cove, and the convoy memorial, so I thought I'd start here. And I wanted to be remote.' Did that sound rather odd?

He turned to face her.

'Gairloch Museum will be your best source, perhaps, but it's closed now, probably till April. They hope to build a convoy museum at Aultbea, but it hasn't happened yet. Winter is not a good time to do research here as places are closed, and events are usually scheduled for the spring and summer. I'll ask around for you. Maybe my mother can give you some background—she lived here during the war and worked in Aultbea. What was your grandfather's name and ship?'

'He was called John Elliott. I don't know what ship or ships he served on, and though I've read lots of interesting books and stuff, none of it is very helpful for this sort of personal research.'

Mr Mackenzie was looking at her rather fixedly. 'How do you spell the surname?'

'E L L I O T T.'

He nodded, turning back to the boxes on the wall. 'Interesting.' Why interesting, Annie wondered. 'I'll see what I can do. By the way, the price per week would be the same as you agreed with Kate if you want to take it.'

She said something neutral and appreciative and continued her exploration, knowing that she already liked the feel of the cottage.

The feeling was reinforced the moment she got upstairs to the two bedrooms overlooking the sea. The wide dormer windows had been extended down almost to floor level, whole panes of glass with nothing to interfere with the view. Annie imagined waking in that bed with the beach and the sea and the mountains right there. Pouring rain, dark scudding clouds, huge seas, bright sunlight, turquoise Loch Ewe, purple mountains. A vast electric delight began to spread through her. Three weeks was suddenly not enough; three months; three years. Alone. She'd bring a table up here, and work looking over this view. Already, the ghosts of melody, the timpani of waves and wind, the bubbling grace notes of rain began to run in her mind, and a sudden sharp desire for a piano overtook her. No flat in London, no texts to meet for coffee, to come to a party; no reminders of Justin and a life that had already flown down the corridors of regret. Just a ballroom of orchestral music.

There was a sudden clatter of feet and her dreamy joy returned from the heavenly realms to the mundane. The boys had stopped in the passage and there was another outburst of wows. She opened the door to find them gazing at the bathroom, which was certainly modern, contained a nice bath and shower, loo and basin, but was not in the celebrity bracket.

'Gosh!' said Christopher as she joined them. 'It is soooo different!'

'What did it look like before?' Annie said curiously.

'Well—it was wood—'

'In little planks, up and down.' Tongue and groove, she thought. Very Scottish.

'Black—sort of dark brown really.'

'The bath was enormous, with brown rings under the taps, and it was really rough on your bum. And it took an age to fill up—'

'And if the water wasn't hot enough the metal stayed cold, and if it *was* hot enough it burnt you. And there was never enough to cover you so the top half of you got goose pimples.'

'And the spiders came through the planks, and there were lots of spider webs, and Mum dusted them up, and put them down the loo, but more always came.'

'And Mum always screeched cos she doesn't—didn't—like spiders,' Christopher added. Annie thought the time had come to discover why Mum was absent. His use of an amended tense was revealing.

'She died,' Seamus said in response to her question, and Christopher added, 'Last year. She had cancer.'

'I am so sorry,' Annie said, because when push comes to shove, what can you possibly say to two boys who have lost their mother?

'We're still very sad,' said Seamus, and he did indeed sound very sad.

'I bet,' said Annie. 'My mum died, too, but when I was a baby, so I don't remember her, but I got a wonderful new one, and I would be really, really sad if she died.'

'I remember mine, and I don't want a new one,' Christopher said. He sounded angry. 'I want my old one.' Annie wished she hadn't mentioned replacements.

It was also from the boys that Annie discovered that their great-grandmother was called Varri, spelt Mhairi, that Daddy's cooking wasn't as good as Mum's, and that they had to polish their shoes all by themselves. She wished that David had told her about his wife himself, prior to the invitation to come and see the cottage. It explained his sad, tired eyes, and once again put her own tribulations into perspective.

Annie heard a footstep and glanced towards the stairs. David came up and leant against the top banister. His face was guarded, although he was smiling, and Annie hoped he hadn't heard her asking about his wife.

'What do you think of the bathroom, boys? It's a nicer floor, isn't it?'

Seamus was disapproving. 'I liked the planks better than this, didn't you, Chris?'

Christopher regarded the thick cork tiles doubtfully. 'It's OK. I got a splinter in my toe from the planks once.'

'And this is waterproof,' their father said, 'which the planks weren't, to the detriment of the kitchen ceiling. So, do you approve, boys?'

'It's OK,' said Seamus eventually. 'I suppose. I liked it better before.'

'Tell Gee Gee what it's like and what you think. She may not want to climb the stairs today.'

They finished inspecting the bedrooms, storage cupboards, and the roof spaces, to their approval all unchanged, and clattered downstairs.

'They hate change,' David said with a rueful smile. 'They liked it just the way it was, though honestly, it wasn't as bad as they described it—just old-fashioned.'

Annie expelled a breath, unaware that she'd been holding it. 'I wouldn't have minded. Kate said it was old-fashioned, but the heating and hot water worked—and it had an internet connection. It's all—lovely. And please, I'd love to come, if that's OK. I mean after I broke the window and everything. Of course, I'll pay for it, the window, and the extra—'

'Extra?' He was laughing and relaxed. 'There isn't any 'extra' anything. And the window will be covered by the insurance.'

'But the kitchen and bathroom improvements—those must increase the rental—'

'Next year. And I daresay you've noticed that the painting hasn't been done, and there are no blinds in the kitchen. I wasn't expecting any tenants this winter, and interior decorating is not my major attribute. I'll be replacing the window hopefully tomorrow morning, maybe the next day, but you can move in any time you like. You already have the key Kate sent you, I think?'

She couldn't help the smile spreading across her face. Excitement and anticipation, of what she wasn't quite sure, but here was her dream remoteness, a vast distance from

Justin and their bitter recriminations, from job problems, from the gossip and from her own wretched disappointments. Yet there was also the comfort, for a city girl, of a pleasant family down the road who would be there in the face of any disaster. And it seemed that David Mackenzie was a sort of fellow traveller along life's bumpy road, as well as being attractively competent. He was looking at her silly grin and smiling in response, grey eyes crinkling at the corners.

12

December 1942

John emerged triumphantly from Hamleys with a Jack-in-the Box, a Dinky toy, and a Hornby train set—for whose entertainment he asked himself with a self-conscious grin—and in his other hand a Fortnum's bag which screamed wealth and luxury, containing a silky peach-coloured nightgown and robe for Elspeth. In a fit of guilt, he had also bought in Fortnum's a box of expensive violet creams for her mother.

Convoy PQ18 had faded like a dream, though shreds of terror still floated into his mind at unexpected moments. Christmas anticipation bubbled up as if he were a child again, and his step felt as light and joyful as his heart at what was in store for the four of them.

Elspeth had been unable to evict her mother from their flat, but this initial setback had proved to be a blessing in disguise. He had contacted a well-to-do naval friend who had an empty flat in Richmond and arranged to rent it for ten days. His mother-in-law could go to stay with a friend (if she had one) or remain in their flat in Portsmouth, he wrote, but they would not be there. He intended to take Elspeth and the boys away for Christmas. It was the first time he had put his foot down. Perhaps dicing with death on the convoys had something to do with his resolve and the discarding of his habitual courtesy towards his mother-in-law. He was truly looking forward to this leave. He hadn't had a reply from Elspeth, but he had been on the move, and though irritated, he wasn't surprised.

In Richmond, he ordered as many Christmas foodstuffs and treats as were available and organised their delivery to the flat. Having collected the key from the housekeeper, he found the beds made up and clean towels in the bathroom. The flat was spacious, spotless and delightfully decorated, only the blackout curtains deferring to the times.

He stored the food delivery in the refrigerator—a piece of equipment he was unfamiliar with—and unpacked his small case in the luxurious bedroom. Leaving the parcels—except for the violet creams—on the dining table, he took a cab to the station. The anticipation of seeing Elspeth and the boys, of a real family Christmas, of treats and presents, Elspeth in a pretty dress, her green eyes surely restored to the gleaming ones he remembered when they were first married, rose in him again. Humming Bing Crosby's latest song, 'White Christmas', he smiled with seasonal goodwill at everyone he saw as the train rattled down to Portsmouth.

* * *

John stared at his wife in disbelief.

'You're not coming?' He was stupefied into open-mouthed shock. She wrenched her hands together, twisting them till the knuckles cracked and whitened, her untidy hair smearing about her face as her head jerked with each sob. Richard stared at John warily, his little fingers gripping her skirts, but Peter slept on.

'But it's all arranged!' He was outraged. 'Ten days. I've arranged everything. All the food is bought, all the presents. Everything. I wrote and told you.' Anger began to overtake the stupefaction. 'Didn't you get my letters?'

He could see she was tempted to deny it, but then thought better of it. 'I couldn't let you know. Mother can't be left—she's really ill.'

'She isn't.' He was nearly shouting. 'She is ill at her convenience, as we have discussed on many occasions.' He was stern now, his voice steadying. 'She became ill when you told her my plans, didn't she? And why did I make those plans, Elspeth? To give us the chance to be a family, just for once. You, me and the boys, without her carping tongue and unreasonable complaints.' He hadn't lowered his voice, hoping that the woman in the bedroom would hear. Elspeth cast a panicked look at the door and tried to shush him. He disregarded her.

'Well, she can be as ill as she likes. We are going to have Christmas in Richmond. The four of us. If you haven't made arrangements for her as I asked you to, then she will have to stay here, prepare her own food, or starve. Which-ever she likes.'

'But we can't leave her!' The sobs had turned into wailing.

'We can,' he said, astounded by his own harsh words. 'She has tyrannised you and me enough. She has tyrannised the children enough. It can't go on. I came to collect you, so go get your things—you should be packed already as I asked you to—and let's go.'

'I can't.' He could only hear a whisper. 'I can't. I prom-ised her.'

'You can.' The whole situation had slid out of his con-trol. Whatever he said, or did, the woman in the bedroom was wielding the power and calling the shots. He stared at her in the silence, knowing already that he had lost. 'If you stay here, you stay without me. In any case, there is no-where for me to sleep. I'd take the children if I could, but I think they'd be terrified without you. Richard will have no birthday party. They will have no Christmas, and nor will you and nor will I. Which is more important to you, our marriage, or your mother? That's the choice, Elspeth, and the choice is yours.' His anger threatened to overwhelm him, to the extent that he no longer cared about the final result. Even if she came with him now, he didn't think he could forgive her. The war, the terror of the convoys, the arrangements for the Richmond flat, the presents, the food, the theatre tickets, the ghastly travel from Glasgow, the huge outlay of money he could ill afford; all was useless, pointless, a vast waste of emotion.

'Are you going to come, or are you staying?' He got to his feet, looking down at his weeping wife, the stylish girl he had married lost in drab, creased clothes, her face devoid of even lipstick, her once beautiful hair greasily scrunched at her nape. She didn't answer, her sobs ever louder, but she shook her head.

John picked up his greatcoat.

'Happy Christmas.' The bitter sarcasm shamed him as he returned to Richmond and lay restless and alone and utterly miserable in the huge comfortable bed, his thoughts cartwheeling between Elspeth and the children, in a flat with not a single Christmas decoration, let alone a tree, and Mhairi in Inverasdale where her paper chain cut from coloured magazines hung cheerily in the kitchen. Could he have done anything differently? He should have given an ultimatum to his mother-in-law face to face, but Elspeth's choice had cut him to the bone—disarmed and enfeebled him. How had he allowed this situation to arise in the first place?

A few evenings in the local undamaged pub brought him intoxication and an unconsciousness of sorts, and the fact that the Germans had mostly ceased their night bombing raids seemed to give the local population a cheerful optimism which, though infuriating to John, was at least an improvement on the fear and misery of the blitz. Still burning from Elspeth's decision, he sent her Christmas present to Mhairi instead, his letter uncharacteristically untidy and distraught. And, he realised, disloyal to Elspeth. How he longed for Mhairi's teasing laughter and sharp observations and her quick understanding of his feelings and moods. He looked up old friends and accompanied them to the theatres which were still standing and had a cast. By the end of his ten days in London, his rage had subsided, and misery was uppermost. He made one final unannounced visit to Portsmouth.

The family was in no better state than before. Elspeth was obviously still spending her nights on the sofa with her mother in their bed and she looked exhausted, ill and deeply unhappy.

John lifted Richard into his arms and kissed him. 'Happy Birthday, big boy.' A throat- catching wave of emotion swept him as the little hands stroked his moustache curiously, and explored his ears, tugging gently at his hair. This fragile part of him that had never experienced anything except deprivation, war, uncertainty, and a grandmother's aversion.

'I've got a birthday present for you and a Christmas present too!' But nothing for you, Elspeth, and it was clear that she had nothing for him. Or for the children either. 'Shall we open the parcels and look?' There was no verbal response, just a vigorous nodding of the big head on the delicate stem of his neck. He helped Richard open the box and extract the Dinky toy. It was a scarlet post office van which the child wheeled about making quiet purring noises. They explored the train set, John setting up the tracks and helping the child to place the engine on the rails and attach the carriages. His focus faded after a few minutes and John brought out the third parcel.

'This is for Peter. Would you like to help open it and show it to him?' Again he nodded, and John noticed a little sideways look towards the bedroom where Elspeth's mother lay. The child scrabbled at the cheap paper around the box and the Jack-in-the-Box made a sharp squeaking sound as it jumped out. Richard flinched and turned in big-eyed alarm towards the bedroom. John frowned in consternation.

'Elspeth, is he not speaking because he's afraid of her?' He was aware of the sharpness in his voice and tried to soften it. 'He always used to chatter like a monkey, but he hasn't said a word since I've been here and now it seems he's fearful of making a noise.'

Elspeth compressed her lips. 'Maybe. Mother does get cross. She finds the noise disturbing.' On the beat there came a strident call from the bedroom. Elspeth scrambled to get up.

'Don't go the moment she demands you! She's living with two small children. Noise is normal. They shouldn't have to keep silence in their own home. You really must assert yourself—this is our home, not hers. If she doesn't like it, she can go elsewhere.'

Elspeth shook her head miserably. 'I try, really I do, but it just makes her worse. I can't find anyone who will take her in.' John wasn't surprised. 'And I've offered to pay for her lodging as you told me. She won't go, and no one will have her.'

The problem seemed insurmountable and John's temper flared again. 'It's not good for the children to live like this. Or you either. And it means I can't come home. She has effectively locked me out of my own house. I've just spent ten days in a delightful flat, where we four should all have been together celebrating Christmas and because of your mother we have all had a perfectly horrible time separated from each other. And now I have to get the night train to Glasgow after a leave which has been less than restful or enjoyable. Frankly, my ship is preferable.' And, he thought,

Inverasdale is the place I want to be, and Mhairi is the person I'd like to be with. 'But if we have many more of these northern convoys you may find that one day the ship and I simply don't come back. There may not be many more leaves to take.'

On the train, rumbling its slow way northwards, he was ashamed of losing his temper, of making her cry again, of threatening her with a possibility which every convoy made more likely. In his saner moments he could see that she was between a rock and a hard place, but his frustration at being unable to solve the problem enraged him. He pulled out his notebook and wrote again to Mhairi, the writing almost unreadable as the train jerked and swayed, braked and accelerated. As he wrote, his mood lifted. There were good times to be had amongst the dreary wartime restrictions. He would do something special with Mhairi on her twenty-first birthday next month, though what it would be was beyond his imagination at this moment. When the train was at a station, he addressed an envelope to himself at Aultbea post office, stamped it and put a tiny M on the back, before giving it to a porter to post.

13

5th January 2012

Annie moved to the cottage the following morning and set about making it home. As she had promised herself, she placed a table at the bedroom window with music notation sheets and a sharpened pencil at the ready. To her surprise, the woodburning stove lit without any fuss and she felt positively triumphant as the warmth spread through the cottage. Outside it began to snow and she settled down beside the fire with a cup of coffee. After exchanging emails with Charlotte, she continued to research John Elliott, finding information about his family, but nothing about him or his naval history. However, her mother's enthusiasm and encouragement had given her an added determination to discover this man and help Charlotte find her roots. Her memory flitted to David's father, in-specting pipes and wiring; his surprise when she told him the name, his questioning of the spelling. A look almost of apprehension.

'Interesting,' he had said. She wondered again why 'in-teresting'? Had he heard the name before? She would ask him. And Mhairi Gillespie had worked in Aultbea during the war. That was a line of enquiry she would follow too. She now had several books and research papers about the

Russian convoys. She stretched out her feet to the fire and began to read.

* * *

The damaged window remained where it was for a further twenty-four hours because the replacement hadn't arrived, and David had somehow been pleased that he'd had to phone to tell Annie. Her voice had initially been cool and cautious, but then became cheerful and friendly when she realised who was calling. Had she been expecting someone else to call? Someone she was nervous about speaking to? He wondered if the missing husband knew where she was, or a boyfriend, or perhaps some other member of the family who worried her.

In the distance, he could see the post van preceding him as he drove up the road to Inverasdale with the new window. Backing up to the gate, he ducked through the wet wind to the back door, gave a hard bang and let himself into the warmth of the cottage. Leaving boots and oilskin dripping on to the boot-room floor, he knocked again on the inner door. Annie opened it, holding a letter in her hand.

He was startled and concerned by the change in her, and in those few seconds, before she visibly pulled herself together, he thought he saw fear. There was certainly no sign of Sunday's joy.

'Oh—David. I quite forgot you were coming. Good morning.'

'Are you all right?' he said abruptly. 'Are you scared up here on your own? You don't have to stay, you know. You can go back to the hotel if it's too lonely.' But he knew instinctively that wasn't her problem.

She looked at him uncomprehendingly. 'Scared? Oh

no! It's wonderful! I love it—the noise of the sea and the wind and rain. And then the gulls land on the roof and thunder about as if they're wearing boots—'

'What's wrong then?' He glanced at the paper in her hand and moved towards the kettle. 'Have you had bad news?'

She sat down on a chair and expelled a breath. In the silence, he put coffee in the cafetière and plonked two mugs, the paper carton of sugar and the milk on the table.

Something must be wrong, and he was a little surprised that he cared. Since Shona, he had been unable to think much further than Christopher and Seamus. 'Well?' he said, 'I don't believe in wasting time on *la politesse* if it's important.'

This time she gave a shaky laugh. 'Obviously not. Well, yes, bad news, but not unexpected. And all my own fault. And not life or death.'

'It doesn't have to be life or death to be important, though. Do you want to talk about it? Sometimes talking puts things in proportion.'

She stared at him as if he'd said something in a foreign language.

'Did you do that? Talk to your wife, I mean, when she was ill?' She put a hand to her mouth. 'I'm so sorry, I shouldn't have said that. Your boys told me your wife—their mother died.' She looked acutely uncomfortable, and he was again surprised at his desire to put her at ease.

He remembered Shona's pragmatism as she faced death. Her acceptance of what could not be changed, and her determination to make it the best possible departure for him and their children. It had been Shona who had made them talk, and she had made it possible for them all to accept the unacceptable.

'Don't worry, it's fine. Yes. I talked to Shona—and the boys. And yes, I think it helped. Sometimes. So, do you want to? You do seem—' he nearly said 'afraid' and changed it to 'worried by something.'

She gazed into the silence, her eyes unfocused, and drank her coffee absently.

'I did something stupid and as a result lost my job.'

'Fingers in the till?'

She sat upright with a jolt. 'No! Oh no!'

He grinned. 'Not that stupid then. You slept with the boss?'

'No I did not! She was a woman anyway.' Her mouth was beginning to curve up and he was ridiculously pleased that he had caused it.

'Well, these days it does happen. You put the wrong letter in the wrong envelope?'

She wrinkled her nose. 'If only!'

'Go on then, what was the job, and what heinous crime did you commit? Or is it too embarrassing to tell me?'

She sighed and dropped her shoulders. 'I slapped a child in school.'

He could feel his jaw dropping. 'Oh dear,' he said, taking a seat opposite her. 'That wouldn't go down well.' He was amazed. She looked the least likely person he had ever seen to have slapped a child. That would be a good reason to crawl to Wester Ross and never emerge. 'What on earth did the child do?'

She could see his shock and seemed to shrink. 'I doubt you'd want to hear it.'

'I'm a listening ear, but only if you want to talk about it.' He hoped there wouldn't be a stream of self-justification. She smoothed the official-looking letter in silence for a while and then seemed to come to a decision.

'I taught music—in a local comprehensive. I didn't enjoy it much, but I'd been so privileged that I thought I should give something back for all my,' she hesitated, 'all my blessings, as it were. So arrogant. So stupid.' She pulled a strand of the red-brown hair, still damp from the shower, round her finger. 'We—my parents and I—gave the school a baby grand, a Bechstein, new.' He raised an eyebrow. That would probably have cost a cool £35,000. 'My mother is a concert pianist and agreed to do a short performance and master class.'

'And your mother is?'

'Charlotte Elliott.'

He thought he heard embarrassment or some form of discomfiture. Charlotte Elliott was a world-class pianist and a name he recognised immediately. He waited, unable to guess at what disaster could have come from this, but whatever it was, it was distressing.

'The whole school was there, all the teachers, lots of parents. When she went on stage, I heard the giggles. I just knew something horrible was going to happen. I thought they might have sabotaged the piano stool. She sat down and—and put her hands on the keys, and nothing happened. No sound, no movement of the keyboard. Nothing.'

Colour had drained from her face and tears were balanced on her lower lashes. 'It was the ultimate humiliation. They'd put Superglue down between the notes—all except three of them. Mum—'

Her voice cracked and then she was crying, the tears pouring out and down her face. David got up from the table and pulled her out of the chair and into his arms, holding her face against his shoulder, rubbing her back as he would comfort his children. He realised he had done that quite automatically, without thought, and that his questioning had caused this girl to lose control and cry helplessly in a stranger's arms. She would probably either hit him or leave rapidly for London. Perhaps both. After a minute or so he pulled a square of kitchen towel off the roll, covered her face with it and said, 'Blow!'

She took a gasping breath and grabbed it. Between the

clean-up moppings, she apologised profusely and tried to remove herself from his arms, but he held her firmly until she was under control again and then put her gently back on the chair. He might as well finish the job now that he'd started.

'That can't be the end of the story. What happened?'

Annie hiccupped and sniffed. 'I knew who'd done it. Or I thought I did. There was a group of Year 11s. They were sniggering at the back of the concert hall, and one of them I knew was the ringleader of the group. I walked to the back and slapped him. You can't do that—assault children, I mean. However much they deserve it.' She paused, and her shoulders hunched, 'and of course he denied it; they all did. I'm not one hundred per cent sure it was them.'

He tried to keep his voice even. Non-judgemental. 'So, you were told not to come back?'

She nodded. 'And more. Police, prosecution, tribunal. Criminal record. Today brought the preliminary court hearing date. I just made it worse for my parents—both of them. And Justin, my husband, said it was the final straw. They're all in the public eye and the media had a field day and will do again when it gets to court. Most of my friends don't want to know me.'

He could well imagine. 'I see. An expensive loss of temper, even under severe provocation. I don't suppose anyone apologised to you and your mother about the piano? Gave you back your money?'

She shook her head. 'Not after what I did. They might have done if I hadn't been so stupid. The piano was a gift—it was the school's to throw away. That loss of control was very expensive indeed. What would you do if a teacher slapped Christopher?'

'I'd be very angry, but I'd be very angry with him, too, if he had done such a thing as to damage equipment. He'd get a punishment from me.' He resisted the inclination to give comfort with another hug and instead said, 'What you need is a good lawyer and lots of righteous anger.'

She looked up at him with a faint and tremulous smile. 'I guess we'll manage a good lawyer, but the righteous anger is trickier. Trying to justify oneself is not a pretty sight, is it? And as the head teacher said to me, "You're old enough to know that you must manage your anger, not let it manage you."'

He tipped his head in dubious agreement. 'Easier in some cases than in others. Apologise for the slap, but stand up for yourself would be my advice.' He put his mug on the draining board. 'That's the misery—so what are you frightened of?'

She dropped her eyes and didn't answer.

'Think they'll lock you up? They won't. Common assault is so common these days they hardly get a wagging finger. Anyway, there's no room in the prisons.' She flushed, and he was immediately contrite for having made light of something so important. 'You may get a fine, but that won't be the end of the world. What's left—media attention? Do what the royal family do—or should do—keep quiet, don't respond, ignore it. If there is no conversation, it dies. The next story comes up the next day, and yours just gets forgotten.'

'You're shocked, aren't you?'

'Yes, I am shocked. I'm also shocked that any child could think of committing that sort of vandalism. Nobody teaches respect these days.' He sensed she needed some light teasing after such an emotional outburst. 'Stop being ashamed of turning over the temple tables. I guess you won't be slapping more children any time soon.' He looked at his watch. 'I must get on with this window. Keep the living room door shut and ignore the noise. It'll all happen from the outside.'

Annie smiled rather damply, but she looked less dreary.

What a very public disaster for both her and her family. She didn't look like the sort of person who might have a rage problem, but he supposed looks could be deceptive. And her husband had said it was the final straw. What had the previous straws been, and how many?

14

6th January 2012

Jem sat at the kitchen table while Fiona chopped vege-tables. Four large carrots. Two onions. One parsnip. One head of celery.

'It could be just a coincidence,' she said rather uncer-tainly. 'It's a common name. Well, John is, anyway.'

'I know,' he said unhappily, 'but still. And Mother has history.'

'And that's a fact! After all these years, we don't know much about your mother's history—before Walter anyway.'

Three large potatoes joined the mountain of chopped veg.

'It's the Elliott bit,' she said. 'If Annie Devereux is researching a naval John Elliott, then she's going to find your name. Lots of people here know it, and your mother worked in Aultbea. The girl is bound to want to talk to her, isn't she?'

Jem pursed his lips in annoyance. 'I told her she should talk to Mother just before I asked her grandfather's name. I was just so taken aback when she told me, I couldn't think what to say.' He tapped his fingers together thoughtfully. 'Mother shouldn't be taking a secret like that to the grave, but she gets annoyed whenever I bring the subject up. Which isn't often these days, because it always seems to upset her.' He chewed his lip in thought. 'She doesn't know why Annie Devereux is here, but I think I'll tell her, and get them together on the basis of research into Aultbea during the war and see what happens.' He looked at Fiona doubtfully. 'She may refuse to see her, of course.'

Fiona put her knife down on the chopping board and stretched her back. 'I wonder if she's afraid of telling you? Afraid of your reaction?' It wasn't exactly a question, Jem thought, more an excursion into possible reasons. They'd been this way before, but Annie Devereux's grandfather was the new ingredient.

'Maybe,' Jem said. 'But it's ridiculous to go on keeping it secret. I do have a right to know. And it's nearly seventy years on, for goodness sake. Why shouldn't I know?'

She cocked an eyebrow at him. 'You be careful, Jem. You may be opening a Pandora's box. Discovering more than you want to.'

He looked at her gravely. 'I realise that.'

Fiona squeezed his shoulder. Comforting and supportive, as always.

'What's she like, this lass? You've all been to a deal of trouble over the cottage for her.'

He wrinkled his nose, thinking. 'Tall. Nice figure, dresses casually, but still manages to look smart. She looks wealthy, but she's chosen a cheap bothy for her month in Scotland and maybe there's less money than I thought. She's—nice.'

Fiona was tossing the vegetables in the vast frying pan and glanced up in amusement.

'Nice! Pretty? Should I be watching you? Or Patrick? Or David?'

'*David*? You must be joking! He's a long way from getting over Shona, wouldn't you think? And not Patrick—she was angry with him, I'm not sure why. He bullied her into playing at the *ceilidh*, but I think it was more than that.

Perhaps she discovered that he'd looked in her handbag. That was out of order.' He grinned at her. 'You needn't watch me. I've got my hands full with you.' He ducked as she threw a carrot round accurately at his head.

'She's a musician.' He said it as a flat statement. 'David says her mother is the concert pianist Charlotte Elliott.'

Fiona's eyebrows rose.

'Well! Quite a celebrity! So why is she here? You don't have to do on-the-spot wartime research these days—at least not at this time of year.'

'Why indeed. Wanting somewhere remote in the depths of winter is quite strange. I'm guessing at an unhappy marriage, or a wobbling one anyway. She's got a wedding ring—but no husband in tow. Parent trouble? Illness? She's not pretty, really. Nice-looking, sort of beautiful in an odd way. You wouldn't forget her. Handsome, I suppose. Sad, but merry, poised and well-dressed, but a mess inside I'd say.'

'Very succinct.' Fiona was dry. 'OK. See if your mother is willing to talk to her some time this week and ask her to stay for a meal.'

He looked up at her uneasily. 'Mother may refuse to talk about a specific John Elliott, but I guess wartime in Aultbea would be a good start.'

Pandora's box, Jem thought, and a faint tremor shivered through him. He hoped that prising open the lid would not give his mother a heart attack. Or himself.

Fiona was watching him with concern in her eyes. She turned her veg into an enormous pan and added stock from an even vaster stockpot simmering on the back burner. 'Go and see her now, Jem. And supper in an hour, boyo.'

* * *

'That Annie lass is researching her grandfather who was here during the war. I said that you had worked in Aultbea then and could probably tell her lots about what it was like.'

'Oh, aye?' Mhairi looked surprised and then considered the suggestion. 'Well, I suppose I could, not that working in the post office was very exciting. What was her grandfather doing?'

'He was in the navy. Killed on the convoys.' He could see that she tensed a little and added cautiously, 'A bit later I asked what his name was.' He breathed in. 'She said, John Elliott.'

He looked at his mother, searching her face for some reaction.

She said nothing, but she was clearly perturbed.

'Anyway,' he said, when the silence became too uncomfortable, 'she's a nice lass, and it would be a kindness to tell her a bit about what it was like in Aultbea during the war with all those ships coming and going.'

Mhairi sniffed. 'That's all I'd be telling her. I'm not having strangers asking personal questions.'

He had achieved something, if only winning a small skirmish. 'That's fine, Mother. I think she'd be interested and grateful.' Would he risk any more? 'But it would be good if you told her my name before I have to. And I will have to.'

Her eyes became thoughtful; calculating. At least he was giving her time to think over how she was going to do that.

15

February 1943

Archie was waiting across the road from the post office when Mhairi finished work. It was only half past three, but the winter sky was dark with fast-moving clouds spattering water drops without actually raining. She tensed in anticipation of the disagreeable mixture of possessiveness and malice. The thrill of being known as his girlfriend was beginning to be replaced by feeling trapped in a relationship she knew was unhealthy and disreputable and now unpleasant. She half waved at him, hunched herself inside her coat and headed for the bicycle rack.

He followed her. 'Not saying hello, then? Am I not grand enough for you these days?'

'Don't be daft, Archie! I thought you were waiting to see someone, and I wanted to get off home before the rain came on.'

'I was waiting to see you, wasn't I? I was going to offer you a lift home, bicycle and all, as your fancy man John seems to be away. Or are you going to Rhionna?'

She hesitated. 'Well, no. Rhionna's out this evening. I was going home, but it's a long way, Archie, and the petrol—'

His eyes glittered in the gloom. 'Don't you worry about the petrol, *mo ghràidh*. I've got plenty of coupons. And plenty of other things too. Let's go, then. The van is round the back.'

She knew she had to make a stand sometime, and it was best to do it here, where he couldn't accuse her of using him again.

'Archie—look, it's right kind of you, but I feel bad about it. You shouldn't get black-market petrol—if you get caught, what would happen? It's dangerous, isn't it? And I'd be in trouble too.' His eyes were narrowed in the handsome face, but she couldn't read his expression. 'And—and I wouldn't be asking you to stay—'

'Oh aye! Only the handsome Lieutenant Elliott gets to stay, and what a cosy little billet he's got. I wonder what your father would think of the arrangement in just the one room—poor old faithful Archie doesn't get a look in now.' His voice was thick with spite.

She hoped he couldn't see her flush in the gloom. Her last comment had been unwise.

'No. Well. As I say, it's a long way and will take up a lot of your time. Thanks for the offer, but I'll stick with the bike.'

Archie shot her a venomous look. 'You'll regret it before you get home.' She stared at him with her chin up, trying to pierce what sounded nastily like a threat. But a threat of what? Getting cold and wet? Or something else?

Archie might be handsome, but he was also dangerous and sharp. She didn't want him as an enemy. She had seen how he bullied younger boys, denigrating their looks, their achievements, their courage. Getting them to drink too much, encouraging dishonesty and bad behaviour and then getting them to boast about it. He took pleasure in getting others into trouble, and he could get her into trouble too.

Later, when she put the bicycle away in the shed and hung up her wet clothes, she felt restless and uneasy. She had known for a long time that he was involved in illegal trading, and she had enjoyed the whiff of danger that it brought. Many people traded on the black market for things they couldn't get with a ration book, but Archie was a smart man, and she guessed he was on a criminal career path designed to give him a substantial and sustainable income. It wasn't wise to cross him, and though she now didn't want to have anything more to do with him, she was unable to climb out of the hole she had dug herself into. Archie could, should he wish to, get her dismissed from the post office, where integrity and discretion were essential attributes. How she regretted the small and petty dishonesties, the acceptance of what had seemed like minor gifts, but in retrospect and in their number, amounted to quite considerable duplicities.

She wished desperately that John was still here. His presence was a solid buffer against Archie. But his ship had left three weeks earlier, and Archie's frequent and menacing visits made her increasingly nervous about being at the croft on her own.

Mhairi wanted John at Inveruidh, and not just for her own protection. She wanted to look after him, to cook and mend for him. She wanted his company and his intellect, she wanted the help he gave her on the croft, she wanted his gentle humour and encouragement. She wanted to be the one he needed and desired, her body naked alongside his.

She seethed with fierce jealousy that John should have a wife and children. I am twelve years younger than him, but I give him more than this puling wife who never ceases her pathetic complaints. Banging the kettle down on the hob, she seemed to hear his calm voice soothing her disquiet.

She made herself a cup of tea, guiltily aware that Archie had provided it, and sat down at the table with John's letters and the silky lingerie that had arrived just before Christmas. They were redolent with his distress and defiant rage. She buried her face in the nightgown, imagining the faint scent of his hands, agonising again for his disappointment yet thrilled at his anger with his wife. The excitement of war-time luxury easily overcame any feelings of this gift being second hand and as she touched the beautiful card of tiny shells and seaweed fronds he had made for her twenty-first birthday, her belly coiled with desire. Inside was a formal birthday wish, but she rewrote it in her mind. *Mhairi, with my deepest love and affection. Mhairi, I wish you were mine. Mhairi, until we are together again.* She re-read the letters he had sent during his disastrous Christmas leave over and over again, and they made her breathless with longing. I am wicked, she thought, but I don't care. The scribbled, almost illegible sheets of paper were testament to his frustration and fury. Again, she experienced the guilty sense of triumph that it was to her, Mhairi Mackenzie, that John had turned, and her craving for him completely drowned out the old excitement that she had felt for Archie.

16

8th January 2012

Jem had advised Annie to keep to unspecific questions about wartime life. He seemed uncomfortable and a little apprehensive. Were her enquiries bringing back bad memories for his mother?

'Sometimes she remembers things quite clearly, but often the details escape her, and she gets cross—with herself. She hasn't ever told me much about what she did, so I'll be interested to hear.'

And the old lady was not at ease, her hands restless and one foot in its sheepskin slipper tapping on the rug.

'It's a long time since I've even thought about those years,' she said. 'It's a long time since I was twenty-one, and because we were all told not to speak of it, or write anything down, I never have. One forgets.' Her fingers curled round her coffee cup, arthritic, bony, the thin skin purpled with age. 'I had to sign the Official Secrets Act because I worked in the post office and dealt with a lot of official papers and telegrams. The postmistress, Mrs Reid, was something fierce! I never dared gossip!'

'Did you get to know the military and naval personnel?'

Mrs Gillespie shook her head. 'We all knew the senior officers by sight, like the base captain and the medical people, but not to speak to unless they came into the post office for some reason. Of course, the sailors and soldiers came in for their mail, or to buy a stamp, but in those days there was nothing to buy like there is now. The post offices are in shops these days. It's all changed.' She said it in such a way that Annie was left in no doubt that the changes were, in her view, not for the better.

'What was it like when a convoy was getting ready? There must have been lots of ships in the loch, and all the seamen coming and going.'

She closed her eyes and put her head back into her chair. 'Oh, my goodness, yes indeed. It was frantic—a sort of organised chaos. Endless lines of lorries filling up the tenders with food and water, ammunition, general supplies. The tannoys blasting out movement instructions—very noisy it was.' She was full of anecdotes and stories and Annie loved listening to her voice, which seemed to become more West Highland as the memories came back, the words drawn out into their separate sibilant syllables. 'And the lads would write their last letters home—for some, it really was the last letter home— and the post office would get very, very busy. So sad, just young boys they were.' Her eyes opened wearily, and Annie wondered if she was tiring. She remembered Jem's admonition to keep things unspecific, but time was running out and she might not be able to talk to her again.

'My grandfather was based here for a time. He was an RNVR lieutenant killed on a convoy in 1945, I think. I'm trying to find out about him for my mother. You might have come across him, his name—'

Mrs Gillespie interrupted. 'I didn't really know any individuals.'

She pushed back in her chair as if easing aching joints. 'I'm so sorry, my dear, but I'm feeling rather drained. I haven't thought about those days for so long.' Her head dropped a little. 'I think I need to rest. Can you find your way out?'

'Of course I can,' Annie said, startled. 'I'm so sorry to have tired you. Thank you so much for talking to me. It's been really interesting.' What an odd and abrupt dismissal.

Closing the outer door behind her, she found a neat but ample lady unloading boxes of groceries in the rain from a car parked beside hers.

'Hello,' she said cheerfully. 'You must be Annie, visiting Mhairi. I'm Fiona, Jem's wife.'

Annie smiled in greeting. 'Hello. Yes, I've had a fascinating afternoon with her, and she's told me all sorts of intriguing facts and stories, but I think she's quite tired now.' She eyed the boxes. 'Can I help carry some of these in for you?'

Fiona gave her a direct assessing look. 'That's very kind, and yes, it would be a great help as it's raining. Stay for a cup of tea and tell us how you got on.'

In the big kitchen, Fiona put the kettle on the Aga and started putting the stores away.

She called Jem. 'Here's Annie, just left your mother. Lots of stories, apparently.'

'Well, I feel that I've got a lot of first-hand knowledge about wartime Aultbea, and I rather wish I could have recorded it. I took as many notes as I could.'

Jem put mugs and milk on the table. 'So she was happy to talk about what it was like during the war?'

Annie smiled. 'At first, it seemed quite difficult for her, but as the stories came out, she seemed to remember more and more.'

'And your grandfather? Did she know the name?' He had his back to her, making the tea.

'Well, I never got to tell her his name. I was about to, but she said she never knew any individual service people, and she suddenly seemed very tired, so I left.'

Annie saw Jem and Fiona exchange a glance. Jem's mouth had tightened, almost in irritation, and remorse flooded through her.

'I'm so sorry if I've exhausted her. I shouldn't have stayed so long.'

He put the tea down with a short laugh. 'I very much doubt that you've exhausted her. She's a good actress!' Annie thought he sounded almost bitter. 'Fiona, isn't there a very old lady at the Sandy Brae care home who came from Aultbea? She might remember wartime stuff too. I can't think of anyone else and those who were around then are pretty old now, if they're not dead.'

Fiona steepled her fingertips in thought. 'Susan Mac-Connachie is probably who you mean. She's in her late nineties, but quite *compos mentis*. I'm doing a regular visit there on Monday, and I'll enquire if Annie could have a chat with her.' She seemed a little troubled. And Annie wondered if there was something they weren't telling her.

17

11th January 2012

Sitting duvet-snuggled with her laptop warm on her thighs, Annie looked out through the open curtains. The daylight was slow in coming, although it was nearly eight o'clock, and last night's satin sea had metamorphosed into rough grey and white in the gloom, great waves crashing on the shore and sending up huge plumes on the rocks, ivory spume bowling along the beach and spray driven almost horizontally along with the driving snow. Deep contentment filled her as she revelled in the warmth in front of the huge, long, low window. There was no one to make her feel guilty. There was a freezer full of food, plenty of wine and fresh supplies, peat, coal and driftwood for the fire, and central heating which would cost a fortune. There were some things about wealth, she reflected, which were particularly pleasant, and not worrying about the fuel bills was one of them.

Buried in her subconscious was the knowledge that at some point the emails and letters would have to be tackled. So far, she had only communicated with her parents and had looked at the replies to her queries about John Elliott from various naval sources, and the Births, Marriages and Deaths information. All else was on hold. Justin, Justin's lawyers, the school governors, the tribunal, and a few 'Where are you?' friends.

She didn't miss Justin, or his friends, or the shooting, or the country house, or the London house either. Cowardice? Hoping all the problems would just go away?

Her brief forays into the wider world had been to the store and a visit to the bank in Gairloch to finalise a new, unmarried, account. The bank officer was the singer from the *ceilidh* and her lapel badge said Isla Thompson. Annie paid tribute to her voice, but Ms Thompson hardly acknowledged the compliment and dealt with the paperwork with brisk efficiency and an unfriendliness which bordered on rudeness.

She looked down at the computer screen. Her notes were taking shape, and a shadowy John Elliott was beginning to take shape too. His marriage in 1937, his parents' names and his siblings, all long dead. Charlotte's unknown uncles and aunts.

She was beginning to feel the human-ness, almost the personalities, of these unknown forbears of Charlotte, began to feel their hopes and fears, the pain and loss of birth and death. She wasn't just searching for knowledge of Charlotte's father; she was starting to peel back the thin layers of family and relationships. Downloading a genealogy tree, Annie began to enter information, often frustrated by making technical mistakes and putting things in the wrong places, but with thanks to Google, plus bursts of membership fees to access information, piece by piece the picture enlarged.

Eventually, hunger got her out of bed. She ate cornflakes gazing out at the driving snow, lit the fire and felt no compulsion for fresh air.

The desire to continue the addictive habit of genealogy had to be resisted because disregarding incoming emails and unanswered post was beginning to bother her. She dealt miserably with the tribunal paperwork and distastefully with the divorce lawyer, answered the urgent emails and phoned Charlotte and Will in South Africa. Charlotte's arthritis had faded in the warmth, and her parents were enjoying seeing old friends and relaxing in the sun. They were also relieved that Annie was happy in her Highland fastness and had laughed with her over the somewhat light-hearted story of her arrival and subsequent rescue. Annie had said little about her search for John Elliott's history, not wishing Charlotte to anticipate success, but the *ceilidh*, the exciting weather, the sea, the walks, the music had all been described, and Charlotte's relief and pleasure were palpable.

By lunchtime the snowfall had covered the surrounding countryside in a glorious ermine cloak; sea, land and sky glittered under a sudden brilliant eye-watering sun. With a sense of release, she celebrated with a glass of white wine and half a steak and ale pie from Mace Stores in Poolewe, home-made in a foil pie case. Then, encased in cold-defying accessories, she set out to explore. Turning north-west up the road, she came to the huge beach at Firemore. A plaque informed her that when the glens had been cleared to make way for sheep, the evicted families had established a fishing and crofting community here. It also told her impenetrable things about anti-aircraft batteries and guns, command posts and portable radar units, and the defence of the loch.

Gazing at the empty land and sea, she found it difficult to people them with soldiers and lorries and guns, with concrete barracks and canteens, with ships and sailors and minefields. An odd sense of sadness perturbed her that she could not be part of this history, could not share in these people's fear and exhaustion, apprehension, boredom. Cold. Annie shivered and strode on, past Mellongaun lookout post, past old crofts and new cottages, until she came at last to the village sign for Cove, a substantial community. A surprising number of people lived, worked and farmed at the end of the world.

Suddenly she noticed that the sun had gone, the snow on the hills around her was gunmetal grey, and the sea had turned a deep and sinister purple. A bitter wind gusted at her back, and turning, she realised she would be walking back straight into it. Thank goodness she hadn't struck out on to the moor, which had been her first intention after lunch, because in just a few minutes the clouds had blotted out the sky and visibility was diminishing with another onslaught of snow. She had come about three miles, had been passed by one car, and needed to get back. Un-English and rather disquieting, she thought, as she turned back down the empty road.

When at last she closed the heavy door of Inveruidh behind her, she slumped against it in relief and triumph. Then she heard the phone, and on opening the door to the kitchen its shrill insistent ring prickled her skin with alarm.

'Hello?' she said, cautious and rather breathless.

A man's voice, anxious and a little harassed, said, 'You're OK then? You haven't been answering the phone. I thought you'd been caught in the storm.' It sounded like David's father and she took a breath. Since when was she his responsibility? Making her voice calm and expressionless, she said, 'I'm fine, Mr Mackenzie. Thank you. Sorry I was out. Were you ringing me about something?'

There was a fractional pause. 'It's David, by the way.' Mistaking the son for the father was a bit of a blunder. 'Yes, to say that my mother was visiting Sandy Brae, the care home, today, and asked the matron if you could visit Mrs MacConnachie. The answer was yes, so long as you came with someone Mrs MacConnachie knew. She knows me, and I've got to go there tomorrow to do some work, so I can take you if you want to go, and bring you back, come to that, as I can pick up the boys at the same time.' He paused. 'I rang about two, and about three, and it's now after four, and I need to plan my day and—' He added belatedly, 'I was a bit worried you'd gone out and got caught in that blizzard.'

'Oh! That was kind of your mother to organise it. Your parents said they'd try to arrange a meeting with her.' Feeling remorseful about the trouble she'd put him to, she confessed to her walk, made light of the blizzard, and arranged to meet him at Poolewe Hotel at one-thirty the next day. Putting the phone down and going to run a hot bath to thaw out, she considered the prospect of going with David. Was she nervous? Both the window episode and her tearful breakdown in the kitchen were uncomfortable memories, but he emanated safe and unthreatening company, mourning a much-loved wife. She decided not to think about how attractive she found him.

18

12th January 2012

She was there before him, leaning over the fence, gazing across the loch. Slim legs in blue jeans, with long leather boots, one foot resting on its toe behind her, her bag slung over her shoulder. A scarf which matched the blue of her eyes was wound round the lower half of her face and the hood of the thick coat covered her hair. Very attractive, but very different to Shona, whose comfortable shape and round face had been appealing and friendly. Not that Anne Devereux was exactly unfriendly, he thought, as he tooted the horn, turned the car in the hotel car park and came to a halt beside her. As she stepped towards him, naturally graceful, he had a faint impression of nervousness, or diffidence, whereas Shona would have called a smiling greeting even to a stranger.

Throwing back the hood, she unwound the scarf, letting the straight, silky hair fall loose. It glinted red in the sparse sun. She thanked him for the lift to Gairloch and he noticed that she held her scarf and bag on her lap with rather tense hands. Long-fingered; short oval nails with no polish. The car took the steep snowy slope with ease.

'Are you still enjoying the cottage, or is the remoteness getting to you?'

'I love it!' she said, her face lifting with the declaration,

'And I love the remoteness. It's warm and cosy, the water's hot and everything works. And everything is so beautiful, even the bad weather. I could stay for ever.'

'I think you might find the long, dark winter quite trying after a while. Most southerners cope for a few years, but eventually the miserable darkness gets the better of them, and back they go south of the border. Living and working, especially crofting, in perpetual rain and darkness is pretty depressing.'

'Maybe you're right,' she acknowledged, 'but London can be pretty depressing too.' She indicated the platforms in the loch. 'Is that a fish farm? I thought salmon were farmed in the sea?'

'Yes, they are. This is a trout farm. I prefer to catch my own, and my boys love fishing too. Have you ever fished?'

She laughed. 'My grandmother tried to teach me, without much success, when I was about nine. She was less than patient.'

He hadn't expected an affirmative or indeed a female influence into what he had considered a male domain.

'Your grandmother? The wife of the grandfather you're researching?'

'Yes, John Elliott's wife, Elspeth. She was taught to fish by her foster father after the war. The Gibbons were sort of adopted parents after her own parents died in the war. My mother Charlotte was a baby when granny moved out of Portsmouth to their pub, The Muddy Punt, on the River Test, and the fish they served was fresh trout—and whatever else you catch in the Test. My mother said they were better than any grandparents she could imagine. If it wasn't for them, she wouldn't have gone to the Royal Academy of Music. Grandma Gibbons insisted that she have piano lessons in Romsey after school and she used to play wartime songs and music hall favourites to the pub customers. Apparently, it brought in a huge amount of custom.'

'Did you know them, the Gibbons, or had they died before you were born?'

'They both died in the late seventies, so I never knew them. That's partly why we're interested in John Elliott's past—Charlotte's musical gifts must have come from somewhere, and it wasn't her mother. He played the violin, but after his death it never came back to her, sadly.'

He digested the information, still uncomfortable that his father had not told Annie the truth. For the first time, he wondered where his father's violin had come from. 'And how is your research going? Are you making progress?'

'Slow—I'm beginning to get the hang of all the different source websites, but with the museum closed until April, I can't do anything there. It doesn't matter—I've explored Loch Ewe and Aultbea, and Gairloch, and read lots about the convoys. Perhaps I'll come back, once everything is—sorted. I could bring my parents; I think they'd love it. Perhaps I could rent Inveruidh in the summer? It just mustn't rain.'

He was amused. 'Of course,' he said. 'Get in touch with Kate about dates.' They hadn't sacked Kate—it was too much trouble to replace her, and in any case, it hadn't been entirely her fault. Was it the fall-out of the piano fiasco that had to be sorted, or her marriage? Perhaps both.

'Why mustn't it rain? The English think it always rains in Scotland.'

'My mother is getting arthritis in her hands, and damp conditions make it worse. That's why they go to South Africa in the winter—so she gets some sun and warmth.'

'I'm so sorry. That's awful for a pianist.' Or for any energetic person. He thought of Shona, always on the move, always busy doing something, hating the exhaustion after treatment, the way the cancer had constrained what little life she had left. 'Why don't they live somewhere warm all the time? The UK can be wet and cold all year round.'

She smiled and shrugged. 'Well, we're English, and my father's job is in the UK. They may decide to spend more time in South Africa in the future.'

And you, Annie Devereux? What are you going to do with your life now that you've messed up teaching music by slapping a pupil? He turned right at the Gairloch Museum.

'Now, Mrs MacConnachie. Apparently, she was a nurse at the wartime hospital, now the Gairloch Hotel, and she's ninety-eight, and sometimes a little confused, so don't expect too much.' A thought struck him. 'I think I've got a little booklet about Aultbea during the war—memories of local people, that sort of thing. Would you like me to dig it out if I can find it?'

'I'd love to have a look at it. But you're busy.' She sounded a little embarrassed. 'I wouldn't want you to waste time looking for it.'

He smiled at her. 'No bother.' The self-deprecation was endearing; perhaps a sign of sensitivity towards other people, perhaps just lack of confidence. He was alarmed that he found it so attractive and in self-defence turned his thoughts to Shona. To her friendly self-assurance, her assumptions that her willingness to help meant that everyone else was willing too. Shona would not have hesitated to either ask for or accept a kindness. Or to give one.

As he parked the car outside the old people's home she asked, 'What time shall I meet you?'

'I shouldn't be more than an hour—I've got to go to the bank, as well as check on the generator here. They had a power cut yesterday and it's got hiccups, but I doubt it's serious. I'll come along to her room to see if you're still with her, but if you've run out of conversation, I suggest you go to the café opposite the post office and I'll pick you up from there. But no later than three o'clock, to collect the boys, OK?'

Mrs MacConnachie was as broad as Mhairi was thin, legs and arms swollen with fluid. Heart problems, David guessed. She was in a wheelchair in the dayroom along with several other residents, around a table covered in flowers and greenery, wire and tape. A middle-aged woman was clearly about to embark on a floristry class. The warden greeted David and Annie and wheeled the old lady out and down the passage.

'I didn't mean to interfere with Mrs MacConnachie's afternoon. I can come back at a better time,' Annie said and again David noticed her diffidence. She didn't like to be a nuisance and he found it an appealing characteristic.

The old lady cackled. 'What would I want with making wedding bouquets? No one's going to marry me now, and the young ones don't bother with weddings these days! No, no, you're as good an excuse as any to get me out of that activity. Now then, young David, how are those wee boys of yours?'

After a few minutes, David clarified again why Annie was there and left them to it, although he rather wished he could have stayed. He would have liked to hear whether she had known a John Elliott in the war. He tried to ignore his desire for the company of Annie Devereux.

* * *

The old lady was happy to reminisce about the war and her time as a nurse in Gairloch, but as so often happens there was an assumption that her listener knew what she was talking about. Annie concentrated hard, taking as many notes as she could, and bit by bit hospital life came into focus, with its starched caps and aprons, fierce matron, long working shifts, the local lads who carried the stretchers and manned the morgue—now Room Five of the Gairloch Hotel. 'Who'd sleep in there without seeing ghosts?' Mrs MacConnachie said with relish.

'Do you remember ever meeting a young naval officer called John Elliott?' Annie asked. 'He was my grandfather and was based at Aultbea. He was killed on convoy in 1945 but that's really all we know.'

Mrs MacConnachie screwed up her face in thought. 'I remember the name, vaguely. Wait a minute now.' After a time, she nodded to herself. 'There was a young man with peritonitis. I think he was called Elliott. Your grandfather, you say? He very nearly died.' This information came as a shock. She might have lost him before she'd found him. 'No penicillin in those days,' Mrs MacConnachie went on, shaking her head, 'not for us anyway. More often they came in with terrible injuries, dreadful burns, shrapnel wounds. Many had to have amputations after being in the freezing water and many didn't survive, even having got to hospital. Discharged officers were sent to the Loch Maree Hotel to recuperate.'

'Is that where John Elliott went?' Annie was finding it tricky to keep her focussed on him.

'Oh yes, and he came back to the hospital a couple of times, later. He had a hand injury.' She seemed pleased with herself for retrieving the memory. 'He was a nice man. I met him in Aultbea too. All the girls in the village liked him, and he was around more than most because of his operation. Used to tease us about our red capes, said he'd like one too.' She cackled. 'They were funny uniforms, looking back at it—all those pin tucks…'

'Did you know Mrs Gillespie, David's granny, in those days?' Annie asked hastily before she could ramble off again.

'Oh aye! Mhairi Mackenzie she was then. She worked in the post office for Mrs Reid.' She sharpened. 'Now *she* knew that boy. Elliott.' Annie jumped. That was a surprise.

At the mention of the post office Mrs MacConnachie's memory seemed to have hopped on the mail bus as it carried her to Aultbea for a dance at the NAAFI.

'Everyone watched for the bus coming down the hill in the evening. That bus carried everything: mail, chickens, locals, the library. All sorts.' She shifted in her wheelchair to get more comfortable. 'I remember that dance because I was on the bus and my Kynoch—I married him a while later—was having a right how-de-do—shouting and fisticuffs—with Archie Mackinnon.' She sucked her false teeth at the memory.

'Archie was drunk and had been bawling Mhairi out for two-timing him, and Kynoch didn't approve of women being shouted at.' It sounded as if this Archie had been Mhairi's boyfriend. 'He was a big man and strong, but he was a gentle giant and would never have really hurt Archie, though he was angry that day. And he detested Archie. Archie was into the black market.' She shook her head disapprovingly. 'He'd once tried to involve Kynoch, who wasn't having any of it. The dance was right uncomfortable!'

'Two-timing him with who?'

'Well, Archie was shouting about the naval officer and I remember his name now. John, it was. John Elliott.' Excitement gathered in Annie's stomach. This was a personal recollection.

'Was John Elliott there, at that dance?'

She screwed her face up in an effort to remember. 'Maybe he was, I don't remember.'

'Can you remember what year it was?'

Mrs MacConnachie shook her head. 'No. But I remember Kynoch and Archie circling each other like dogs, while all the girls danced with the American and British lads.' The old lady chuckled at the memory and then leaned forward conspiratorially, her voice dropping.

'But Archie came to a bad end! He washed up on

the anti-submarine boom across the loch one winter. Murdered!'

With the requisite widened eyes and indrawn breath, Annie gasped. 'Really! Why? Who did it?'

'Nothing was ever proved,' Mrs MacConnachie said dramatically. It was obvious she enjoyed this raking up of an ancient scandal. 'But it was said—' her voice dropped again to a whisper as if the room were awash with listening ears, '—it was said that he assaulted Mhairi—tried, you know—' she bobbed her head meaningfully, 'and she killed him. Her face was fair bruised. All sorts of people were questioned by the police: Mhairi, crofters, soldiers, sailors, local shopkeepers.' She leant back and repeated, 'Nothing was ever proved.'

A little uncomfortable at hearing that Mrs Gillespie had been suspected of killing someone, intriguing though it might be, Annie tried to divert the conversation away from her and back to John Elliott, but Mrs MacConnachie remembered nothing more and she realised that the old lady was beginning to repeat herself, past and present merging. Time to go. Saying her thanks and goodbyes, she left her to snooze and made her way down the street to the café. The possibility that Mhairi had been assaulted by this man Archie must have been quite a piece of gossip for the community and the inference had been more than assault. 'It was said that she killed him.' She would look at Mhairi Mackenzie with new eyes now. Annie wondered if David knew that particular piece of gossip. Or if Jem Mackenzie did. It was an uncomfortable feeling that she might now be party to information that the family might not know.

The generator had taken longer than David had antici-pated, so it was almost three by the time he met her at the café, and they hurried to collect Seamus and Christopher. The boys fell out in the tumbled rush and bursting energy that release from school produces and scrambled loudly and untidily into the back of David's car. They didn't bother to speak to either their father or Annie beyond saying 'Hi!'. David's question about Mrs MacConnachie was lost when the boys began to bicker.

'Tell me later,' David said, handing the boys a banana each. 'If you come back with us, I'll feed the monsters—it's hunger that makes them bad-tempered—and give you that booklet. I think I've remembered where it is. I'll let you collect your car and you can follow me back.'

'OK. Thanks. What happens to the boys when you have to work?'

'They go to Hugh and Catherine's or get off the school bus at my parents' house. It's not ideal, but the best I can do at the moment. Sometimes they go to a friend's house, but I don't like to do that too often as I can't reciprocate much—I keep it for emergencies.'

'You're lucky to have family who can do that.'

He glanced at her. 'I am indeed,' he said. 'Otherwise I'd have to employ an au pair or something, which would drive me berserk, I'm sure.' He sounded fatigued by the idea. 'What happened to you when your mother was away on concert tours?'

'I went to a boarding school in Hampshire. At weekends, if Mum and Dad were away, I used to go to my grandmother, who by that time owned the Muddy Punt. I liked going there—I used to help lay-up and serve the food, and do the rooms, and the flowers. Lots of things—I always felt useful, and I used to play the piano to entertain the customers. Good fun, really.'

On collecting her car, she followed him back to a big stone house on the hill above Poolewe and sat with them in a spacious and Aga-warm kitchen while the boys consumed large jam sandwiches and they all had slices of Granny Fiona's chocolate cake. She liked the way their father was so patient with the squabbling and just produced what they needed to restore energy and good nature after a school day. The boys disappeared in a welter of discarded uniform and she told David what Mrs MacConnachie had said about a John Elliott with peritonitis.

'If she hadn't been a nurse at the hospital, I'd never have discovered that,' Annie said incredulously. 'I suppose it must have been him, but she couldn't recall any dates. She also repeated some gossip about a man who was murdered. Did you ever hear about that?' David shook his head in surprise. 'She said your grandmother knew him, but no one was ever convicted.'

They discussed Mrs MacConnachie's revelations for a few minutes. When he went away in search of the booklet, she picked up school blazers and sweaters from the floor and put them on a chair by the Aga. David hadn't heard of this man Archie, but it puzzled her that he seemed uncomfortable talking about John Elliott. She heard Chopsticks being banged out on a piano and David's roar of exasperation from upstairs. Chopsticks continued, a little quieter. The phone rang and was answered, and Annie followed the maddening piano noise to its source.

* * *

David came downstairs quietly because Chopsticks had given way to one of Scott Joplin's syncopated piano rags, clearly played by Annie. But then to his surprise, the simple bass was thumped out by one of the boys, uneven at first, with the melody played competently on top, accommodating the uncertain bass notes. There were a lot of giggles, and the syncopation improved as the bass got the rhythm. He heard Christopher demand a turn; the playing stopped and then started again. The tune became a little faster, and he could hear Annie telling him which notes to play. David put his head round the corner to find both boys sitting on the piano stool, with Annie standing behind them playing with her right hand and pointing out the bass notes with her left. Then Christopher gave way to Seamus again, and he could see his younger son using his two forefingers to play as Annie added the tune. They were all laughing, Annie enjoying their amusement. An unexpected surge of resentment assaulted him, immediately overlaid by pleasure, emotion he couldn't analyse, at seeing his boys and this woman playing a simple tune at the piano. Not Shona. Her absence screamed at him, and as always, he found the unexpectedness of his emotions frightening. Pulling himself together, he waited until Annie had thumped in the final chords, and then joined them.

He was surprised by the look on her face—a wide smile which transformed the grave look which had seemed to be her default expression. She was beautiful. Beautiful in the odd way that faces of character have when they are unbalanced, or beak-nosed, or deep-chinned. She had none of those deficits, except a slightly crooked nose, and he realised that it was happiness that had crept out of sadness, and that he recognised the place where she had been.

She turned immediately, and taking the booklet, thanked him for the lift and his trouble, and left them. The boys disappeared upstairs to homework and Lego respectively, knowing they wouldn't be allowed to watch TV, and David went slowly, with a cup of tea, into his study. He gazed out into the four o'clock darkness, seeming to glimpse a reflection of red-brown hair in the panes, and for some time he did no work at all.

19

13th January 2012

Jem took Mhairi's supper into her room which, unusually, was cluttered with her old leather case and papers and old letters and little packages. She gathered them up in a heap to one side as he set out the cutlery and food on the table, and he noticed that her hands were trembling a little and she looked more frail than usual.

He sat down in the chair opposite her and reached across the table for her hand, the bones sharp under the thin skin.

'You look tired tonight, Mother. Do you feel all right? Is the thought of those birthday teas worrying you?' Her ninetieth birthday was the following week and they had arranged a series of small tea parties over the coming weekend.

Her eyes flicked over him, evasive, wary. 'I'm all right. Just been lifting more than I should. I'd forgotten how much rubbish I'd kept in that case, and I got the urge to purge.'

They both smiled at her joke. Jem peered down at the wastepaper basket, emptied by Fiona this morning, and still empty.

'Not much purging, I'm glad to see. Whose history are you thinking of ditching? Yours? Mine?'

Her eyes sharpened and she pulled her hand away.

'No, boy. Not yet. Anyway, how can I throw history away without you knowing?'

He straightened, startled. 'Good God, Mother! I don't—we don't—spy on you or interfere in your business. I'd not want you to think—'

'No, no, I know that! Still, if I had secrets, I'd not put them in the bin, I'd get you to bring me that scrunchy thing.' She was smiling a bit severely. 'Go away while I eat this' she eyed the home-made soup and buttered toast, 'while it's hot. And come back later. I think it's time to talk a bit.'

He got up slowly. 'Do you want me to bring you the shredder?'

There was a long moment of silence as she looked up at him, debating. Her face had lost the humour and had dropped into its tracing of lines, grave and a little sad. 'No. No shredder. Not yet.'

As it turned out, Mhairi found it difficult to talk. She sat in her chair by the fire, with her little table pulled up in front of her, pushing the papers and envelopes and packets into separate little piles, then pushing them together again. Her expression was tight, mouth pursed into a thin line and Jem knew that there was no point in asking her what the matter was. She'd either tell him, or she wouldn't. He leant back in his chair, watching and waiting.

'It was my fault Walter didn't treat you as he should have.'

Jem blinked. This admission was more than sixty years late and he had never held the undoubted truth of it against her. He said nothing, but it was a comfortable sort of silence.

She glanced up at him ruefully. 'But I'm not telling you anything new, am I?'

He shook his head with a smile. He had no desire

to increase her self-condemnation if that's what it was. He looked at the papers and packets. Had the arrival of Annie Devereux induced her to discuss the past? His own memory slid back to the man who had housed, fed and clothed him, and paid for his excellent education. Walter had done all that he should, but had withheld that great necessity, affection. But Jem also knew that affection—love—had been withheld from Walter, by a sort of osmosis of understanding between mother and son.

Mhairi seemed to read his mind. 'We needed him, you know. We needed him, but I gave him good value even so.' This, he thought, was true. He had always known, in the way a child knows, that Walter was only there, only tolerated, because Mhairi needed him for her son. She herself had never really needed him; she had used the security he gave, his name, his house, his money, for her son. And Walter had known it. In that sense, it was indeed her fault that Walter had treated him as he did.

'But there was more to how he behaved towards you—and me—than just resenting that he was being used, wasn't there?' Jem leant back in his chair, allowing the childhood puzzlement to creep back into his memory. 'He changed from being a devoted suitor to being a bitter, carping husband. He became angry, didn't he? I was only eight or nine, but I remember that change.'

Looking at his mother he saw a sadness fall over her. She took a deep breath and raised her head.

'It wasn't what I intended, but there seemed to be no way round it except to tell the truth,' she replied. 'When we married, it seemed my previous marriage certificate was required, I think so that enquiries could be made to ensure my former husband really was dead, and that I hadn't just left him. Of course, not only did I not have a marriage certificate, but I wouldn't—couldn't—tell them my husband's name. I had to tell Walter that I had not been married at all, and that fact meant that you were—'

'—illegitimate.'

'He never forgave me. And he took it out on you.' She repeated her justification. 'I was a good wife to him. A good cook. A good housekeeper.'

Jem knew that she was trying, perhaps for the first time, to say sorry.

'You did well, Mother. No need to apologise. It must have been humiliating for him to have to bring up his wife's illegitimate child. Walter was a passable father—if a little Victorian. What's brought all this on? You've never worried about it before, so what's bothering you now?'

Her lined face cracked into a web of deeper lines around her tightened mouth. 'He punished you because he couldn't—' She hesitated. 'There wasn't anything he could do that would trouble me, except hurting you.'

Jem reached for her hand, wanting to lighten this surprising burden of guilt that had seemingly appeared out of nowhere.

'It didn't trouble me much, either. I seem to remember that any thrashing he gave me was well deserved. What's in your box that's reminded you of bad memories?'

'Nothing. I've only kept good memories. I have nothing of Walter in my box.' She was brusque, sounding almost contemptuous.

He was assaulted by a sudden and almost physical pain for her. No good memory of sixteen years of marriage. What an appalling and tragic waste of life and happiness, and all for him.

'Was it worth it, Mother?' He immediately regretted the question.

She turned her face towards him, and the restless uncertainty left her.

'Oh yes. It was worth it, boy. I knew you were clever like—' She stopped.

'Like my father?' he said.

She nodded, but her expression was uncertain, anxious. 'Yes. Like your father.' She ignored his unspoken question.

'Look at you now! I couldn't have given you that education—put you through university. I'm a wealthy woman thanks to Walter, and I have a son and grandchildren I'm proud of. It didn't matter about Walter.' She grinned—a naughty, derisory expression. 'I don't miss him, you know, I don't miss him one bit.'

'Honestly, Mother!' He was laughing. 'Don't go saying that to anyone else, they'll think you murdered him—put arsenic in his whisky.' He looked at her sharply. 'What's the matter? I was only joking!'

She was looking grey—horrified. Frightened even.

'Mother! I was only joking!' He took a deep breath. 'You didn't, did you? I mean, even if you did, I wouldn't tell anyone, but don't tell me, for God's sake!'

She heaved in a breath. 'Murder Walter? No, of course I didn't.' Her colour was coming back, but Jem wasn't sure how genuine she sounded.

Walter had died of a heart attack in 1970 aged fifty-five. At least, Jem thought he had. Did his mother, if not feeding his stepfather arsenic, tip the scales on the heart attack with cake? Walter had been a big man. Unattractively big.

By then he himself was twenty-five years old and living with friends in a flat in Gogarburn, near the engineering firm that employed him. He had left Walter's large merchant's mansion in Morningside with relief, and in the way of young men, without a thought for his mother left behind in it. Had Walter abused her? Been violent with her as he had been with Jem as a child? He didn't have the courage to ask.

Mhairi had got herself under control. 'There were times when I wanted to. He drove me mad with his pernickety ways and endless harping on about what a bad housekeeper I was, and how I wasted money—which I most certainly did not. Men change when they marry, different priorities. He wanted to be seen as a solid citizen, and you and I threatened that perception.' It was irritated amusement. 'He was a most attentive suitor and a most annoying husband. But no, no arsenic in the whisky.' She sat up straight and gathered all the papers together and back into the case. Whatever had come to the surface was pushed under again as she snapped the fastenings.

As he put the case on the floor beside her chair, he saw her mouth tighten with determination. He had the impression that she was forcing herself to do something she didn't want to do.

'That girl's grandfather was called John Elliott.'

'Yes, I told you,' he said neutrally and waited.

'I remember a Lieutenant Elliott.'

'And?'

She shrugged.

'I'd like to talk to that girl again.'

20

February 1943

There was a bang on the door. Mhairi knew from the familiar flat sound of his palm on the wood that it was Archie. Her breath caught in apprehension and she opened the door reluctantly, still holding the wicker basket she was mending as if it could protect her. A man in military uniform was standing behind him. For a stomach-lurching moment she thought she was about to be arrested for some black-market misdemeanour, but then realised he was a boy, a raw soldier.

'Hello, *mo ghràidh*. This is Alan, on his way back to the guns at Cove. We've got a favour to ask you.' He pushed past her and came inside, the young soldier trailing nervously. Mhairi followed them into the kitchen, already at a disadvantage. She did not offer them her normal hospitality of a cup of tea, from a pack that Archie had provided weeks ago, but stood wordless, wicker basket held in both hands while they leant against the warm range.

'We're in need of a bit of storage space in a few days' time, and the shed here would be just right.' He wasn't asking a favour, she realised. He was telling her. Her mouth opened, like a fish. Archie's hard brown eyes held hers. 'So the shed key, if you please, Mhairi.'

She found her voice. 'Storage for what? I've no spare

space and I can't have the shed locked—I need it all the time.'

He shook his head. 'No you don't.'

His insolence both astounded and infuriated her.

'So I do! I have the feed and hay and tools stored there, and my bike.'

'You can keep what you need in the outhouse.'

Fury boiled up in her. 'How dare you, Archie! Telling me how to run my croft and where I can keep my things and where I can't! And I've no need to ask what you want to store in my shed. It's black-market goods, for sure, and I'm not having it.' She had never spoken to him like that before. She had never spoken to *anyone* like that. It made her tremble and her throat was thick and tight. Whether it was anger or fear she didn't know. Both perhaps.

Archie's eyes were like ice pebbles, boring into her. 'It's never bothered you before, girl. There's been plenty of fine goods that came your way and you were pleased to take them, so what's the problem now? What's made you holier than thou all of a sudden?'

'There's a difference,' she said. 'Storing black market stuff on my property is different, and I won't do it.' She was glad she had the wicker basket to grip, to still her trembling.

Archie shrugged. 'OK. If that's how you want it.' That sounded like a threat too. 'There would have been thank-you gifts left behind, for just the few days of storage, but if you're not interested—that's fine. No need to be rude and get on your high horse.' Her breath shortened. She had not just offended him, but shown him up in front of the soldier. Not wise.

She watched them go, the van's darkened headlamps barely illuminating the track, and shivered. Not from cold.

For some reason she had not anticipated that he would return that night and because the wind had risen, she didn't hear the van's engine. She jumped with fright as the door banged, and he came in unannounced and unapologetic, pulling a chair from the table and straddling it reversed, his arms folded on the back under his chin. Observing the nervous twitch of her hands, a faint look of satisfaction crossed his face.

'Well, I had not enough time earlier to explain that your shed is just the most ideal and convenient spot for us all,' he said, the pleasant tone at odds with the sharpness of his gaze. 'But I'm sure I can make it quite clear now.' He looked around the kitchen. 'Did I not leave a drop of whisky here? I was sure a wee bottle came your way, but maybe your friend John enjoyed it all, knowing where it came from.'

Mhairi said nothing, but got the bottle out of the cupboard and snapped it down with a tumbler beside him.

'Are you not joining me?' he said, pouring himself a generous tot. 'Perhaps a mug of tea for you? It was best Lipton, as I remember. Good old Archie came up with the tea, didn't he?' Mhairi shook her head, though she would have liked to keep her hands busy with tea-making. It had seemed a joke at the time to accept those gifts, but now each one had the potential to blow her up, like unstable gunpowder.

'You need to be careful who you offer whisky and tea to.' He lifted the tumbler to his mouth, his eyes never leaving her face, 'There's no knowing these days who might drop a word in Mrs Reid's ear or tell the kirk elders or even the MPs, and you don't want them visiting, do you? Poking their noses into your larder, asking about all that butter and cheese. Querying the weight of a meat joint, counting the eggs. And lipsticks, and American nylons and dress material—where did all that come from?'

'I'd tell them they came from you,' she said hardily. 'And they know all about you already.'

He shook his head. 'I don't think so,' he said easily, 'but I wouldn't be here, would I? I'd be long gone, unlike you, caught red-handed as they say.'

'They wouldn't be finding anything,' she snapped, trying to sound fiercer than she felt.

'Well, you just never know who might turn up on your doorstep, do you? There'd be all sorts of things in funny places around the croft, and plenty of folk impatient to tell your father when he gets back, and the lovely John and his captain, too, and the base captain. I'm thinking Mrs Reid wouldn't approve at all.' He rocked the chair back, shaking his head in mock dismay.

So this is what blackmail feels like, she thought. Her job, her reputation in the community, her father's violent outrage, and worst of all the damage to John and his reputation and career if there was any taint of her involvement in the black market. These were not just threats; this was Archie telling her exactly what would happen. A sickness swelled in her throat, a terror that threatened to rise like the tide over shingle, the inevitable, unstoppable power of Archie's malice.

There was silence for a while, just the old wall clock ticking its uneven coughing tock. Then she got up and unhooked the shed key from the nail behind the door, folding it into the palm of her hand. 'How long? You said a few days. What does that mean? John will be back any day and he'll ask why the shed is locked.'

He shrugged. 'I'll know when John gets back. Nothing will be in there very long; stuff goes in and stuff goes out.' He looked up at her, a malevolent grin splitting his face. 'The shed'll be there for however long I need it. And so will you, Mhairi, *mo ghràidh*.' He leant forward and one by one forced her fingers open, the key lying on her palm like a sacrifice.

'Handsome John isn't here now, but you are, Mhairi.'

The disconcerting brown eyes travelled down her body and undressed her. As fear trickled down her spine, she knew he saw her shudder.

21

March 1943

The *Countess of Minto* limped home having spent, as John dryly put it, weeks being repaired in Kola to a worse state than she had arrived in, and they had lost one crew member in the same attack that had damaged John. Mhairi's relief for his safety was clear as she gripped him round the waist, avoiding touching his left arm, which was in a sling, and pressed her face to his chest.

'What happened? Is your arm broken?'

He put a reassuring right arm round her shoulders. He wanted to kiss away her fears, but it was far too public to do that.

'No. It's my hand only.' A broken arm would have been preferable. He knew from the instant he saw what the shrapnel had done that this would not mend like a broken arm. The pain after the initial numbing hit had been excruciating and the rough kindness of the only first-aider on board had been equally agonising in spite of the ice used to anaesthetise it.

She exhaled with relief, released her hold on him and picked up his kit bag and the scruffy violin case which had been deposited on the quay by a shipmate.

'Have you to see your captain again? Can you come home now?'

He sighed. Nothing would be more pleasant than the croft, some decent food, and forty-eight hours of uninterrupted pain-free sleep.

'I have to report to the base commander and then to the hospital.'

'What have you done to your hand?' She was puzzled and concerned. 'Is it bad?'

'It's a bit of a mess,' he said, trying for a bit of humour. 'Jerry took a potshot at me. Maybe the medics will straighten it out. I think my fiddle-playing days are over, though.'

Her eyes widened in dismay. 'Oh! John! I'm that sorry.'

When the officers had been debriefed, he found Mhairi loitering outside Flag Officer in Command's (FOIC's) office and she walked with him down to where the transport to the hospital waited. Out of the corner of his eye, he saw Archie watching them and knew from the tension of her arm on his that Mhairi had seen him too.

'He doesn't like it that I pay him no attention now,' she said quietly. 'People here give him the shoulder, but he still stays. I don't know why.'

Because you're here, John thought. He wants you, and I need to watch out for you, and I need to watch my own back too. His perpetual naval duties worried at his mind. Mhairi's safety was not within his power when he was away, and his skin prickled with anxiety, along with the thudding pain in his hand. Her safety was not within his power, even when he was here, he thought with gloomy discontent

* * *

He had been given local leave due to his wounded hand, and the thought of being at the croft instead of battling down to Portsmouth to see Elspeth and the children was an intense relief, not even blighted by guilt. The hospital had repaired his hand to an extent, thankfully under chloroform, but they were not encouraging about him regaining full use of it. Not only was it painful, but he was clumsily reliant on his right hand and any small manipulations were awkward and inelegant. He wrote a short and chaotic-looking letter to inform Elspeth.

'What! No potatoes peeled?' Mhairi teased in response to his apology for achieving nothing but sleep during the day while she had been at work. 'And I suppose it took you an hour to get dressed as well?' She slipped off her boots and put them to dry by the range. 'Look what I've got!' She fetched her bag and tipped two enormous parsnips on to the kitchen table. 'We are going to feast like kings this weekend. Mrs MacRae gave them to me, the darling lady.' She did a little skip in anticipation. 'Oh, and I've got a letter for you from your captain. I hope he isn't trying to get you back?' She sounded anxious as she slit the envelope and pulled half the letter out for him.

'I hope not too,' he said, ineptly opening the sheet, and running his eye down it. 'He wants to see me tomorrow and is sending a car at two o'clock.'

Mhairi frowned. 'Why? He surely knows you've not even been discharged. You have to see the surgeon again next week.'

He shook his head. 'I don't know.' Several disagreeable options went through his mind. Local leave becoming home leave. Local leave cancelled. The ship going in for refit. The captain taking leave and needing his second officer in charge. 'I expect it's just to clarify the report on the last convoy.' That was the least likely option, but there was no point in telling Mhairi that.

* * *

The interview was in the Aultbea Hotel, his captain seated behind a table and John standing before it. He was bewildered by the uncomfortable and unaccustomed formality and his shock on hearing the accusation that he and Mhairi were having an affair was profound and his anger genuine.

'This allegation is baseless and untrue, sir. I have not and never would do such a thing. I have never approached Miss Mackenzie in such a way, and she has never approached me. We are both entirely innocent of this charge, and with a wife and two children, all of whom I love dearly, I find the accusation hurtful and viciously irresponsible.' The heat of his fury spread through his body. 'May I ask, sir, who has had the impertinence to suggest that either myself or Miss Mackenzie is behaving in such a way?'

His captain raised an eyebrow at the undisciplined anger, but John was beyond apology.

'I am not able to specify where this accusation has stemmed from, Lieutenant.' He paused. 'I was wondering whether you yourself might have an explanation?'

John stared at him. Tardily, he remembered a bad-tempered exchange with an officious female administrator who objected to him being billeted so far from Aultbea. He had just come off convoy and had not been his usual gracious self.

'No, sir. I have no explanation as to why anyone would make this baseless allegation.'

His captain sighed. 'I have worked with you long enough to know that such actions are alien to you. However, I am obliged to make enquiries and FOIC will want to see that I have done so. Although I accept your assurance that both you and Miss Mackenzie have behaved with propriety, the service does not want to have complaints or even gossip about the billeting arrangements.' He looked at John's bandaged hand. 'The surgeons seem to think you will be out of action for some months. Do you want me to recommend you for a desk job in London? You'll not be much use to us while we're in Liverpool for a refit.'

John had a flash of dismay. 'I'd prefer not, sir. Could you find me a desk job up here instead? They've said I must not put any pressure on the bones and the thought of a train commute to London with briefcase and umbrella fills me with dread,' he added, with a little surprise that it was true. 'I don't want to leave the ship, sir.'

His captain looked at him thoughtfully. He gave a faint nod. 'It may depend on how your hand mends. A gunner without two hands is a liability for the ship. I'll do my best, but no promises.' He paused for thought. 'If you do get a posting here, rather than in England, it might be a good idea to transfer your shore accommodation either to the officers' mess or to a family home.' He rose and rocked on his heels. 'I will leave you to make provision in due course as you see fit. Dismissed.'

John saluted, but even as he marched out, he thought that 'make provision in due course as you see fit' was a peculiarly un-naval-like expression, and hardly an order.

He left the Aultbea Hotel as the sky was beginning to darken and waited for Mhairi to finish work, the anger bubbling like a volcano. What should he tell her? It would be easy to say it was a discussion about his future postings, due to his wound.

His official transport returned them both to Inveras-dale, her bicycle hooked on to the back. He spoke in brief generalities until the croft door was closed behind them and then she turned to him, her face concerned.

'What is it, John? Something's wrong. What did your captain want? You're not being posted away, are you?'

She wouldn't let it go, he knew. She was too intelligent to have any wool pulled over her eyes.

He sat down at the table, his hand throbbing from the tension. 'It was a disciplinary hearing.'

'Disciplinary? Why? What have you done?' Anger flared. 'Don't tell me they expected you back on board with a hand in full working order!'

He sighed. 'Let's have tea, Mhairi. Have you any rations left?' She banged the kettle on to the hob and sat down opposite him, her eyes dark and wide.

He straightened his back. 'There has been an—allegation. About us.' His throat closed and he swallowed. 'That we have behaved improperly.'

She didn't move, but her eyes widened further. 'An allegation? From who?'

He shrugged. 'He wouldn't say. But I suppose there are a few people who could insinuate that sort of thing, and I've been foolish to think that because we *have* behaved properly, other people would think the same. I think it's my fault. Before Christmas the Accommodation Officer wanted me to move nearer Aultbea and I refused. I think she's getting her own back.'

Mhairi was very still, and then she laughed. A harsh unamused laugh. 'Oh John! What an innocent you are! Accommodation officers don't do that!' The kettle started to sing, and she got up abruptly to make the tea. 'But I know who does. Archie Mackinnon wants you out of here. He's jealous, and he's out to make trouble.' His skin prickled with shock. 'And what does "He wouldn't say" mean? Wouldn't? Or couldn't, because it was an anonymous accusation?'

'I don't know.' Alarm was overtaking the shock. How stupid he was. 'I'm so sorry. I've been so thoughtless, and now your reputation may be damaged because of me. My captain advised me to move to the officers' mess or find another billet with a family, and I was going to do that as soon as possible—but…'

'But if you do, it will be as good as an admission of guilt.' Her tone was dry.

And if I do, she'll have no protection. Archie will be back in her life again. He'll have Mhairi under his thumb again. There was misery in her eyes, and he wondered if it was caused by more than just Archie's jealousy.

She got to her feet, fingertips on the table. 'I need to tell you about Archie.'

'You do,' he said tersely. Had they been lovers? Were they still lovers when he was away?

The grubby tale of manipulation and blackmail infuriated him.

'I'm so sorry. I tried not to let him, but he took the key. I couldn't stop him.'

'Why didn't you tell someone? Mrs Reid? FOIC? The Military Police?'

She shook her head. 'I'd accepted things from him.' She looked up at John pleadingly. 'They were little things. Nylons, tea, butter. He said he'd tell Mrs Reid, and I knew I'd lose my job. And the MacRaes wouldn't have me in their house or let me be friends with Rhionna. And she'd be in terrible trouble too. He said he'd get you into trouble with the navy.' Her eyes were bright with angry tears and she looked down, trying to hide them.

'He succeeded there.' He wrapped his good hand round the mug of tea she had poured. 'Blackmail never ends once it starts. The only way is to expose it immediately. The consequences are never as bad as trying to conceal it.' She looked crushed. 'You must tell Mrs Reid. Even if you do lose that job, it means Archie can't blackmail you.'

She hesitated. 'I'll think about it. Think about how to tell her, and what to tell her.' She looked at his dubious expression. 'I will, John.'

Part of him was angry with her, but the rest of him longed to gather her into his one good arm and comfort her. His anxiety about what Archie Mackinnon had done, and might do in the future, lay heavy on his mind and heart.

22

13 January 2012

'I have a summons for you,' David announced over the phone.

'A summons?' Annie tried to ignore the warmth rising in her chest.

'It seems my grandmother would like to talk to you again.'

'Oh? Has she recalled more wartime memories?' Why did she think that Mrs Gillespie was a rather calculating lady?

'Maybe. I don't know. But she's asked if you would come at eleven o'clock tomorrow.' Annie contemplated the imperiousness of old age.

'I could come and collect you if you like,' he said. 'You've been driving quite some distances lately.' Was he concerned about all the driving she was doing or was he making sure she deferred to Mrs Gillespie's wishes? She suspected the latter.

'I think I can manage the trek to Poolewe,' she said. 'Thank you. I'll be there at eleven.' She later wished she hadn't been so prickly.

The next morning, she presented herself at Jem and Fiona's back door, let herself in and called. She had hoped that David would be there so that she could reverse the effect of being prickly, but Mhairi was sitting alone in her lug chair by the fire, with papers and envelopes on the table pulled up before her. After cups of coffee and Fiona's home-made chocolate biscuits, and the fire stoked, the old lady settled back in her chair, and professed herself ready for more questions about wartime Aultbea. When Annie mentioned that she had been to see Susan MacConnachie, her chin became pointed and the slippered toes twitched.

'She's an old gossip, is Susan.' She was irritated at being upstaged, Annie thought in amusement. 'Very unreliable. Jem told me your grandfather was called John Elliott.'

Annie nodded neutrally, remembering Mhairi's firm statement that she had not known any individuals and the abrupt dismissal when John Elliott's name was about to be revealed.

'I remember John Elliott.' Her old lined eyes narrowed on memory, and she shot a straight and searching look at Annie perched on the tapestry stool opposite her. 'He was a lovely man.' Her head tilted, all the lines creasing into a shadow of a pretty girl, a memory of a beautiful woman. 'He came off escorts in—' her mouth pursed as she tried to pinpoint a date '—I think, March 1942, with a burst appendix. He was in a bad way.'

'Mrs MacConnachie remembered him arriving at the hospital—'

'I remember it because I worked in the post office and saw him nearly fall.' Annie hid a smile at her obvious annoyance about Mrs MacConnachie. 'It was me got the sick bay attendant to him and they took him into the hospital. He took a long time to recover.' She shot a glance at Annie. 'He was a dear man.'

A lovely man. A dear man. At last, she was getting real evidence about a real person. Excitement bubbled in her chest.

Mrs Gillespie went on dredging up memories. 'He

was a gunner and Number Two of a trawler. What was her name.' It wasn't a question, just irritation that she couldn't bring it to mind. She lapsed into thought and then exclaimed, 'Peppermint!' in triumph. She laughed a little, then sharpened suddenly. 'Yes! She was the *Countess of Minto*. I remember now.'

'Who was?' said Annie, mystified.

'That was his ship. Yes, the trawler, the *Countess of Minto*.'

That was a significant piece of information, a point of reference for research, and Annie added it into her notebook.

'One winter, very bitter, he lost two fingers of his left hand. A bit of shrapnel while he was on the Lewis.' She paused, her eyes seeing far-off events. 'He couldn't play his fiddle after that. Sad, he was. But better to lose a couple of fingers than your life.' Her expression altered, a surprising anger in her taut mouth.

Confused, Annie enquired tentatively, 'The Lewis? You don't mean the island of Lewis?'

'No. It was a gun. Mounted on the deck and not much use really. Those trawlers were equipped with AA guns, but they iced up solid on the winter runs. They were anti-submarine trawlers, with depth charges, which malfunctioned often enough.'

'You said he couldn't play his fiddle after being wounded. Did he play well?' The old lady pursed her lips. Shrugged. Nodded.

Annie persevered. 'I wonder what happened to it. His wife said it wasn't ever given back to her, so perhaps it was lost when he was killed.'

Mrs Gillespie shook her head and began to say something, changed her mind and stared at the wall behind Annie's head. There was an odd look on her face. Wariness; a tense determination.

She refocused on Annie. 'There wasn't much opportunity to play on those trips unless they were stuck in Russia.' Her voice became brighter. 'But lots of ships could rustle up a wee band and they sometimes played at the socials. There were all sorts—the American negroes had fine voices, and I remember one who played the saxophone—real dreamy, that was.' She went on talking, but Annie had the feeling that she had decisively taken her memories from the personal ones about John Elliott to the generalities of wartime experience. She tried to bring the conversation back to John, but the old lady didn't take the hint. Her reminiscences became harder to follow and further from John Elliott. Annie told her of Mrs MacConnachie's memory of Kynoch fighting a man called Archie.

'I remember that fight,' she said, gazing up at the ceiling. 'Kynoch MacConnachie was a big man then, though he faded away to just a feather before he died. Kynoch Whaler they called him. He crewed one of the fleet supply whalers. He was a God-fearing man was Kynoch, but he couldn't abide Archie or any that supplied the black market.' She brought her gaze down to Annie's face.

'Archie had no conscience. He cared only for his pocket.' A little secret half-smile crept on to her face. 'But Archie didn't get to keep his pickings, sure enough.'

'Was he arrested for it?' Annie said, even though she knew the answer. She wanted to know what Mrs Gillespie would say.

'Not he. He'd have wriggled out, such a worm he was.' Her voice was loaded with contempt. 'No, Archie died. Drowned.' The smile was broader now. 'And lots of problems died with him.' *It was said that he assaulted her, and she killed him.* Was it possible?

Mrs Gillespie tilted her head, the fine white hair with its meticulous waves glinting in the weak sunlight. 'He was dangerous, true enough, but there was a thrill to being with

Archie. There was many a girl envied me my nights out with him.'

So she had been Archie's girlfriend, although she made it sound as if the fight had been about Archie's nefarious activities rather than her two-timing him with John Elliott.

The old lady's expression slid back to that secret smile. 'Archie got his come-uppance, for sure.' There was a note of finality in her voice as if the subject of Archie was now closed.

She wasn't sad or regretful about the man's death, Annie realised with a renewed sense of shock. Perhaps she really had murdered him?

'And John Elliott? Can you tell me about him? What did he look like, what sort of person was he? My mother knows so little.'

Mrs Gillespie hesitated a moment. 'You learn the difference between good and bad when you meet a good one.' She directed a straight look at Annie. 'John Elliott was a good one. And a brave one too. He knew the chances of coming back got thinner every time they went, but still they went. I seldom heard any of those men, merchantmen or naval officers, whinge about convoy duty, even though it must have been like hell for every one of them.' She blinked rapidly as if trying to disperse the memories. 'What did he look like?' She considered Annie, her head on one side, almost surprised. 'You don't have a look of him. He was a gentle man.'

With her Highland lilt, the way she said it sounded old-fashioned, using gentleman in the true sense of the word. Which sounded as if she thought Annie was not a gentle woman. She wasn't surprised she didn't have a look of him, and had Mhairi suggested it, she knew she would have been distrustful of everything she said.

'He was kind, and he had a lovely sense of humour. He teased me no end. But he could be firm too—a man

135

of conscience he was. His hair was dark, though there was grey in it, and thick. It flopped in his eyes when it got too long. I cut it a bit before he went away, but not too much for they needed all the warmth they could get.'

Annie kept her surprise to herself. Cutting a man's hair was surely a most intimate service. She had a vision of a row of sailors lining up outside the post office to get their hair cut.

The old eyes had become unfocused, the lines of her face softening. 'Yes. He was a handsome man, tall. Calm. It took a lot to anger him, though I saw him angry a few times. Yes indeed.' She nodded to herself.

'All the naval officers looked so fine and handsome in their uniforms, but in the northern sea they wore all the thick clothing they could get on. It was never enough. The cold was awful. He came back from one convoy with a terrible mark across his face—he said one of the rigging lines came loose in the gale and as it hit him it froze to his skin.' A deep breath. 'He had to rip it off, and of course the skin came too.'

Annie gasped, and the old lady glanced at her. 'There were things happened then no one could imagine now. My cousin Kenny was torpedoed off Spitzbergen—he was picked up, but he died on deck—been in the water too long. My God, what a waste it all was.' Her sad eyes shimmered.

'Yes,' Annie murmured. 'What a waste. How old was your cousin Kenny?'

'Seventeen, thereabouts. His memorial's in Gairloch Old Burial Ground, along with many another.'

'And between the convoys, how much time did they have to spend here, and where did they all live? Did they stay on board their ships?'

She didn't answer immediately. 'Sometimes there was a quick turnaround, and they went straight back on the

Russian road. Sometimes if their ships were damaged or needed a refit they went down to Liverpool, or Belfast, or Clyde and then they'd have sea trials. If they were here the officers and men were either on their ships or in the messes in Aultbea—and dreich comfortless places they were—Nissen huts, basic, damp, cold. Those that were lucky got billets with local families.'

'And John Elliott, do you know where he was? After he left hospital did he go home?'

She looked at Annie, frowning, debating with herself. But eventually she seemed to come to some conclusion and shook her head slowly. 'No, he couldn't go home. After he came out of hospital in 1942, he was billeted on Mhairi Mackenzie at Inveruidh.' She smiled a little at Annie's astounded face. 'He still looked shocking and I had a feeling that the officers' mess wouldn't improve matters. He got extra rations, so I did quite well out of it. My father was in a prisoner-of-war camp in Germany and the croft was hard work for a single girl—and I was working in Aultbea Post Office most of the war too.'

John had stayed with Mhairi? In the same house Annie was now staying in? A ridiculous sense of shock, as if she had unexpectedly been transported back to an era of entirely different values. What must the locals have thought of two young people sharing a small house? And surely Scotland was quite repressive about that sort of arrangement during the war?

It was clear Mrs Gillespie guessed what she was thinking. 'Don't get me wrong, girl, it was just a billet! Many of the locals provided billets if they could.' She seemed amused by Annie's embarrassed blush. 'He was a gentleman, John Elliott was. He never took advantage of anyone, but he helped me when he could, on the croft.'

Annie's head was spinning. Never had it crossed her mind that her researches would uncover an actual human connection with the shadowy person of John Elliott, or his presence all those years ago in the same village, the same house that she was living in. She was dazed by the revelation. Here, finally, was someone who had known this man well, who had lived in the same house, heard him speak, cooked his food, done his washing.

'Can you remember when his hand was wounded? Which convoy?' What a feeble question, when there were so many other more important things to discover.

Mrs Gillespie squinted in thought. '1943? March? It was a right mess when he came back.' The linked hands tensed briefly. 'They had to amputate two fingers. He stayed in Wester Ross until his medical discharge, and it took a long while to recover enough to go back on duty.' Annie saw that her face had tightened.

'I wonder why he wasn't invalided out,' Annie said, puzzled.

Mhairi turned in her chair to face her directly. 'He didn't want to leave his ship. He was given light duties and did escorts in the Bristol Channel and things like that for about a year.' She hesitated a little, seeing Annie's confusion. 'Did you know that he couldn't go home to Portsmouth?'

Annie frowned. 'I thought their house wasn't bombed until August 1944? Why couldn't he go home?'

The old lady's thin fingers tensed and her eyes dropped. 'I don't know that I should be telling you any of this.'

Annie stared at her. Was this the betrayal that Elspeth had spoken about? John had fallen for Mhairi Mackenzie and abandoned Elspeth in the middle of the war? Anger at his disloyalty flooded her mind.

'Elspeth's mother went to live with her after her own house was destroyed. She took over John and Elspeth's bedroom and Elspeth slept on the sofa.' She heaved in a breath. 'There was no room for John. He visited a few times, but he couldn't go home.'

Annie's head jerked up. 'That simply can't be true! Elspeth wouldn't—couldn't— have allowed her mother to do that.'

Mrs Gillespie's expression was almost mocking. 'It's hard to hear hard truths. I found it difficult to believe, too, but I know it's true.' She shrugged it away.

'So he was at Inveruidh a lot of the time. Oh aye, John was a help, though he knew nothing of sheep! He was a fast learner, and good with his hands, too, before he lost those fingers. He fixed fencing and gates, and roofs and sheds, and heaven knows what.' Her eyes crinkled in memory and a ghost of a smile touched her mouth.

'You said he never played his violin again. Do you really not know what happened to it?'

'No.' Her voice sounded harsh. 'No, I don't recall.'

But she does. Annie experienced a stab of frustration. She was not telling her something. Now she tipped half the contents of an old envelope on to the table with a little rattle. A folded card, some tiny pebbles and little shells, some of them crushed, bits of faded ribbon, grains of sand. And a pack of letters wrapped round with a fraying piece of thin cotton material, faded to grey. She pushed the card across to Annie.

'He was clever with his hands, John was. He made that for my twenty-first birthday and it was the only card I got. That card was a bit special.'

The annoyance faded as Annie lifted it gently. She held something that she knew John Elliott had touched, and not just touched, but handled, with care. With love? Her eyes watered.

The card was rough, a grimy cream and smeared with the remnants of ancient glue, now darkened to brown, tiny shards splitting off even as she held it. Miniature shell halves, some not even a centimetre wide, clams, limpets, blue mussels, cuttle fish, tiny pebbles and little desiccated fronds of seaweed delineated the words 'To Mhairi, Happy 21st Birthday'. Many of the shells had come loose as the glue had disintegrated over the years and lay on the table between them. Annie had the feeling that the intervening seventy years were like the little shells, falling away in fading memory, only their shape held by the dark outline of the glue.

The card was folded over and she had a reluctance to go further, almost fearing an unwelcome revelation inside.

The sad eyes were watching her. 'You can open it,' she said, her voice even.

No more creation. Just faded black ink in beautiful copperplate. 'With my thanks and best regards, John Elliott'.

'When were you twenty-one, Mrs Gillespie?' Annie's voice was unsteady and her eyes rather blurred.

'19th January 1943. A few days before, we'd walked the beach at Mellon Charles and he was collecting shells after the storms. A fine bright day it was, cold, mind you. He said it was like the Caribbean compared with the northern waters. He'd wanted to do something special on my birthday, but his convoy left earlier and he could only give me the card. But it was special to me, right enough.'

She put her head on one side, considering Annie, picking her words carefully.

'That Christmas before my birthday he went to visit them. He'd made such wonderful arrangements for the family, rented a flat in London for the four of them. But when he got there, she wouldn't leave her mother. John couldn't stay in the house and he spent Christmas alone in the rented flat. It was something that truly hurt him. He never got over it.'

Could this possibly be true? Was this not the petulant lover exaggerating, if not fabricating, a story? Her throat tightened and she swallowed the lump.

Mrs Gillespie went on, 'It was difficult—very difficult—to get enough leave between convoys and refits. As an officer he had to stay with his ship more than the crew, so don't think badly of him for not visiting much. Portsmouth was about as far as it was possible to go—it could take three days or even a week just to get there.'

'I never knew,' Annie said. 'I don't think badly of him. Perhaps my grandmother did, because she didn't speak of him much, and as a child I just never thought to ask about him. It's only now that I wish—I wish I had known him, I wish I'd asked about him, and so does my mother. She's really sad about that, about not knowing anything. That's why she encouraged me to find out more about him. He never even saw my mother. She was born after he was killed.'

There was an odd look on Mhairi's face. 'Was she now? And with the wee boys gone she was a lone bairn, like—like me.'

She stretched out her hand for the card. 'Don't know why I keep it, it's all falling apart. Like me. Getting old is no fun.' Her voice was sharp with frustration. 'Sometimes I think it would be better to go senile—like most of my friends, past and present.'

Annie thought that any comment would be a platitude, so didn't make one. 'Would you like me to get some more modern glue and we could put the card back together again? It was so pretty and it seems a shame to let all the shells fall off.'

'No.' She wasn't quite as dismissive as Annie thought she'd like to be and picked up a handful of childish pictures. 'I'm having a sort-out. All this rubbish I've kept over the years, Jem's and the grandchildren, and the greats. It takes up space and it's time it all went.'

Annie was horrified. 'Oh no! It's memories! Part of you! Part of your family and their history. I love seeing all the things I made when I was a child—awful clay models and jewellery made of Fimo plasticine which she used to wear to please me, and home-made cards for my parents. My mother kept them all.' And her mother had kept so many other mementoes for her, too, so many photographs and reviews and concert programmes, albums which were opened and discussed, memories which were not allowed to fade.

The old lady smiled rather grimly. 'I wonder if she'll keep them all when the next generation starts producing their artistic offerings! Have you brothers and sisters?'

'No. Only me.'

'Why only you?'

Annie was startled. She supposed that great age gave a person licence to ask impolite questions, but somehow she found herself answering.

'My mother, Charlotte, couldn't have children of her own. My real mother was my father's first wife and Charlotte's best friend and she died when I was born. Charlotte brought me up. She's really my stepmother.'

Mhairi stared at her for some time, then nodded, pursing her lips and looking sideways at Annie's wedding ring. 'And no bairns of your own?'

'No. We haven't been married long.' A whopping untruth. She had been married for eight years and wasn't married now. Shame prickled and she edged away from the topic. 'My real mother was a violinist and that's why I was interested in John Elliott's violin.' She wondered if Mhairi would pick up on the reference, but she didn't. 'Your family are musical too—do they get that from you?'

Mhairi shot her a glance and half laughed. 'Not from me or my family, though my father had a fine voice before the war. When he came back, he had infected lungs from POW camp, and I don't think he ever sang again.'

'How sad,' Annie commiserated. Where had the musicality come from then? 'But it must have been wonderful to have him back, and to have him helping you on the croft again.'

Her mouth tightened, and she took a moment before replying. 'He came back in 1945, but the war had changed a lot of people. I stretched my wings and went down to live in Edinburgh.'

How curious. What had happened to make her leave her home and a long-absent father?

'I'm sorry. Had he been wounded?' Mhairi just shook her head and Annie retreated. 'And John Elliott—which was his last convoy—the one he died on?'

Mhairi seemed glad to change the subject. 'He left at the end of 1944, after Christmas. I don't know when he died, but the ship came back without him months later—after repairs in Russia. Did the navy not tell his wife what happened?' She sounded puzzled as well as sad.

Annie shook her head. 'I don't think so. They sent a telegram to say he'd died on active service in January 1945. Nothing else so far as I know. Perhaps I can find out now from the Admiralty records. It's seventy years after the events now.'

Mhairi took a deep breath. 'Maybe. Poor man, so far from home. I don't know how many convoys he did. They seemed endless. Every time they went, the chances got slimmer. I think he knew he wasn't going to come back.' She sighed, and her voice sank to a whisper. 'Such a waste. My God, such a waste. So many letters undelivered and returned to sender.' She shook her head as if to clear away the memories and started to gather up the envelopes. Annie drew the side of one hand across the table and brushed shells and sand into her other palm before tipping it back into its envelope with John Elliott's card. Slipping it into the large envelope containing all the papers, she saw a thin sheet of folded yellowed writing paper amongst the contents, and clearly, in a large bold hand, below some writing on the inner fold which she could not at that instant decipher, a familiar signature. *'Elspeth'*.

The earth shifted. What was a letter from her grandmother doing in Mhairi's possession? How could they possibly have known one another? Was it a letter from Elspeth to John and if so, why had it not been returned to Elspeth? Or had Elspeth written to Mhairi perhaps warning her off John? Had Mhairi kept things she should not have done? Annie's heart thumped in her ears. There might never be another opportunity to ask about that letter. She took a breath, but the old lady spoke first.

'I suppose you could bring that glue.' Her bony hands trembled. 'It was a pretty card and it'll remind me that once upon a time I was twenty-one!'

'I'll do that,' Annie said. 'Maybe you'll remember other things about him too.'

23

March 1943

His anger overwhelmed his common sense and when he went looking for Archie the following evening it was too late to retrieve it. He found him in one of the village bars drinking with off-duty military riff-raff. The air was thick with cigarette smoke and the rancid smell of beer and sweat. All of them turned to look at him as he let the door swing shut behind him. Archie lifted his glass slowly to his mouth.

How could a brown-eyed man look so hard? Those eyes should have been soft, but they were sharp and harsh. He had a thin, unkind mouth, John thought, feeling the anger bubbling up again.

'Well, if it isn't the lovely John, Mhairi's darling. And it's back to the warm bed, isn't it, John? With good home cooking and butter on the tatties. Soap to wash the clothes, oil for the lamps, a pretty dress and silky nylons to make a man slather, eh?' Archie's mouth twisted in a grin, the eyes glinting.

The men around him laughed, their body language arrogant. Had Archie told all his cronies how he'd set him up?

'I'd like a word with you in private, Archie.' John had dealt with insolence before. His voice was even, and he looked each man in the eye, letting them know they were observed and scrutinised. He wished now that he had come in uniform.

Archie tilted his head and considered John's words with lazy amusement. 'In private, is it? I have no secrets from my friends here, so you're welcome to make the word public.'

'I don't think you'd like them to hear what I think of you.'

'Do you know, John, I think I'd be very flattered. So go ahead and tell us all what's bothering you. Is our Mhairi going about the town with other lads and leaving you out in the cold? She's inclined to do that, I'm afraid.'

'Are you afraid, Archie? Is that why you haven't the guts to be in private with me? You must have the safety of a band of small-minded men to back you up, is that it?'

Archie shrugged and glanced round at the men. 'Small-minded, are they? That doesn't sound very polite to my friends.' He looked back at John and dropped his eyes to his bandaged hand. 'Maybe you need the advice of these small-minded men as well as me when it comes to Mhairi. 'He pushed his beer mug at a neighbour. 'Get me a refill.' He transferred his attention back to John. 'We could all give you good advice about Mhairi, and it would be a kindness to a man who must be fair desperate after all those weeks on a wee boat with not a lassie in sight. It's not just dancing she likes, is it, boys? What else? Kissing, eh? She's a right good kisser, eh boys?' There was laughter and the courage that comes from being in the pack.

John itched to put his fist in Archie's face. He had trained in the boxing ring at school and knew that his right punch carried fair power.

'And of course, kissing is just the beginning.' He was watching for John's reaction, enjoying the anger. 'We could all tell you what happens after that, couldn't we, lads? While the fleet's away the mice will play, John.' He shook his head in mournful parody. 'She's a good one, and she doesn't complain if it's not a soft bed—any old place will do for a bitch on heat. Oh! She's a right little player is our Mhairi, and we can all testify to that, can't we, lads?' There were grins and laughter and nodding heads.

A red tide of fury rose up in him, a longing to put his fingers round Archie's throat, a visceral desire to make him scream for mercy.

'You are a liar, a coward and a criminal. Don't think for one moment that the authorities believe a word of what you've tried to fabricate round Mhairi Mackenzie—or me. They know what you are. It's you they'll be coming after, both civilian and military police, and—' he turned his glare on the men around him '—if you don't want to be contaminated by Archie Mackinnon's criminal activities, I suggest you keep well away from him.' He paused. 'And this is not a suggestion, Archie. Keep away from Mhairi Mackenzie and keep away from her croft.'

He turned away towards the door. In the space of seconds, a blow hit his left side and an excruciating agony travelled like a lightning bolt from his hand throughout his whole upper body. Somebody screamed, piercingly, and lightning exploded into his head, the flash instantly blackening and blinding as the floor rose up to hit him, drowning him in swamping pain. The sour smell of beer washed across his brain, discordant with noise; crashing boots, crunching glass, voices, shouts. The kick to his kidneys brought the agony exploding in again, but he forced his eyes to open, to focus on the centre of the pain so close to his head, but not in his head. The centre of the pain was inside the bloodied bandages wrapping his left hand.

Archie's voice came from above him. 'And this is not a suggestion, John. Keep away from Mhairi Mackenzie. And keep away from her croft. And just one other thing, John. One word about what happened this evening—to anyone at all—and our Mhairi will wish you at the bottom of the ocean. Yes indeed. Mhairi will be very, very sorry that you mentioned it.' Beer slopped on to his face in a stinking stream. 'Oh dear! My beer must have slipped from my hand. So sorry, John. Let me help you up, get you on your feet again.' He leant down and grasped the broken hand within the bandages, tugging his arm up, pulling the whole weight of John's body into a focussed agony in the smashed bones which flung him again into a tunnel of black oblivion. The black blurred into grey mist, swirling in a vortex of pain, and the grey mist thinned into shadows of light and dark. The dark shapes clarified fractionally, chair and table legs, moving figures, noise, shouts. And then close up, expensive leather shoes in his sightline, a swinging foot, his stomach, curling from the blow, and then the tunnel of agony once more.

24

January 2012

'She knew John Elliott,' Annie said, still astonished by the revelation, over a cold salad lunch with Jem and Fiona. 'He was billeted at Inveruidh! I can hardly believe it!'

Jem looked astonished too. 'He was billeted at Inveruidh? So she knew him well?'

'Yes. She said he was "a lovely man".' She saw Jem and Fiona exchange a glance. There was more than surprise in it. Trepidation? Disquiet? 'It was seventy years ago, and she remembers that he had a burst appendix and nearly died on arrival here. Mrs MacConnachie remembered that too, but—' she hesitated, not wanting them to think she was criticising Mrs Gillespie '—it was odd really. She didn't mention anything about it until I asked directly about where he'd gone after his medical discharge. I wonder if she would have mentioned it if I hadn't asked.' And I wonder how much more information I could get if I knew what questions to ask.

His mother's revelations fascinated Jem, and Annie told them all she could remember.

'I think my visit to Mrs MacConnachie irritated her. She wanted me to hear *her* memories, not Mrs MacConnachie's, and it seemed the more she talked, the more she remembered.'

After lunch, Fiona produced cake with their coffee. 'Your cake is to die for, Mrs Mackenzie,' Annie complimented her. 'I had some of your chocolate cake with the boys at David's house after visiting Mrs MacConnachie, and about half disappeared at one sitting!'

Fiona laughed. 'Annie, please call us Jem and Fiona, or some other Mackenzie will answer. And I enjoy baking— just as well, really, as the family enjoy eating them. I bake for the wee café at the museum in the summer, and for the stores as well. Mhairi taught me as a new wife—said it was the best way to a man's heart. How right she was!'

'*Not* the best way to a man's heart, actually,' Jem said, cutting himself not a generous slice, but not a sliver either. 'Probably lethal. Still,' he said cheerfully, 'all the children and grandchildren seem to be as thin as rakes, but whether that's nature or nurture I have no idea.'

Annie laughed. 'My parents and I eat like horses, but we never put much weight on. I think it's unfair on those who eat little and sensibly and get fat. Genetics and metabolism are probably more relevant than amount or exercise. My father, whose intake of social and work-related food and alcohol must be enormous, is as lean as he was when he married.'

'What does he do, your father?' Fiona's voice held only idle interest, but Annie flushed. She hadn't meant to provoke the question and was irritated by her own carelessness.

'He's a sort of financial adviser.'

Fiona looked interested, her eyebrows lifting in an invitation for further information.

'For the government. For banks,' Annie said, feeling a familiar discomfort. People were sometimes resentful or critical of Will's job, and she now tended not to mention it.

'So Charlotte Elliott is your mother, but that's her professional name, her maiden name,' Jem said. 'What did you exchange to become Devereux? I always feel it's rather bad luck on women to lose their family names on marriage.'

As quite often happened, she wondered if she should explain her family in a little more detail as she had to Mhairi. Most of the time it didn't matter and she didn't bother, but now the conversation was getting more complicated.

'Our surname is odd—Meredith. Everyone thinks it's a girl's name.'

'Unlike Mackenzie.' Fiona's laugh was infectious. 'As you have no doubt realised, everybody round here is called Mackenzie, and if you're not called Mackenzie, they look at you sideways and wonder where on earth you came from. It's just not done, being called anything but Mackenzie.'

'Don't exaggerate, woman,' Jem said peaceably.

'But how does anyone know who you're talking about?' Annie said, laughing now that the awkward moment had passed.

'They've all got nicknames, or descriptions, or sometimes the house name, or their father's name, or the village, or some boat or rock. It's all madness to a sensible Edinburgh lass like me, who had the perfectly good name of Ross, which I had to turn in for a common-as-muck Mackenzie.'

'So how do I differentiate between Mr and Mrs Mackenzie of the Poolewe Hotel, and you? And all the little Mackenzies. Oh! And Mr Mackenzie at the Gairloch shop?'

Fiona put her head back and pealed with laughter. 'Well, Jem is Jem Stone, because we're builders, I suppose, Jan and Les at the Poolewe Hotel are Mackenzie Hotel, Mace Stores are Mackenzie Shop, Angus Mackenzie, the laird's ghillie, is Mackenzie Fish, the pharmacist at Gairloch is Old Bear Mackenzie—he's called Rupert, then there's Roddy Mackenzie Aultbea, Roddy Mackenzie Naast, Roddy Mackenzie, Grease—he's the car mechanic at the garage. And so on.'

Annie was amused. 'I like Jem Stone. What is Jem short for? Jeremiah? James?'

There was a little silence and Annie wondered if she'd been a bit rude and was about to apologise.

'She didn't tell you?'

Annie stared at Jem. 'Who didn't tell me what?'

Fiona gave her husband a severe look. 'Jem, just because your mother isn't coming clean it's no excuse for you to stay quiet. You ought to tell Annie—it may mean nothing, may just be a coincidence, or it may not. But if you don't tell her, you can be sure someone else will.'

Jem sighed and gave Annie a sideways look. His mouth was compressed, almost as if he were angry.

'I'm known by all and sundry by my initials. Jem, J. E. M., but my name is John. John Elliott Mackenzie.' He let the pause lengthen. 'Mackenzie was my mother's maiden name, and after the war she moved down to Edinburgh with me and married. For the first time. A man called Walter Gillespie. They had no children.'

Her mind stalled and then raced. No wonder he had muttered 'interesting' when she had mentioned John Elliott's name. How dare he say nothing! How could he fail to mention that he had the same name? And if Walter Gillespie had not been his father...

Conscious that her mouth was open she closed it smartly. Jem slid another sideways glance at her before continuing. 'I never changed my surname to Gillespie, which would have been much simpler. For her, for Walter. And for me. The Elliott is spelt the same way—two ls, two ts. Nothing in that, really, Elliott in all its spellings being a fairly common name.'

'Less common as a first name in the forties,' Annie said with a gasp. 'And it wasn't a family name?' He shook his head.

'She said they were just names she chose because she liked them, and I didn't particularly mind or think about it. Not till you came. It's certainly made me wonder.'

'And I've stirred up all sorts of things I never intended to. I'm really so sorry.' It was quite likely, quite possible, that Mhairi had named him after a man she liked and respected. Perhaps in memory of his death. But it was also possible that John Elliott was Jem's father. Discomfort churned in her stomach. 'It was pure coincidence that I chose Inveruidh—if I hadn't, I wouldn't have met any of you and none of this would have surfaced. I'd have gone to the museum and found it closed and maybe found out a bit about him by asking around and looking on the internet. And then I'd have gone home without disturbing any of you.'

'I wouldn't be too sure of that!' Fiona's voice was resigned. 'Enquiries about a wartime John Elliott might easily have reminded someone what Jem's initials stood for. And that his mother wasn't married. Anyway, we don't know if there is a connection, and there's no guarantee that Mhairi would tell us, one way or another. She can be like a clam if she wants to.'

Jem was sitting with his elbows on the table, his hands steepled under his chin. He exchanged another glance with Fiona.

'Don't fret, Annie. Maybe this is the moment to do some mutual research. I've always wanted to know who my father was, and she's never answered my questions. Perhaps you are the catalyst I've been waiting for. I told my mother I would tell you my names if she didn't. But you realise, don't you, that there are implications for both our families if your grandfather turns out to be my father?'

Annie felt out of control, frightened almost. It was all going too fast, and the fabric and structure of two established families were beginning to be stretched and strained.

He eyed his last mouthful of cake thoughtfully. 'What else did she tell you about him?'

Annie thought of Jem accompanying her at the New

Year *ceilidh*. 'He played the violin but was wounded in 1943 and lost two fingers on his left hand. He was left-handed—' and so was Jem, she had noticed '—and couldn't play any more after that. She said she didn't know what happened to his violin, but it didn't get returned to our family.' She recounted Mhairi's other memories of John. 'Now that I know the name of his ship, I can find out lots more from The Imperial War Museum and naval records.' Her eyes met Jem's. 'Both Mrs MacConnachie and Mrs Gillespie said they knew a man, a criminal, called Archie Mackinnon who drowned—or was killed—and it sounded as if John Elliott knew him too. I wondered if you knew anything about that?'

Jem looked mystified and shook his head. 'Never heard of him. Really, my mother is the most secretive woman I ever knew! You've discovered more about her murky past than I ever have.' He glanced outside to see fat snowflakes slide-slipping to the ground. 'It's snowing hard, Annie. We can continue this another day, but I think you should go back to Inveruidh before the weather gets worse.'

As she said her thanks and goodbyes, David's car drew up in the driveway and her breath shortened unexpectedly.

'Hi,' he said easily, depositing a large package for his father in the hallway and shedding snow on to the floor. 'How was your visit to Granny?'

Ridiculously tongue-tied, she said, 'Very interesting.' This man could be her cousin, her mother's nephew. She found herself staring at him as if he had transmogrified into another being. Her pulse thumped and she put a hand up to her throat in case it showed.

'I'd love to hear about it,' he said, 'but I must go and do the school run.' With which he departed, leaving tyre tracks in the snow. Annie wished she was on the school run too. How ridiculous to be envious of a man because he had to do a school run.

On the way back, pushing her reaction to David to the back of her mind, she found herself astounded by the thought that John Elliott might have been Jem's father. Mhairi had made so much of his good qualities and moral virtues, and the fact that officers were often billeted on locals, that it seemed altogether implausible that they had been lovers. Maybe Mhairi really had just used the name of a man she admired, in memory of him. But maybe not. Jem could be Mum's brother. What an extraordinary thought.

She walked a while on the beach in front of the cottage, listening to the sad cries of seagulls flying landward and the noisy susurration of foamy wavelets. Bending to collect some tiny shells from the water line, she watched the snowflakes gently falling to instant oblivion on the sand.

Why had Mhairi got a letter from Elspeth? The more she thought about it the odder it seemed. Was it something to do with Elspeth saying John had betrayed her? Had she known about Mhairi? She would go back, armed with glue and these shells to replace the broken ones, and she would ask Mhairi why she had a letter from Elspeth Elliott. Good manners would have to take second place to finding out the truth.

As the early darkness slid across the sky, the cold seeped into her and she retreated to the warmth of the fire with a cup of tea. It was odd to think that John had stayed here, had seen the same view, even if the present cottage was very different from the one he had known. The frisson of shock at the possibility of these familial connections shook her again. Just because Charlotte was not her biological mother, it didn't mean those connections wouldn't be real ones. What had her innocent and slightly self-interested explorations revealed, and what complications, what emotional traumas might result from them?

Annie had enjoyed their company; this possible uncle's untidy and somewhat dour exterior had concealed a dry ironic humour offset by a possible aunt's friendliness and brisk intelligence. She wondered what David, her possible cousin, was doing now. Homework with his boys perhaps. Again, that odd feeling of being on the outside looking in. Envy. Had things turned out differently, she might have had a child of Seamus's age. She might be helping with homework too.

A rattle of snow, or perhaps hail, on the window brought an odd excitement at the idea of extreme weather and being holed up in her warm cottage while the world froze round her. The wind dropped as the sky cleared, the stars sharp as pinpricks, the sea like silver satin.

She closed the shutters and drew the curtains across.

25

August 1944

This time, John's departure seemed worse than ever. Mhairi's heart was heavy as the next convoy readied for departure and finally slid away through the boom. Waking and sleeping, her thoughts were of John. In her saner moments, she berated herself for becoming infatuated with an older man. And a married man. With two children. In the more frequent insane moments, her thoughts turned to immoral longings, to desires that shamed her. She imagined his face close to hers, his mouth under that enticing moustache, even though she knew that both beard and moustache would be as long and bushy as he could grow them. She thought that he felt the same for her, but not until the last day, before they left the cottage, did she lift her face to his and kiss him on the lips. His tightening arms and his involuntary loving response gave her a joy she had never experienced before. Even in the face of his apology and his guilt, she ached to entice him to abandon his family, to come and be with her for all time. She found her own fingers on her lips to re-imagine the sensation of his. She ran her fingers through her own hair re-imagining John's hands. Her sleep was splintered with memories: shards of his laughter, slivers of imparted knowledge, fragments of music. Without comment, he had left his violin in the croft and sometimes she took it out of the case and gently plucked the strings just to evoke his spirit.

Mrs Reid seemed to sense the change in her assistant and Mhairi found that she had exhaustive extra duties which did not allow for either dreaming or introspection. As she sorted incoming letters, Mhairi saw a flurry that arrived for John, some official, some with strange handwriting. As regulations required, they were put into a large manilla envelope in his pigeonhole to await his return. They seemed to have an actual presence, and she found herself glancing involuntarily at the little compartment. Why the increase in number, and why so much official mail?

As the weeks slid past, there was no information on any convoys, and Archie became a constant presence. He hovered on the edges of her vision, watching, waiting, appearing at odd times at Inverasdale. As a result, she did not fulfil her promise to John to tell Mrs Reid the situation, and the fact that Archie didn't always bother to come to the cottage, but just used the shed was in a sense more frightening. It was as if he owned the place and Mhairi was just a temporary inhabitant. Often she saw that he had been there in her absence; tyre marks in wet mud, bits of cardboard blowing about the yard. The time to confess his activities to the authorities had long passed and she was now an accomplice to his illegal trading. Frightened to go back to Inverasdale, she spent as many nights as she could with Rhionna and her parents.

'What if the ship is sunk?' she asked Rhionna. 'Torpedoed, or bombed? He'll have drowned or been blown up. Such terrible stories they're telling of the German submarines and bombers, all those ships on fire, all those men killed.' Her mind teemed with images of John in the sea, burnt or wounded. 'Why is there no news? The sailors have named the ships they saw lost, but why haven't they news of the trawler escort?'

Rhionna hugged her through the tearful breakdowns and night-time horrors. By the end of September Mhairi was frantic.

'I've not found a single seaman who knows why the *Countess* hasn't come back with the return convoy,' she wailed to Rhionna. 'It's more than six weeks, and plenty of stragglers are back with not a word of them.'

Rhionna said nothing and Mhairi knew that she too thought that the absence of the *Countess of Minto* was ominous. She confided her fears about Archie.

'Without John there, he comes any time he likes, and I don't know what's in the shed and I don't know how to stop him. He just walks in on me. But what can I do? I put the bolt across yesterday, but he banged and banged and shouted until I opened it. I thought he was going to hit me.'

She wept into Rhionna's arms. 'I can't tell anyone, and nobody could do anything in any case. I'd be arrested, and he'd just walk away.'

'They wouldn't arrest you if they knew Archie was using you,' Rhionna said uncertainly, but they both knew that Archie would involve them equally. Rhionna had accepted Archie's 'gifts' almost as much as Mhairi had. Her father was a kirk elder and the community's censure would shame and ruin him. For Mhairi, this haven of their house would be withdrawn, her work at the post office would cease and she would only have the croft to go back to, with a predator stalking her.

At last, at the beginning of October, the ship returned. Kynoch Whaler opened the post office door and shouted that the *Countess of Minto* had anchored. The relief and joy made her shake, but Mrs Reid pursed her lips and forbade her to go to the quayside. An hour later the tender came alongside and the men disembarked. John and the crew were intact but exhausted and malnourished, and Mhairi had recovered a semblance of normality. Later they came to collect their mail and she couldn't help giving him an enormous welcoming smile as she handed over the manilla envelope. Her thought that the thickness and officialness of its contents might signal a change of posting gave her relief that he might be safer, together with fear that he would have to leave her.

As he leafed through the envelopes, he gave her a conspiratorial smile and went to stand in the October sun to read them. She saw through the window his sudden stillness, and then a sort of inner collapse, his shoulders dropping, his head jerking forwards on to his chest. The rest of his mail dropped from his hands, fluttering down to the ground, and he staggered as if he had been punched. A sudden horror drenched her, and she ran from behind the counter, pushing through the men waiting for their mail, a nightmarish sense of paralysis gripping her. He had collapsed on to the steps and under his beard the skin had drained to white. She knelt beside him and gripped his hands, the empty sockets where his fingers had been jolting her afresh.

'John! John! What is it?' It was almost a repetition of his first arrival with appendicitis. 'What's happened? Are you ill?'

His eyes turned to her uncomprehendingly, as if she were a stranger. He shook his head slightly. Mrs Reid appeared briefly above her, then disappeared and was quickly replaced by two of his crew members. In a daze she watched them lift him, steady him on his feet, and escort him away towards the naval HQ. She remained kneeling on the wooden steps, staring after them, a nameless dread soaking into her, the envelopes and pieces of paper scuttering around her in the wind. Mrs Reid appeared again, putting an authoritative hand on her shoulder.

'Pick up the mail and come inside. Finish what you have to do.'

She knew she should not look at his letters, but nevertheless her eyes skimmed down the open pages until the typewritten page from the Admiralty shook her into understanding. She stood motionless until Mrs Reid dispersed the remaining crew and took the papers out of her hand.

'They're dead!' Mhairi whispered. 'His little boys are dead.'

* * *

The handwritten letter had been written by a neighbour, Nellie, but Elspeth had signed it. The signature was so shaky that it was almost unrecognisable. While Elspeth was out queuing for her rations, the house had been hit by a doodlebug—Mhairi saw it was on the same day that John's convoy had departed—and totally destroyed, her mother and the two children killed. Through her shock, Mhairi was thankful that the news had come after his departure so that at least he was spared seven weeks of being unable to communicate with his wife. She couldn't imagine losing your children. How could Elspeth remain sane, losing her mother and children simultaneously?

An official letter informed him that his house had been bombed on 15th August with the death of both his sons and mother-in-law. The Admiralty granted him two weeks leave to rehouse his wife.

When he left FOIC's office he was wordless and helpless. She could only hold him in his frozen horror. The Admiralty might have given him leave, but they failed to provide transport. Even his captain was unable to immediately conjure a vehicle further than Gairloch. In desperation, seeing John's state of utter exhaustion, hunger and inability to solve the problem, she went to Archie.

'Just twenty-four hours, that's all.' She loathed having to beg and knew there would be a price to pay for it.

'What's it for?' He was slitty-eyed with suspicion.

'I can't tell you, but Mrs Reid has given me the time off, and it's urgent. Really urgent.'

Archie was unimpressed. 'Well, I'd need to know what my van was being used for, and where it was going, wouldn't I?'

She hesitated. 'Achnasheen, that's all. I have to collect something and its important.'

He shook his head regretfully. 'But I'm needing it myself. I've got business in Ullapool tomorrow and it would be a deal of inconvenience to change it all.' He was watching her, calculating how desperate she was.

'I'd pay you for the petrol.' Which would be a large part of her small pay.

Archie snorted in derision. 'I don't need payment for the petrol. But the van is loaded, and you'd have to empty it first. Can't have the first checkpoint looking at all that. You can put it all in your shed along with the other stuff, so long as you lock it again afterwards.' He took the shed key out of his pocket and idly tipped it from hand to hand, watching her face.

She had always refused to handle Archie's goods personally, but now he was forcing her to if she wanted to use his van, and she would be guilty of having the key in her possession. Another manipulation which he could use against her. She shivered.

'All right.'

'And then there is the little matter of compensating me for all the bother and aggravation of changing my plans. And I'm not talking petrol. Shall we discuss that another day?' His face was hard and knowing, and although she knew what he was insinuating, her brain refused to accept it.

She took a long time to answer. 'All right,' she said eventually.

Mhairi took John to Inverasdale where she force-fed him her week's meat ration. He had not even noticed that it was Archie's van she was driving, or that it was full of mysterious boxes and bundles. When she had persuaded him to go to bed, she went out and unloaded the contents into the shed. In the horror of what was happening she closed her mind to Archie's threats. In spite of John's exhaustion, she could hear him tossing and turning all night, sometimes dozing off, but continually jerking awake with muffled cries.

As she drove him to the train at Achnasheen the next morning, helpless tears slipped down his face, and at the station he put his head down on her shoulder and sobbed like a child. She held herself together until the train had steamed out of sight. Why had she fallen in love with a married man of integrity when the world must contain other men without those complications? Or was the rest of the world full of men like Archie? Fear of Archie bubbled up through her chest and squeezed her throat and she deliberately closed her mind to him and opened it to thoughts of John. How much more painful was her love for John than her hatred for Archie. Her nose and eyes ran with moisture as she blindly navigated the narrow, rutted road back to Aultbea, her handkerchief sodden and useless within a mile and involuntary sobs making her swerve. She did not know what would happen after he had been back home to grieve with his wife. Would his sense of duty and morality win? They had, after all, nothing more than a wartime friendship, even if she knew that it was, in their hearts and minds if not in actuality, much, much more. Would he come back to her?

*　*　*

When he eventually returned to Loch Ewe, he was bone weary, but Mhairi knew it wasn't just physical tiredness, although there was that too. It was grief which had seeped into his bones, crumbling his optimism, blackening the light in his grey eyes. It was not a weariness that sleep could ease or work alleviate, and indeed his sleep was an aching agony for them both, as hideous as the convoy nightmares and infinitely more distressing. His recall from Portsmouth for sea trials had been abrupt and ships were now gathering for a convoy which had no leaving date except 'soon'.

'There is nothing there,' he said, his voice infinitely sad. 'Just two outside walls. No floors. I could see the wallpaper of the boys' bedroom and the fireplace. They found their bodies in the rubble.' Mhairi gripped his hands across the table, silently allowing him the space to let the horror out. 'They were buried together. In the one grave. There was a handwritten notice on it and they had Richard's birth date wrong.' He bent forward and rested his head on Mhairi's hands for a moment. 'She hadn't done anything about a memorial stone for them—or her parents. She was still in shock, I suppose, but she hadn't done anything at all. I was relieved that her mother wasn't in the same plot—she was buried with her husband. We did arrange the memorials.' He lifted his head and stared into space. 'There was nothing left. How can that be?' He spoke in a dull, automatic tone as if giving evidence in court.

'How can we have brought two children into this world and have nothing left?' He shook his head in a sort of bewildered stupefaction. 'An old friend, Nellie, took her in, and me too. She's a nurse and has seen it all, I think. Portsmouth is such a mess, but she wouldn't leave—wouldn't let me get her out to the country. I suppose she needs to be with a friend. I'll have to try to sort it when I get back. She can't stay there, in someone else's house, for ever.' As always, the possibility of him not coming back was left unsaid.

John wept in the night. He wept in his sleep when at last sleep came for him. He wept for his children and Elspeth and himself. He wept in guilt and hopelessness and helplessness, and Mhairi lay above him in the rafters and cried too, noiselessly, exhaustedly.

'Soon' became 'shortly', and 'shortly' became 'tomorrow'. Mhairi's self-control broke. She came down her ladder, left a silky peach-coloured nightgown on the sheepskin beside the bed and slid under John's blankets. Her arms enclosed him, and her comfort permeated his misery, infiltrated his desolation, brought blessing.

26

16th January 2012

Annie bumped into Fiona Mackenzie in the store at Poolewe, and on hearing that Annie had arranged to visit Mhairi later in the morning, Fiona invited her back to the house for coffee before their meeting. The coffee was strong and real, and the coffee cake thick with butter icing. Jem came out of his office next to the kitchen to join them and the conversation returned to the theme of Jem's name.

He was a stranger and a generation older and she was uncomfortable theorising as to why his mother had named him as she did. It could involve the complication of her acquiring an uncle and aunt, and several cousins. For her mother, the complication of acquiring a brother—anyway a half-brother—and a greatly expanded family. For Jem, of acquiring a half-sister. And Mhairi. What about Mhairi? Was she really the mistress of a man dead for nearly seventy years and mother of his child? A sudden, ludicrous thought came to mind of her mother and herself wrapping piles of Christmas presents for this enormous unknown family.

'May I ask when your mother was born?' Jem said.

'1945. 18th August.'

'And I was born in 1945 on 5th October, to an unmarried twenty-three-year-old, father unknown.' Jem's voice was quite flat, expressionless, but the words were a kind of challenge.

It proved nothing, but John had visited Portsmouth in the autumn of 1944 and had left on his last convoy from Loch Ewe in late December.

Annie's shoulders tensed. 'I feel I've disturbed and worried Mrs Gillespie, and I'm really sorry.'

Jem and Fiona were silent for a few moments and then Jem said carefully, 'My dear, my mother *is* rather disturbed and there are things on her mind which I get the impression need to be resolved, though whether they are anything to do with your grandfather or my father, I don't know. Did you have some more questions for her?'

Annie thought of the letter with Elspeth's signature. 'There were photos and letters she was going to show me, and I offered to help her mend something and she asked me to come back today and do it.'

'Mend something?' Jem looked puzzled. 'I can do any mending for her—or Fiona. What was it?'

'She was showing me an old home-made card.' The awkwardness of this conversation was getting to her. She was a stranger interfering in personal affairs, even though she hadn't intended to. 'All the bits stuck to it had come off and I offered to glue them on again.' Both Jem and Fiona seemed surprised.

'An old card? One of Jem's? Or the grandchildren's?' Fiona asked.

Annie shook her head. 'No. Look, I don't think I—she showed it to me, but I don't know if I—I suppose I'd rather she showed you what it was and got you to repair it, but I don't think I—' For the life of her she couldn't see how to finish this without either Jem and Fiona being offended, or Mhairi's confidences being revealed.

'A card from who?' queried Fiona, quickly interrupted by Jem.

'No, leave it. Mother showed something privately to Annie, who quite rightly doesn't wish to gossip about it. It's fine, Annie. Go ahead with whatever you arranged with her. She enjoyed your company, even if it's brought up a few, possibly painful, memories. And maybe it will help her to tell me who my father was.'

Annie looked at him gratefully. 'If you came through with me, perhaps she'd show it to you. I expect you've seen it lots of times, but I'd feel more comfortable.'

'Well, I'll do that and see what transpires. I can't remember ever seeing an old card.'

Fiona picked up the cake and put it back in its tin, decorated with a child's version of heaven. Blue sea with white seagulls, yellow sand, purple mountains, and various stick people with ear-to-ear grins. Some of the poster paint was peeling off. Annie brought the plates and mugs over and admired the painting.

'One of our granddaughters painted it for my birthday a few years back. Jem tells me to throw it away, but I can't bring myself to do it.' She ran her fingers over the battered tin.

'It certainly isn't airtight any more. Everything goes stale.'

'Rubbish, man! With you around the house, nothing's in there long enough to go stale.' There was a familiar and pleasurable tone to their banter. Annie recognised it from her own parents' relationship. Did it take forty years of marriage to achieve? She didn't recollect any such ease with Justin after eight years.

'Thank you for the delicious cake and coffee.'

Jem got up from the kitchen table and winked at Annie. 'You'll be expected to have more with her, so brace yourself. I'll come with you so that I get some more too.' She was grateful for the wink and the normality it brought.

Initially, Mhairi couldn't be bothered, or was too tired,

to get out her little suitcase of memories and extract the old card. Or, as Annie suspected, she wasn't going to do so while Jem was there, even though he offered to get the case for her, so having had another slice of cake and declining the coffee he took himself off with another wink for Annie and a kiss on the top of his mother's head.

Annie thought that if this was going to be her last meeting with Mhairi she might as well risk all—though she did hope she wouldn't be the cause of the old lady's sudden demise.

'Mr and Mrs Mackenzie asked me to call them by their first names,' she said diffidently. 'And I asked whether Jem was a shortening of James or Jeremiah.' There was a little silence and the old lady gave her a look over the top of her glasses.

'And I wondered,' Annie continued, 'whether there was… a connection?' She stopped. She really could not suggest that they had been lovers and that Jem was the illegitimate child of John Elliott and Mhairi.

Mhairi lifted her chin and inspected her ceiling. 'John Elliott was a lovely man, that he was. A brave man. A gentle man.' Again, that Highland way of saying 'gentleman' which was so affecting. 'The war destroyed so much for him and yet brought good things to others. I felt it was right to name my son after a man I respected deeply. Oh yes, John Elliott is a grandfather to be proud of, so he is. You tell your mother, his daughter, she can be proud of him.'

Annie nodded, feeling her eyelids pricking. 'I will.' Mhairi had told her nothing. And she was none the wiser.

'Let's do that card,' she said into the ensuing silence, and because Mhairi did not disagree, she lifted the little case on to the table so that Mhairi could reach the clasps. 'I'm going to go home soon,' she said. 'My parents will be back from South Africa, and I have a lot of things to see to, which I've been putting off since I've been here. I can't go on doing that any longer.'

Mhairi undid the clasps but left the lid closed. She put her head on one side. 'Been doing some thinking at Inveruidh, have you? A bit of quiet always helps.' She nodded towards Annie's left hand. 'You had a wedding ring when you first came, and now it's gone.' There was no question, just a statement of fact.

Annie smiled faintly. 'It seemed rather dishonest, somehow. My husband divorced me a few months ago, but I found it difficult to discard eight years of marriage.' She wasn't quite sure what induced her to confide in the old lady, but it was quite helpful to unload a bit and she somehow doubted that anything would be passed on.

Opening her bag, she put the various tubes and pots of glue on the table. 'May I get some saucers, and perhaps an egg cup for the sand, then we could put the various shells and things where you could see them and direct operations?' She retrieved an envelope from her bag. 'I found some tiny shells on the beach which might replace some of the broken ones.'

Mhairi nodded, and when Annie returned there was a slither of black and white grainy unfocused photos and some papers on the table.

'I had an old box Brownie. John gave it to me,' she said. 'Terrible photos, but that was the best to be had in those days. Not like the young ones now, with their mobile phones and digital this and that. Still, they take beautiful pictures, right enough, all colour and crisp-looking. They show me on the computer and it's like you're right there.' She picked one up. 'That's Inveruidh before the boy got his hands on it.'

Annie looked at the long, low, single-storey croft. It had rough stone walls and a thinly thatched roof with big stones hanging all round and what looked like dilapidated farm buildings round the back. She could just see Loch Ewe in the corner of the picture.

'My grandfather was here? Is this what it looked like during the war?' It bore no resemblance to the present cottage.

Mhairi nodded. 'Aye, and generations before that. There was a byre at one end, and the kine gave warmth to that end of the house in the winter. I only had sheep during the war. It was difficult to keep a cow then because I didn't always manage to get home at nights from Aultbea to do the milking. When my father came home in '45, he said he'd get another, but then I was away down to Edinburgh and I doubted he would do much milking.' There was a distinct note of humour and a suppressed smile.

Annie considered the small space taken up by the kitchen. 'But where did the family live and cook and sleep if there wasn't an upstairs?'

Mhairi laughed. 'There was only the two of us. The kitchen was quite big. It was where we lived, there was no separate sitting room, then in the middle was the bedroom. Our beds were built into the wall and curtained off, though my father floored between the roof beams when I was older and put my cot bed up there. I climbed the wee ladder and there I was, queen of all the house, and I could look down on the cows next door too. Oh, I loved that wee space—it was all mine! I came back in the seventies when my father had a stroke, and after he died Jem messed it all about, and put an upstairs in and heaven knows what. And it wasn't the same. There wasn't anything left of the old croft really.' She sounded a bit sad, but then brightened. 'Not that it wasn't quite nice to have a bedroom and bathroom upstairs, and a proper kitchen, and not to have to go down the garden to the privy in winter. But look at it now! Young David's done it all over again. Such a waste of money.'

She was so disapproving that Annie had to laugh. 'But

it is gorgeous now—and though I can see you're sad about the changes, we do have to move with the times, I suppose. What does Inveruidh mean, or doesn't it mean anything?'

'Oh aye, everything in the Gaelic has a meaning. Inver means river mouth and Uidh is the name of the wee burn that runs out down the garden. That was our water supply, lovely and peaty brown it was, but now the Hydro sends us horrible stuff that smells of chlorine.'

She picked up more photos, of the house from different angles, with a girl, Mhairi she assumed, in a mid-calf skirt and headscarf, laughing into the wind, some sheep, a cat sitting on the garden wall, the girl again on the beach, bending to pick something up, someone's hands (John Elliott's before losing his fingers?) holding a huge posy of monochrome flowers, bluebells perhaps, a young man astride a great rock, silhouetted against the sky.

'Is that—my grandfather?' The figure was too far away to be distinct.

Mhairi took it, peering closely. 'No, I think it's my cousin Kenny. I think John took the photos, though—can't think who else could have done.'

Annie was disappointed. 'Do you have one of John? It's just that, well, I don't know what he looked like, or how tall he was, or anything. If you did, perhaps I could photocopy it? It wouldn't be damaged or anything, it just takes a photo of a photo.'

'Jem's got a machine in the office.' She appeared to be considering the idea, perhaps debating whether or not to agree, but in fact, it seemed she was trying to remember what photos she had. She opened the case again, fumbling amongst the contents, bringing out two more envelopes, creased with many handlings. Annie gathered the little photographs together, keeping a few aside. Even if she could show her mother where her father had been during the war, that would be more than she had now. Mhairi had pulled out the contents of one of the envelopes, and looking briefly at each item, she passed them across to Annie. Roughly typed play flyers for amateur dramatics and socials, ticket stubs, passes for trains and buses. Timetables, shipping lists, crew lists, identification papers. And then a handwritten note. 'Please thank Murdo for the tot last night—very warming!' in that copperplate hand.

She held it up to Mhairi. 'Is this his handwriting?'

She nodded. 'Aye.' And then curiously, 'Had you never seen his writing, then?'

'No, not from the war. We have virtually nothing. It was all destroyed by the bomb which killed my uncles. We have no photos, no letters, nothing. The bomb took the whole house, her mother and her two little boys and Granny was left in the clothes she stood up in.'

The old lady looked at her with compassion, an emotion that Annie thought was not typical of her, and then she focused on the papers again. 'I have photos of him. There's one in uniform and one taken as they left for a refit. Those were illegal—you couldn't take photos on the base. It was a court martial offence. They did, of course.' She picked up another smaller envelope from the pile of papers. 'It was me gave him the letter telling him about his mother-in-law and his wee boys. That was a bad day for him, poor man. Sometimes working in the post office was a grim job.' She had found what she was looking for and with a grunt of triumph handed over three black and white photos.

For the first time Annie saw her grandfather; an old, young face, a gentle face with a sharply razored moustache, standing to attention in his dark uniform with a single gold band around the cuff. He looked straight at the camera, the eyes seeming light-coloured, but with a dark outline, giving them a penetrating, piercing look. A class of boys would have paid attention to those eyes. Jem's eyes were dark brown, like Mhairi's. David's eyes were—what? Grey? Not brown. Not gentle.

'What colour were his eyes?' she asked, and Mhairi answered without hesitation.

'Grey, they were. Pale but sharp. His captain said he had excellent eyesight—could see a U-boat periscope when no one else could. He didn't say that to me, mind, but I heard it. I'd gone up to the office to see if I could get news, and I heard him. I knew he hadn't come back, see.'

'How?' Annie's voice caught in her throat so that she had to clear it. 'How did you know?'

Mhairi turned her head towards the window. 'I don't know. I knew when he left on that convoy that he wasn't coming back, and I knew that he hadn't come back even though the ship got back. I just knew.' The flat tone of her voice covered a real sadness, even after all the years.

'So what happened? If the ship came back, how did he die?' She felt frustrated by the lack of detail, but at the same time almost voyeuristic. Was it indecent to want to know?

Mhairi was still turned towards the grey overcast sky. Her profile seemed to have sagged, the cheeks drooping, eyes half closed, mouth lax. She took a deeper breath and her shoulders dropped forward as she breathed out.

'They were torpedoed—it hit the depth charges and they exploded. He was on the gun above that hold.' Her voice was even. Matter-of-fact.

'Where? Where were they?' Mhairi shrugged, lips pursing in ignorance. 'Did they bury him at sea, or was he brought back? Does he have a grave?'

The old lady twisted to face her; sympathy, irritation, impatience.

'My dear, no. No. An explosion like that—there was nothing. Five of the crew were killed beside John. I don't think they found any of them. His grave is the northern ocean. He wasn't wounded—he was killed. I believe he didn't suffer—he was just—gone.'

27

January 1945

The northern ocean was black, mountainous and vicious. John knew the convoy was a mess because none of the ships could see each other beyond the few seconds they were at the top of a forty-foot wave crest, and then you couldn't see anyone else if they were at the bottom of a trough. As far as he was concerned, they weren't escorting anything.

Like a bucking horse, the ship lurched through the vast waves. The explosive crack of the hull ramming down as she pitched forward, her screws screaming as they thrashed air, was deafening. Then the bows plunged under metres of water, the sea exploding up and over the entire ship as she headed for the ocean floor. Her downward plunge checked as her nose lifted, water pouring and streaming off her decks as she began the climb up the other side, until she seemed almost vertical and on the verge of falling over backwards. The crew were roped on, but were still thrown like dolls around the mess decks, loose objects hitting them from all sides as cupboards sprang open, and equipment slid lethally end to end and side to side. John doubted there would be any intact crockery to eat off or drink out of, should this storm ever lessen. Hardened seamen were throwing up their guts. He was aware, as he clutched Mhairi's hunk of sheep's wool, of praying, not coherent prayers, but a continuous call for help, for life, for courage, to do his job as he was needed. His captain, tied, as John was, to stable uprights in the wheelhouse, was calm and competent. He called his instructions to the engine room in a steady voice which carried above the scream of the storm.

The likelihood of colliding with another ship was high in nil visibility, except for the fact that they were probably all dispersed over about a hundred square miles of sea. 'Escort duty' was a misrepresentation of fact. Much more likely, his captain shouted over the noise of the storm, was that they would ram a large piece of ice which would send them to the bottom in short order unless the watch saw it first. As the watch was blinded by ice-cold salt spray, John didn't hold out any hope of this. The only good thing about this storm was that the enemy couldn't see them either.

John's damaged hand ached sullenly with the cold, but he welcomed both the physical discomfort and the responsibilities which served to dilute his anguish. There was no opportunity to consider Mhairi's actions and his disloyalty. No room for their mutual consolation or for his guilt. There was no place for Elspeth here. No space for loss.

A faint shout penetrated the howl of the wind. 'Bridge!'

He braced against the heaving deck, put his head out into the screaming storm and winced as the bitter salt spray hit him like a fist. 'Ship to port, about 300 yards.'

Much too close for comfort. His heart hammered as he ordered alteration of course and noted the log. What ship? There were about forty possible answers. His captain's eye caught his, and they exchanged rueful grins.

During the night, the wind eased as quickly as it had risen, and by dawn, the sea was a heavy swell but hardly breaking the tops. The storm clouds had lifted slightly, and the chaotic remnant of the convoy showed as smudges of smoke spread over many miles. On the northern horizon he glimpsed the white edge of the ice sheet. Without being able to use telegraph which would have revealed positions, it took time to round up some of the scattered ships and set the signals for a new course east from Bear Island. The ships began to clatter through broken ice, and John saw his captain's eye on the fuel gauge. Oiling at sea was never easy, but in bad weather it was almost impossible. The oilers were the number one targets for the enemy and the escorts circled them like sheepdogs, depth charges exploding like malevolent geysers.

With the subsiding of the storm and return of fair weather came a worse prospect: the reconnaissance planes, reporting their position to German airfields in Norway, to be followed by the JU88s and the torpedo bombers, and the noiseless wolves who slid from under the waves to deliver their deadly consignment of torpedoes. John found that he was hallucinating attacks, his heart thumping in his chest. Why did it never get easier? Why couldn't he get used to it? The ever-present misery of the boys' deaths was blocked out by the anxiety of the present moment. He thought he was ravenous, but the occasional distribution of dry biscuits and bread for all hands was futile. He couldn't swallow, however hard he chewed, his throat tight with strain. He pushed the remains into the pocket of his oilskins and chipped at the frozen spray adhering to the Lewis gun.

They didn't have to wait long to be discovered.

When the reconnaissance plane found them, his stomach roiled in the familiar sickness of fear. It circled high up in a great circle above the shattered convoy, now steaming at about six knots to allow the wandering flock to catch up as best they might. John longed to nose in amongst the armed ships, like a sheep escaping wolves. The shadow circled while the whole convoy scanned the winter-dark sky and the heaving sea with ever increasing anxiety.

The shadow swung away. The tension ratcheted up even further with every order from the bridge, every movement. Then John, at his station on the gun, saw the incoming flights of JU 88s. Sweat trickled down his back and underarms and froze on his skin. Planes peeled off with their terrifying screaming noise and dived to mast height to let their loads go and his stomach turned to water. They flew unscathed through the curtain of lead from the escorts, but their bombs, sending up vast plumes of explosive water, hit only one merchantman. The next sequence screamed down, but this time one of them was hit and John flinched as it plunged like a javelin into the sea. Even as he rejoiced that there was one less aircraft to bomb them he thought of the pilot's last desperate moments. When his moment of death came he prayed it would be quick.

He saw periscopes in every wave shadow and the sky seemed to be flecked with aircraft. Then four torpedo bombers were sighted. John raced to get more magazines out of the lockers, but his gloved and damaged hands were clumsy with cold and a magazine fell with a clang to the deck. His awkwardness would be the death of him, he thought, with a suppressed hysterical guffaw of laughter.

The bombers attacked in a broad line down the convoy. John could smell his own fear as he attempted to line his gun sight on the aircraft as the trawler pitched. The din of the magazine emptying deafened him, and the smell of the cordite flared his nostrils. Hit the bloody target, you useless little gun. He never heard the yelled warning, but felt the ship heeling sharply to avoid the bomber's load. In a last moment of clarity John knew the evasion was too late. As the torpedo struck the *Countess of Minto*, in the fraction of time when fear drained away, he knew his luck had at last run out.

28

16th January 2012

Annie stared at Mhairi, mute with sudden loss, a silent gut-wrenching wail of protest. It was as if John had turned the light off, had slammed shut the door of relationship in her face. Ridiculous; she knew he had been killed on that convoy, why the surprise? Why the feeling that she had caught him in her mind's net, and that he had slid through an unseen rip, sinking down into the black unknown of oblivion. She pulled herself together, and looked again at the portrait—what was it that made him look so old-fashioned, so 1940ish? The moustache perhaps, lengthening an already long face. Old-fashioned but still faintly familiar; she tried without success to pin down what it was in Charlotte that resonated with this face. She turned to the next photograph, curling at the edges, slightly out of focus. A group of six men in the foreground with perhaps another ten in the background, all smiling, some waving. They were in civilian clothes except the group in the foreground who were in an untidy sort of uniform, with epaulettes on the shoulders of thick sweaters, leaning against the rail of their ship. There was a gun barrel pointing away to the right behind the crew.

'That was his ship. The *Countess of Minto*. The gun is one of the anti-aircraft guns. They were off to Belfast for a refit, so they were all happy. Some had gone on leave already by the looks of things, as there would have been a crew of over twenty. That's John, second from the left, on the rail. It must have been 1943 or 44, I think. Can you see if his hand is damaged?'

But they couldn't. The photograph was too grainy and John's left arm behind his neighbour.

Annie was disappointed not to have better photographs, but it was better than nothing. She put aside the photos and a few of the documents where he was mentioned, intending to ask if they could be copied. Then a prickle of irritation came into her mind. Mhairi had, as it were, been sitting on this information all Jem's life. Why hadn't she told him? And where was that sheet of paper with the signature 'Elspeth' on it? Why would her grandmother have been writing to Mhairi?

'Did John not leave any of his papers, any possessions, at the croft?' she asked.

There was a slight nod of her head. 'I took what there was to the base, to be returned to his wife. A few civilian clothes. Private letters.'

But not that letter from Elspeth, Annie thought. Frustration got the better of her. 'Oh! It's so sad to have nothing of him. I suppose letters could have been destroyed by Elspeth. She seemed to have disposed of most things.' Elspeth's case had contained little in the way of private correspondence and almost nothing between her and John.

Mhairi sighed and picked up a package of envelopes tied together with a thin faded rag. She handed them to Annie one by one. 'These are letters from John to me.' She hesitated. 'They could be copied for your mother.' Annie was astonished. It seemed an inappropriate suggestion, but as she read them, she realised it was not.

How anodyne they were, how stilted and how respect-ful. Dear Mhairi. With best regards, John Elliott. And between these two were lines of uninformative information, how the refits were going, but not what was being fitted, the visits to Liverpool and Belfast and Greenock, the descriptions of dreary Murmansk and Archangel, the cold, the bad food, his hopes of getting a returning naval ship to take his letters back, and the censor's occasional thick black line, a reproving schoolmaster crossing out some politically incorrect statement. Were these the letters of a lover? Or had he just been careful of their reputations? Just one came from Portsmouth, with a brief mention of Elspeth, her mother and the little boys, all with bad colds, and told of his return date to Aultbea. She wondered again if John Elliott had had any relationship with Mhairi at all, if the whole idea was a figment of her imagination, that Jem was someone else's son and she really had just named him after a man she knew and liked. There were still letters and papers on the table which Mhairi had not given her to look at. Could she ask to see them?

The irritation at Mhairi was overtaken by resentment that Elspeth had left nothing of John for his daughter, not an item of clothing, not a letter, not a keepsake, and Mhairi had had all this, all these years. Charlotte had this vacuum—this non-father. Neither of them broke the silence that had fallen.

Picking up the envelope with the shell card, she tipped the loose fragments on to a saucer and stirred the little collection of sea debris with her finger. She started to place shells on the card to fit the old glue marks, Mhairi nodding encouragement. Annie suspected that she could neither remember the original design nor really minded if it was put together differently.

The card took shape, the superglue doing a better job than the original. There was a noise from the little kitchen, a door opened and Annie sensed someone behind her. Mhairi lifted her face with an affectionate smile.

'Good morning, boy.'

'Good morning, Granny. Morning, Annie.' At the sound of David's voice, her stomach lurched unexpectedly.

Annie turned her head to greet him. He had grey eyes, the irises darkly, sharply, outlined.

'Mother has sent me in with fresh supplies—lemon drizzle, I think, and a chunk of her soggy gingerbread. Who wants coffee, or tea?'

Mugs and plates distributed, David slid the card from Annie's fingers, and his hand touched hers. A tingling awareness raced through her, so electric that it must surely have transmitted to him.

'So this is what Annie's mending.' He read the shell message and then opened it.

'With my thanks and best regards, John Elliott.' He laid it down carefully. 'Goodness, that's a bit sexy! It does make one wonder, Granny. You and Annie have been having a good talk, then?'

Both Annie and Mhairi were silent. Annie out of a shortening of breath and because she had noticed for the first time that David was left-handed too. Mhairi was silent because she was an elder and entitled to silence. Eventually, she made a harrumphing noise in the face of David's teasing smile.

'Yes, a good talk. I've got stuff Annie wants copying, David. Can you do that in the office?'

'I'll do that, Granny. Hand over the family secrets. How many copies? A set for Dad?'

'If you were closer, David, I'd—'

'Box my ears. I know. I never sit too close for that precise reason. Do you want the copies now?' He winked at Annie and she couldn't help grinning back, her tummy cramping.

'Cheeky devil. No, we're not finished. John Elliott was a wartime billet and a nice man and Annie's grandfather, and I was telling her what I remember of him, so don't you go making assumptions where none are to be made.'

182

David gave his grandmother a straight look and Annie bent her head to hide her smile and stuck more shells and pebbles on, distributing a dusting of sand over the gluey surface for aesthetic purposes. David picked up a handful of paper. He came to a yellowed folded sheet and flicked it open, reading without embarrassment. Mhairi's hand twitched and then was still.

After a few moments, he said, 'Elspeth? John's wife?' He sounded shocked.

She nodded. 'John was dead when that letter arrived,' she said softly.

Annie felt entitled to read it herself and took it out of David's hand. It was headed Portsmouth and dated 'Jan 30th 45'.

My dear John, I know you won't receive this until your return, which must be soon I think, but I cannot delay writing what will I think be good news for you, though I am unable to feel any joy myself, as I am sure you will understand. I think I find myself pregnant—and tho I can hardly believe it after all my losses—My losses? Annie jerked as if the letter had burnt her—*the memories of which are in my nightmares and all my waking hours, I fear it is so, and wish it were not. I hope in time to have my thoughts taken up by this child which, Deo gratias, may console us in our tragedy perhaps. It is not a good time, nor a good place, to be expecting a child. The town is still in a dreadful state, with half the streets impassable, and water a severe difficulty. I must go three, sometimes four streets to find a standpipe, and of course the stirrup pumps must be kept filled before clothes can be washed or we ourselves. The incendiaries are however less frequent, though I find it impossible to sleep for fear of the bombing starting again. Nellie is a good friend, but Norman I know wants me out of his house, and now I suppose there is nothing to keep me here, nor indeed have I any desire to remain. If I can find somewhere outside the city I will let you know. By the time you read this I think you will be returned from this trip*—She made it sound as if the convoys were a holiday, Annie thought incredulously—*and I hope you will be given leave to help me during the pregnancy and can get away from Scotland and your boat. It is galling to think of your comfortable lodgings amidst those peaceful mountains and lakes while we suffer here. The child will be due around mid-August, as you may calculate for yourself. I have to say that I feel perfectly wretched and very unwell. I will look forward to hearing from you. Your Elspeth*

Annie stared at the sheet, numb with shock. What an extraordinary letter, sent to a husband who she must have known was on yet another voyage from which it was quite likely he would not return, and indeed did not. She found her eyes were full of tears—for John Elliott, for Charlotte. For Elspeth, too, she supposed, who must have been in the grip of severe depression to have written such a letter at such a time.

She blinked and rubbed her eyes. The old lined face opposite was regarding her with dispassionate gravity.

'A letter I was glad that John did not receive,' she said in a level voice. 'I hadn't read it for years, but after you came, I looked at it again and was undecided whether or not to show it to you. David's interference sorted that. I suppose I ought never to have read it in the first place—but of course, the censor had opened it and I worked in the post office, so it was easy for me. I should have given it to his captain to send back with his things, but I didn't. I would have burnt it, but it wasn't mine to burn.'

It was as if she'd been hit in the stomach. Annie inhaled a long breath. Blundering to her feet, she stammered, 'I... I don't think... That's awful... I don't know what to...' She was incapable of moving or speaking for a second or two and then forced a shallow normality. 'I must go. It must be nearly your lunchtime and I've taken up too much of your time.'

'Annie—I'm so sorry.' David sounded mortified. 'I never dreamt that letter… I wouldn't have…'

He, too, seemed lost for words. She gestured blindly at the scattered photographs and then turned to him. 'No, of course not. Neither of us expected that. David, would you be kind enough to take copies of anything you or Mrs Gillespie might think of interest to my mother? I could collect them when I'm passing.' Gathering up the tubes of glue she put them in her bag, aware that her hands were as unsteady as her voice, and shrugged her coat on.

'Thank you for all the coffee and cake—and for your time and memories, Mrs Gillespie. I am truly grateful.'

David walked with her to her car and the cold wind on her face brought a welcome return to normality.

Opening the car door, he put a hand on her wrist. 'Will you be all right?' She heard the anxiety and remorse in the senseless question.

'Yes, of course I will. What Elspeth wrote seventy years ago is hardly your fault, is it? I just found it rather shocking.'

'I'm sorry,' he said again, helplessly.

In the mirror, she saw him watching her leave and she drove slowly back up the lochside to Inveruidh. The letter had been a dose of unpleasant reality—like a slosh of cold water on what had been just dry and dusty research; John and Elspeth Elliott had emerged from the historical past into the realms of real people, suffering real pain, and she, too, was glad that John had never read that letter. She did some mental calculations: her mother had been born on August 18th 1945. Nine months prior to August 1945 was November 1944. Annie knew from her endless forays on the internet that convoy JW63 had left Loch Ewe on December 30th 1944. Elspeth had conceived Charlotte on his last leave. John Elliott never saw his daughter; he never even knew that Elspeth was pregnant. And if—if—Mhairi Mackenzie had been pregnant by him, then he never knew about or saw his son either. As she thought about the weight of all that loss, Annie found that she was reaching for the tissues in her bag.

29

September 1945

There was no water again. The pipe had burst, and Elspeth had to go to the standpipe two streets away with her two cans. She sighed with relief when she got back—at least the kitchen was on the ground floor—and Nellie helped her pour the water into the various awaiting receptacles: kettle, tin bath and the buckets and after she had fed the baby she went back for another load. They had all learnt to fill every available container whenever possible as the water supplies were intermittent at best. Elspeth avoided looking in a mirror and bound her long hair back into a loose bun with the ease of long practice. She knew that her beauty had disappeared and had no wish to be reminded. Her high cheekbones were gaunt and ugly, her eyes huge in the dark circles surrounding them, and her soul was as dry and empty as her eyes.

At the standpipe, she put down the cans as she waited in line again, putting her hands loosely over her belly, still slack and stretched from the baby's birth. What a leaving present he had given her, during that brief visit before his last convoy. It had been worse than if he had never come at all. And then to die, in the cold arms of the sea, the last to leave her after father, mother and her children. A sob shook her unexpectedly, the sound making the women in the queue turn towards her apprehensively. Oh, God! The absences, the voids, the nothingness. The night-on-night wakefulness in Nellie's little spare bedroom, the baby's snuffling noises, so unlike the sounds the boys used to make. The realisation that there would never again be the fellowship of her husband, the painful admission that her failure to stand up to her mother had caused his anger and distress and their separation; had thrown him into the arms of another woman. That woman was a mirage, a blurred silhouette, standing with open welcoming arms for Elspeth's husband, while she, his wife, had blocked the doorway to his home, to her, to his children. This baby girl he had left her with was incapable as yet of loving her, and she was incapable of loving it. Her skin flared hot in guilt and the misery shook her bones again.

The baby, Charlotte, was six weeks old. Hideous, wakeful, fretful, perpetually hungry, but vomiting out her mother's thin milk as soon as she received it. The baby was not loveable. She thought that there must be something fundamentally wrong with the tiny tyrant, but the doctor had shrugged wearily and told her not to worry, many children were born like it. The child would grow out of it.

The line moved forward and Elspeth filled her containers. The weight dragged at her shoulders, the cans banging bruisingly against her legs as she carried them back. She could hear Charlotte's wail from the corner of the street, and putting the water cans down in the kitchen, hurried to try to quieten her. Nellie gave her a tired smile.

'She started as soon as you left.'

Nellie was an old friend, sympathetic, hospitable and kind, but her husband Norman's patience had worn thin. He was employed in the dockyard, shoring up the broken quays and loading bays, manning cranes and trucks, working from early dawn, returning home tired and impatient. Elspeth had heard him, not bothering to lower his voice, as he complained to his wife.

'She turns my stomach, with that puling baby sicking up and her creeping around snivelling. For God's sake get her out of my house!'

Nellie's sympathy was wearing thin, too, and Elspeth knew that she had far exceeded their goodwill and welcome after a year, even with the substantial rent she paid. They craved peace with their own family, with children who went out and played in the street after their tea and were quiet when told to be. Norman did not want a strange miserable woman in his house, whose manners served only to show up his own lack of them, and her sudden inexplicable—to him—collapses into distraught sobs. The house smelt of vomited breastmilk, sour and sharp, and never seemed to be without the thin wail of Charlotte's dissatisfaction. Norman wanted them out, making his views clear to both women.

'I'm making enquiries,' she told Nellie, rubbing her bruised shins with one hand while rocking the baby with the other. 'I've put a notice up in the post office and the council offices, for accommodation. I'm sure to get somewhere soon. Oh! Why does she cry so much? I only fed her an hour ago!' She was tearfully exasperated.

Nellie shook her head. 'Some are colicky, some not. You just have to be patient. Norman doesn't mean to be rude. He's tired at the end of the day, that's all. But you do need to make a new life now and stop living with all those regrets and bad memories. There are people in the town who've been through the same and they're having to make new lives too.'

And that's a slap on the wrist, Elspeth thought. I'm not the only person in this war who's lost everything. I just feel that I am.

Eventually, she found rooms above a pub in a village near Romsey, on the understanding that she would 'help out' the publican's wife when required. The publican himself was now employed as a quartermaster in Southampton.

To her surprise, she and the brusque Mrs Gibbons came to respect each other, if liking was still a step too far. Elspeth paid her rent on time, and the small navy pension stretched far enough, together with the decent amount John and her parents had left her. Mrs Gibbons had no truck with self-pity and set her to work clearing the dead garden vegetation when the weather was fine, and on sewing and scrubbing and checking the apple boxes when it wasn't. She had brought up five children, and there was little she didn't know about child-rearing. Bald baby Charlotte spent much time in an old battered pram, rescued from an outhouse, wrapped in blankets with only her red nose and cheeks showing. The blasts of fresh air made her sleep, and the vomiting lessened. The apple tree waved above her, the occasional falling fruit hitting the pram hood with a bang that made her briefly shriek and jump, her greeny eyes following the dancing branches and the skimming, swooping fall of autumn leaves. The skinny little body began to put on flesh and by the time she was shovelling in mashed potatoes and gravy, she became, if not beautiful, less ugly.

'Ugly babies often turn out the best-looking,' Mrs Gibbons said, not bothering to consider Elspeth's feelings in the interests of truth. 'You would be a good-looking lass if you smiled more and stopped being so droopy.'

But Elspeth was haunted by the echo of John's bitter farewell and buried the memory of her own cold responses to his last lovemaking; her stiff body, the turned shoulder. Her inference that his pain and loss could not compare with hers. That he had hardly known his children and therefore their loss must be so much less for him; that her mother's death was devastating to her, whereas in truth, it had been a guilty relief. And in the end, his reaction, his hitting back, the comparison of her selfish behaviour with another woman. A girl in Scotland, an uncomplaining, optimistic, hard-working, good-housekeeping girl. Who cooked what little she had well, who kept her house bright and shining, went to work, and efficiently managed her croft and sheep. Elspeth's guilt and jealousy consumed her memory of John.

Mr and Mrs Gibbons watched patiently and compassionately and week by week, month by month, they saw Elspeth come, resentfully, to terms with a situation she could not alter, and with experiences which were by no means unique to her. John's perceived betrayal was a different matter and the maggot of unforgiveness ate away at the good times and bloated the bad.

Charlotte, at any rate, said Mrs Gibbons to her husband with brisk approval, was in significantly better shape since their arrival, even if Elspeth was not.

30

17th January 2012

Annie studied her notes on the people she had already researched. None of it threw much light on John Elliott, although each person must have known or at least met him, one way or another. She was running out of leads. Mrs Reid's grandson, who had been ten years old in 1945, still lived in the old family croft on the Mellon Charles road and Annie went to see him.

He had creaky knees and entertained her with strong black tea and chocolate Hobnobs while he shuffled out old post office ledgers on to the kitchen table, all the while dripping memories and anecdotes of his schooldays.

She could see from the bowed shelves of the cupboard that they went back far beyond the war, and probably for years after. Grandam had been a power in the land, he said admiringly, and knew everything about everything seeing as she ran the post office for forty-seven years. A pillar of propriety she was, but with a Godly Heart. Had she misheard? But Mr Reid junior extolled her rather severe form of care and compassion to such an extent that she decided probably not. The ledgers revealed wartime records of ration books, identity cards, telegrams, letters, packages, telephone calls, stamps and stationery and much else, incoming and outgoing, in tiny amounts of pounds, shillings and pence. A time when, to Annie's amazement, a stamp cost two pence. Two old pence. She couldn't work out what sort of a fraction of metric pence that would be.

The entries for the war years were in two distinct hands, one the clearest, neatest and most miniature handwriting she had ever seen, the other a little larger, though pedantically educated, and there, sprinkled among the hundreds of entries, she found the names of Lieutenant John Elliott and many other *Countess of Minto* officers and crew. She noted down names and ranks and dates in her notebook, marvelling at the wealth of detail. On enquiry, Mr Reid proudly professed the miniature handwriting to be 'Grandam's' and dismissed the larger one as her assistant's.

'Would that be Mrs Gillespie?' Annie asked cautiously. 'I understand she worked in the post office during the war.'

'Aye, Mhairi Mackenzie she was.' He nodded his thick thatch of grey hair. 'She was right pretty in them days, and a bouncy girl full of laughs and always a kind word for those poor men off the ships. She liked the children too. At the beginning of the war, when there was still sugar, she would hide them wee sweets, barley sugars I think they were, in her apron pocket and put them into our hand when she thought Grandam wasn't looking. Oh ay, the children loved her right enough, and she thought Grandam never knew, but she did. She told me years later that she turned a blind eye, though the barley sugars in the jar were fewer than the pennies to pay for them. Later, of course, the sugar was rationed and there were no sweeties in the jars.'

She was incredulous. 'You don't tell me she did stock-taking on the sweetie jars?'

He gave a rich throaty chuckle. 'Oh aye, she had a sharp eye, and a sharp tongue, too, but for all that, she had a Godly Heart.' She hadn't misheard. Annie thought it was a curiously touching description. 'When Mhairi had to leave,' he went on, 'it was Grandam that stood by her. She never let folk gossip—she could freeze out the blether and the cuts, inside the post office anyway. I only knew that when I was older. As a wee boy I just knew I'd get boxed ears if she heard me tittle-tattling.' The old man looked sideways, as if the ghost of his grandmother stood at his elbow, ready to box his ears. 'Oh, she lived by the book did my Grandam.'

When Mhairi had to leave was an interesting remark. She looked again at the ledgers. After April 1945 there were no more entries in Mhairi's handwriting. A pregnancy would have been showing. 'We could do with a few more like her these days,' she said.

'Things changed after the war,' he said, sounding a bit wistful, Annie thought. 'The ships went, the guns went, they dismantled the boom; there was no trade then, no employment.'

'Did your grandmother lose her job at the post office, too, because of the war ending?'

'Och, no! The post office has always been there—always will be.' Annie felt unsure about that but said nothing. 'She ran it for years afterwards, but the village became quiet again, do you see, and there was no need for the extra staff.'

'How old was she when she died?'

He nodded his head admiringly. 'She lived to be one hundred years old. Born in 1887 she was. She was a great lady, so she was.'

'I went to see Mrs Gillespie and she told me lots about your grandmother. Fierce but fair, she said. She loved her time at the post office. I suppose you don't remember a Lieutenant John Elliott? He was killed on a convoy in 1945.'

He shook his head. 'There were hundreds of sailors and military men, coming in and out, all through the war. Us children never knew any of them.'

Frustrated, she wondered what other connections she could follow. She remembered her conversation with Susan MacConnachie. There was at least one other person, Archie, who had known John, or at least known of him as a possible rival for Mhairi's affections. Would Mr Reid know anything about that? Should she even be asking? It was a very long shot.

'Does the name Archie Mackinnon mean anything to you?'

There was no mistaking the wary look. 'No,' he said firmly. 'I was just a lad.'

He gave her a straight look. 'Sometimes digging things up is no' very healthy.' He closed the ledgers up with sharp snaps and began putting them back in the cupboard. 'Things happened in the war which are best forgotten now.' It was clear that Mr Reid wasn't going to repeat any ancient gossip.

He wasn't to be drawn any further, and she had driven back to Inveruidh through yet another gale, with the wind-screen wipers at full speed, wondering why Archie Mack-innon was beginning to establish his presence so strongly. Mrs MacConnachie and Mhairi herself had described him as an unpleasant black marketeer whose death had been a case of 'good riddance to bad rubbish' and now Mr Reid had declined to talk about him, although it was obvious he remembered Archie too.

Rumours of murder were certainly intriguing, but she had come here to find out about John Elliott, not to delve into a murder case. She should go back to London and sort out the mess she had made of her life. Find a job. Find somewhere to live. Make new friends and break connec-tions with some existing ones. She should leave Jem to find out if John Elliott was his father, and if he was Charlotte's half-brother, although the possible relationship fascinated her, and would fascinate Charlotte too. She should suppress her attraction to David Mackenzie and leave him to grieve for his dead wife. Nevertheless, the reluctance to return to London was like a lump of Blu Tack sticking her to Wester Ross. Wester Ross held intrigue, an unsolved murder, new adventure, new interest. And David. Suppression was easier said than done. And it would be easier to stay than to face the world.

31

January 2012

It was nearly time to pack up Inveruidh and return to real life. A life Annie was not looking forward to. To sort out how she would live as a single woman after eight years of being married to a man who didn't really want his wife working. She never had discovered why. Perhaps it had offended Justin's ideal of a little woman waiting at home just to look after him. Perhaps he was aware that she had a good brain and might show him up as rich and idle, and possibly not very clever. She doubted that David Mackenzie would have discouraged his wife from having a career. Putting a stop to the ironic twist her thoughts had taken, she looked out at the rain sweeping up Loch Ewe in grey bucketfuls, solid and dense, gusted forwards by the clawing, punching wind. David and the Mackenzie family would be battling the weather to gather today for Mhairi's ninetieth birthday. Was Mhairi looking back down the years to Jem's father? John Elliott, or perhaps this Archie Mackinnon? Or maybe even someone else. Ninety years. What a colossal weight of memory must have accumulated in that time. And much of that memory had been kept hidden. Annie was certain it hadn't been forgotten.

* * *

The following day it was still raining, but she resisted the temptation to cosy up by the fire and took herself off to the archives in the County Library in Ullapool. The young man at the front counter took her, on payment of a small fee, to the appropriate microfiches and explained how the search function worked. Nothing relevant under Aultbea, HMS *Helicon*, Russian convoys, or John Elliott. No mention of the *Countess of Minto* or military units. By twelve-thirty her stomach began to growl, and in a final bid for some nugget, she guiltily typed in 'Mhairi Mackenzie'. Up popped several results, and another name caught her eye. Archie Mackinnon.

The rather dry wartime journalese was, she thought, more revealing than the lubricious tabloid scandals of today.

Archie's death was an open verdict. He had last been seen alive on 24th January 1945. In the opinion of the coroner, he could have been killed by a person or persons unknown; his lungs had little water in them, although he had been in the sea for at least a month before his body was found in March 1945. There were marks on his face concomitant (what a lovely word, she thought) with being hit with a heavy chain, and the wound on the side of his head, according to the police forensic expert, would appear to have been made prior to him entering the water. How could they possibly have known that?

Various people had been called in for questioning, including a Miss Rhionna MacRae and a Miss Mhairi Mackenzie. She pondered about Rhionna MacRae. Who was she? Unless she had been a young woman—perhaps a rival for Archie's affections?—she would be dead. But it was possible, just possible, that she was still alive. Others had given evidence at the coroner's hearing: Mrs Reid of Aultbea, a Mr Angus Mackinley of Inverasdale, plus a Private Alan Norburn and numerous other military personnel, sentries and shopkeepers. Maybe some of them were still alive. She noted down names. It seemed that Mhairi Mackenzie was number one suspect, but as nobody could prove she did it, no one was charged. There was no reference to John Elliott.

Annie paid for copies of the relevant sheets and then, hungrier than ever, took herself through the driving rain to a harbour-front café for a late and indifferent lunch. Archie Mackinnon was taking centre stage instead of John Elliott and she was annoyed by it. Was there anything more she could find out about John? Was there anything more *to* find out? Mhairi had told her all that she was going to. The internet had filled in the convoy dates, a few other postings and a certain amount of information about the *Countess of Minto*'s refits and sea trials. She should type it all up nice and tidily for her mother and go back to London. Go back and pull her life together. Stop putting off a fresh start. Stop hovering around David Mackenzie, however much she was attracted by him and to him. She finished her lunch and scurried through the rain to her car with her coat hood pulled down to her eyes, the weather making her feel depressed for the first time.

32

25th January 1945

Mhairi hung her snow-covered coat on the hook and unwound the scarf before turning to face Mrs Reid.

Mrs Reid's mouth dropped open. 'Dear Lord Almighty! Whatever happened?'

Mhairi gave her a lop-sided smile because half her face didn't work. 'I'm sorry I'm late. Last night's storm was a bit of a disaster.' There had been plenty of time on the long bike ride to get the disaster story sorted out in her head, although her head was one clanging, throbbing, incoherent tangle.

Mrs Reid continued to stare. 'Well? What happened? Did the roof come off?'

Mhairi shook her head and wished she hadn't. 'I had an accident with the sheep.' Suddenly rather wobbly, she sat down on the little stool behind the pigeonholes. 'I got trampled in the storm. So stupid. All my own fault.'

'Trampled?' Mrs Reid's voice was seldom raised, but it was now. 'An accident with the *sheep?*' For a long speculative moment she stared at Mhairi's swollen face and black eyes, then suddenly pulled herself together. 'My Lord! You look terrible and you'd better have a hot cup of tea before you keel over.' Although her tone didn't change, Mhairi recognised Mrs Reid's severe form of sympathy and a whimper nearly escaped as a little bit of the suppressed shock surfaced.

'Silly girl, you should have stayed at home. Someone could have brought me a message.' She clanged cups and kettle. 'What were you doing out in that blizzard with the sheep? Are you mad then?'

Mhairi took a breath. 'I wanted them off the moor. Out of the drifts and safe, if I couldn't get back from Aultbea. Seven I found and put inside the garden with hay. Then when I found more, I opened the gate to put them in, and the first lot all rushed out and knocked me over.'

Mrs Reid's chin nearly tucked itself into her blouse as she looked over the top of her spectacles. 'Oh yes?'

'The path was a sheet of ice,' Mhairi said defensively. 'They just trampled all over me.'

Mrs Reid made the tea and put the cup and saucer down with a sharp clack.

'Humph,' she said. 'You'll go to Mrs MacRae now and stay tonight, and never mind the sheep. Tomorrow you'll stay indoors, and the next day you can come back to work. Maybe.' She put her head on one side and considered Mhairi's grazed hands. 'And did the sheep only tread on your face or is the rest of you in the same state?' Her eyes dropped to the thick stockings.

'There's a few more hoof prints,' Mhairi admitted with an attempt at a grin, recalling how the pain in her ribs had made her breath whistle as she bicycled.

Mrs Reid fisted her hands on her hips. 'You'll look like a rainbow for a week, but you'll just have to cope with being the butt of all the village jokes.'

The day had crept past with a headache which made her clutch her temples, and every now and then there was a flash of memory, panic and pain.

Mrs Reid must have gone to the greengrocer's to warn Mrs Macrae. There was a truckle bed made up instead of the normal mattress on the floor and hot flannel-wrapped stones to warm it. Rhionna had obviously been told not to chatter or ask questions, but she looked on in fascinated horror as her mother anointed bruises and grazes with Pommade Divine. Dosed with half a tumbler of whisky, Mhairi sank into sleep fragmented by shrieking wind, driving snow, the banging of the gate, or was it the door? Running footsteps, falling, a foul taste in her mouth. Ropes. Hay. Tarpaulins.

Once, during the night, she woke both herself and Rhionna as she screamed. A nightmare of running as if through water, struggling forwards, getting nowhere. Someone or something coming after her, a faceless evil just behind, pulling at her shoulder, catching her foot. Something plunging on to her as she struggled to move, and flashing pain, again and again and again.

Rhionna knelt beside the bed, her arms around her as she thrashed out from the nightmare.

'I'm here, I'm here. It's me. Quiet now. It's all right.' Her hand stroked back the sweaty strands of hair from Mhairi's twisting forehead. 'It was only a dream. A horrible dream.'

Her heart was bursting, hammering in her chest so that her whole body shook with the frantic banging, her ears pounding with the noise of it. Even as she woke, she remembered, and the dream was not a dream. It was real.

33

20th January 2012

As she drove back from Ullapool, the rain eased off and on a sudden impulse Annie turned down into Aultbea village, following the road beside the restless, grey waters, wondering where she could go to ask the questions. The Aultbea Hotel looked closed, but further on there was the shop and post office. An elderly man behind the counter was placing sheets of stamps into a large book with meticulous precision and conversing with an equally elderly lady on the shop side. Both stopped speaking for a moment, looked at her in what appeared to be amazement and then continued their conversation. In due course the lady departed, tying a rain hood over her tight permanent waves. Annie suspected that the damp would create a splendid frizz, plastic or no plastic.

The postmaster asked whether he could help her, in the tone of voice which intimated that it was highly unlikely. He shuffled his stamp book shut as if he were about to close up and go home.

'I hope you can,' she said. 'I'm trying to trace various people who lived and worked in Aultbea during the war.' The door opened and shut, and she glanced over her shoulder at the newcomer, a young woman with a rash of freckles and flaming red curly hair spangled with raindrops.

She smiled at Annie and put a bulging plastic bag and her elbows on the counter.

'I've been to see Mr Reid, the grandson of the wartime postmistress,' Annie said hastily, in case he started to serve Red Hair instead of her, 'who has been most helpful, and I 'm trying to discover what happened to someone called Rhionna MacRae who lived in Aultbea then, and I wondered if you might perhaps know the name?'

He didn't even hesitate, which made her suspect that he didn't want to bother with thinking about it. 'No. There are many MacRaes hereabouts, but I don't know that person.' He was so offhand as to be rude. Annie put a lid on her annoyance.

'I wasn't thinking you'd actually know her. She would be at least ninety by now and has probably died. I wondered if there was anyone in the village who might remember her or know what happened to her. She might have been a friend of Mrs Gillespie at Poolewe.'

'I cannot be of any help. I don't know that lady either.'

'But I do!' suddenly chimed in Red Hair. 'If you'll wait while I put the post through, we could have a wee chat, the two of us.' She gave Annie a friendly grin and a flicker of a conspiratorial wink. The postmaster looked as if he was sucking lemons.

Five minutes later they sat in Red Hair's smart silver Subaru, the engine running to keep the heat up. 'He's a right dour old codger, no one gets any help from him, and unless you ken what you're doing, he'll let you overstamp and underweigh, and then fine you! I'm Kate Mackinley. I'm the secretary at Mackenzie Brothers, and you're Annie, if I'm not mistaken. I've been meaning to come and see you, but it's been a bit frantic since I got back. I owe you an apology for what I hear was a bit of a disaster over the cottage. I'm really sorry.'

Kate's accent was strong and brisk and had none of the West Coast lilt. Annie was warmed by her friendliness.

'Well, it was a bit of a disaster at the time, but they've all been extremely kind and helpful since and I'm loving being there, new kitchen and all. You heard about my efforts at burglary?'

Kate looked sympathetic. 'That must have been horrible, and David confessed he was horrible too. Typical man, as if they didn't leave their wallets and phones all over the place. Iain's hopeless with receipts, which is endearing at the moment, but I don't think that will last.'

Annie remembered that Kate was newly married.

'Congratulations—I gather you just got back from honeymoon. Somewhere hot and sunny, I hope?'

Kate grinned again. 'Three weeks in Sri Lanka. Bliss! Fab!' She waved a hand at a dark grey seascape studded with light grey flying waves, against a backdrop of dark grey sweeping clouds and rain. 'Back to the good old West Coast! And back to a cross David who said I deserved the sack for not telling him about your booking. I told him he deserved the sack for not telling me he intended to put in a new kitchen as well as the bathroom—which I did know about.'

'Yes, you'd told me about the bathroom and that it would all be done by Christmas. The kitchen, which looked like a bomb site that first night, is beautiful.'

'Well, I'm glad about that. David is amazing. Plumbing, electrics, woodwork, you name it, he does it. Turns his hand to anything really, and since Shona died—did you know his wife died?' Annie nodded. 'Since she died, he's worked like a maniac. Must have a project going all the time. I must come and see the kitchen. Iain's parents live in Inverasdale, so I can kill two birds with one stone. If you don't mind me visiting, that is?'

A penny dropped in Annie's mind with a loud clang. Inverasdale. Mackinley.

'I'd be delighted. Tomorrow? I guess not during the day, but how about after work?'

'I could do that.' She frowned, 'Were you asking for someone in the village when I came in?'

'Well, yes,' Annie said, conscious she was raking up names from some irrelevant murder investigation. 'I'm researching a naval officer, John Elliott, who served here in the war. Mrs Gillespie knew him. A Miss Rhionna MacRae was mentioned in a newspaper report during the war and I thought she might remember my grandfather if she was an unmarried girl then.' She heaved a sigh. 'She could have been an ancient spinster, of course, in which case she's long dead.'

Kate wrinkled her nose in thought. 'Rhionna MacRae. It means nothing to me, but I'll ask around.'

'Your surname was there too—a Mr Mackinley of Inverasdale, so I was a bit startled to hear you say your in-laws lived in Inverasdale. I wonder if there is a connection?'

'Och, bound to be! The croft has been in the family for generations, same as the Mackenzies. My Iain's father was the first to leave crofting as an occupation. Now they have a flooring business. God knows why it works—he's no' the most efficient businessman.' She chuckled, a rich throaty good-natured sound. 'Iain'll take it on when his father retires, and he's got plenty of get up and go. Unlike most of these West Coast lads here, who'll always do it—but tomorrow!'

'You're not West Coast then,' Annie said curiously. 'You do sound different.'

'I'm from the Borders—Galashiels. I came up one summer a few years ago. I just loved it, and the Mackenzies were advertising for a secretary, so I stayed. I met Iain then, he does a lot of work for them, and here I am, a married woman with her feckless Highlander. According to my dad, all Highlanders are feckless.' She chuckled again. 'So what was the newspaper report you saw the name in?'

'Well, I don't think it had anything to do with my

grandfather. I think the Mr Mackinley was a witness in some murder investigation during the war.'

Her eyes rounded. 'That would be my Iain's grandfather, I'm guessing. Murder! Who was murdered?'

Annie wrinkled her forehead. 'Some man had come to a bad end because he dealt on the black market.'

Kate pursed her lips. 'I wonder if father-in-law knows of it? I could ask him.'

'It was rather fascinating, and I just went on reading, although it had nothing to do with my research—you know how the eye wanders on from article to article.' She picked up her bag, conscious that she was babbling slightly. 'I must be going, and so I'm sure, must you. Are you going back to the office?'

'No, I'm going home, but I'll be working.' She indicated behind her, and glancing round Annie saw a laptop on the back seat. Kate smiled again, 'Great to put a face to the emails, and I'm sorry again for the bad start to your holiday. Not that it's exactly holiday weather. I should think you can't wait to leave!'

'Oh no! I don't want to leave at all. I'd like to stay for ever!' Kate's eyebrows rose in faint astonishment and Annie, embarrassed, realised how vehement she sounded. 'I just love it—the cottage, the snow, wind, rain. Everything.'

Kate smiled. 'Well, each to his own!' Annie grinned and got out into the damp roaring wind, calling her thanks.

'See you tomorrow afternoon, then.'

'Aye. Look forward to it.'

By the time she reached Poolewe the rain had stopped, so she drew in at the stores to get supplies, the Ullapool Tesco having been elusive. Inside, she found David and the two boys with a small trolley into which the boys were dropping unsuitable goods which David was half-heartedly trying to put back on the shelves and replace with more suitable items.

Her tummy did a little cartwheel at the sight of him. 'Hello,' she said to the boys. 'How are you? Hungry by the looks of it!' She looked up at David. 'How was the party? Did she enjoy it?'

'She did. She presided over the clan gathering all afternoon and we deferred to her every whim and waited on her hand and foot.' The grey eyes creased in affectionate amusement and attraction tightened again in her stomach.

'And how many guests did she have?'

He laughed. 'No guests. Only close family, but that was quite enough for her. We were fourteen in all.' Annie blinked. How could you possibly have that many close family?

Seamus threw a tin of alphabet spaghetti into the trolley and grabbed Annie's hand. 'I've got a new skateboard!' he said, pulling her towards the door, 'and I can do really good jumps on it. Come and see, it's outside.'

For some reason, this seemed a better option than talking to David, who made her feel a little breathless. 'OK,' she said. 'I expect Dad might get on faster without you trying to buy everything he doesn't want!' David smiled in agreement. She put her basket back on the pile. 'Is it your birthday, that you've got a new skateboard?'

'No,' he said confidingly. 'It's not really new, it was in the Community Shop and it only cost three pounds. That's good, isn't it? It looks new. It's a bit dirty underneath, and there's a few scratches, but it's pretty wicked. The wheels are on ball bearings so it's really smooth.' Reaching the car, he pulled out the skateboard and embarked on a demonstration through the puddles.

'Let's go to the hotel car park,' Annie suggested. 'Then at least you won't get run over in the dark.' Not that there was a moving vehicle in sight. 'It certainly is a super-duper skateboard. Does Christopher have one too?'

'Yep. His is bigger than mine.' The jumps needed lots

of practice. 'We got them for our birthdays from Tom and Tilly. But one of my wheels broke, so I didn't have one for yonks and yonks—and then we saw this one and Dad got it for me.' He set off on another ill-fated gymnastic run. 'Watch! Watch me!'

'Who are Tom and Tilly?' Annie asked idly, pulling him out of a puddle and righting the skateboard with her foot. The car park gleamed slick in the light of the single streetlamp.

'Oh, they're Mum's Mum and Dad. We have holidays with them and sometimes they come and stay with us. They sleep in the room at the top, where Chris and I have our Lego, and Tom helps us build spaceships. They give us chocolate biscuits in their bed in the morning and they have cups of tea, cos they have a kettle beside the bed.'

A pang of envy. Tom and Tilly sounded rather cosy, and she remembered the slightly formal, chilly graciousness of Justin's parents. She couldn't imagine them making early morning tea and eating chocolate biscuits in bed. Even with an heir. Charlotte and Will would have loved to have snuggles in bed with grandchildren, but would never have the opportunity. Seamus was still intent on his practice jumps, but suddenly brought the board to a halt beside her.

'Do you want a go? It's easy.'

She laughed. 'Oh yes? It doesn't look easy, but if you say so! Do you think I'll break it? I'm much heavier than you.'

'No, of course you won't! Go on.' He held her hand in gentlemanly fashion, which was most unhelpful to the balancing act, and both of them were giggling idiotically as she lurched from side to side up the car park.

David was standing at the gateway watching them. She thought his face looked taut and expressionless in the pallid lamplight. She had been presumptuous to have played like that with his son. He clearly didn't like it. Annie, praying that her flushed face would cool, made her way back and headed for the shop.

'Bye, Seamus, 'bye David,' she called over her shoulder and waved at Christopher who seemed to be intent on some gadget in the car. The shopping was done without much thought. She felt uncomfortable, as if she had committed some social solecism. He could not, after all, know that her day's research had focused more on his grandmother, rather than on John Elliott.

As she pulled the shop door shut behind her, someone came towards her. It took a moment to realise it was David and that he was still parked next to her. She was shaken by a moment of unreasoning panic.

'Annie, I've got those photocopies for you at home, and the boys would love you to come back for tea. They are dying to learn another Scott Joplin rag—me too, as the present one has got almost as bad as Chopsticks.' There was nothing in his voice or manner except pleasant friendliness. 'Unless you're busy, and have to get back, that is.'

'Oh! I—no,' she gulped. 'Isn't that a perfect nuisance for you? I mean—I ought to go back. I've got frozen stuff—peas—' She looked down at her plastic bags. He was looking amused.

'Nothing will melt in this weather. We can put the peas in the freezer and write a Post-It note to remind you when you leave. And no, it's not a perfect nuisance for me, otherwise I wouldn't have suggested it. We have my mother's gingerbread.' As if this last were the clinching argument.

'The boys will be disappointed if you don't and you don't need to stay long—I expect you've got lots to do at the cottage.' She glanced up at him, uncertain whether she had heard a note of irony, but his face was unreadable; only the grey eyes glinted. She couldn't think of anything to say that wouldn't sound rude and in any case, she was curious to have Mhairi's photocopies.

The bag of frozen food went in the freezer and he made a pot of tea as he cooked pasta for the boys. They ladled on spoonfuls of pesto while she grated white drifts of Parmesan over the bowls. Under direction, she cut hunks of sticky gingerbread and poured mugs of milk for the boys, impressed that they didn't even ask for fizzy drinks. They were silent for the few minutes it took to consume this feast, and he asked about her day in Ullapool, listened in amusement to the description of the Aultbea postmaster and seemed pleased that she had met Kate.

'Don't you eat with them?' she said, indicating the disappearing pasta.

'Yes, we'll eat about seven when they've done their homework. This is a temporary stopgap.' He laughed at her incredulity. 'I don't always give them anything hot for tea, but today they had extra stuff at school—gym and badminton— and they're ravenous after it. My mother has done a vast cauliflower cheese for supper, bless her. God knows what I'd do without her extra cooking.'

Annie contemplated the enormity of boys' appetites with some awe. What on earth would the consumption be when they were teenagers?

'I hear you want to learn another Scott Joplin rag,' she said to them. 'Will you play me the other one?'

She was astonished at how good they were. The syncopation was rhythmic and natural, and Christopher played the melody clearly. It appeared that they had taught each other the reverse hands and both boys were pleased with themselves, enjoying their triumph. David came and leant against the doorframe, and she could see he was proud of them. He caught her eye, smiling, and a warmth spread through her.

She played them 'Alexander's Ragtime Band' and was touched by their enthusiasm to learn it. Much later, the doorbell rang, and David answered it. There was a murmur of voices, one female.

'I must go, boys. I hadn't realised how late it was,' Annie

said, dismayed at how long she had been there. In the hall she heard the voices were now slightly raised and she shrugged her coat on, instinctively making a noise with a chair as she did so, and nervously went into the kitchen to collect her bag and the photocopies. David was leaning against the Aga and looked bad-tempered and mutinous. Isla Thompson of the beautiful voice and the bank was standing close to him. She, too, looked angry. Her dark hair was cut in a close, sharp, elfin style, and she was dressed in a smart black skirt and jacket, making Annie feel too tall and too big. She turned to Annie, smiling with her mouth, but not with her eyes. Not at all pleased to find me here, Annie thought.

'Hello, Miss Thompson. We meet again. I'm just off, David. I fear the boys will drive you crazy with this one, too, but at least there will be a choice of crazy. Thank you so much for tea.' She indicated the envelope beside her bag, 'And these are for me, are they? I'm so grateful. I'll let myself out.'

As she started the car a figure passed in front of the headlights and opened the passenger door. 'Your peas,' he said gravely, depositing the bag on the seat. There was no trace of the bad temper as he smiled at her. Her heart thumped and warmth spread through her again. He was a most attractive, good-looking man, at ease in his jeans and heavy sweater. The grey eyes were very crinkly when he smiled. She reminded herself that he had recently lost his wife and was not looking for another relationship. Not that I'm looking for another relationship either, she told herself crossly. I thought Justin was the be-all and end-all, but he turned out to be nothing of the sort. I'm a bad judge of character, therefore people I think are attractive, are almost undoubtedly not. You're on the rebound, Annie.

* * *

The following day, Kate came after work as promised, and looked with interest at the new installation. Annie was impressed by her thoroughness as she made notes about decoration requirements, and familiarised herself with stopcocks, meters and wiring, before driving them both to the Mackinley house about a mile further.

Mr Mackinley senior led them into a conservatory which was warm and comfortable, with thick cushions on white wicker sofas and glass-topped occasional tables. The low windowsills held a collection of driftwood sculptures, rough and unfinished but somehow evocative of wild nature.

'What a lovely room!' Annie exclaimed. 'This must be wonderful all year, but in winter it must be bliss to sit here all cosy with the weather going crazy outside!'

Mr Mackinley looked at her curiously. 'Do you like to see the rain and wind then? There's many folk who pull down the blinds and try to pretend it's not there. I leave them open. I like to see the loch wild, and the rain blattering and the snow drifting.'

Annie beamed at him. 'Me too—Inveruidh has huge windows upstairs, facing the loch, and I never draw the curtains. During that storm the other night I lay and watched the lightning and counted the seconds before the thunderclaps.'

Disappointingly, he had no knowledge of John Elliott and only a memory of gossip about Archie's death during a bad storm. He was interested in the newspaper report.

'Your father was a witness at the coroner's hearing, apparently,' Kate said. 'Had he seen something? I can't believe he was involved in a murder!'

'Oh no! He wasn't involved at all, but he'd got up in

213

the middle of the night because his old dog was barking, and they thought the Germans had landed! He found Mhairi Mackenzie up on the moor, looking for her sheep. Apparently, he saw terrible cuts and bruising on Mhairi's face and the speculation was that Archie Mackinnon had beaten her up and either she or the naval boyfriend killed him. But she said she'd fallen chasing her sheep or something.' The equivalent of 'slipping in the shower'? Annie wondered. Again, he paused for thought. 'Of course, I only heard this story long after the war, because I wasn't born until 1949, but I'm fairly certain they said the naval officer couldn't have done it because he was on convoy at the time and was killed. Would that have been your grandfather?'

Annie nodded. 'I would think so. He was killed in January 1945.'

'Mhairi was a bit of a loose cannon in her younger days from all accounts. I think everyone thought she'd had something to do with his disappearance, but nothing was ever proved.' Mr Mackinley smiled and shrugged. 'Who knows? Anyway, it was my father's moment of glory—well, his moment in the limelight anyway.' He tapped his fingers on his knee in thought.

'The story went that when Mhairi's father came back from the war, she had had a baby but wouldn't say who the father was. Her father took to the bottle—or perhaps returned to it—and one day he attacked the baby and she ran to my parents for help and they put her on the bus for Achnasheen.' Annie put a hand to her mouth, remembering Mhairi saying she 'stretched her wings and went down to Edinburgh'. What a lot she hadn't said.

Mr Mackinley went on. 'Father gave her a ten-shilling note which she repaid later with a thank you note.' He sipped his dram thoughtfully. 'Don't know where she went to, but she came back when the old man had a stroke. By that time the baby, who must be Jem Mackenzie, was grown. She looked after her father until he died and then, of course, the croft was hers. More than that, I suppose only Mhairi knows.'

Mr Mackinley had put a new twist on Mhairi's story. How terrifying to have your father attack your baby and have to run. She thought of Will and was flooded with thankfulness.

34

March 1945

Detective Inspector Melhuish sighed. The Aultbea Hotel was old and cold, with ancient and deeply uncomfortable furniture, and the plumbing was even older. Wartime military occupancy had not improved matters, and the beer was pulled into jam jars in the absence of pint mugs. He put the thought of his wife and comfortable home in Inverness out of his mind and closed his eyes in order to review the evidence.

There were some certainties:

Firstly, Archie Mackinnon's body had washed up on the boom at the mouth of Loch Ewe.

Secondly, he had died from a blow to the head, not from drowning.

Thirdly, Archie had last been seen on 24th January 1945.

Fourth certainty, Mhairi Mackenzie had been seen with a heavily cut and bruised face, including two black eyes, at about three in the morning of 25th January 1945.

Fifth certainty: Archie and Mhairi had been involved with each other and had had public arguments.

Sixth certainty: Archie Mackinnon's snow-covered van was seen parked about two miles south of Inverasdale later in the morning of 25th January. It contained boxes of illegal goods.

And that was about it for the certainties, he thought. All the rest was very uncertain. He shifted uncomfortably in the sagging brown armchair and brought the jam jar to his lips.

A sheep was very heavy, James Headley, Aultbea's local policeman, had said, especially with snow on the fleece. Nobody other than Rhionna and Mrs MacRae had seen what the rest of Mhairi looked like after being trampled by a flock of sheep, but they said she was 'fair bruised' and thought some ribs were cracked. DI Melhuish thought a man could crack ribs as well as a sheep, but then could you kill a man if you had cracked ribs? And if you did, could you move him somewhere else? Anyway, Rhionna was Mhairi's friend and an unreliable witness.

Perhaps Archie had persuaded, or forced her, into his van and driven the two miles down the loch. He could have raped her, or they could have quarrelled, perhaps about the goods, and she then killed him and somehow dumped his body in the loch. But everybody, the local community, farmers and fishermen, were all adamant that the storm was from the Atlantic. A body would not float or be blown out to sea, but inland, towards Poolewe, whatever the state of the tide. And Archie's body had been found outside the boom, on the seaward side. DI Melhuish sucked his teeth.

The discomfort of the chair and the irritation of the case got him to his feet. He would tackle the dining room and the tasteless single offering on the lunch menu before interviewing Mhairi Mackenzie.

* * *

Had there been a disagreement? Had Archie attacked her? Archie had been a jealous man, and no doubt resented Mhairi's friendship with John Elliott who, he understood, was sometimes billeted with Mhairi between convoys. From Ben Bradley he knew about John Elliott's burst appendix in 1942 and that Mhairi had visited him in hospital. Melhuish could see that she was startled by his knowledge and his thoroughness.

He knew all about Archie, and Archie's sources of income, about his van and what he carried in it, and about his friends, of whom Mhairi was one.

She was even more startled to find that he knew she had taken John home with her in Archie's van after his children were killed and had driven him to Achnasheen in the van. He didn't tell her that Alan Norburn had been the source of that information. He wanted her to be nervous of his omniscience. He wondered whether there had been goods in the van?

'Definitely not!' she said. 'I made sure there was nothing in the van, because if John had seen or suspected he wouldn't have gone in it, and he'd have informed FOIC, even though he was that upset. I used the van because there was no transport for him, and he couldn't get to the train.' She sat up straighter. 'The van was empty.'

Melhuish nodded his head in thought. 'I see. But on the night Archie Mackinnon disappeared it seems the van was loaded. When Constable Headley opened it, it was full of goods. According to Private Norburn, they were put in your shed for storage before they left.'

Mhairi sighed. 'Not with my permission. I've said it all, over and over. They both came, wanting to use the shed, and I refused. I told them I wouldn't do it.' She looked hunted. 'I'd have lost my job if I'd been caught with black market stuff.'

'And then? How did he react? What did they do?'

'Archie was cross and said I was stupid. He'd have paid me with something nice, he said, but if I didn't want it, then too bad for me. They drove away. He said he was taking the soldier back to barracks at Cove.'

'With the van full of illegal goods? Did you watch them drive away?'

Her shoulders dropped. 'No.'

'So they could have put it all in your shed, couldn't they? Before leaving?'

She hesitated. 'I don't know. Yes, I suppose so.'

Melhuish sucked in his cheeks. 'I think that Archie threatened you, Mhairi. Perhaps suggested he might frame you. Had he said he might tip off the authorities if you didn't help provide storage for him?'

She shook her head emphatically.

'And what happened when he came back?'

Mhairi stared at him. 'He didn't come back. Or if he did, I wasn't there. The storm was getting worse and I went out to bring in as many sheep as I could.' He saw her swallow involuntarily. 'You're saying I killed him because he threatened me? Well, I didn't kill him, and he didn't threaten me like that. If he came back, he must have reloaded his stuff and driven off. I heard he drowned, but if you think he was killed, it wasn't me. He must have met somebody else and they killed him. God knows, he was hardly popular.'

Melhuish rocked slightly in his chair and didn't mention the box of cigarettes on the beach or Archie's hat in the sea. 'He was a very nasty, dangerous sort of man, wasn't he? Did he really never threaten you?' She shook her head. 'Nothing physical? Nothing sexual?' Mhairi's eyes widened like a rabbit caught in headlamps and she shook it again. 'Did he ever threaten to harm Lieutenant Elliott?'

She licked her lips. 'No.'

Melhuish left a silence and looked at her without blinking. She was lying. Maybe Headley's theory about her marching him off the rocks at the point of a gun was right.

'Did your father leave a gun at the croft?'

Her mouth opened in what appeared to be astonishment. 'No! Where would he have got a gun?'

'Or perhaps Lieutenant Elliott left you a gun for your protection?'

Now she looked angry. 'No! Of course not! Was Archie shot then?'

Again, Melhuish left a silence as he looked at her.

'I'm thinking that a man like that was not above a bit of bribery. Perhaps things not on the ration book? Food perhaps?'

She sighed, her eyes dropping. 'He gave me some tea. And some butter. And once, a pair of nylon stockings. It wasn't bribery. He just gave them to me.' She looked as if she might cry. Melhuish didn't tell her that Norburn had listed quite a few other gifts that Archie had given her.

'I'm going to lose my job, aren't I?'

He wondered if she was acting up, and then thought, probably not. He nodded slowly. 'I think that is likely, yes.'

He changed tack and became a policeman again. 'I'm thinking, Mhairi, that you met Archie again that night. I think he came back to change your mind about storing his merchandise. It seems that he intended to—what shall we say—persuade you. I'm thinking you went with him in his van and he parked a way down the loch and tried to blackmail you and somehow you had to stop him?'

Her eyes widened in disbelief, almost in humour.

'For sure I did nothing of the sort! He never came back, and that weather was right horrible. I went up on the moor and brought down as many beasts as would come. Then I went back to see if I could find more.'

'And did you?' She shook her head. 'A few. Four more I found, but then I couldn't see, and I'd gone out without the compass. I came back in.'

Melhuish leant forward, his forearms on his knees. 'Why, Mhairi? The crofters leave the sheep out in all weathers.'

'And they have to go hunting for them in the drifts the

next day!' She was impatient. 'I wanted as many as I could find inside the walls, where I can give them hay easily. I have to go to work, don't I?'

Melhuish pursed his lips. He supposed it was a possible reason. 'And you went on looking until three in the morning when you met Mr Mackinley?'

She looked embarrassed. 'Well, no, not exactly.' Was he going to hear something more interesting? 'When I opened the gate to put the four inside, the others rushed out and took me flat on my back. The path was sheet ice, and I got trampled all over and lost the lot of them, the stupid beasts. I went inside and cleaned up a bit. I was that shaken, for they're heavy, and I sat a while cursing and crying—and then—' She seemed even more discomfited. 'I lay on the bed and went to sleep.' He waited patiently, and she concluded, 'When I woke up it was after midnight.'

'Was it not Archie that woke you?'

She shook her head. 'No. It was hunger. And all of me ached. And my ribs were that painful. I had some food and felt a bit better, and I took the torch and a compass and went out to look for them.'

Very biblical. 'It's not quite what you told Constable Headley.'

Her eyes dropped. 'He'd have thought I was daft.' She lifted her head and looked at him. 'I *was* daft. I don't know what I was doing. I got lost, even with the compass, and I never found the beasts. I near passed out in that storm, and if I had I wouldn't be here now. I was that relieved to find the crofts and Mr Mackinley.' She did sound genuinely frightened by what might have happened, Melhuish thought.

Detective Inspector Melhuish had already sent policemen to search the cottage again, as well as all the sheds and outhouses, and the surrounding land. They found little except some papers and letters, and a few small items which might have come via the black market. The letters were not hidden—they had been in the kitchen table drawer, bound together with a sliver of old curtain fabric—and they certainly did not create the impression that John was her lover or that Archie was jealous and that they had had a quarrel. There had been eight letters in the drawer, and Lieutenant Elliott had written, often with humour, of his hopes and fears, the cold, the ice on his cabin bulkhead, the water that came down the chimney and put the cook's fire out so they had nothing hot to drink or eat for four days, the torpedo they saw coming and the evasive action they took which saw it slide down their side. Eight letters. He read them again and suspected that there had been others. There were phrases, 'as I told you,' 'did you manage to get the wool for the sweater?' which indicated longer correspondence. But there was nothing of Archie and nothing from Archie.

Melhuish talked about blackmail, and how it never ended. He talked about the mounting evidence that she had been the last person to see Archie alive. She said nothing, just looked at him with calm, assessing eyes.

He gazed at the peeling ceiling of the Aultbea Hotel lounge after Mhairi had gone. His every instinct told him that she had killed Archie Mackinnon.

But as he couldn't work out how she had disposed of his body in the sea at least three miles away, in a driving storm, without the sentries seeing any kind of transport, he could not prove it, and worryingly, it didn't really bother him.

He had a sneaking admiration for Mhairi Mackenzie.

35

January 24th 1945

Mhairi came out of the hotel in the same calm state that she had been in during the whole interview and walked firmly along the lochside to the MacRaes' house, unlocked and unoccupied at this time of day. In Rhionna's room, she sat on the bed and her body began to shake; a little tremor at first and then convulsive spasms. Her vision swung crazily, one moment spinning, the next a sort of tunnel, like looking through the wrong end of John's telescope. She lay flat, but the effect was worse, and she pushed herself upright again. The policeman had so clearly seen Archie's manipulation, his blackmail, his intentions. She let out an involuntary moan. He had somehow known it all. She had so nearly told him everything about Archie. She closed her eyes and against her will her memory rewound, the sickness enveloping her again.

* * *

Archie pushing past her into the scullery, pulling the door closed behind him as he pocketed the shed key. His mouth was set in a hard line and his face pinched and blue with cold, the result, she guessed, of reloading goods into his van after taking Alan back to barracks. She experienced a vindictive pleasure that his vanity prevented him from wearing warm clothes.

He knew John had sailed, and he was back like a wasp to meat bones, wanting to use the cottage again for meetings, and for storing more goods in her shed. Her stomach contracted nervously.

'I want the key back, Archie. I don't want to talk about it again. I'm not going to store any of your stuff any more. I'd not just lose my job if I was found out. We'd both of us be put in prison—or worse. I won't have it any longer, and if you try to insist, I'll tell Mrs Reid and take the consequences.'

He became aggressive. 'It's a bit late for that, girl. How many years have you been helping my war effort? If you try that, Mhairi, I'll have to do something about it. There are always ways to stop someone blethering. The ingratitude of it! All those things you were so glad to have—food and nylons, that nice new bicycle, the use of my van and petrol, to mention but a few. Oh, I'm thinking there's a lot of information I could give them too—and your lover John would be quite shocked, wouldn't he?'

She shook her head, though she was trembling inside. John had gone, and a heavy sense of disaster lay like wet peat in her spirit.

'I never asked for them, and you gave them to me—I never paid. You said they were presents.'

'And it never occurred to you to wonder where they came from?' The sarcasm was biting. 'Well, I'm asking you to pay for them now, in the form of a shed. That's hardly expensive, is it?'

'No!' she said violently. 'I've decided. I'm not having your stuff here, and I'm not having your friends here either, and I'll thank you to leave now.'

He was still then, just looking at her in a narrow-eyed,

calculating way. 'All right then,' he said softly, 'if that's your attitude.' He turned as if to go, his hand on the backdoor latch, 'But I wonder what the navy will think about you taking the van that wee while ago.'

He lifted the latch and let in a shaft of freezing wind and a drift of snow.

'What are you on about? It was navy business—there wasn't a transport free.'

'Oh, but I don't think it was all navy business, was it? The van all packed with good things—meat and butter and eggs, and a whole box of nice new ration books, and two dozen bags of American sugar. I expect quite a lot of those things went into his pack and away down to Portsmouth. I expect a few things changed hands in the trains along the way too.' His words hit her like a punch in the stomach.

'That's not true! You told me to empty the van and I did! I put the boxes in the shed and there was nothing in the van. I put John's bag in the back and it was empty! John can swear to it as well.'

'But John isn't here, is he?'

The accusation was so outrageous that she was rendered speechless, and with a malicious grin, Archie went on. 'And if he didn't take it all, which I admit would have been difficult, I think the navy would find a few things hidden away on the croft for you to sell on a wee bit later.'

Furious, she found her voice. 'And who do you think you'd be persuading with those lies, Archie? I put it all back in the van, as you very well know. When I brought the van back everything was there.' She banged her fists down on the table. 'Everyone knows you're a thief and a black-market dealer. Who do you think they'll believe? Me and John, or Archie Mackinnon?'

'Mud sticks,' he threw at her, 'and I can be right convincing when I choose. Yes, maybe they know about me, but they'll know about you too. Think of your precious John's reputation, and how interesting a search of the croft would be. And you two canoodling all cosy by the fire all those months—you don't think anyone believes it's all innocent, do you? I've seen you on the beach and swimming together. I've seen you holding hands, and kissing. You were all over him every time you saw him. And that night you took the van, hugging and petting like a bitch on heat.'

A vast tide of anger washed over her as he turned and went out and she had to jump to prevent him slamming the door behind him. She pulled it open and automatically tugged it shut behind her, shutting them both into a black, icy maelstrom of wind and snow. She pulled on his arm and shouted at him.

'How dare you! The man had just heard that his house had been bombed. His two children were killed. His wife's mother was killed. The captain gave me permission to drive him to Achnasheen.'

He shook his head. 'But you didn't drive him to Achnasheen, did you, *mo ghràidh?*' He turned his back to the wind and his shouted words were spat into her face. 'Not that day. You came back to Inverasdale and into his bed, didn't you? You drove him to the train the next day, with all my goods to sell.'

She tried to intervene. 'That's not true and well you know it!' He shook his head again and continued as if she hadn't spoken. 'And you, losing your looks you are and terrible anxious about your lover. Could that be because there's a bun in your oven, Mhairi?'

He had put into crude words her own fear. She was never regular, but it had been a long time since her last bleed.

Archie was staring at her intently, the brown eyes black holes in the darkness. 'Yes!' He was slyly triumphant. 'Well, well! You little whore! But you won't be wanting the world to know you seduced a married man, will you now? It seems to me that if you fucked him, you'd be happy to fuck me, would you not?'

She was aghast. Horrified at the filth of his language and the sheer parody of the truth. A stronger gust of icy wind nearly blew her over, reducing her thick sweater to summer muslin. She had to stop him somehow, but her brain wouldn't function.

'For God's sake, Archie, none of that is true.' The cold and the noise and power of the rising gale beat at her mercilessly. 'We can't talk out here. Come back inside.'

Even in the gloom, she could sense his satisfaction. Taking her arm in a tight grip he thrust her over the threshold. There was a sudden silence as the noise of the wind was cut off when he banged the door shut. The smile on his face as he looked at her made her face and hands prickle as if she had nearly stepped on an adder. She saw his eyes rest on the silky nightgown airing on the cord above the range, and again her skin lifted in a shudder of fear.

'Archie, the man was devastated—he'd lost his bairns, and he'd just come off convoy. They'd had a bad time, a really bad time. It would be kicking a man when he's down. I felt right sorry for him, that's all. Don't go telling lies about him. He was just that shocked by the news.' She hated having to plead with him; it was a humiliation that chilled her as much as the wind. He put a hand to her cheek and stroked it down to her chin, holding her face up to his in a painful grip.

'Well, *mo ghràidh*, I ought to do my duty and inform the authorities. My van lent in good faith but used for illegal purposes, a naval officer in your bed.' Again he ignored her protest. 'And a lassie with his babe in her belly.' She shook her head violently, but his hand dropped from her face down to her throat, 'Still, you might save the day by changing your mind about the shed.' He stepped closer to her, one hand holding her face as he bent to kiss her on the mouth, the other hand on her breast. Disgust flooded her throat. 'Fair dos, eh, Mhairi? If you can take a filthy convoy man who hasn't washed or shaved in a month, you could put your hypocrisy on hold and take me, couldn't you?'

Every muscle screamed to resist, to fight his hands, but she forced herself to remain pliable, even as his hands moved on her, sliding under her sweaters, pulling at the clips of her brassiere, fingers scrabbling on her skin. She brought her hands up to his wrists, weakly.

'Wait, Archie, wait a minute. Your van's outside for all the world to see—if you promise not to tell, you can put it in the big shed and then we can come back. If you promise not to say any of those things, you can have the key.'

He laughed. 'No bargaining required, and I already have the key. No one's going to bother about my van. They'll just guess I'm paying you a visit on a cold night, and they'll not be surprised to find us tucked up in a warm bed, will they, considering where your boyfriend is usually to be found?' The tone changed, the threat clear. 'And if you think to cheat on me, if you so much as blink about our storage arrangement, there's no promise, and you'll be in so deep you'll never surface.'

36

22nd January 2012

David had suggested coming for supper at Inveruidh because he was mending a satellite dish that had blown down in Cove and he'd be passing the house on his way back. Amused to hear the slight panic in her voice as she confessed to having only frozen meals, he said he'd do the honours and bring food. Enjoyment, or looking forward to something, normally made him feel ashamed. It was irrational, this guilt about feeling pleasure. Shona would have been the first to condemn it. Oddly, today he didn't feel guilt; anticipation, freedom, an inclination to smile. But not guilt. As he moved about the cottage kitchen, throwing together a chicken casserole from the contents of his bags, he pondered his irritability with Isla and his enjoyment of Annie's company.

'I gather from Kate that you visited Mr Mackinley senior. How did you come to dig him out as a possible source of information?'

'When I went to Ullapool to look up the archives, his name was listed as a coroner's witness, at the hearing about Archie Mackinnon's death.' She sounded a bit defensive, he thought. 'When Kate told me her name, I put two and two together. I thought he might know something about John as the two crofts are so close.'

'A proper little detective, you are!' he said with a smile, suspecting that the defensiveness was to do with searching an irrelevant lead. 'And did he come up with anything interesting?'

'Nothing about John really, except that he'd known a naval officer was billeted at Inveruidh. They didn't suspect John in Archie Mackinnon's death as he was found to be on his ship. In fact, I think he was killed before Archie died.' She sipped the wine he'd poured out for her. 'But surprisingly, he remembered hearing about his father finding Mhairi on the moor in a storm at half past three in the morning, looking very beaten up, and that he'd had to give court evidence.' She hesitated and seemed a little embarrassed as she told him about Mhairi's father attacking the baby. 'I expect you know all this already. I really was trying to find out about John Elliott, but instead got all this information about Archie Mackinnon and your grandmother.'

He put the casserole in the oven and leant back against the counter. He hadn't known, and was fairly sure his father didn't know, that Mhairi had run to Edinburgh to escape her violent father. Looking up, he saw Annie's anxious eyes and experienced an unexpectedly strong desire to reassure her.

'I'm fascinated,' he said. 'Especially about the ten-shilling note! It's a shame we haven't found out more about John Elliott, but it's brought considerable light into our murky family history.' He tipped some crisps into a bowl. 'Let's have a sit down by the fire while supper's cooking and see where else we could go for information.' Her long legs nearly reached his across the hearthrug and he resisted an inclination to rub his ankles against hers.

'Have you told your mother about your discoveries?'

'Not really in any detail and now they're on their annual romantic getaway. Daddy's taken her to their favourite gorgeous hotel in South Africa—in Constantia. They go to the same place every year on their wedding anniversary.' There was a smile in her voice. Recognisable affection.

'That *is* romantic! Every year the same place?'

Annie laughed. 'Yes. No concerts, no meetings, no socialising and very private! The diary date is sacrosanct.'

He thought it sounded delightful. 'And which anniversary is it?'

'Twenty-eighth. And they'll do exactly the same next year.'

His brain churned. A memory of Patrick telling the family that Lady Devereux was thirty. It was perfectly possible that they had a child before they married, but still, he thought, it was rather surprising.

'I know why your mother travels so much, but what does your father do?'

She hesitated. 'He works for the IMF and the Bank of England. He does a lot of travelling too.' There was a small silence. He had a feeling that she was understating her father's work, but she clearly didn't want to expand any further, so he brought the subject back to Archie Mackinnon.

'It's a horrible thought that this man Archie might be my grandfather. Perhaps if we find Rhionna she'll know more. DNA tests on you and me would answer the question too. If we had a mutual grandfather, that would be proof. Or if we didn't.'

Annie stared at him in consternation. 'Oh! I've been so stupid! I suppose I never told you, but it wasn't on purpose. I kept meaning to.'

He frowned. 'Never told me what?'

Her eyes squeezed shut in apologetic embarrassment. 'Charlotte isn't my biological mother. My mother was Rebecca Jordan. She was a violinist and Charlotte's best friend. She was married to Will, my father, and died when I was born, and Charlotte looked after us both.'

He was so taken aback it took time to absorb the information. 'Why on earth didn't you say so?' He felt a fool and as a result, sounded cross. She wasn't John Elliott's granddaughter at all and was unrelated to him or the Mackenzie family. The realisation brought an odd sense of relief which he couldn't immediately analyse.

She got up from her chair, her hands twisting together. 'I'm really sorry I never explained. I thought I had.' She looked mortified. 'I did tell Mhairi, and I suppose I thought she would tell everyone. Charlotte gave up her career for two years, looking after me and my father. When I was two, they got married. Charlotte is legally my stepmother, but of course I've never known any other and as far as I'm concerned, she is my mother. I forget that it's sometimes important. It's Charlotte who needs to give the DNA sample, not me.'

How typical of his grandmother not to have passed it on. Some might call her discreet, but in fact she was downright secretive. Annie's father had lost his wife too. An odd connection. An odd coincidence. Various snippets of memory came back to him. Patrick quoting from her driving licence—The Lady Anne J. Devereux. He guessed that J was for Jordan. And Annie had almost always referred to John Elliott as her mother's father, rather than her grandfather.

'That explains a lot of things,' he said. 'But not why you're researching a man who isn't in fact, your grandfather.' Did that sound accusatory? He didn't know how to soften it.

Annie paused before answering and when she did, he knew that he had indeed sounded harsh. Her voice was subdued. 'Various reasons, I suppose. I wanted to do something for Mum. Her mother was less than forthcoming about John Elliott. More than that, Mum says she was—' she searched for the word '—dismissive? Oddly unwilling to tell her anything about him. What he was like. Honestly, he could have been a criminal or a bigamist. We've wondered about both scenarios. Mum has always wanted to know about him. Then she was pretty upset about Justin and me.' And that was another unexplained scenario, he thought. Had the episode over the piano been the final straw in their marriage break-up?

'And you?' he said more gently. 'Was it something to focus on after your marriage broke up?'

She nodded. Looked away out of the window. 'Yes. I was angry, too, I suppose. Otherwise I don't think I'd have lost control over the piano fiasco. Everything was so *public*. Emails, even sympathetic ones, Facebook, Twitter. My father is incredibly discreet—he has to be, doing the financial work he does, and there he was, plastered all over the papers.' Her face tightened.

He wanted to put his arms around her, to bring comfort, but he was afraid she'd be embarrassed, as she had been the day she got the tribunal letter.

'I wanted to get away from London and people who looked at me and whispered scandal and gossip. Wester Ross seemed ideal. I wanted to focus on something that wasn't me and my failures, so I ran away from them. It's difficult, being labelled a major disappointment by your husband.'

A failure. A disappointment. Why would a wife be labelled a failure? Or sufficiently disappointing to merit divorce?

There were all sorts of reasons for running away, some better than others, he thought with wry self-knowledge. It seemed Mhairi had run from a violent father to protect her baby, Annie had run from a failed marriage and he himself had run from—what? Memories? Responsibilities?

'Failure to be what? Or do what?' He was genuinely puzzled.

She turned her face towards him with a tight little smile. 'Oh. I can't have children. I couldn't give him an heir.'

After an instant of shock, he was appalled by his own self-pity. He'd had a loving wife, two beautiful children, a large and happy family.

'He couldn't have divorced you just because you couldn't have children!' The shock had become outrage. He also realised that he had virtually accused her of not telling the whole truth.

Annie straightened in her chair. 'Well, he could. And he did.' She changed the subject abruptly. 'Where are the boys tonight?'

His reaction had been aggressive and she had rebuked him. 'Seamus has a sleepover with a friend, and Christopher has gone to his cousins. The cousins may be girls, but they are boys at heart and Christopher loves going there. They climb trees, make bridges, dam burns, dig ditches. I'll collect him on my way home after supper.' He looked at his watch, 'Talking of which, I think it'll be nearly cooked so let's go and put the veg on.'

Annie was standing in front of the salt pot and he put his hands on her shoulders and gently moved her sideways in order to reach it. Without warning, the touch of her body nearly overwhelmed him. Desire assaulted him. and he wanted to inbreathe for ever the now familiar fragrance that she wore. He wanted to keep hold of her, to bend his face to hers, to taste her mouth. Fighting to withstand it, he forced his hands to release her. He saw a mutual awareness in the wideness of her eyes, her lips soft and a little apart and even in the moment of his own confusion, as he stepped away, he saw something else. Disappointment? Rejection? That look of insecurity, as if she was unsure of her attraction or desirability. She had wanted to touch him. She had wanted to be touched.

With a sense that he had nearly fallen off a cliff, he

added salt to the pan. Did Shona's death justify his continued avoidance of new relationships? He was attracted to Annie and was almost sure that she was attracted to him. Was that so wrong, so disloyal? He was not the only person to have ever lost someone. Annie's father had seen his wife die giving birth to their child. And his own great-grandfather had lost his wife in childbirth too—his drinking problem was possibly due to that trauma. And what had Mhairi been through as an unmarried mother in such a community as this? Having to flee her home, her lover long gone?

It must have been lonely for Annie, since her divorce. Just as lonely as being without Shona. Or Will without Rebecca. Or Mhairi without the father of her child. Of them all, he knew it was him, David, that needed to move on.

37

November 1945

The croft was shining, gleaming. She wished he could have seen it when the flowers in the meadow were heart-achingly brilliant, buttercups, red and white clover, magenta mallow and wild pink orchids, the deep yellow broom thick and scented, cow parsley throwing its lace veils over field and ditch. Now the land was empty, harvested. The hay was in, stacked ready for winter, and the sheep, lifting their heads heavy with lazy, full-bellied grazing, welcomed the homecoming soldier.

She had the baby over her shoulder and was stirring a pan of broth when he pushed the door open and came in, without a knock or a call, dropping his kitbag on the floor. For a long moment she could not think who he was, even though she had been expecting him for weeks. She ran to him in initial joy and welcome and relief, the baby held in one arm and her other going about his neck and clutching him to her, but almost immediately she felt his withdrawal and silence, his foreknowledge and his disapproval. She disengaged from him and put the still sleeping baby in the makeshift cot beside the range, asking questions about his journey, his transport. She busied at the kettle, made the tea, using proper cups and saucers, put out milk in a jug and sugar, saved from the rations, in a bowl, the seed cake she had baked in anticipation of his coming. His replies were monosyllabic; the journey tiresome, the trains delayed, the bus crowded, the final walk long. His eyes flittered everywhere, not, she felt, in enjoyment at being back amongst familiar things, but searching for changes, noticing baby clothes drying on the range rail, the cord she had put up to hang washing on. He didn't mention how well everything looked, the bright metal of the range, the washed and shining stones of the floor, the beauty of the autumn day.

He looked bony, his hair pale and thin on his scalp, so unlike the thick mane he'd gone away with before the army got at it with their razors. His moustache was pale and scraggy, too, and he hadn't shaved. His face still seemed to have a winter pallor—almost like a pale slug from under a stone, she thought with distaste, and then deliberately changed the emotion to pity.

'Were they terrible, those camps? Your letters never gave much idea. I suppose you weren't allowed to write what it was like. They didn't feed you enough, I can see that. It must have been awful, locked up, but often I was glad for it, for you weren't killed. Why did they send you to Bremerhaven—was it all of you from the regiment, from the camp?'

She heard herself chattering. Gabbling. He drank his tea without responding, and then he interrupted the flow of her words as if he hadn't heard a single one. As if all his thoughts were centred on the one subject.

'What's with the bairn?'

His harsh voice, the putting-down of the interruption, the force of his displeasure crushed her like stones on a butterfly. Inside herself, there was a hopelessness about how she could possibly change his attitude which already, in the half hour of his return, and in those few words, had pooled into a sludge of disapproval, and was now setting into concrete condemnation.

'The bairn is not to be blamed. Things happen in wartime.'

'I'm not blaming the bairn. Whose is it? I haven't missed a wedding, have I? One of those things that happen in wartime?'

The sarcasm was overlaid with anger. She tried to fill in the gaps of the few letters she had been allowed to send him. Her job with Mrs Reid and the MacRae's kindnesses, the naval officer billeted at the croft after an illness.

He put his elbow on the table, chin in his hand, the knuckle of his forefinger rubbing up and down his nose, his eyes boring into her, stony hard. He had heard, and with a sinking heart she wondered who from, that she'd been involved with another fellow, a good-for-nothing criminal, that she'd been dealing on the black market, in trouble with the police. There was a death, he understood. Murder, was it not? Was the baby his, or this fancy navy man's? Or didn't she know? How many other men had she gone with, prostituting herself while men died for their country?

She was determined that, no matter what else might be revealed, John Elliott's name should remain unblemished, that her father's anger should not be allowed to tarnish John's service—his death for his country—in conditions that had far outweighed in horror her father's incarceration.

'Archie Mackinnon he was called,' she said quietly. 'He's dead for sure because they found him on the boom. But murder? Nothing was proved. I was questioned, along with others who knew him. And yes, it turned out he was a bad lot.' And because she knew that if he hadn't been told already, someone would tell him soon, she said, 'He wanted to use the croft to store things for his business, in the sheds. I didn't like it and said so. The police came and looked, and they found nothing. It was a horrible time, and I wished you were here. They never found out how he died, though there's plenty of theories flying about.' She heard the bitterness in her own voice.

'Is the bairn his?' There was no softening of his tone. She closed her eyes tightly, hearing the snuffling of the baby, his shifting body, precursors to waking and hunger.

Although normally she would have left the baby to wake fully, she picked him out of the cot and put him to her shoulder.

'I'm not saying whose bairn he is—that way the only blame is mine. His father's dead. The baby needs a feed now.'

He snorted in derision. 'You're not saying because you don't know. You're a whore! You've been with so many men you don't know who the father is!'

'As he's dead it makes no difference. There won't be a marriage.'

Before her father could respond she had taken the baby through to the bedroom, putting her heel to the door. The click of the latch was loud in her ear, but the thumping of her heart was louder.

She had known, deep down, what his reaction would be, but because she could not stop him coming home, nor could she not have the baby, there had been a kind of mental full stop. A fantasy in her tired brain which seemed to be the only way of coping with an impossible situation. A fantasy that he would be understanding, that he would love the baby on sight, that he would love him because he loved her. Yet she knew that because her mother had died giving birth to her, he had often resented her. She had tried, as a child, to be her mother. To keep the house clean, to learn to cook, to wash the clothes, to garden, to farm the croft, but she had learnt that however hard she tried, it was never enough.

In the weeks after his return, the disapproval and condemnation did not lessen. He never called John by his name, he didn't ask how the birth had been managed, he pushed the little pile of napkins on to the floor and told her to take all the 'clobber' up the stair ladder to the rafters where she had returned to sleep. Perforce she had to take the baby up and down the ladder too, and she was terrified that he would wriggle out of her arms and fall—that they both would fall. She was lonelier with her father in the house than she had ever felt when he was absent, or when John was absent. Rhionna came when she could, but Mhairi knew that she had to keep her visits secret from her parents and was uncomfortable about deceiving them. Sometimes Rhionna's brother came over by boat, bringing a note from her, or some small gift of scones. Sometimes she sent fresh vegetables which she knew Mhairi could not grow in the garden.

Her father's visits to Aultbea were to buy alcohol, and it soon became evident that he was drinking enough to be dangerous, and enough to be useless. Mhairi was afraid to leave John in the house when he was there, so she tied him to her back in a shawl when she was working in the garden or on the croft. She learnt to be wary of his fists. She knew that his war, largely unfought, and the knowledge that now he was simply not required, was the main pivot of all his frustrations, but her own presence and the often noisy presence of the baby just added to the melting pot of his anger, and his frequent shout that she should 'Get out and take that squawling brat with you,' rang in her head daily.

Inevitably the day came when she failed to avoid his fist. In the midst of her grogginess, as she groped blindly up from the floor where the blow had sent her, she sensed his purposeful movement towards the crying baby in the cot. Terror at what he might do gave her strength, but her grab at his leg missed, and he kicked at her, connecting with her head again. He lunged violently at the cot and in horror she saw the baby flipped out on to the stone floor.

The baby's crying instantly became a penetrating scream, doubled in force by Mhairi's. A primeval fury swamped her as he went to kick the child, and this time her fingers caught his trousers in a deathlike grip. As he fell headlong, blackness came over her like a winter's night and John's screams faded.

When the darkness receded a little, she saw that the whisky had taken its toll. He was unconscious on the flagstones. Staggering to her feet, she saw two babies and two fathers. Two of everything. Trying to squeeze the sensation away, she scooped the screaming baby off the floor and stumbled to the Mackinley's croft, a mile up the road.

'He'll kill John.' Mhairi dabbed a wet cloth on the bleeding graze on the still screaming baby's head, as Mrs Mackinley cleaned up her bloody nose and put sheep fat on the bruises.

'I can't stay. He wants me out. I'm leaving.'

'You can't, Mhairi! The bairn is too small. Where would you go?'

She put her head in her hands. 'I don't know. But I can't stay. When he's at the bottle he's out of his mind. He would have killed the baby if he could.' She was trembling like an aspen leaf. 'He'd have killed me.'

'Oh Lord have mercy! Never!'

But they know, Mhairi thought helplessly. They know he drinks all his money away. They know he's violent. What do they expect me do? Lie down while he murders the both of us? As her head cleared anger took over from fear.

Reluctantly the older woman sat with John while Mhairi returned to her house. Fearfully skirting her snoring father as he lay on the floor, she packed a bag of essentials for herself and the baby, and along with her ration book, put all her savings into her purse. It was frighteningly little, she thought grimly. Then she left, closing the door quietly behind her.

While she was feeding the baby, Mr Mackinley, meekly obeying his wife's instructions, put the trailer on the tractor and drove them to the main road in time to meet the southbound bus. As she put a foot to the step, he touched her arm and thrust a mauve ten-shilling note into her hand. This kindness, after the fear and tension of the day, reduced her to tears again. They dropped damply on to the baby's shawled head, his uncomprehending eyes roving round his new and noisy environment and over his mother's bruised and swollen face. The bus roared and chugged its way through Gairloch and Kinlochewe, and over the narrow pass of Glen Docherty to Achnasheen and a train into the unknown.

38

24th January 2012

Gloom and apprehension fogged her mind as she packed her suitcase and shut down the laptop for the final time. London had never been such an unattractive option. But it was, after all, her home. The city she had grown up in, the sounds and smells and sights familiar, the transport easy, the people suspicious and unfriendly in their customary way. She couldn't run away for ever, making excuses to avoid what had gone before.

She folded sheets and towels and tea towels into a pile. Put the few left-overs on to one shelf of the fridge. Turned the heating down and checked that she had completed Kate's exit list. For the last time, she stood at the huge windows in the bedroom, trying to imprint the mountains and the sea on her memory, even though she had a hundred photographs of this view, in every possible light and weather. Running her hand down the stripped pine banister her thumb sought out the knothole near the bottom, a familiar comforting dent.

For a month this little house had been her shelter, security and home. It had accepted her without accusation or demands. The only memories she would have of it would be good ones and she had a ridiculous desire to stay for ever. To be in the same place as David. The attraction was mutual, she was almost sure. Two nights ago, she had thought he was going to kiss her and then he had withdrawn abruptly. Had it been her fault? Had she somehow given off the wrong signals? Had she been too forward, or too cool?

On the beat of the thought, his car drew up in the yard and his legs in the habitual tatty jeans swung down on to the wet gravel. Her tummy looped the loop. Persuade me to stay. Tell me you want me here. Stupid thought, Annie. This widower is still grieving his lost wife.

He came in, wiping his work boots on the mat, his eyes creasing on his smile, making her tummy do more somersaults.

'Hi,' she said, feeling oddly shy. 'I wasn't expecting you.'

'Thought I'd see you safely off the premises, to make up for your arrival.' His teasing tone made her smile back. 'The weather forecast is just rain, so it won't be as ghastly a drive as it was coming. Are you looking forward to going home?'

'No.' She looked out across the loch. 'I'd much rather stay here.' And that was quite enough baring of her soul. 'Will you go on searching for Rhionna MacRae?'

'Yes. Now you've got Mr Reid to divulge that her married name was Fletcher—a lightbulb moment on your part—I can search parish records and voting and census records. I should be able to find out if she died or whether she's still with us. Dad is keen to find out as much as he can. He's very disappointed that Granny can't—or won't—give him a definitive answer about his father.'

'It seems so extraordinary, looking back just a month, that we discovered the connection with John Elliott. I still feel that I have stirred up rather a hornets' nest.'

'The hornets' nest was necessary though, wasn't it? We wouldn't have discovered the connection without you, and I feel that there's a lot more that Granny isn't telling us.'

244

She took courage in both hands. 'Will you keep in touch with me? Tell me what you discover? Whether your grandmother has more photos or letters? And I'll keep looking for more information on John, too, in naval records and things.'

'Of course I'll keep in touch, and tell you anything we find out about him.' He hesitated, and his eyes on hers looked a little anxious. 'I have to come to London occasionally. Can I come and see you? It's not a place I feel that comfortable in on my own.' His expression was a mixture of embarrassment and hope.

She couldn't help the grin, even though she tried to hold her lips together. 'I should be delighted. I'll give you my email.'

'I've got it,' he said, with a smile of his own. 'It was on the booking form.'

He loaded her case and laptop into the car, put his hands on her shoulders and kissed her on the cheek, and then lightly on the mouth. She inhaled the woody male smell of him. Those light kisses weren't just friendship and warmth. They spoke of attraction and desire. Her skin tingled and her breath shortened.

'Drive carefully. I'll be in touch.'

For some reason, the panic in her stomach had gone, and London seemed not quite so horrible a destination.

39

November 1945

The train terminated in Inverness. The east coast weather was the opposite of the west, windy, cold and damp, and she hated the gusty streets, smelling of sea dirt, rather than the salt fishy smell of home.

She did not feel safe. The Mackinleys would inevitably tell someone where she had gone and she would be traced here; made to return to her father's drunken violence and the unbearable harassment and judgmental attitudes of the community. Anything would be better than that. She bought a ticket to Edinburgh, which seemed as far as she could possibly go from Aultbea, paying over an alarming proportion of her remaining money. Taking herself to the women's toilet, she fed the baby in a cubicle, sordidly perched on the rim of the filthy, seatless lavatory, afterwards laying him in the sink to change his napkin. Wrapping him firmly in the shawl, she tied him on to her back where he sank back into sleep, while she rinsed the dirty cloth, wrung it out and folded it damply into a square of oiled paper. She settled hungrily in the waiting room to await the morning train.

The journey was a long grey memory, which often came back to her in dreams. The baby missing, the shawl on her back empty, her frantic searches, pushing through air thick as porridge, doors closing in her face, food being carried past her, train doors slamming, finding herself on a platform with the train leaving the station, carrying John with it.

She spoke to no one, except once to an old lady getting out at Perth, giving her a threepenny bit to buy her a pie at the station buffet, afraid to leave John and her case on the train lest it leave without her. The pie was an appalling weight of heavy pastry with virtually no filling, but to her it tasted like the nectar of the gods. Even better, there was a penny change. Where would she go in Edinburgh to find accommodation and work? She must avoid contact with any agency through whom she might be traced.

At Waverley Station, she stood bemused in the welter of hurrying passengers and shouting porters, the case at her feet and rocking John in her arms. An elderly porter pushing a flat trolley laden with parcels looked at her battered face curiously, and a few moments later returned without the trolley.

'Now then, young lady, you and the bairn look as if you just arrived on the moon. Where are you going? The trams are all up there and I can take your bag up for you.' He indicated the steep steps beyond.

Mhairi was grateful for his brisk kindness and confessed her bewilderment. 'I've nowhere to go and need a room. Is there a hostel nearby?'

He clicked his tongue in concern. 'Oh, deary me! Do you not know anybody in the town?' She shook her head, still rocking the baby. 'Well now, the Sally Army have hostels, but they'll not be in the centre I'm thinking. Tell you what, see that telephone booth there? You stand in the queue and when it's free you look in the directory under Salvation Army Hostels and find some addresses. I'll come back in ten minutes and tell you which tram to get for the nearest one.'

He was as good as his word, and though she said she could carry the case up the steps, he took it for her anyway and declined the penny she tentatively offered him. He pointed out the tram stop, told her where to get off, and disappeared down the steps

The city was bewildering and alien. Clanging tram bells made her jump nervously, and the pushing crowds made her dizzy. Her arms ached with carrying the baby and her case. When she at last found the hostel, having initially walked in the wrong direction after getting off the tram, a sensible non-judgemental Captain Alice Baker put her into her little office.

'Wait there a minute, while I take the vegetables to the kitchen. You could put the kettle on for I'm ready for a cup and maybe you are too.'

Gratefully she laid John on a little camp bed in the corner, filled the kettle at the sink and put it on the gas ring. There were several teacups upturned on the wooden drainer, along with a chipped teapot, and she found the tea in an ancient tin marked 'Wherry's Mints'. John started to stir and whimper. Beginning to tremble with overwhelming fatigue, she was afraid that a howling baby would adversely affect her chances of accommodation.

On her return the captain was sharp-eyed and brisk. 'When did you last eat?'

'I've not had anything since morning.' The pie at Perth was a distant memory.

'You can feed the baby while I fetch something for you.'

Later, she would remember with enormous gratitude the hot food, and a clean if ragged bed. Captain Baker's hostel was able, seemingly, to expand and contract at will—or at her suggestion. A woman who had a little cupboard room of her own was moved into a dormitory and Mhairi and the baby installed. She was able to wash the baby, herself, and the nappies, and fell into an exhausted sleep only broken by having to get up to feed John. The following morning, when she handed over her ration book, she felt an entirely different person and Captain Alice Baker noticed it.

Finding a job, however, was an exhausting and debilitating exercise. A young girl with a baby seemed to be an impossible starting point. There was a suspicion of her Highland identity, and together with the baby, all she received were rejections. She got a temporary job cleaning offices, John wrapped up in shawls and put in a little shopping basket that Captain Baker had procured from somewhere, and tucked into a corner while she scrubbed floors, cleaned toilets and dusted and polished desks. There was a little money in her pocket at the end of the week, and she could contribute a small amount to the hostel for her keep. There were occasional Saturday jobs at the local greengrocer, humping crates of fruit and vegetables, and arranging the displays, and even serving and running the till, albeit under the greengrocer's watchful eye. John lay in his little basket on the sacks of potatoes, batting at the string of walnuts Mhairi had hung from the handle. She enjoyed those mornings, even though it was a cold and windy March, and flourished in the earthy atmosphere. There was often a bag of not-so-fresh vegetables to take back to the hostel, as well as wages for the few hours of work. She had had high hopes of a place at the post office after her training in Aultbea, but the postmaster had no need of extra help. Captain Baker suggested she enquire at the main Edinburgh Post Office in George Street, but they wanted a reference and were suspicious of her reluctance to give her previous employer's name. Her explanations of a husband dead in the war and a violent father who might track her down provoked pursed lips of disapproval, but she knew that any communication with home might result in the destruction of her new identity as a widow.

One evening Captain Baker called her into the house-keeper's room. Untying her bonnet, she told Mhairi that her regular quarterly meeting with her immediate superior and some of their local lay supporters—soldiers they were called—would be the next Friday morning. She would present Mhairi to them with a recommendation that they keep her in mind for employment of a better sort; an office job, or administration of some kind. She suggested that Mhairi make herself as tidy and clean as was possible and that she leave John in her room for the brief interview with the committee. She smiled at Mhairi's excitement and gratitude, but cautioned her not to expect too much from it.

On Friday she fed John earlier than normal, rubbed her good shoes with a cloth to shine them, and dressed in her one tidy frock, kept for Sundays. She waited nervously in her room until Captain Baker came to fetch her.

She was introduced to the four ladies, a blur of matrons, and shook hands with them, standing straight, making herself look them in the eye. Major Savanner, in her trim uniform and close bonnet, inspected her carefully, taking in the work-roughened hands and thin frame, the clean, shining hair and the worn but tidy dress. An upright chair was indicated and Mhairi perched on the edge, hands gripped on her knees to control their trembling.

'We understand, Mrs Mackenzie, that you are looking for employment, but finding it difficult on account of your little boy?' The Major's voice was matter-of-fact; brisk.

'Yes, ma'am. I've been looking for proper employment for some weeks now, but I can only find temporary work, and I know I can do better—contribute more,' she amend-ed hastily. 'The baby is easy. Captain Baker found me a wee basket and he just comes along and smiles and sleeps!' The ladies looked faintly disbelieving.

'Would you tell us how you came to Edinburgh and

what you think you might—contribute?' There was a faint undertone of humour.

The story was more or less the truth, except for the omission of Archie's life and death, which seemed to Mhairi to have no bearing at all on the present. The other exception was the fact that she had not been married.

'So I have run a household, managed the sheep and grown the vegetables. I worked in the post office under the postmistress, managed the ledgers, accounts, petty cash, telegrams and sorted the letters.' In case this all sounded too good to be true, and the postmistress redundant, she added humbly, 'All directed by Mrs Reid, of course. She taught me it all.'

The matrons blinked. 'And can this Mrs Reid not give you a reference?' one of them asked reasonably.

Mhairi took a breath and shook her head. There was a short silence.

'I think if you wish us to try to help you, you must explain why your previous employer should not be asked for a reference. I'm afraid it gives an impression of your trying to hide something dishonourable.'

She was genuinely horrified. 'Dishonourable? You mean stealing or some such? Oh no! It isn't that at all. I don't want you to think that at all, for it isn't so.' Her distress was palpable, but Major Savanner was made of stern stuff.

'Well then, Mrs Mackenzie, if there is a good reason, you may tell us. No one here will let it go further unless what you tell us is unlawful, and then I'm afraid we would have to think again.'

Mhairi lifted her head and looked Salvation Army godliness in the eye.

'After John was killed and I had the baby, I farmed the croft as I told you. The navy base was run down with the war ended and I wasn't needed at the post office any more—anyway I had wee John to look after. Then my father came home. He'd been a prisoner-of-war for five years, and he was—different. He didn't like it that I was running the croft and managing everything. He didn't like it that I'd married and had the bairn. He was—difficult. He made me sleep up the ladder in the rafters which I'd done as a child, and so I had to carry the baby up with me. It was dangerous, and I near dropped him one night.'

'Where was your mother in all this?' interrupted one of the ladies.

'Mother died when I was born. Father said it was my fault and I suppose in a way it was. The postmistress had helped look after me after Mother died and I think that was why she gave me the job. But I'm afraid she'll tell him where I am if you write to her. I know she will. If he knows where I am, he'll come after me.'

'Was he violent towards you? Does he drink?' It was the same lady asking the questions.

Mhairi nodded. Her face flamed in shame. 'He hit me, and I thought he was going to kill John, the day I left. He knocked over the cot and threw the baby on the floor. I just picked him up and ran. Father was dead drunk. I don't want him to find me.'

'Mrs Mackenzie arrived here with a cut and bruised face, and as many of the women are knocked about, we don't find it unusual,' Captain Baker said baldly. 'If we feel that we have all the information we require, we could let Mrs Mackenzie go while we discuss her case. Do you have any more questions?'

They did not, and Mhairi sat on the little truckle bed, rocking John in her arms. All her energy had seeped away and her reasons for not writing to Mrs Reid seemed to be flimsy excuses. A reference request need not give her whereabouts, and Mrs Reid wouldn't tell her father in any case, she was almost sure. But what she would tell them was that Mhairi Mackenzie was not 'Mrs' Mackenzie and that her child was illegitimate. Inside her, the determination to start her new life as a respectable widow faded a little bit more.

Two weeks later, Captain Baker called her into the little office to tell her that a Mrs Wenham, the daughter of an acquaintance of one of the committee members, was in need of a nursemaid for her three-year-old daughter and was open to interviewing the young widow with the baby.

'Should I take John?' she asked anxiously. 'Where could I leave him if I don't?' Captain Baker had made it clear from the start that she could not undertake child-minding duties, and Mhairi was wary about leaving him in the care of any of the other residents for any length of time.

'Take him and let him charm the lady,' said Captain Baker comfortably. 'He's a dear wee thing, and it will be an indication to you whether Mrs Wenham is going to welcome him. I feel that she would never have agreed to see you if she was not willing to have another child in the house. I hear she is a godly, churchgoing woman and her husband is in the law. See to it that she finds you a responsible, sober person, fit to care for her child. She has been told why you do not wish to give a reference, but I cannot say if that will be acceptable to her and her husband.'

On the appointed day Mhairi took the tram up to the New Town, again in her tidy frock and polished shoes. The captain lent her a pair of gloves which didn't have holes in the fingertips, and her hat was of red velveteen, made by Mhairi from an old pair of curtains found in the hostel sewing room. John was getting larger and heavier these days, but he seemed to enjoy his journeys from the vantage point of his mother's shoulder and beamed involuntarily at anyone who took the trouble to smile at him. Walking up the steep hill to Roxburgh Terrace, her shoes clacking on the cobbles, she became ever more nervous. By the time she stood on the wide shallow step in front of the great black door with its gleaming brass plate and door furnishings, her heart was thumping fit to deafen her. She took several deep breaths before pulling on the bell pull. It rang with a deep clanging somewhere in the depths of the house and after long moments the door was opened by an elderly man in a black morning suit. For a confused moment she thought that it must be Mr Wenham, but then realised he was a manservant.

She told him her business, and he ushered her into a large hallway, a great Indian carpet on the floor, and heavy furniture glinting in the sunshine pouring through a large sashed window opposite the front door.

'Wait here,' he said heavily. 'Mrs Wenham will call you up when she is ready.' He disappeared through a small door and she heard him descending uncarpeted stone treads. She shifted John on to her other shoulder and gazed around her. Never in her life had she seen a house like this, except the laird's from a distance. There was a floor below, and at least two floors above. Was it all one house? A great vase of flowers stood on a silver salver on a table and through the window she could see a sensational view out to what she assumed was the Forth estuary. A door opened upstairs, and a lady came to the top of the stairs.

'Mrs Mackenzie, will you come up please?' The voice was cultured and pleasant. Like John's, Mhairi thought with a pang.

Mrs Wenham was pale and beautiful and her clothes, though rather pre-war in fashion, were tasteful and well designed. The interview was thorough and searching, but Mhairi did not feel that she was looking for faults, rather that she was concerned not to make a mistake in her assessment. John smiled at her and gripped the finger that she proffered him. She appeared to think Mhairi might be suitable. She had been pleased by her enquiry as to whether she would be able to attend a church service on a Sunday and whether the baby could be taken or if not, whether he could be minded in her absence. Mrs Wenham said she would enquire from the minister and suggested that Mrs Brydon the housekeeper might agree to take charge of the children during the service. Mhairi thought that church attendance once a week would be a small price to pay for Mrs Wenham to be impressed by her godliness and therefore her desirability as a nurse for her child. Indeed, it seemed that she thought her education and previous position were adequate, though she was cautioned not to speak Gaelic at any time. Mhairi guessed that to take in a young war widow and her baby would be an acknowledged Christian action. Mrs Wenham was evidently not accustomed to looking after her own child and the loss of a previous nursemaid had been an inconvenience. She thought that a young mother and her child would give Emily an enjoyment and interest which was not presently hers in the company of the butler and housekeeper.

They came at last to the matter of the reference. Mhairi had had long enough to think about this sticking point in obtaining a position.

'I know that my father will come after me—he wants me at home to housekeep for him and to run the croft. He's seldom—' she hesitated '—seldom well enough to manage the garden or the farm, or to run the house. In any case, he doesn't think it's his job, but mine. He didn't expect to find me married or a mother after five years of war. But he'll hear soon enough that a reference is being sought, and he'll come for me.'

'What do you mean when you say he's not "well enough"?' Mhairi dropped her head and wished she did not have to confess to an alcoholic father.

'He had a bad war, ma'am. The whole regiment was taken prisoner, and they were in a camp for the whole five years. I think it nearly drove him out of his mind.'

Mrs Wenham looked at her closely. 'So why did you not stay to look after him if he was ill?'

'Well, not exactly ill, ma'am.' She looked away. 'I'm afraid he'll hurt the baby. If it was just me, I could have stayed.'

'You mean he's violent?'

Mhairi nodded, flushing.

'I could ask my husband to write from his law office,' said Mrs Wenham carefully. 'That way your father wouldn't know where to find you, but I fear he would not allow me to employ anyone without a reference.' There was a note of finality in her voice. Mhairi knew when she was beaten.

'Very well, ma'am. If I may have your undertaking not to give any indication of my whereabouts, I will agree to the reference being taken up. Before I give it you, please may I meet your daughter and see the proposed accommodation for myself and John should I be offered the post?'

Mrs Wenham looked slightly startled, but not displeased at this evidence of strong-mindedness and rose to press a bell beside the fireplace.

'I will ask Mrs Brydon to bring Emily upstairs and to show you the nursery and the accommodation generally. If the situation is satisfactory to you, perhaps you will return to the drawing room and give me the details required to take up the reference. I will explain to my husband the reasons for using his office address. If the reference is satisfactory, I will ask you to come for a further interview with my husband.'

Mhairi tensed unhappily. If the reference is satisfactory. The likelihood was remote, and along with the revelation of her non-marriage would come, she supposed, the loss of this opportunity and expulsion from the hostel.

Mrs Brydon, breathless from her climb from the basement, was glad to have a chance to recover while the baby was introduced to Emily. As Mhairi expected, the little girl was fascinated by John's waving, clutching hands and thought a new toy had been given her. The accommodation for the nursery maid was a small, though to Mhairi's eyes a sizeable room off the nursery, and there was plenty of space for John. Emily slept in the nursery in a white high-sided cot with little paintings of rabbits on the head and base boards, and a rag doll was propped up at the bottom of the bed. There was a small fireplace with a high brass-railed guard round it, a decent armchair and a table, highchair and upright chair. A single gas ring, for warming milk she was told, stood on a small table below a cupboard. On the other side of the nursery was a door to a bathroom with plumbed-in bath, a sink and a toilet. Mhairi was open-mouthed, never having seen such an arrangement. The Wenhams must be exceedingly rich, she thought. The space was intoxicating, and though Mrs Brydon told her she would have to descend to the basement to collect their meals, and for the washing, she was not at all daunted. All she felt was an overwhelming desire to have this job, to live in this luxury, to be so necessary to this family that they would be unable to exist without her. But first, she had to deal with the reference.

Mrs Brydon said she would stay in the nursery with the children while Mrs Mackenzie returned to see Mrs Wenham and would bring them down when the bell rang. Mhairi provided Mrs Reid's name, with the post office as the address, with a sense of despairing inevitability.

* * *

Two weeks later, when Mhairi had given up all hope of the placement, a note was delivered to the hostel. Mrs Wenham was pleased to inform her that the reference was satisfactory and if Mrs Mackenzie would present herself the following Saturday at 2.30 p.m., her husband would be at home to finalise their interviews. Perhaps it would be best if she came without the baby. If he also was satisfied, she should present herself at Roxburgh Terrace with her belongings at 6 p.m. on Sunday, ready to commence her duties on Monday morning.

Mhairi was so astonished and delighted that she gave Captain Baker an impromptu hug, knocking her bonnet sideways and bringing a smile of pleasure to her kind, plain face. On Saturday she looked Mhairi over: dress, stockings and shoes, twitched her hair more tidily under the hat, pinched her cheeks to give them more colour and despatched her to the tram, words of interview wisdom ringing in her ears, and assurances that she would see to John's care just this once, mind.

This time Mhairi took in much more of the journey, the city, the beautiful houses of the New Town, with their wide steps and huge windows. There was a certain shabbiness about the unkempt gardens and the dusty basement areas full of leaf debris—the war had not dealt these great houses many favours, but the steep climb up from the tram stop, the cobbled streets, the green parks and gardens, many without railings, all served to lift her spirits and fill her with joy and excitement. She had no idea how her reference could have passed muster, but she was going to make sure that Mr and Mrs Wenham would find her more than satisfactory.

Mr Wenham was a tall, elegant man in his thirties and he interviewed her in his book-lined study, papers on the desk, everything neat; pens and pencils in a little silver tray in front of the inkwell and blotter, a white rose in a tiny crystal vase to one side. His eyes were like a buzzard's, she thought uncomfortably. Penetrating. He indicated a chair for her and enquired after her journey, the location of the hostel, the quality of the accommodation. How long she had been in Edinburgh and the difficulties she had had of finding a position. How different Edinburgh must be from her home in the Highlands, did she miss the beauty of the hills and the sea? His voice was moderate and kind and encouraged confidences. As their conversation progressed, she realised that within only a few minutes he had extracted a great deal of personal information from her. Information about her character and her values. She was alarmed at how much she had revealed.

Eventually, he picked out a sheet of paper from a folder and she recognised Mrs Reid's beautiful, precise handwriting. Her heart thumped.

'Your previous employer has written a complimentary recommendation,' Mr Wenham said gravely. 'She says you are hard-working, kind, discreet, intelligent and resourceful.' He paused, and the raptor's eyes pinned her where she sat. She felt the colour drain out of her and then flood back in a deep flush. 'She tells me that during your father's absence in the war you not only worked well and reliably in the post office, but also successfully ran your father's croft and sheep, keeping house and land in good order until he came home. She says that he was violent towards both you and your baby and that you left home to protect the child.' Mhairi should have been encouraged by this, but in fact felt it was only a precursor to something unpleasant.

Mr Wenham leant forward on his desk, his fingers steepled at his clean-shaven chin.

'She says a good deal about you, Mrs Mackenzie, but also leaves out a good deal, which makes me curious. She refers to you as Mhairi Mackenzie and does not, for instance, mention your husband at all.' There was a silence in which he waited, watching her, and Mhairi sat like a hypnotised rabbit, unable to move or speak. Eventually, he leant back in his chair.

'My wife seems to think you suitable, and Emily was

very taken with your small son.' He glanced down at the paper. 'Mrs Reid believes that you would be a kind and reliable nursemaid. My wife and I are prepared to give you and your son that chance. I hope you will not let us down.' His tone was grave, and there was the faintest question in his last phrase.

All the air had been pressed out of her. It was quite evident that Mrs Reid had told no untruths and it was also evident that Mr Wenham was no fool. She raised her head with an effort and looked him in the eye.

'Thank you, sir. I am truly grateful for the opportunity, and I give you my word that I will work to the best of my ability for you and Mrs Wenham, and for Emily.'

The penetrating eyes held hers for a long speculative moment, and then he nodded and dismissed Mhairi to see his wife for more detailed instructions about her duties.

Her elation vied with astonishment and thankfulness that she had passed this test. Mr Wenham had understood her situation perfectly yet had given her this chance. Her home community had judged her without compassion; Mr Wenham had extended mercy. This is a new beginning. John will grow up in a just and fair and censure-free atmosphere and I will be judged not by my mistakes, but by my achievements. I will serve you to the very best of my ability, she vowed again to the Wenhams in the quiet space of the nursery, as the two children slept.

40

May 2012

David was elated by his discovery of Rhionna. Here was someone who had known John Elliott and remembered him well. Letters had been exchanged, and then telephone calls and an invitation to visit.

'Rhionna Fletcher is widowed, and she sounds completely on the ball,' he had said to Annie. 'She and Mhairi were close friends, but for some reason, they never communicated after Mhairi moved to Edinburgh. It seems so odd.'

'Perhaps Rhionna knew something about what happened to Archie which Mhairi was afraid she might reveal?'

'It's possible. Let's go to see her when I'm in London in May for my lecture week. She's in Lymington so only a couple of hours by car.' He hesitated. 'Unless you want to go sooner, by yourself?' He hoped she didn't. Although their meetings since January had been sparse, their friendship had gathered momentum through the exchanges of phone calls, emails and WhatsApps. He liked the way she wrote—wry and funny—and the easy conversations which always seemed to be interested in what he and his family were doing. But despite his growing attraction to her, he was wary of his feelings, having seen enough of his friends rebounding from divorce or break-ups into disastrous and short-lived relationships. He hadn't yet pushed any further than friendship.

'Oh no!' Annie sounded quite unnerved by the prospect. 'I'd much rather go with you. After all, she was Mhairi's friend, not John Elliott's. Have you still not told Mhairi about finding her?'

'No.' Not for the first time, he felt uncomfortable about it. 'Not yet. I still don't understand why they lost touch. They might have had some horrible argument and if Granny told me she didn't want me to see her, it would be difficult to go against her wishes. This way seemed better. A *fait accompli* as it were.' He was chagrined that his grandmother's disapproval was something he avoided. They arranged for David to collect her after his Friday lecture at Imperial College.

On the designated afternoon, Annie, superficially calm but with tension in her voice, called with a warning about a news-hack ringing her doorbell and a photographer outside. It was therefore no surprise to David to see a spotty youth, with harsh eyes and unhealthy, tufty hair, standing outside her door as he got out of the car. He advanced towards David, swinging up a big-lensed camera.

'Don't even think about it,' David said. 'What the hell do you think you're doing?' Anger on Annie's behalf made him unusually belligerent. Was this something to do with her parents? Earlier internet searches had revealed that the concert pianist Charlotte Elliott was married to Sir William Meredith, whose financial credentials were high, to say the least. He put out his free hand and swallowed the lens in his palm, holding it firmly as the youth tried to pull the camera away.

'That's assault!' The man's voice was accusatory and the words, David thought, well practised.

'Too right it is. Who gave you permission to invade my privacy?'

The youth backed off as far as he could without losing his camera to a man substantially larger than he was, but David pulled him towards the door and thumped on it with his foot.

'Now, young man. If you don't want a thrashing, I suggest that you get out of here and don't come back. Otherwise, I'll want to know your name and who your employer is, and I'll have that memory card, too, as evidence of harassment, and report you to the police.'

Annie had been watching through a chink in the curtains and half opened the door. David shoved the youth away, releasing the camera, and stepped inside, shutting the door in the man's face.

'Will he go?' He heard the tremor in her voice.

'Yes.' He turned to take her in his arms. He hadn't seen her for three weeks and he realised his entire being longed for this closeness. She flopped against him, boneless and distressed, and he remembered that other occasion, in the new kitchen at Inveruidh, when he had comforted her like a child. Her body against his was a disturbing pleasure.

'It's OK. You'll be away all weekend, by which time they'll have lost interest.'

She seemed unable to respond. He disengaged himself and held her away from him, examining her tense face.

'The phone's been ringing and ringing. How did they find me?' She looked so vulnerable he enclosed her in his arms again. Why did someone want to find her?

'I don't know. Turn your phone off. If you need to phone anyone, you can use mine. Have you packed a bag?' She nodded. 'Enough for a weekend?' She nodded again, summoning a small smile.

'I've been totally obedient—I think. But I'm not sure I'm functioning awfully well. I expect I've forgotten something essential.'

'Hairbrush? Make-up? Clean undies times three? Wellies, something waterproof, something glamorous times two; jewellery, lots?' She looked uncertain and he laughed. 'Your laptop, or notepad and pencil. I've got the recording equipment. Go check, girl, and let's go.'

She looked at him gratefully and leant briefly against his chest. 'You're so good for me. And to me.' As had happened every time he saw her, he wished the brief moment was longer, and then felt shame about wishing it.

While she went upstairs, he turned her phone off. Were the media revisiting the slapped pupil episode? He looked again at the modern, reasonably spacious mews house, its characterless right angles softened with some good figurative drawings and paintings, shelves of books, a few ornaments and a mass of music. The CDs were an eclectic mix; classical, but with a good sprinkling of crossover and modern. An empty case on the player featured a young Charlotte Elliott on piano and Rebecca Jordan on violin, playing baroque music. Recorded in 1979. He frowned, wondering why Rebecca Jordan should look vaguely familiar before he remembered—this was Annie's birth mother.

In the centre of the sitting room was a Steinway baby grand, the lid down, covered in piles of music, manuscripts, scoring and notation notebooks. The sofa and chairs were modern, comfortable, white, and the adjacent kitchen tiny and well-designed but terribly clean and characterless. Somehow it seemed a lonely environment. Shona's kitchen had been cluttered; surfaces covered in drifts of flour and icing sugar, the boys' mess everywhere. He opened the fridge to find only the basics and guessed that the freezer would contain several supermarket ready meals.

'Not a sign of the paparazzi,' he said comfortingly as he loaded her case into the hire car. 'I must have put the fear of God into him.'

Annie had recovered her aplomb in the relief of rescue. 'You'll be on the cover of *Hello!* magazine, or front-page news. Undernourished photographer assaulted by protection officer. I hope he didn't get a picture of you.'

'I don't think so, but even if I'm plastered over the tabloids, I doubt they'll discover my identity. What I would like to know is why they were here?'

Annie put her hand on his arm, which made him feel absurdly happy. 'I am hugely grateful. It's utterly pathetic, and I don't know why I've allowed myself to be upset by it, but Justin has announced his engagement to a beautiful new girlfriend, the daughter of a duke, no less, who, wait for it, is pregnant with his child. As he divorced me because I couldn't provide the heir, I suppose they just want to rake up my failure and the shiny mags will get a month's worth of sales.' Her voice was light, but he guessed that a new and pregnant Lady Devereux hardly a year on from the divorce was deeply humiliating. He squeezed her hand.

'Well, I'm no reader of *Hello!* so the goings-on of the upper classes and so-called celebrities pass me by. I'd let them pass you by, too.'

The Friday traffic was heavy, but he relished the time with her on the way to the hotel in the New Forest. The coppery hair was drawn low at her neck, inviting his palm to slide down the silky tail, and as she talked, he enjoyed the deep inflection of her voice. She was unaware of how attractive she was. But his body was acutely aware.

Over dinner, their talk turned to his lectures at Imperial College.

'I thought you said you were at Edinburgh University,' she said, sounding puzzled. 'How come you're lecturing at Imperial and not Edinburgh?'

'I did Materials Science and Engineering at Edinburgh, and then an internship with a company in Aberdeen and finally a PhD at Imperial.' Her eyes were round and he grinned. 'You need not be impressed. These first-year students are a bright bunch, and no shrinking violets either. They'll run rings round me before they're finished.'

She gave him a disbelieving raised eyebrow.

'Did you meet your wife in Edinburgh or London?'

Again, he heard that old diffidence, as if she was nervous of causing offence.

'I met her first in Edinburgh, but got to know her properly in Aberdeen. She was teaching at Aberdeen Grammar School and had warm and comfortable digs near the centre, whereas I had cold and uncomfortable ones on the outskirts. In those days I was always broke, and interns were just unpaid skivvies. Shona was earning extra money baking for a tea shop, and she used to give me free cakes.'

Annie laughed. 'Cakes seem to be a recurring theme in your family! My mother should have sent me to cookery school as neither of us is much good. I hadn't a clue when I married. It was fast learning, though. I had to cook endless shooting lunches which gave me more stress than you'd believe possible. I'd hardly ever had game before, and suddenly I was jointing pheasants, cooking whole partridge and deciding on whether to have haunch or leg of venison. I am not the world's greatest cook.'

Unlike Shona, who, in his view anyway, *had* been the world's greatest cook. He pushed away the thought and concentrated on Annie. 'Well, for a girl who doesn't like cooking, you don't seem to have any hang-ups about eating.' She had had a rare steak, and he eyed her clean plate. 'Did Justin like cooking?'

She gurgled with amusement. 'I think he could manage a boiled egg and toast, but that was about it. The Devereux clan must always have had staff, I think, and my mother-in-law wouldn't have been seen dead in an apron. She was not cosy. Unlike your in-laws, who Christopher portrayed as the ultimate grandparents—feeding the boys chocolate digestives in bed along with their early morning cuppa! They sound lovely.'

He laughed. 'They are, indeed, extremely good grandparents. And talking of grandparents, shall we embark on our new investigations about John Elliott tomorrow around nine-thirty? It won't take us more than an hour and I told Mrs Fletcher we'd try to be with her about ten-thirty. Now we could have some sticky pudding and a coffee and a good night's sleep, or—' he hesitated '—shall we do something else?' He saw a little wash of pink come into her cheeks and her upper teeth gripped her lip, not quite controlling a smile. He was relieved that she wasn't upset by the idea, and the pink was not just endearing, but altogether sexy. She looked straight at him, blue eyes wide and her expression now rather solemn. Sudden desire shortened his breath. She was considering the suggestion.

Then she gave a slight shake of her head. 'We could. But perhaps better not.'

He needed to release the tension, or she might back off further. He was aware that he did not want her to back off.

'You could always join me in bed for tea and chocolate biscuits tomorrow morning, say at eight o'clock?'

She took the proffered joke gratefully and shuddered dramatically. 'No thanks. I have an aversion to crumbs between the sheets. I will meet you over the breakfast table at eight-thirty sharp, toast crumbs on the table.'

Outside her room, he kissed her on the cheek and then turned her face to his and let his lips touch hers, very lightly. She did not withdraw, but he had a sense, not for the first time, that she was doubtful, sceptical. As if she could not believe that his attraction to her could be genuine. He opened her door for her and turned away with a smiling 'Good night, sleep well.'

As he prepared for the following day, checking emails, charging phone and laptop, putting papers and notes ready, he thought that Justin had chipped away at her self-worth to such an extent that she was nervous of making any relationship at all, friend or lover. Shona, on the other hand, had been a self-believer, supremely confident in her abilities, in her attraction to everyone, male or female. Shona had been very uncomplicated.

41

May 2012

David liked it that Annie was ready to leave on time. He didn't want to be stressed by being late in the heavy traffic.

'I feel really curious about meeting Rhionna, don't you?' he said as he navigated down to Lymington. 'I just hope that she and Granny didn't part as enemies.'

She put her head back and contemplated the roof of the car. 'I hope so too. It does seem odd that they lost touch.' She was quiet for a moment. 'Something else I'm curious about is how she knew that your grandfather had had a stroke in Inverasdale if she had no contact with anyone there. She came back to look after him. Your father told me that. She must have been in touch with *someone*.'

'Perhaps she was in touch with Rhionna after all? We'll ask her.'

Rhionna Fletcher lived in a pleasant modern bungalow set in a neat garden bursting with spring cherry blossom and magnolia bloom.

She had been a tall, strong woman and her face, though weather-beaten, held the remnants of beauty, the bones sharp under the skin, her straight cropped hair the steely grey which develops from original red or brunette colour. Faded eyes behind thick glasses. Nothing soft, cosy or gentle about this lady. In fact, she was rather like Mhairi.

Perhaps that was why they had been friends—or perhaps it was just that in old age there wasn't time for polite untruths. David liked her immediately. He had already asked for and received her agreement to record her memories, and he placed the recorder next to the lemon drizzle cake on the coffee table in front of her.

'So you,' she said, looking intently at him, 'are Mhairi's grandson. You have a strong look of her. Are you like her in character too?'

He laughed. 'I'm not as feisty as her. I think my parents have softened the genetics a bit. Father is pretty easy-going.'

'Is he now?' This pause for reflection seemed to hold some sort of evaluation. 'She was always sparky, for sure. Always wanted the last word and made her decisions and stuck to them. I'm glad she's well. We were a tough generation, for it was no easy life and she had it tougher than most.' She turned to Annie, considering her carefully. 'And you are John Elliott's granddaughter! You've no likeness to him at all. He had a long face and sharp grey eyes under a widow's peak. Very dark hair.' David wondered if Annie would say something then, but she didn't. Sliding the photograph out from the documents, he handed it to Rhionna and she studied it with interest and a certain sadness.

'Yes indeed. Dear John. I never knew his wife had another child after her boys were killed. Was it another boy she had?'

Annie shook her head. 'No. A girl. She was born in 1945. After he was killed.'

Rhionna considered that and nodded slowly. 'Poor John. He was out of his mind with grief and guilt at not being there during that bombing raid, and then he died himself on the next convoy. He was a dear man, and a good one, too, whatever people said about that billet.' She sighed. 'But I'll tell you the story from the beginning, otherwise it will be such a jumble of memories, nothing will make any sense.' She sipped her coffee from the big mug beside her. 'My family lived in Aultbea village and Mhairi would often stay the night if the weather was bad. It was a long road to a lonely croft at Inverasdale. My parents thought it was too far to go in the dark especially. She had the sheep to care for on the croft, but she didn't have to grow much as she had a job at the post office, and they let people off the farming if they had war jobs.'

'They?' David queried. 'Do you mean the landowner or government?'

'It was the elders who ruled the roost then.' She chuckled. 'They had eyes in the backs of their heads, they did, helped by a puckle of mealy-mouthed tell-tits to let on that you'd ducked out of Sunday kirk, or hung the washing on the line on the Sabbath, even if it was the only sunny day in a week.' She put her head back and laughed. 'My parents were strict, and the Sabbath was a holy day, but if the other elders got over-puritan, my father gave them a large dose of common sense and reminded them that they'd been lads too, once.' She laughed again.

'Did you have a job too, Mrs Fletcher?' Annie asked.

'I helped my mum at the greengrocer's. Mrs Reid took Mhairi on because I think she'd been friends with her mother. She was fond of Mhairi, though she was a right feisty woman and you didn't try having a gossip with Mhairi when she was there! She ran that post office slick as oil.' She rocked a little in her chair.

'The first day Mhairi set eyes on John she fancied him. He had a burst appendix and I think he might have died if she hadn't got him to hospital. After he was discharged, she got him billeted at Inverasdale and looked after him. That was the beginning of the end of her relationship with Archie. Do you know about Archie Mackinnon? Mhairi's boyfriend?'

'A little,' Annie said. 'A rather nasty man who drowned—or was killed.'

Mrs Fletcher flicked her a glance and nodded.

'Eventually, John went back on convoy—late summer, I think, pretty well recovered. Archie was glad to see him go and thought he'd be back in Mhairi's good books, but she was getting fed up with his jealousy and coming to realise what a manipulative, nasty piece of work he was, compared to John Elliott.'

She gazed at the ceiling, remembering. 'John was a true gentleman, and I think Mhairi wished he wasn't.' She laughed suddenly. 'I know Mhairi wished he wasn't!' David was a little startled by how she was presenting his grandmother. 'She was sick to death of Archie, who had to be physically fended off, but also frustrated by John who was too much of a gentleman to touch her!' There was a short pause while Annie and David digested this evidence of the eternal chemical reactions in a previous generation.

'While John was at Inverasdale, Archie couldn't influence her, but once John left on convoy, or navy business, Archie was back. He had a lot of military customers up at Cove so her croft would have been very convenient to store his black-market goods in. At first, she wouldn't let him, but he kept coming back and pressurising her to let him use her sheds. He threatened to tell the authorities about her.'

'Tell them what?' David asked. 'That John Elliott was living in her croft? Would that have been frowned on?'

'Oh no. The navy knew all about that, and though the community, or anyway the elders, disapproved, the navy needed every billet they could lay their hands on.' She seemed hesitant, as if deciding whether to say more. 'Archie threatened to tell the authorities that she'd handled illegal goods. He'd given her—and me—"presents" every now and then. Lots of people were guilty, to a degree, of handling black-market goods. Little luxuries meant a lot and none of us was perfect, or entirely honest.' She sighed.

'It's hard to visualise, but a new lipstick was enough to send us into ecstasies, and enough to take risks for too. But she was afraid—rightly—that she'd lose her job at the post office, and that her father would be informed. And she was worried for me, too, getting into trouble, and my parents wouldn't have let her stay in our house. Whenever John had to leave, Archie always sent her into a tailspin, and in the end she agreed to her sheds being used to store his stuff, and he "paid" for it in kind. Meat, or butter, or eggs, or nylons, and then he used that to bully her. It was just a spiral of manipulation, and John never knew how much he protected her from it when he was there.'

She gave David a straight look. 'Don't underestimate what it was like for her. She was nineteen only, her mother dead. Her father was a difficult man, and a drinker, and then he was a prisoner of war, and she was all on her own. We were hardly more than children, though you grew up quick in the war. No wonder that John Elliott was heaven-sent. She fell in love with him.' Her mouth compressed sardonically. 'My detached and self-sufficient friend fell hopelessly in love with a married man.'

With difficulty, David tried to visualise his ninety-year-old grandmother as a teenager in love. After a moment Annie cleared her throat.

'Do you know much about his life before the war?'

Mrs Fletcher settled more comfortably in her armchair. 'He was a teacher. He was lovely to listen to. He told you lots of things without seeming to. He never made us feel ignorant and he always listened. John was a gentle soul—I never could see him keeping control of a class of youngsters, but he always said he loved teaching. Perhaps wains took to him because he probably didn't raise his voice to them.'

Annie leant forwards. 'Do you know what school, or where it was?'

She shook her head. 'I'd guess in or near Portsmouth. Music was his great love. He played the violin beautifully and carried his violin about everywhere he went, convoys and all, until—until his hand was wounded.'

'Mhairi mentioned that. He lost two fingers in an air attack, she said.'

Mrs Fletcher gave her a sharp look. 'Anything more?'

'No,' Annie said, sounding puzzled. 'Isn't that what happened?'

Mrs Fletcher uncrossed her ankles and crossed them again the other way. 'Well, it is true he was wounded,' she said at last. 'But it's not the whole story.'

42

March 1943

As usual, Rhionna had taken the short cut home from the greengrocer's. She hurried through the narrow lane, head down, her coat pulled tight across her in the bitter east wind which brought the smell of fuel oil with it. She nearly missed the crumpled body lying close to the wall in deep shadow and her stomach lurched when she realised this was not a drunk soldier, but an unconscious—possibly a dead—man. Not till she knelt beside him and peered at the bloodied face in the twilight did she realise it was John Elliott. Her horrified gasp brought a groan from his lips, and his swollen eyes opened a fraction, focussing on her with a perceivable effort.

'John!' Her voice cracked as she took in the smashed hand, the slack bandages soaked in blood. 'What happened? Can you get up?'

He licked at a split lip, shifted his body a fraction and groaned. 'Get me sitting.' His voice was thickened and slurred.

He was heavy, a dead weight, and she knew he'd not get upright with only one hand and half conscious. When at last he had his back against the wall, she took off her coat and covered him.

'What happened?' she asked again, trembling from the

effort of moving him, and now wondering whether she should have done so.

'Got stamped on.' His eyes closed and she wondered if he had lost consciousness again.

'Someone stamped on your hand?' She was incredulous. 'Who? Who did this?' He said nothing and she had to leave it, realising that it was not just his hand that had been stamped on. 'I'm going to get help. I'll be right back.' Her voice was unsteady.

Why had John been attacked? She almost retched at the thought of someone stamping on that broken hand. Was it safe to leave him alone? What if they were still around? What if they were watching now? A judder of fear shook her as she looked up and down the apparently empty lane.

She bolted back to the shop to fetch her parents, her breath raw in her throat. Later, as a white-faced Mhairi clambered into the Red Cross truck alongside John's stretcher, Rhionna saw Archie leaning comfortably against the wall of the hotel, hands in his pockets. As the truck passed him, he pushed himself upright and gave a sardonic half-salute before turning away. The answer to who had done it came to her, clear as a bell. Fear rose like sickness. If Archie could do that to John, what might he do to Mhairi?

43

May 2012

'His fingers were amputated later that night,' Rhionna said, almost matter-of-factly.

'But the doctors must have known what happened!' Annie's stomach cringed in horror and indignation. 'If they had to amputate, why wasn't Archie arrested? Why didn't the navy protect him?'

Rhionna shrugged. 'Wartime, my dear. And I don't believe that John told anyone that it was Archie who'd attacked him. But Mhairi and I knew it was him and it terrified us. Archie had demonstrated both his power and his cruelty, and she was afraid for John and herself. She'd fallen in love with him, but knew it couldn't go anywhere because he was married.'

She said nothing for a time, thinking. 'His hand took a long time to heal and he was on sick leave and light duties. He didn't go down to Portsmouth much. He stayed on at the croft because he knew it protected Mhairi and Archie had to keep clear of her while he was around, which must have annoyed him. Beating John up hadn't had the desired effect.

'John recovered and eventually had to go back to his ship. She knew he was safe, but she was right miserable as well as frightened. She missed him. And when John was gone, Archie came back. She didn't go out with him and tried to keep away from him, but he'd got his nails into her and she was afraid of him.'

There was a loud scratching noise at the door and Annie jumped.

'David,' Rhionna said. 'Would you let him in, otherwise *his* nails will be into *my* door.'

An enormous marmalade cat stalked through and surveyed the room before jumping on to Rhionna's lap and putting his front paws up to her neck. She ignored him and he jumped down and transferred himself to Annie.

'Do you mind cats?' Rhionna asked.

'Love them,' Annie said. A cat's companionship came with no strings attached and gave her a sense of being wanted just for herself. She stroked him from head to the base of his tail, whereupon the tail twitched in ecstasy and he started a loud rumbling purr.

Mrs Fletcher continued her story. '1944, that summer, that was a happy time for Mhairi and John.' She heaved in a sigh and her fingers tensed on the arm of her chair. 'And then the Germans sent those horrible doodlebugs over. The last raids on Portsmouth, I think. It was a V2 rocket that killed his little boys.' She turned her head towards Annie. 'They would have been your uncles.'

Annie rubbed her cheek. 'August 15th.' There was a long silence after this, only broken by the purring of the cat.

'Poor John. His ship left just before it happened, and he didn't hear the news until October. Such a tragedy. And his poor wife— Mhairi didn't know about it either but she was almost ill with anxiety because they didn't get back for weeks.'

She rolled cake crumbs round her plate and a line creased her forehead. 'What with John's absence and Archie's manipulation—Archie was using the croft, with or without her permission— she got tearful easily, which was just not like her. Normally she was practical and self-sufficient, detached—not emotional, you know?'

'Yes, that's her,' David said. 'I've never seen her cry.'

She shook her head mournfully. 'Although I wasn't vastly aware at that age, even I realised she was in love with John. Oh dear! A married man! And Mrs Reid must have realised, too, for she worked her to the bone to keep her mind occupied! Lots of official letters arrived for John and they were all put into an envelope in his pigeonhole.'

A sudden sharp breeze blew in through the patio doors and she asked David to shut them.

'And then the ship got back, and he got that awful news.'

'I found the letter they sent! They gave him two weeks leave to rehouse his wife,' Annie said indignantly. 'I couldn't believe it.'

Rhionna's mouth turned down. 'Wartime. There wasn't too much sympathy available. But then Mhairi made a bad mistake and got herself embroiled with Archie again.'

Annie's heart sank as if this was contemporary information, not seventy years in the past.

'He got that news the same day the ship got back to Loch Ewe. They were all exhausted. John was given leave, but for some reason there was no transport available so Mhairi borrowed Archie's van, took time off from the post office, took John to Inverasdale and put him to bed. The next morning, she drove him to get the train south.'

Annie was puzzled. 'Did she take the van without Archie's permission?'

'Oh no. She asked him. Archie used the fact to blackmail her. He said the van had "goods" in it, and that John and Mhairi had stolen them.' She shook her head wearily. 'But that was later—after his ship left. John was called back from Portsmouth for sea trials before the convoy—his last convoy—left at the end of December.'

The cat suddenly looked up, ceased his purring and transferred itself to David. It must have sensed her tension, she thought.

'And that convoy must have been JW63,' David said, checking dates on his tablet above his head while the cat got comfortable on his long thighs. 'It left on 30th December 1944.'

'I don't know what its number was,' Mrs Fletcher said, with a frown of concentration, 'but the weeks passed and the ships from that convoy began to come back, though not the *Countess of Minto*. Mhairi got so anxious. Of course, none of us could get official news, but we heard they'd been attacked, and several ships had been lost, and some had been towed into Murmansk, and some had got back to Iceland and some to the Clyde. She didn't know where the ship was, or where John was.' Rhionna shook her head. 'We didn't know then, about John. She worried, but she still hoped to hear from him. The only good thing was that Archie had disappeared, and therefore wasn't harassing her, and I for one was relieved about that.'

She turned her mug absently backwards and forwards on the table beside her. 'Mhairi was—odd. Sometimes she was laughing and back to her old self, and sometimes she was crying for no reason. And that was just not like her. But she wasn't frightened any more. Not of Archie. It was as if she knew he wouldn't come back. She was anxious, though, and I assumed it was just worry about John's safety.'

Annie felt David's glance, but focused her eyes on the recorder and tried to relax her tense fingers.

'But there was still no news of him,' Mrs Fletcher continued. 'By this time, it was nearly March and Mhairi began to lose her looks, she got thin in the face and looked more and more desperate.' She hesitated a little. 'It was then I began to wonder if there was more to Mhairi's desperation than just anxiety for John. I think Mrs Reid wondered too. She wouldn't go out much, but she wouldn't tell me anything for a long time.'

David leant forward. 'But she did tell you? That she was pregnant?'

'Yes. By April it was becoming noticeable. She wouldn't say who the father was.' She looked straight at David. 'If it was John Elliott, she wasn't going to hurt his reputation, whether he was living or dead. She really pitied his wife, losing her babies and her mother, in the bombing. She wasn't going to damage that family more if she could help it.'

David looked back at her. 'And if not John Elliott, who? You said she hated Archie by this time.'

The thick hair silvered in a ray of sunshine as she bent her head downwards. The first time that resolute gaze had become less than direct.

'If she was pregnant by Archie, it was rape or coercion, because by then she loathed him, especially after he beat John up and smashed his hand. I did wonder—after that storm when she got so badly trampled by the sheep and stayed with us. She had terrible nightmares. She would shout and thrash about.' Her face twisted. 'The shouting wasn't about the sheep. It was Archie's name she screamed, and she was frightened. When I asked her, she clammed up. She was terrified by something, and I guessed it was Archie threatening her with something. Or something he'd already done.'

The cat transferred itself back to Annie's lap and resumed rumbling. 'Anyway,' Rhionna continued, 'she was in a daze. Grey. Just existing, living at the croft, getting through each day, going to work at the post office, not speaking hardly. Then Archie's body was found, and the police were convinced she'd had something to do with it because it seemed he'd died of a head wound, not from drowning, but they couldn't prove anything, and in the end, they went away. It wasn't as if anyone was mourning Archie.

'So Mhairi was pregnant, and eventually, she couldn't hide it but she still wouldn't say who the father was, only, to me, that John Elliott was "not to blame".' Mrs Fletcher pursed her lips. 'Rather obscure, that was. She was rejected by the whole community when it was realised, and a lot of people assumed it was Archie's, and that she'd had something to do with his death. They would have nothing to do with her.'

She shook her head. 'But I am getting this story all out of order, and it's John Elliott you want to hear about.' She screwed her face up trying to get things in the right order. 'His hand had healed—minus those fingers—but of course, he never played his violin again. I don't know what happened to it. Maybe he sent it back to his wife.' She looked enquiringly at Annie, who shook her head.

'No, my grandmother never got it back. Maybe he left it with Mhairi, and perhaps her father destroyed it.'

David interrupted her. 'I think she must have left it in the cottage, probably up in her little room in the rafters, where he wouldn't—couldn't—have gone. She gave a violin to my father, years later, after she came back to the croft.' His head tilted in thought. 'And the likelihood is that it was John Elliott's. He still has it, and he still plays it.'

Mhairi had denied all knowledge of his violin, but Annie's memory flashed back to Jem playing with her at the *ceilidh*.

'That's possible,' Mrs Fletcher said. She added carefully, 'I think John knew—no, that's too strong a word, for he wasn't given to fanciful thoughts. I think he felt his luck was running out and he might not come back. He was sad—depressed—not unsurprising given he'd just lost his two little boys. Anyway, his luck did run out.

'The ship spent weeks in Russia getting repaired and

came back to Scapa Flow in Orkney—April Fool's Day it was, 1945—and we got news, oh, weeks later. Six crew lost from a torpedo strike, including John. Mhairi was fair out of her mind. Oh! It was a bad time for her—for all of us, for we were all that fond of John—but much worse for her. She was like a ghost.'

She heaved in a sigh and the faded eyes blinked behind the glasses.

'Everyone had thought Mhairi was overdoing the reaction a bit—she wasn't the first lass to have lost a sailor boyfriend. It was only later that they realised why she was so upset.' Mrs Fletcher exhaled a long breath. 'Some things can't be hidden, and nature takes its course.'

'Do you think Mhairi herself might not have known who the father was?' David asked.

She made a little moue of pursed lips and took her time about answering. 'I don't know. Not for sure. I know that she loved John Elliott and would have loved his child. It would have been difficult for her as he was already married, and the child therefore illegitimate, and John himself was a man of—of—' she seemed lost for words. 'A man of virtue. A moral man. It seems so unlike him.' The surprise was still evident in her voice. 'I do know that Mhairi hated Archie Mackinnon, but if he could do what he did to John, he could have raped her. I think he was blackmailing her, maybe for sex, or he could have guessed that she was pregnant, though he disappeared that January, so he couldn't have known for sure. Blackmail need not always be about money,' she continued, her eyes looking beyond them. 'I *hoped* the father was John Elliott, and that she would not admit it in order to protect his reputation. But I really do not know, and sadly I think the baby was probably Archie's.'

David gazed into the distance, his expression sombre. Annie knew that he was thinking that if Mhairi had known for sure who John's father was, there would have been no reason to keep it a secret for the whole of Jem's lifetime.

As if to fill the awkward silence, Rhionna resumed her story.

'By April, the police investigation was over, and everyone knew Mhairi was pregnant.' She was tapping her fingertips against each other, her eyes looking inwards. 'Folk were really unkind and called her a whore. She'd go in a shop and they'd all stop talking or make horrible remarks in her hearing. The shopkeepers wouldn't serve her, or they'd serve everyone else first and make her wait. I was warned not to be friends with her or even speak to her, and if I did someone would always tell my parents. The minister preached against her openly, the elders wagged their fingers and told everyone what to think and how to think. Oh! The hypocrisy! It was a hard time for her, but she had nowhere else to go. When she had the baby, she was on her own in the croft. She had got all prepared for the birth, and she'd asked me to be with her—not that I'd have been much use—but my parents forbade me to go, and I didn't have the courage to disobey them.' She sighed. 'I think a bit of her was hoping that both she and the baby would die, then all those folk would have been guilty of—of their murder, almost.'

The shock of her statement made Annie's heart jump and the cat looked up in disapproval. The image of a young woman giving birth friendless and alone, shunned by her neighbours, was so outrageous that she was speechless. Mrs Fletcher was tight-lipped, her face tense with an old anger that had never died.

'Her job at the post office had long since gone. Even Mrs Reid couldn't stand in the face of the elders' disapproval. I feel bad to this day that I wasn't there for her, that I didn't have the courage to stand up to them. I argued with my parents about going to see her once, and they locked me in my room, which they'd never done in my life. But I didn't have the courage, and you can't turn the clock back. The consequences of what you do, and what you don't do in your life stay with you for ever. Sins of omission, and all that.' Her sadness was palpable. 'Mhairi and I were never quite the same after that, although of course I did visit when I could. She didn't go out if she could help it, she just stayed at the croft and looked after the baby. He was a dear wee thing, dark hair, placid. Used to fall asleep tied in a shawl on her back when she worked the land—after leaving the post office, she had to start farming again. The minister refused to baptise him and maybe he never was baptised.' She looked enquiringly at David.

'I don't know,' he said. 'Mhairi has never been madly enthusiastic about the church. You can't blame her.'

'Indeed not,' Rhionna said. 'He was a dreadful hypocrite, that minister.'

She paused, her eyes looking inward again. 'And then her father came back.' She stopped. Annie held her breath and her hands were so tense in the cat's fur that the animal leapt down in offence and began to wash furiously. She knew it had not been a happy homecoming.

Rhionna told them how Mhairi's father had returned to find his daughter in disgrace, how he turned to drink and eventually, as Mr Mackinley had told Annie, to violence. 'And that was it. When she came to, she took the baby and ran.'

Rhionna Fletcher cocked her head sideways. 'And he never had a good word for how she'd kept the croft, with sheep in good fettle, oats in the ground, and the house as bright as a new pin. He told everyone he'd packed her off without a penny, and he was glad to be rid of her—good riddance to bad rubbish. Even the community took a breath at that, for it was known he drank all his money away, and there were some folk who'd been loud against her who thought he'd no right to turn her off destitute. I never saw her to say goodbye, and I never knew where she went, though I learnt later that neighbours put her and the baby on the bus to Achnasheen, and she wrote later to thank them. The postmark was Edinburgh, but she never sent an address. She never wrote to me, and I never knew what happened to her, how she managed, how she brought up that wee mite.' Rhionna sounded distressed, even after all the years. Annie surreptitiously dabbed the back of her wrist on her cheekbone.

Abruptly the cat rushed to the patio doors. A magpie strutted on the terrace and eyed the frantic feline inside with derision. The frustrated cat made them all laugh and broke the tension, and Rhionna ordained a coffee break

'Will you tell her you've been to visit me?' She sounded uncertain, anxious even, and Annie guessed she still regretted not being there for the baby's birth.

'I'd like to,' David said. 'I think Mhairi would be pleased to hear news of you. And there are people who are affected by not knowing what happened because she's never told anyone. My father grew up in Edinburgh knowing nothing of John Elliott or this story. We'd never heard of Archie Mackinnon until Annie found his name in the course of her research. But Dad has always wanted to know who his father was, and Mhairi wouldn't—or couldn't—tell him. It may be easier for her to tell her story now, knowing that part of it has already been told.'

She half nodded, just a little duck of her head. 'Tell her—tell her—Oh! I don't know! We're both so old I'm not sure if any of it matters now. Tell her I missed her all those years and thought of her often. Did she marry? Did she have other children? Was she happy?' Her questions were almost rhetorical, but David answered her briefly.

'She married a man called Walter Gillespie in Edinburgh, but they had no children. He brought my father up, paid for his education, and a good one at that. Walter died in 1970 of a heart attack and then Mhairi's father had a stroke.' He paused. 'She came back and looked after him until he died in 1973, and we wondered how she knew he'd had the stroke. It wasn't you that told her?'

'No, it wasn't me. I never knew where she'd gone.' Her eyes narrowed thoughtfully. 'I didn't think anyone knew where she was, but perhaps Mrs Reid knew. She was discretion personified, that lady.'

What a vast unknown story lay in those seventy years, Annie thought. Maybe Rhionna would be the key to unlocking it and giving Jem some answers.

Rhionna shrugged. 'Well, the croft would have been hers, house and land, after he died, but even so, it must have taken some courage to go back.' There was admiration in her voice. 'What's she like now, our Mhairi?'

David chuckled. 'She's very like you—full of energy still—all the marbles rattling around and her memory still good. She's got a snappy sense of humour, nothing sentimental about her.'

'We didn't tell you,' Annie said, suddenly remembering. 'Mhairi named him John Elliott Mackenzie.'

Rhionna stared at her. 'Did she now?' She thought it over. 'It still doesn't prove anything, except that she liked the man enough to use his name. She'd never have called the bairn Archie, that's for sure.'

It was almost like a bad joke, but they knew it wasn't.

When they were leaving, Rhionna picked up a thick envelope from her sideboard.

'I found these at the back of my cupboard at Aultbea when I packed up to get married. Mhairi must have hidden them there after Archie disappeared when she was staying with us and the police were swarming all over her croft. I assumed they were letters she didn't want them to see, and I took them with me when I left because of course I didn't know how to get them back to her. I've never read them, and I sealed them in that outer envelope so I couldn't be tempted!' She held the package carefully as if it was fragile. 'They are in John Elliott's handwriting and addressed to John Elliott at the Aultbea post office. I believe they did that in order to keep their correspondence secret and I think now is the moment to give them back to Mhairi. Even though perhaps they ought to belong to your mother, Annie.' She looked at them both. 'Will you give them to Mhairi, without reading them?'

Letters. At last the possibility of something personal between Mhairi and John. Maybe the proof that they were lovers. Her throat tightened. How would Charlotte feel if that was the case? She stared at the package.

'I promise not to read them.' She turned to David, seeing an unexpected sympathy in his eyes. 'Will you give them to Mhairi? And tell me what she says?'

He nodded agreement. 'I won't read them either. But although they may reveal their love story, they won't confirm her pregnancy. He must have written them all before his last convoy.' She knew the elation of finding this personal connection must be mixed with disappointment for his father. The elusive proof might not be here either.

44

May 2012

They had a pub lunch by the river and as he watched her it was as though he'd consumed an entire bottle of wine instead of the alcohol-free beers they had both drunk. Annie sat across from him, elbows on the table, the long tail of her hair falling to her collarbone. His fingers itched to run along the line of that collarbone and their eyes kept meeting in a way that made him wonder if she knew what he was thinking. They spoke of their meeting with Rhionna, but his focus was on Annie. He tried to concentrate on Shona's memory and on the boys, but his mind and eyes and body were embarrassingly aware of Annie and he despaired of his inability to control his thoughts. Why should he suddenly be consumed by this unwanted desire? Except that it wasn't sudden. Ever since January, his thoughts had slid back to her; he had made excuses to contact her, had worked to discover more about Rhionna, about wartime Aultbea, in order to keep this connection alive. It wasn't just for his father, he acknowledged tardily.

As if trying to remind himself just how inappropriate his feelings were, he steered the conversation towards their respective marriages. She told him more about Justin; the first exciting, heady days, the new and different clothes suitable for country activities, the great family mansion in Sussex.

'My mother-in-law was quite shocked when I suggested boxing in the pipework or putting in modern bathrooms and loos. Honestly, the spiders and the spider webs were horrendous, but it would have "destroyed the integrity of the building".' She shuddered and laughter bubbled in his throat.

'Then there were shooting parties, and hunting friends, and in the summer he went fishing with his men friends, wives not invited.' She tipped her head back and contemplated the ceiling, and he imagined running his fingertips down that exposed throat, into the valley between her breasts.

She rocked upright and he withdrew his gaze abruptly.

'I am so ashamed now of how naïve and easily impressed I was—the young trophy wife, with a famous mother and I suppose a famous father to those in the financial know. And of course, he was in the financial know.'

She told him about the misery of the divorce, the restless and unfulfilled search for a job that satisfied, and he leant back and watched her over their coffee. He crossed his legs as affection and desire surged through him. She was an endearing mixture of self-assurance and insecurities, he thought. The smart urban girl, knowing which bus to catch, versus the out-of-her-depth country wife, juggling her pheasants and haunches of venison and not knowing the difference between French and runner beans.

He told her about moving from Edinburgh to Poolewe after Shona's death. Leaving his job, selling the flat, already too small for growing rumbustious boys, wanting to get away from the surroundings of her illness.

'My in-laws tried to be supportive, but they just drove me mad with their funeral and memorial services, the endless designs for her headstone, marble or granite, or a dozen other choices, black lettering or gold. The wording, the epitaph. The visits to her grave.' He glanced up at Annie in slight embarrassment. 'It all seemed totally irrelevant, and I could only think of how much I didn't want to be reminded that she was dead.' He drank the last of his coffee. 'It is all much easier now. The boys go to stay with them at some point in the holidays, and they come to stay in Poolewe at reasonably frequent intervals. The boys adore them—the crumbs in the bed syndrome—and they adore the boys.'

'Talking of crumbs—I'm going to eat that last mint.' She licked the chocolate off her thumb and his stomach lurched at the unwitting sexiness of it as if he were in a dropping lift. 'Were you running away, like me? Hoping that you'd feel better somewhere else?'

Had he? 'Maybe. I didn't feel that much better, but at least it was different work, and I came back to a house which had never had her in it—no memories. I felt guilty about taking the boys away from Tom and Tilly, and from their school and friends.'

'Was it the right choice, looking back?'

He rubbed his thumbnail over the tablecloth, leaving a faint line in the fabric.

'I'm not sure. The school is adequate, but not brilliant. They teach the children in Gaelic, and the boys talk to Mhairi in Gaelic, all very culturally amazing, but not madly useful in the wider world. Christopher has a good brain, but he's becoming idle and slightly wild and I don't think is challenged sufficiently, and for me, working in Dad's business is convenient but undemanding.'

'Which is why you enjoy a change lecturing at Imperial College?'

He laughed. 'I guess so. It certainly stirs my brain up.' Like you do, he thought. You, Annie Devereux, have stirred everything up.

* * *

He stopped the car near Burley in the New Forest hoping that fresh air might get him into a more sensible frame of mind. They walked briskly down tracks on the heathland, the horizon seeming low and the huge sky tumbling with dark clouds, meeting ponies behind every gorse bush, and much more infrequently, fellow walkers. He wanted to hold her hand, like a teenager, but didn't quite have the courage to try it.

'It's as if all those people have walked out of the shadows, isn't it?' Annie said, breaking off a twig of pussy willow and stroking the fluffy buds. 'Rhionna was just a name and now she's a lovely person we actually know. And she's made John alive again, and Mrs Reid, and all those other peripheral people.'

'Particularly nasty Archie. I wonder what on earth happened to him. Quite a mystery, seemingly.'

'It's odd, though. I started to research John Elliott, yet somehow everything comes back to your grandmother. I can't even begin to imagine what it can have been like to give birth to a child, entirely alone, no telephone, when every single person in your community has turned against you.' She sounded so sad that he used it as an excuse to put his arm round her shoulders. 'Do you think your father knows any of that?'

'I very much doubt it. He's certainly never spoken about it.'

'And I bet you've never asked. That's a major difference between men and women,' she said. 'As sad as it was for me to hear sometimes, and as painful as it must have been for her, my mother has always told me everything about my birth and Rebecca's death. But men seem to have a complete lack of curiosity about other people's emotions

292

and feelings. What do women talk about when they get together? Everything but sport or politics or property or finance!'

'But that doesn't leave anything else to talk about,' David said. She stuck a foot out and he stumbled over it, grabbing her hand for balance and not relinquishing it. He was aware of the casing over the bones, the soft, fine texture of the skin at the joint of thumb and forefinger, and he had a sudden desire to bring her hand to his mouth, to smooth his lips over it, to touch it with his tongue.

A cold wind suddenly whipped up and drops of rain rattled on their windcheaters. They turned and headed back towards the car, at least a mile away. The rain quickly became heavier, climaxing in a startling downpour. They ran the last hundred yards splashily, breathlessly, before collapsing in a wet heap in the car. Stripping off his coat and throwing it on to the back seat, he turned to help Annie out of hers, which had stuck damply to her wrists and pinioned her hands behind her. She leant forward, struggling to get the clinging fabric off and without volition, without thought, he kissed her on the lips, even as he pulled the sleeves off inside out and threw the coat after his. Then his arms went around her, and he kissed her again, properly, and her mouth opened under his in response. Tasting and touching her was the culmination of a craving, a longing which had crept up on him ever since the first night he met her when she had stalked out of Inveruidh to a car with no petrol. All those moments of reminding himself of Shona and then allowing her to fade into the background again. The craving had become a drug, taking his thoughts captive, and without any effort on her part, he had become addicted. As he kissed her, a long-forgotten sense of happiness swept through him, together with an odd inclination to let that happiness express itself in laughter.

When they drew apart, Annie pulled away from him a little, looking bemused, and pushed a swathe of hair behind her ear. He tried to look apologetic, but the good feeling inside him made it difficult.

'I'm really sorry. I honestly didn't intend to—I mean it just happened—but somehow you looked very, er, kissable just at that moment. Damp and kissable.' The apology had become an effort not to laugh, and he thought she was deciding whether to be offended.

Her teeth gripped her lower lip and with relief, he saw that she wasn't offended at all. She was trying not to smile. 'Oh! John Elliott would never have done that!'

He did laugh then. 'We don't know, do we? I retract my apology. You were damp and kissable, and I'm not at all sorry. Can I kiss you again?'

She drew in a sharp breath. 'Honestly! The brass neck of you!' She leant forwards and put her arms around him. 'Yes.'

At some point they disentangled, straightening clothes and hair, touching face and hands and lips. He ran his forefinger down the length of her nose, ending in the soft valley of her upper lip.

'That was—good. Wonderful. Did you enjoy that as much as I did?'

She smiled. 'Mmm. You're not a bad kisser, as they go.' Her fingers smoothed his hair down. 'You're disgracefully tousled.'

He did the same, removing the hairclip and gathering the chestnut strands into his fingers, the feel of her skin, the curve of her neck giving him that strange mixture of desire and affection. As he clipped it back, he kissed the tip of her nose and inhaled a steadying breath.

'I would dearly love to make you very tousled indeed, but feel that a public carpark really isn't the place. Shall we go back to the hotel and have cucumber and Marmite sandwiches and a pot of Earl Grey?'

'I hate cucumber and Marmite,' she said, sounding as tipsy as he felt. ' I shall have scones with cream and jam and charge them to your account as punishment for leading me astray. And you must promise not to kiss me in the hotel reception.'

He grinned. 'OK. Not in reception.' No prohibition on anywhere else, though.

They did have tea in a secluded corner of the glass walled conservatory, the intermittent showers and bursts of evening sunshine gleaming on the wet lawns and dripping oak trees. The dynamic of the day had changed after that kiss, even though they spoke of Rhionna and Mhairi and John Elliott, and the contrasts between the two families. Annie's singleness, compared to his rowdy, unpeaceful houseful of siblings. Mhairi growing up alone and motherless. Every time there was a pause, the pauses in themselves perfectly comfortable, he thought of that kiss, remembered her shoulders echoing to the touch of his hands, remembered her mouth, tentative at first, then lifting and responding. Every now and then her eyes met his and there was an astonishment, a not-quite-believing-what-had-happened look in them. Might it have been the first time she'd been kissed since her divorce?

'Look at the time,' she said once the last cake had been eaten. 'Perhaps we should go upstairs—' she eyed him with pseudo-severe gravity '—and concentrate on transcribing her memories.'

He grinned at her as he got up. 'I'd much prefer to do something else. But I suppose you're right. I'm going to experiment with Google's voice dictation. It may not work, but we could try.'

They worked their way through the recordings, snorting with laughter at the malapropisms and misunderstandings, the misheard and inappropriate words, haywire punctuation and mad grammar. Eventually, breathless with hilarity, he turned it all off.

'Oh dear. It really isn't funny material,' he said, wiping his eyes. 'If only Google could see the result. Tomorrow we can correct all that and add in our own questions.' His thoughts sobered. 'It seems more than possible that Mhairi did not know for sure who the father of her baby was. She and John Elliott might well have been lovers, but if Rhionna was correct, Archie Mackinnon could also have raped her. All those rows and arguments might have been the result—or might have led to him losing control?'

'Or her losing control,' Annie said soberly. 'What a horrible idea.' Her arms tightened around herself. 'I suppose it is possible. I should hate to ask her that question. In fact, I should hate her to see all that transcript, some of the things Rhionna told us.'

It was certainly an uncomfortable thought. 'My father would have to have the final say as to what information she was given.' He slid a hand behind her neck and stroked his thumb down to the bone at the top of her spine. The gentle, repetitive movement seemed to relax her, and her tension slackened. Her skin was translucent, smooth and unblemished, waiting for summer sun to tint it to gold and to give that chestnut hair tongues of flame. The scent of her skin was faint yet intoxicating and he couldn't tell whether it was her own scent or man-made. He had a strong urge to bury his face in her shoulder and breathe her in, but she gave a deep sigh and gently moved away.

Had he pushed her too far? Moved too fast? Perhaps kissing and gentle flirting in public was one thing, but now, in private, she was having second thoughts about being close to him? He brought normality back reluctantly, ringing his parents and speaking to his boys. Their fishing trip had been a great success with everyone catching fish, but to their disgust, the girls catching more than them. Grandpa had played backgammon with them and built another platform on the tree house. Granny Fiona had made a new sort of gingerbread, so sticky that they had to eat it with a spoon.

His father asked after their researches and the meeting with Rhionna Fletcher.

'Did she throw any light on John Elliott? Did she remember him?' His voice betrayed an unfamiliar eagerness.

'She certainly did. He was obviously a delightful man and she said Granny was deeply in love with him. But she didn't know for sure who your father was.' He could feel both his father's disappointment and his surprise. 'If we take DNA samples from you and Charlotte, we may know more. But there's a strong possibility it may not be what you want to hear, Dad, because there's more to the Archie Mackinnon story than we realised, which I'll explain when I get back. And Mrs Fletcher has produced a large envelope full of letters written between Granny and John, which I'm bringing back for her.'

He finished the call, looking thoughtful.

'My guess is that he'll talk to my grandmother again and tell her that we've found and visited her old friend.' He smiled a little. 'It might be interesting to set up a Face Time meeting for them. I can't see them travelling to meet each other at their age, but it would be good to get them talking again.'

'Mrs Fletcher still feels bad about what happened, doesn't she?' Annie said. 'It would be so lovely for them both to have the slate wiped clean, after all these years. I think that Mhairi might feel guilty because she was the one who never made contact.'

'Perhaps. In fact, probably.' He got up from the bed. 'Let's change and have dinner. My sandwiches and cake are just a memory and I need a drink.'

Room service produced a glass of white wine and a whisky, and Annie went away for a shower, reappearing in black silk trousers and a deep turquoise glittery tunic, and chunky turquoise and silver jewellery, the heavy coppery hair clipped back in a straight shining fall. Her black stilettos brought her to the same height as David.

'Wow!' he said impulsively. 'You look fabulous.' He had an intense desire, reluctantly suppressed, to slide his hands through that hair.

She twinkled. 'I can scrub up reasonably well. You had specified glamour and jewellery, so I tried to oblige, in spite of *Hello!* magazine. You look all right yourself.'

He was in chinos with a blue shirt and tidy jacket, his big frame restrained by fashion, but he knew he still looked as if he should be on the rugby field.

'Not quite in the same league.'

Their dinner and good wine engendered easy conversation which once again drifted, somehow, back towards their past marriages. It was as if the subject were inescapable.

She expanded on Justin's recent engagement to his pregnant aristocratic girlfriend, which had resulted in the raking up of journalistic curiosity about Annie, the previous wife.

'So he was making sure this one could produce an heir before he made an honest woman of her?' He kept his tone light and humorous.

'I suppose so,' she said with a faint smile. 'He couldn't afford to make the same mistake twice. If he doesn't have a son, the title and estates will go to a rather dissipated cousin who he detests.'

'It may be a daughter,' he said, topping up their glasses. 'What happens then?'

'I suppose he'll go on having children until he gets a boy. He's only forty-seven.'

David briefly contemplated the thought of fatherhood at his age of thirty-five. 'Rather him than me,' he said dryly. 'Think of those sleepless nights, dirty nappies and porridge-encrusted surfaces. We had ours when we were both young, and we needed every bit of that youthful energy. I think I'd die of exhaustion now. And children get much more interesting as they get older.'

He reached across the table and touched the back of her hand.

'Sorry. That was wonderfully insensitive. Do you still love him?'

The pause lengthened, and she looked at him, top teeth nibbling at her lower lip, unfocused, not really seeing him, trying to consider the question unemotionally.

'I don't like him now, and I did, before he became unlikeable, if you know what I mean.' He wasn't sure that he did. 'Love is different, isn't it? I mean, one falls *in* love, which means that one can fall *out* again, I suppose, but somehow, it's a slower process than liking or not liking. Loving someone is much more of a commitment—kind of, I don't know, deeper. You don't just stop loving, it's more like a slow death. A sort of withering. Like a tree that's blown over in a gale, it doesn't die immediately—the buds will open, the leaves are still green, but it's dying, and you can't do anything about it.' She focused on him again. 'And then you turn around and find that it's happened. It's gone dry and brown and withered. There isn't any love any more. That's how it's happened for me. But that's only one sort of losing love—there's a reason for losing it. You haven't fallen out of love with your wife, have you? She just happens to be absent.'

Absent. He hadn't thought of it that way. 'How did he become unlikeable?'

Her pursed lips curved downwards as she examined the question.

'The feeling that he wanted me more as a brood mare than as a desirable wife, and that my failure to conceive was a personal insult to him. I don't think I imagined all that. There was an underlying accusation that I was unwilling to be a mother, which became more obvious as time went on.'

Unlikeable might be a good definition of Justin, David thought

'He made me go for tests, which was a real lesson in humiliation.' He saw her shoulders tense. 'Especially as they couldn't find any reason why I shouldn't conceive.'

'Did it make you wonder if perhaps he should have gone for tests too? It takes two, after all, to make a baby.'

'After they couldn't find anything wrong with me, I did wonder. I even suggested it to him. It made him, if anything, angrier. He made comparisons between Charlotte and me. Because neither of us had children, both of us are deeply selfish, according to Justin.'

He could see anger flaring in her eyes. 'He never understood that Charlotte gave up her career for Will and me. She lost two years, and to get back to where she had been before Rebecca died took a vast effort.' She looked at David over the rim of her glass. 'Justin said I was doing it on purpose—not conceiving—which was absolutely not true, and he knew it. Then when his new girlfriend got pregnant, I knew it had to be my fault. But unkindness is not likeable.'

'Fault is not the word.' His stomach twisted in sympathy, and something more. 'No. Definitely not likeable.'

She sighed. 'Love, or what one thinks is love, really is blind. Looking back now, I see that my parents weren't overwhelmingly enthusiastic. They weren't actively against the marriage, at least not in my hearing, but even if they had been, I wonder if it would have made the slightest difference? Probably not, or only to alienate them from me.' She thumped a fist into her palm. 'They could see it so clearly and I was so stupid. Obsessed by a slightly rakish, older man, titled and rich. I just couldn't see it.'

'You aren't the first and you won't be the last.' He put his hand on hers across the table, trying to comfort.

She raised her glass to him in a silent toast. 'Anyway, it's all water under the bridge now, and we've both moved on. I don't like him any more, and I don't love him any more either.'

He sensed she didn't want to pursue the subject, so they moved on to more current concerns. Her life in the last four months seemed to have been a wasteful mix of sorting out her divorce, attending the tribunal, finding somewhere to live, and finding a new job. This last was as a session musician for a recording company.

'It's OK,' she said with a sigh, stirring cream into her after-dinner coffee. 'It's something to get up for and get on a bus to, but the music, in general, is dire. I'm a keyboard player, so don't do much orchestral, so it's mainly pop or rock which is not my favourite sort of music; the bands usually consist of rather unmusical druggies.' She shrugged. 'Still, I'm learning quite a lot about how it's done, mixing and so on.'

'Is there no way you can go back to teaching?'

She shook her head. 'I don't think so. I've got a record. The tribunal was awful—humiliating and embarrassing. It would come up in my CRB check. All that teacher training wasted.'

'What about private lessons for individuals?'

'I suppose I could, but I think I'd have to tell them the whole sorry story and who'd let me loose on children and—' she raised her eyes briefly to his. 'I'm not sure that I've got the courage, especially if they then declined to use me. Anyway, how on earth would I find enough private students to make it a proper job?'

'Is it the money that's stopping you trying? Word of mouth would bring you students over time.'

She gave a low laugh. 'No, it's not money. It's cowardice. If I needed the money, if I really needed to, like Mhairi needed to, I'd get over the cowardice, wouldn't I?' She sounded thoroughly disgusted with herself.

That wave of desire came again, and this time he surrendered. Putting down his coffee cup he got to his feet and put out a hand to her.

'You are not a coward. Don't put lies in your own mouth. Come on, we're going upstairs.'

He placed the plastic key on the touchpad and drew her firmly into his room. The laptop and all their notes and papers lay tidily on the desk, evidence of his self-control before dinner. He kissed her at the foot of the bed, softly at first, then real urgent hunger took hold and her own needs united with his. She saw him reach for his wallet and shook her head.

'You don't need to. No danger of that.' And he turned back to her, sensing the sadness under the bravura.

Later he woke and turned his head on the pillow and saw that her eyes were open, staring at the ceiling, the soft light from the bedside lamp outlining her solemn profile. He put a hand out and touched her cheek.

'What is it?'

After a little silence, she said, 'I feel guilty. As if I've spoilt something lovely that you and Shona had.'

There was another silence—his, this time, and then he breathed deeply. 'The guilt isn't yours. It wouldn't have happened unless I had started it. Would it?'

'No. It might not have happened, but that doesn't mean I wouldn't have wanted it to happen. The thoughts are just as bad as the actions, aren't they?' She turned her head towards him and reached out her own hand to touch his face. He smiled at her.

'Don't feel guilty. Shona died almost two years ago. I shouldn't go on living a memory, however good it was. I have to remember—I do remember her—but I know I also have to move on, and she would have wanted me to. I know it's a horrible cliché, but it's true.' Easier said than done. Where did this weight of shame come from? Not

302

from Shona, nor his parents, but perhaps his upbringing. Perhaps the fact that Christopher and Seamus still missed their mother. There was guilt, exacerbated by Annie's desirability.

'Was it the first time since she died?' Annie was tentative.

'No. No, I'm afraid it wasn't. But it was the first time my—emotions—came into the equation. Before, it was just plain need. Lust. Requirement. Necessity.' He smiled a little ruefully, and propping himself up on an elbow pushed the covers down her body, trailing his fingers over the rounded hills and down the valleys. She closed her eyes tightly, fingers curling into fists as she tried to control her reaction.

'What about you?' he said softly.

She shook her head. 'Yes, the first time. Oddly enough, no one has even tried it on. Or perhaps it isn't odd. When it was all finishing, Justin said I was a cold fish.' She thought about it. 'But I hope that's not true. It was just that, at the end, I felt used. Of no use. As if my only reason for being his wife was to produce children, and because I couldn't, he didn't find me sexy any more. I wasn't desirable which I thought I had been, at first. Perhaps I never was.' She sounded sad. 'Anyway, there hasn't been anyone else. Till now.'

'Not a cold fish. Not at all. And I find you exceedingly sexy.' He moved his hands over her, slowly, deliberately, without the former urgency but intent on rousing her, and they made long, slow love into the early hours of the morning.

45

1st May 2012

'And I've got a surprise for you,' David said after he'd told Mhairi and his father about visiting Rhionna. He handed the packet to her. 'It's a present from Rhionna. I do hope it's a nice one.' His apprehension about their contents had kept him awake at nights. They might or might not contain proof that she and John had been lovers, but there was no certainty that she wouldn't just burn them.

Her head tilted in puzzled interest as she opened the envelope, the old glue cracking easily from the paper.

'Oh my!' Tipping out about ten or twelve smaller envelopes, he was relieved that a broad smile spread across her face. 'The last time I saw these was in 1945! Fancy Rhionna keeping them all these years.' She peeked in the envelopes, checking that the letters were still inside.

'How did you even know about Rhionna? How did you find her? I never thought I'd ever hear of her again!'

'Annie came across her name while she was researching John Elliott. In an old newspaper report.' Mhairi's eyes seemed uneasy as they flickered to David's. 'We tracked her down via old Mrs Reid's grandson who found her married name in those amazing ledgers, and then we found her marriage in the parish register and followed her through the voting registers. She married a ship's chandler from

Ullapool called Peter Fletcher, who's dead now, and she lives in the south of England surrounded by a vast family. She's got all her marbles and is very spry.'

His anxiety had lessened, but he hoped that she wouldn't be angry with Annie. 'Annie really didn't mean to rake up your past, but it seemed every time she looked for John Elliott, you came up, and then Rhionna. And Archie Mackinnon.'

There was a thoughtful silence, Mhairi's fingers tapping gently on the table until he spoke again.

'Rhionna MacRae was obviously a big part of your life in Aultbea, wasn't she?' He watched his father give in to the temptation of another slice of chocolate cake. 'Why did you lose touch?'

She screwed up her face. 'It's a long story. You've seen Rhionna, and you'll have heard most of it. I expect she was furious I never wrote, and I've felt bad about it ever since, but you can't change the past.'

David moved the cake plate away from Jem. 'She doesn't blame you and was tickled pink to hear you were well and had a family, though she was very sad about not knowing what happened to you. She told us what she knew from her perspective. About how John Elliott lost his fingers. About Archie. About your father.'

Mhairi heaved a sigh.

'Not much of the story left for me to tell, then. It was a foolish fear, but I was so terrified that my father might discover where I was that I never wrote or sent my address to anybody, not even Rhionna. Nobody knew. But I had to have a reference from Mrs Reid to get a job. I asked Mr Wenham—he was just plain Mister then, before the knighthood—to write from his office so that she couldn't tell anyone my address. At the time I was so angry at how everyone treated me and you—' she directed a fierce look at Jem '—I didn't want to have anything to do with them ever again. I was upset that Rhionna hadn't helped me when you were born, but that was unfair. She was in trouble herself with the elders and her parents. She couldn't help me. I had no idea what happened to her, or whether she was alive or dead. I might write. I might go and see her.' She fingered the envelopes. 'Fancy her keeping those letters all this time.'

'She said she sealed them up, so she wouldn't be tempted to read them.' David grinned. 'But she did say they were from—and to—John Elliott. Love letters, Gee Gee?'

'Hmph.' But her face softened. 'No. But after Archie died, I just didn't want the police reading them. I left a bunch of other ones for them to find, those ones I showed you and Annie. Nothing personal in those, and nothing that could have harmed him.'

'Why did he address them to himself and how did you know they were for you?' Jem was curious.

She chuckled and turned over the envelopes to show them a tiny M on the bottom right-hand corner. 'We did that so that no one would know he was writing to me. It was just a joke really. He mainly wrote news and general chat, but some of these were personal. When he was going through bad times. The police could have seen he was more of a friend than just a billeted officer, and when—if—he came back they might have questioned him. I didn't want that to happen, it would have looked bad for him, so I took the letters to Rhionna's house and hid them. As it happened, he didn't come back, so it wouldn't have mattered anyway.' She sighed and folded her hands in her lap. 'One of these he wrote on the train coming back after a disastrous leave in Portsmouth. Christmas 1942, I think. I could hardly read it, the train must have been lurching all over the place, and he scribbled it in his notebook and tore out the pages. He was terribly upset, poor man. He sent me a special present that Christmas.' She smiled. 'I still have it.' Shuffling the envelopes, she found what she was looking for. 'The letter he sent with it is here too. Oh! I could have slapped his wife for what she did to him!'

'What had happened?' David asked. He was sitting with his elbows on his knees, hands lightly locked together, no longer teasing.

She looked up at them, considering. 'Maybe it's time to tell the story, though I vowed never to tell anyone, ever.' She regarded Jem rather sadly. 'But even telling the story won't give you the answer you want.' She pursed her lips. 'My Lord, that Annie has a lot to answer for.'

An understatement, David thought. But without Annie, would Mhairi have gone to her grave with her story untold, and his father none the wiser about who his father was or might have been?

Jem said gently, 'David can set up the computer so that you could talk to Rhionna and see her at the same time. Would you like to do that sometime?'

She sat up straighter and looked alarmed. 'She'll give me an earful for never writing.'

David gave a crack of laughter. 'I don't think so, Granny. Mrs Fletcher is terrified you'll give her an earful for letting you down. Anyway, you can think about it.'

Mhairi took a breath, but Jem beat her to it. 'And don't even *think* about travelling to the south of England.'

She sighed in advance defeat, her fingers restless on the arm of her chair. 'Interfering pair! Going and finding her without telling me! And she's an interfering old woman!'

David said nothing and neither did Jem. She sniffed and fingered the envelopes on her table. Eventually, she raised her eyes to Jem and stared at him, her mouth alternately pursing and straightening.

At last, there was another 'Hmph!' and a long pause. 'Well, what do you want to know then?'

'Even if you can't tell me who my father was, tell me

what happened when your own father came home, and when and why and how you did a flit to Edinburgh. How you got employed by the Wenhams. How did you meet Walter? And how did you know that your father had had a stroke if nobody knew where you were?' He leant back with a sigh. 'And I think you kept John's violin and gave it to me when you came back to the croft. That was stealing, Mother!'

'I didn't steal it!' Mhairi was scandalised. 'Stealing means taking something which doesn't belong to you, and I didn't. His violin was in the house, where he had left it. I put it up in the rafters to keep it safe when my father came back, and that's where it stayed until he died.' She huffed in phoney irritation. 'How could I have sent it back to his wife? I hadn't any idea where she was.'

'You should have given it back to the navy in 1945.' Jem sounded uncomfortable. 'They would have made sure his wife got it. I feel really awkward about having it, now I know it was his, and that Elspeth was upset that she never got it back.'

'John always said Elspeth was totally uninterested in music, so what would have been the point?'

Jem sighed, and David shifted in his chair. She was defensive and combative. Not a good combination.

'What's Charlotte going to think? She might be really upset that you held on to her father's violin.'

'You made better use of it than Elspeth would have. She would probably have sold it.' she said, aggression giving way to gloom.

'Mother. That's a terrible thing to say.' Jem was repressing a smile. 'The violin belongs to Charlotte.'

'You can't give it back to her. What will you play?' Her voice was sad.

'I can't not,' he said, and David ached for him.

Mhairi sighed. Then she carefully shuffled the letters into a neat pile and seemed to come to a decision.

'I knew about my father's stroke from Mrs Reid. She was still alive and wrote to me at Sir George Wenham's office. He sent on her letter.' She smiled a little at Jem's surprise. 'I always kept in touch with the Wenhams. They had been very good to me, and I loved Emily. Walter had died the year before and you had flown the nest. There was nothing to keep me in Edinburgh. Mrs Reid was a good woman, and Sir George was a good man. I've been blessed by more good folk than bad in my lifetime.'

She sat up straighter. 'It's that Annie who set all this off, then David, and now Rhionna. A great deal of interference and poking noses where noses shouldn't go. I can't tell you what you've always wanted to know, Jem. I know what I believe is true and want to be true. But I don't know for sure whether it is true.' Her shoulders sagged a little. 'A man died, for sure. I'm really not certain what I should tell you. Heaven alone knows where it might land me.'

David couldn't help but grin. 'They won't lock you up at your age, but I'm not at all sure I want to hear any confessions of murder.'

Mhairi put her head on one side and sighed. 'No murder. But there was self-defence. I think they call it manslaughter these days.' She clasped her hands together on the table. 'Where do you want me to start?'

46

24th January 1945

His hands were all over her, urgent, predatory, vicious. He had managed to unclip her bra and was pressing her against the scullery door, trying to control her thrashing arms and twisting body. Eventually he managed to grab her wrists and drag her through to the kitchen. The terror sucked at her throat as she desperately braced her foot against a table leg. He was taller and heavier, and with a vicious jerk crashed her against the wall. His knee jabbed between her thighs until he forced them apart. Unable even to scream, the horror and inevitability were as heart-stopping as the punch of a cold wave. Ducking her head, she pulled his arm towards her and sank her teeth into his thumb. If she bit it off, he would have to let go. As his blood ran warm and salty on to her tongue, he screamed and, letting go of her other wrist, hit her hard across her nose with the side of his hand. Mhairi heard a crunch inside her head and her sight fogged with the excruciating pain. He hit her again and the agony slid into oblivion.

When awareness slowly returned, she found she was lying on her back across the kitchen table, her sweaters and bra around her neck, and her skirt around her waist. She hurt everywhere, and every second it increased. A noise gave her impetus to turn her head painfully towards it, and through a fast closing eye she saw Archie leaning over the deep sink, the single tap running icy water over his bitten hand. His trousers were obviously unbuttoned, the waistband sagging at his buttocks. She could see his profile, his face tight with his own pain, his eyes clenched shut. A deep ache throbbed in her pelvis and pounded in her head. She closed out the horror of what had happened before it could overwhelm her.

If his eyes were shut, he couldn't see her, and the noise of the storm and the running tap might be loud enough to prevent him from hearing her move. Adrenaline coursed through her, obscuring the debilitating pain in her body. Sliding her feet to the ground, vaguely surprised and relieved that her shoes were still on, her skirt slipped back to cover her, and she swept her bra and sweaters down. Dimly she wondered where her panties were. Two steps to the open scullery door and she cursed herself for touching the latch which made its customary loud clack, a sound which cut through wind and water and the crashing of her heart. She sensed him turning from the sink and heard his roar of anger as he came after her. Banging the door shut on him, her hands fumbled for the only weapon she could think of.

The long chain hung on the coat hooks, used for myriad purposes around the croft, from holding gates to lugging sheep. As he hurled the door wide, she glimpsed his fury and knew, terrified, that if he could rape her, he could kill her. Was she going to survive this?

The chain struck him across the face, bringing bright and immediate blood from the corner of one eye, across his nose to the side of his mouth. He screamed, grabbing at the chain as he lost his balance and staggered back, jerking it out of her hands.

Hauling the door open, she ran into the blackness of the storm. She slammed the door shut behind her—a few seconds more to hold him up. The path was a mixture of slick ice and sharp wind-drift snow, but she knew its cobbles and ruts better than Archie. She ran for his van, knowing there was nowhere on the croft that she could find safety; nowhere he wouldn't find her. Faintly through the racket of the wind, she heard the backdoor crash open and her mind saw him diving through the air like a German bomber, catching her up in one swoop. The van loomed out of the driving snow and against the strength of the gale she managed to wrench open the driver's door and hurl herself in, feeling frantically for the key in the ignition. Her brain refused to believe it wasn't there, and she was still fumbling for it when he pulled open the door, buttoning his trousers with one hand. Even in the dark, she could sense his fury.

'I'll kill you, you stupid little bitch. I'll make you watch what I do to your belly. I'll make it slow and painful and when I've finished with you, you'll wish you'd never been born, you'll wish you were dead long before I'll let you die. Did you think I'd be so stupid as to leave the keys? I never do that, Mhairi. Safe in my pocket they are. And you, out you come, sweetheart, you're going to give Archie a really good time before I finish with you, aren't you now?'

His hand came towards her. In terror, she catapulted back over the gear lever to the far side of the cab. Her fingers found the door handle and she threw herself out into the snow, the wind crashing the van door shut, and she ran like a hare back to the cottage. Once in, she could bolt the door on him, find a weapon.

He caught her as she reached the gate, a hard shove which sent her crashing down on the cobbles beneath the skim of snow, and then he knelt above her, flipped her over and slapped her face viciously.

'Get up, bitch.' He hit her again as he got to his feet, jerking her violently after him.

But under the snow, her fingers had closed on the stone jammed under the gate. She had seen it in her mind's eye as she fell, the stone that tapered from a heavy round end to a thin edge, once sharp but now blunted by the years and general wear and tear. It had been used to wedge the gate open for all of Mhairi's childhood, and for a generation before that, the thin edge jammed under the frame, easily kicked free if the gate needed to be shut, but usually just propping it open.

As he dragged her roughly to her feet, the instant of leverage came sweetly—her right hand swung at his head, her left hand using his grip on her to give momentum to the blow. Although he saw it coming in the last fraction of a second and jerked his head up, it was too late.

47

25th January 1945

It felt and sounded like a spoon cracking through a soft-boiled egg.

Archie made a noise like a steam whistle, his hand fell away as his knees buckled and he crumpled forwards, disintegrating like wet bread. Mhairi rocked on her feet, her vision blurred, looking down a black tunnel to the blackness of the snow-wet path, and the blacker form of the man face down at her feet. She was outside herself, disconnected from those last seconds, disconnected from all the past as if it had happened to a complete stranger. Was he dead? What would she do if he was? And what would she do if he wasn't?

As she sank down into the icy snow beside him, she expected him to turn his head to her, to grab her throat. Swallowing the terror, she held the stone ready again and put a tentative finger below his ear There was no pulse that she could feel except her own, hammering to the exclusion of all else, and pushing the panic back down, she found his wrist and again tried to find the pulse that wasn't there. *I can't have killed him, I can't have killed a man! What am I going to do? How do I move him, and where to? They'll hang me for murder.*

The night swung and shrieked blackly in the wind and

the snow, and now there were needles in the wind and she could hear it rattling on the house windows, black too, outside the blackout curtains. *I will not hang. I will not let them. I will hide him, hide the van, clean the stone, wash away the blood. I will not hang.*

Pushing herself painfully upright, she stumbled to the shed which, thankfully, he had not locked, and despite the pitch darkness, laid her hand immediately on an empty sack and the tarpaulin. Laying it beside Archie, the wind lifting and snapping at the heavy canvas, she knelt on it and put the sack round his head. She tugged and rolled his body on to the tarpaulin and pulled him towards the shed, wincing at a shafting pain in her side which only now was she fully aware of. The snow was glassy with ice and the heavy load slid fairly easily, but when she got to the shed door, it took all her strength to get him over the wooden threshold and inside. Lighting the lamp, she searched his pockets and removed the keys, at every moment expecting him to turn over and grab her—a dead man rising—as the horror threatened to swamp her again. The sacking had loosened, and his head rolled towards her, the eyes open, staring at her. She screamed and jerked back, her ribs spasming, but the eyes did not follow. They stared at the place she had been. Her heart thundered and her vision blurred again. *I will do it. I will succeed. I will not panic. I will not hang.* She pulled the sacking back across his face and dragged the tarpaulin alongside the wall. Tilting a loose bale of hay and a hayfork over it, and placing a bucket in front she stood back, the lamp held high. It was just a pile of tarpaulin covered in hay. Someone would have to do a physical search to find him, and no one was going to come looking on a night like this, even if he'd told anyone where he was going. She extinguished the lamp and left it and the matches on a fish crate. *I will not hang for Archie Mackinnon.*

She returned through the gale to the cottage, her mind like a trapped rabbit zigzagging over the possibilities. If she got him into the van, could she then drive it to the cliffs and somehow run it, with Archie, over the edge? Every part of this idea was immediately fraught with difficulty—how would she lift him in, and how would she move him across into the driver's seat? A dead body in the passenger seat could not be an accident. Even more difficult was the fact that the road did not run past the cliffs, and any vehicle would be seen and noted by the military police at the checkpoints. Her eyes squeezed shut in terror at the thought of being stopped whilst driving a van containing a dead body. Nevertheless, the van would have to be moved. She couldn't have anyone seeing the van here. The van and its contents must be found somewhere else, not on her property.

Inside the cottage, she bolted the door, and in the comparative warmth and shelter, she reacted in shock to her frozen body, and what had happened in the eternity of short minutes since she had left the scullery. Sliding down the wall, she crouched, shuddering with horror and pain, on the cold stone, dark with melting snow and drops of a darker, more viscous fluid. Archie's blood. Or hers. Her mind tripped over her distracted thoughts; what he had done to her, the pain in every part of her body, and so many things to do. The van, his body, the blood on the floor, on the chain, on her clothes and hands and on the path and in the shed. She forced herself up, threw the chain into the sink and scrubbed the floor and the stone clean of blood, finally rinsing the cloth and chain by tipping some fresh water into the scullery sink.

The necessity of cleaning some of the blood off her own face and clothes, painfully pushing a bit of rag up the leaking nostril, washing herself and putting on clean underwear, thick socks, warm clothes and her boots, enabled her to push back the horror again and to think more calmly. Taking her torch, she battled into the shrieking horizontal gale, past the shed to the van. Already the snow had covered the windscreen and she brushed enough off to enable her to see out. Archie's dark trilby was on the dashboard and though she guessed that even if someone saw the van, they wouldn't be able to see who was driving, nevertheless she pushed her coat hood back and put the hat on. She shuddered. It was as if Archie was touching her again.

Blindly she drove a mile or so south, peering through the struggling windscreen wipers, and parked facing the sea above an expanse of shingle. The tide had turned, and her brain automatically calculated that high tide would be around four a.m. If she couldn't hide or get rid of the van, then she would leave it in full sight and hope that no one would connect it with her or Inveruidh. She prayed that the snow would quickly cover the tyre marks and her returning footsteps. Already they were just blurred indentations.

Taking a box from the back, she locked the van. Leaving the box above the high tide mark and throwing his hat into the sea, she returned along the shingle, buffeted by the driving snow and salt spray. When she reached the Inverasdale cottages, the long crofting plots were white and blank through the driving gusts. There were no horses or ponies in this community and the problem of moving Archie's body gnawed at her mind as the cold gnawed at her body, and pain gnawed inside her, and in ribs and back and face, stiffening muscles and movement.

Inveruidh was as dark and lifeless as she had left it, and her nerves shrieked as she passed the shed. Was he really dead? Would he loom out of the blackness and attack her again, or crawl along the path and push the back door open? Perhaps he had already. She remembered his sightless, staring eyes, but was he truly dead? Despite the cold, she found herself sweating.

In the scullery, she pulled her scrambled thoughts together as her clothes dripped melting snow on to the floor. At last, she picked up the icy wet chain, a strong sheep crook, her father's compass and the oil lamp, and taking her courage inside in a great deep breath, opened the door on the storm once more.

On the moorland above Firemore, perhaps half an hour from Inverasdale, there was rumoured to be an Indian army camp. Few people knew of it, and even fewer went there; only the sheep grazed peacefully and without astonishment around it. She had often thought that the Indian soldiers must be the most miserable men on earth, far from their hot and humid jungles, lost and lonely in the frozen wastes of peat hags, heather and inhospitable rocks. She had no idea why they were there or what they did, but rumour had it that they carried their supplies on mules, and a mule seemed like the most desirable form of transport tonight. Mhairi had never seen a mule, let alone handled one, and their existence seemed tenuous, except that on occasions she had found tiny horseshoes, made for fairy horses, on the sheep tracks.

Tonight, she needed a mule, and therefore she had to fetch one. Grasping the crook, she staggered up the hill behind the crofts, avoiding the coast road with its checkpoints and sentries. Her ribs ached as she waded through wet slushy snow accumulating in the pools under the peat cuts, her boots crunching through soft ice which she could feel but not hear. An innate sense of direction born of a life in the hills guided her, but she could see nothing. Not the moorland about her, nor the sea somewhere to her right, nor the sky above. Everything was filled with roaring wind and the snow drove deep into her face, like flung gravel, anaesthetising the pain and freezing the seeping blood from her nose, and she knew that if she could see nothing, no one could see her either. Every few minutes she dug the compass out of her pocket and shone the torch clumsily on the swinging indicator.

Gradually, after what seemed an eternity of struggling up and over and down, her breath whistling from the pain in her side, she registered a change in the atmosphere. The wind and snow were still as strong, the darkness as all-consuming, the noise as loud, but it was different. She stopped. Something faint, familiar, both threatening and friendly. Peat. Peat smoke.

It took her another half hour to find the camp. She had gone far beyond it, and the elusive smell eddied in the fierce air like the bog spirits of Sunderland, which, so it was said, lure the traveller into dangerous paths and eventually drown them.

It was after two in the morning, in one of the worst gales of the winter, and the ugly camp buildings were dark and lifeless. The tang of dung in the wind guided her to open walled sheds where she found six fairy horses, rumps to the gale. Their living presence was an astonishing positive fact in the eternity of terror since Archie came. She stared at them, almost not believing the reality. There was no one to see or hear her as she fumbled with stiff resisting fingers to release one of them and led it, protesting, into the snow and up and over the ridge. Exhaustion had taken over from the adrenaline rush of actually finding the camp, and the desire to crouch in the shelter of the wooden stabling had almost overwhelmed her. But Archie's body lay in her shed, and there might be a search for him tomorrow. She gripped the halter rope fiercely and tugged the reluctant animal behind her, climbing again to put the ridge between herself and the road, slipping and sliding on the icy rocks, the heather stems clutching at her legs and her dragging feet sinking without warning into the snow accumulating in the holes and hollows of the peat bogs. She would have to do this same journey again, and further, with Archie's body on the mule. The very thought of it made her weep with exhaustion and fear.

Suddenly a dog let fly with a fury of barking just a few feet to her left. Her heart hammered in fright and shock and the mule jibbed sharply, pulling her off her feet and sending a savage spear of pain through her ribs. Because of the rock face above, she had been forced too close to the outer boundary of the crofts. The barking went on, furious and vicious, and it penetrated through the sounds of the storm like a needle through canvas. Pulling herself up, she dragged the frightened mule away from the noise and into the temporary shelter of a peat hag filled with water and slush, praying that the dog would quieten. It continued to bark, urgent, insistent, penetrating, as she crouched beside the restless mule, unable to tether it to anything solid, and guessing that it would make a break for home should she lose her hold on the rope.

A man's voice, thinned by the wind, calling and questioning, brought a wave of panic. If he came up his field and let the dog through by the hill gate, she would be discovered, and more seriously, so would the mule. She cast about in the darkness for something, anything, a post, a peat spade, a stone, to tether the mule to, but found nothing except at last a broken slab of wet peat lying in the heather. The voice was coming nearer. She found more peats and desperately piled them up over the rope end, tying it round them. A frail and uncertain weight which would disintegrate if the animal decided to pull away. She left it and slithered back, pain smothered by the urgency, down towards the croft and the still hysterical dog, and the crofter himself. Through the gusting snow, she called out that there was nothing for him or the dog to worry about, she was looking for her sheep and had strayed too close to the crofts. He came up to the fence and shone a torch in her face.

'Mhairi Mackenzie, is it! Jesus, girl, what have you done to your face?' he said, horrified. "Tis no night to clamber aboot the moor! Are you mad, girl, to go a-looking for white sheep on a white hill in the black of night and getting folks out their bed for no reason?' He sounded both astonished and angry. 'Get ye back home and leave honest folk in peace.' He began to turn away, growling at the dog who slunk to his heel. 'And get some sheep fat on those bruises. What the devil happened?'

'I fell on the ice. I'm sorry, Mr Mackinley. It seemed such a storm, I thought I should try to gather them down to the croft. I found some and was worried for the others. Father would have known what to do.'

'Ach—leave the sheep, they've more sense than you. Get you home, Mhairi. You'd best come over the fence and go down to the road. Though its longer, you'll not get lost.'

I won't get lost,' she said, shouting into the wind. 'I've got a compass and a torch too. And I might come upon them on my way.'

She sensed rather than saw his shrug as he made his way back towards his croft. After a moment she turned and started back towards where she had left the mule. Her still thumping heart sank as she saw no sign of it in the peat hag. Then she saw a movement through the snow flurries, and she scrambled after it, finding the rope still dragging the remainder of the peats. She put both arms round the neck of the startled animal and hugged it, her sob of relief loud in her ears.

The journey back seemed shorter and less dreadful than the outgoing one although her legs trembled with tiredness and the fright of encountering Mr Mackinley. At last the cottage loomed out of the snow-filled air and she led the animal into the shed where Archie's body still lay in its hay-covered tarpaulin. It seemed extraordinary that it nosed into the hay seemingly unconcerned by any smell of blood or death, whereas her throat was thick with tension and fear. She needed sustenance. In the house, she took a slug of whisky from a bottle provided by Archie and forced down cold haggis and a slab of Orkney cheese. The idea of getting his body loaded and going out again seemed unthinkable and impossible. *I will not hang for him.*

After the painful process of hoisting Archie on to the mule, via the simple pulley she rigged over the beam, she corded on a thick layer of hay and secured the tarpaulin on top of all. If she were seen, she could confess to borrowing the mule and maybe the story of looking for the sheep and taking them hay might just hold up. The mule was criss-crossed in a web of ropes as she could not afford to have Archie slide to the ground. She could never get him loaded again.

Again, she took to the hill, pulling the animal after her up the steepest slopes. It was sure-footed and seemed not to mind her tugging at the head collar, nor the occasional arm she flung round its neck to keep her balance as she slipped in the now deep snow. She felt more confident of her direction, though she checked the compass at regular intervals, and the horror of all that had happened had receded somewhat in the light of what she had determined to do. An hour's walking had brought her to the point of frozen apathy; if she failed, she failed. More than once she nearly gave in to the temptation to let Archie slide into the oblivion of a loch, but the waters were shallow and eventually his body with its broken skull would be found. What would her boyfriend Archie Mackinnon have been doing wandering the moor in weather like this? And how could he have had a wound like that in this soft peat? No, the sea was her destination, and she prayed it would be her friend and not throw his body back. There would be questions now, but hopefully none later, and no evidence.

After an eternity, she heard the sea. A deep roaring

growl, then a sucking breath, then the growl again. No break in its thumping rhythm, only the wind screaming and sweeping and buffeting in from the icy water. The snow swirled in every direction as the updraft from the cliffs caught the flakes into a madness of chaos, mixed with salt spray which battered at her as she drew closer to the edge.

She had no idea where she was on the cliffs, or whether they sank into deep water or down on to boulders which would hold his body. She did know that there were only rocks here, and therefore his smashed skull would tell of nothing but a fall, should he fail to reach the water. Should that happen, she prayed that she was close enough to the military base at Cove to give the impression that he was meeting someone and perhaps had slipped and fallen—or was pushed. Archie's reputation should lend credence to the theory. The snatching gale made looking over the cliff a dangerous and terrifying experience, and she could see nothing beyond a few feet, blinded by spray and snow and wind.

Wriggling back from the edge, every breath like a knife in her ribs, she tethered the mule by rolling a large boulder on to the rope end, She fumbled to undo the knots, tightened by the strain of the journey, the man's body unbalanced, her eyes blinded by her whipping hair and the ice in the wind. At last it slid to the ground, hay wisps sucked into the flailing air and the tarpaulin flogging in the gale. It would have been ripped away by the wind if his body had not been weighting it. On her knees, she began to push the tarpaulin and its burden over the icy ground towards the cliff edge. When at last he slid free of it, into the black darkness, the tarpaulin snapped back with a crack, enveloping her in its wet and clammy embrace. She lay in it for long minutes, weeping with exhaustion and pain and horror and relief and a dreadful triumph. *I will not hang.*

48

May 2012

'So you see,' Mhairi said, 'it was kill or be killed. I didn't mean to kill him. I meant to stop him killing me.'

Jem and David stared at her.

'And what are you going to do about it?' she said belligerently. 'Hand me in?' She stared back at them. 'You think I should confess to the police? They would have hung me then, but would they now?'

Jem stiffened further than he had already. 'Hand you in?' he said incredulously. 'Don't be mad! You're ninety!' He swallowed. 'It's the most ghastly story outside a crime thriller and you've never breathed a word about what you went through.' He heard David inhaling a long, appalled breath. 'Did you think that I—that we—would blame you for any of that? For what he put you through?' He ran his fingers through his thinning thatch. 'And you've lived with that horror all your life, and never told a soul. Anyone else would have gone mad.' How could she have survived those experiences and still have been the excellent mother and governess and housekeeper and wife that she had been? He got up and put his arms round her. 'I always did think you were astonishing, but I am speechless with—' he couldn't think of the right word.

'Admiration.' David said. 'Granny, you needn't worry

about telling anybody, least of all the police. It was 1945 for heaven's sake. It was self-defence, and surely there must be a Statute of Limitations or something. And you didn't even intend to kill him. I'd have killed him on your behalf, the evil bastard.' He sounded furious.

Jem would have rebuked David's curse had he not thought the same. Nevertheless, he was concerned. Should they tell anyone that the mystery of a seventy-year-old killing had been solved? Might the police want to interview her? He didn't think there was a Statute of Limitations in the UK. Should they just keep quiet?

Mhairi looked at him gravely and he knew that she knew exactly what he was thinking.

He gave her a weak smile. 'We'll wait till you've fallen off your perch and then tell them. They hate having unsolved cases on their books.'

And his still-unsolved case was the identity of his father.

49

July 2012

'They've come,' David said, and Annie could hear the satisfaction in his voice. As always, her spirits lifted with the choking pleasure of speaking to him, and she knew that her excitement was not about the DNA results at all, but about David.

Charlotte had been uncertain about giving a DNA sample to help prove that her father was also Jem's father, but the reflection that she might have a brother and an extended family as a result proved irresistible. Annie did wonder how Mhairi and Jem felt about it—after all, it might prove the opposite. It seemed she was about to find out.

'John Elliott is the genetic link and they are both delighted and relieved. Granny is like the cat with the cream, and Dad is quietly tickled pink. He said he hadn't realised how much he needed to know, and the fact that his dad was John Elliott and not Archie Mackinnon is clearly more important than any of us realised. I'm pretty pleased, too, I have to say.' He hesitated, sounding a little apprehensive. 'I do hope Charlotte is OK with the results. Her initial idea about finding out about her father must have gone way beyond her expectations. To discover an illegitimate brother and a large extended family must be quite a mouthful to swallow.'

'I'll let you know her reaction, but I think it will be positive,' Annie said, sounding more certain than she felt. She hadn't assumed this would be the outcome and part of her wondered if Charlotte *would* react positively. 'Are you going to send the results, or can you bring them?' She heard him sigh and wondered whether it was a sigh of regret or a sigh of annoyance that she was pressurising him. Probably the latter, she thought. 'If you can send them, or copies, that would be great,' she said hastily. 'Mum is in Manchester now at the Bridgewater Hall, and then goes to some piano competition, so she won't be back for a while.'

'Competition? Surely not competing?'

'Judging, I think. Anyway, concentrating on music, not DNA results.' Even to her own ears, she sounded overly brisk. Trying to establish a relationship with someone who lived six hundred miles away was not easy, and she was not sure that he wanted it as much as she did.

'Of course I'll send them! I'd come, but I just can't leave the boys in the holidays.' There was regret in his voice. 'But maybe the three of you could come north for a joint family meeting? It is quite a momentous discovery, isn't it?'

Annie gulped. 'I doubt Mum will have time between concerts until winter, but I'll talk to her.' Joint family! This was not the outcome they had expected when Annie set off to research John Elliott. She was filled with trepidation and wished her father was there to give her advice.

But to her surprise, Charlotte was keen to visit, even though Will could not go with them. They would go to Wester Ross to meet the brother and extended family for a week in August—all that could be managed between concerts. Jem and Fiona had asked them to stay in their house, but both Charlotte and Annie had felt it was too soon to be so intimate, and Inveruidh had been reserved for them. Plane tickets and hire car were booked, the school grand piano available for practice sessions.

Charlotte's excitement about finding a brother and meeting her new relations began to alternate with apprehension.

'How will I cope with all these people calling themselves family?' she wailed to Annie. 'How do I greet my father's mistress? A peck on the cheek? A formal handshake? This Jem, he's virtually my twin! We might loathe each other! Oh, Will! I do wish you could come!' Will, adjusting his white tie in the drawing room mirror for a city dinner, grinned at Annie in amused sympathy.

'Sorry, my darling. Next time.' He touched Charlotte's face gently. 'I promise—given enough notice.'

'Mum, you cope with Japanese and Americans, Eskimos and Africans. I expect you'll cope with the Scots.' Annie giggled and Charlotte looked at her sideways.

'What on earth is the matter with you? You're like a champagne bottle about to explode.'

'The excitement of genealogy? Having a newly discovered family is extraordinary, isn't it? We're not alone any more.'

Charlotte sat down on a stool with a bump. 'Yes, extraordinary. Scary but thrilling.' Her expressive mouth pursed as she contemplated Annie. 'Does it really account for an exploding champagne bottle?' Annie blushed.

The desire to see David again writhed in the pit of her stomach; each conversation, every WhatsApp chat, text and email made her breath shorten and her cheeks hot. She berated herself for feeling like a teenager and behaving like an idiot. She was a moth drawn to the flame, an iron filing to his magnet. She knew it was imprudent to be so attracted to him, because she had no idea if he felt as strongly as she did, but she simply could not help it. She didn't remember feeling like this when Justin was courting her.

It was raining on arrival at Inverness airport, but after having collected their car and the pre-ordered supplies at Tesco, they drove west, and the skies cleared into a spectacular evening. The lochs reflected mirror images of the mountains in placid blue waters and Charlotte was enchanted. She had visited Edinburgh and Pitlochry for concerts in the past but had never penetrated further and now she exclaimed with wonder and got Annie to stop frequently to take photographs until driven back into the car by the midges.

'This is where I left my bag. On the potato sack,' Annie said with a twisted grin as they came down into Kinlochewe. 'It was snowing, and the fuel tank was empty, and the petrol station was shut.'

'So horrible for you!' Charlotte exclaimed. The story had already taken on legendary qualities. 'It must all have been perfectly ghastly and so frightening. Thank goodness I didn't know at the time.'

'I was really scared.' Annie shuddered at the memory. 'But I suppose it was one of those experiences that makes the rest of life seem a complete doddle. And it taught me a lesson about checking hire cars for fuel before driving off! What was so extraordinary was that it was David who was working at Inveruidh and that the Mackenzies turned out to be the connection between us all.' She glanced sideways at her mother. 'Mum, are you really OK with this? I feel I've bounced you into these relationships without asking you. I realise that my feelings about what your father did or didn't do are not the same thing as your feelings about what your father did—or didn't. It's much nearer the bone for you.'

Charlotte sighed. 'Well, I feel sad for my mother, who I think suspected that he had a—that there was someone else. But she should have left Portsmouth, with or without her parents. She made it impossible for John to come home and she must have blamed herself for my brothers' deaths, and her mother's. What can she have felt when she found that little scribble of Peter's in the rubble of her house?' Charlotte's voice cracked. 'What a weight of guilt to carry. I'm not surprised she never got over it.'

Annie said nothing in the silence.

'I just don't know what to think about Mhairi,' Charlotte said eventually. 'A bit of me resents her—and a bit of me is grateful. I suppose she looked after him and comforted him. I suppose she made him happy during those awful months while they prepared to go to Russia and when they came back, and I'm glad for that.' She hesitated and then asked, 'You liked her, didn't you?'

'Yes. I think I do like her. She's a tough cookie and I certainly respect her, especially after hearing everything that happened after your father was killed. What horrible secrets she kept hidden all her life.' Not for the first time, she visualised that once-bloodied wedge of a stone under the gate at Inveruidh. 'I really hope she feels better now she has revealed them.'

Annie swatted at a midge that had invaded the car and hoped that David had wanted them to come for reasons other than Jem and Charlotte meeting each other. On the one occasion he had managed to come to London, his lovemaking was so perfect. Gentle as well as fierce, considerate as well as demanding. But although he never said anything, she suspected that Shona was still on his mind and on his conscience.

Their communications after the visit to Rhionna had been so comfortable, so easy. The little jokes, the one-word messages, the envelopes of photocopied papers and photos from Mhairi's little suitcase with Post-It notes in his precise, meticulous writing. Most of those exchanges hadn't been about John Elliott or Mhairi Mackenzie at all, but about art exhibitions, concerts, descriptions of hilarious recording sessions, and from him Christopher's bagpipe lessons, Seamus's front tooth knocked sideways by a football and the dash to an Invernessian orthodontist.

She opened her emails avidly, disappointed if there was nothing from him. Sometimes she just burst into giggles of happiness at the thought of him, and sometimes she remembered his love for Shona and the boys and cried into her pillow because he seemed so out of reach; mentally, emotionally and physically. Each contact had increased her passion—she no longer termed it attraction or friendship or affection— and she admitted to herself that she had fallen in love with him. Now she was going to see him again, on his home ground, and sometimes that thought made her nervous enough to feel sick. Would they be able to be together, alone? Would the presence of the boys and his home environment prevent any privacy between them? Was he really still mourning Shona? Had the few nights they had been together meant anything deeper than just enjoyment to him? Neither of them had broached the subject of anything more permanent.

This time there had been no keys in the post. On arrival at the cottage, in broad daylight, although it was nearly nine o'clock, with a blessed brisk wind to disperse the midges, there was David, in jeans and short-sleeved shirt, and the boys, as expected. Annie's chest cramped at the sight of him and she couldn't help an enormous smile spreading across her face. He opened the car door for Charlotte and helped her out, before putting his hands on her shoulders and kissing her on both cheeks.

'It's allowed, don't you think?' he said. 'Welcome to Inveruidh.'

He kissed Annie, too, also on her cheeks, but his hands were warm and enclosing, thumbs seeking out the hollows above her breastbone. She could feel her nipples harden and closed her eyes in brief ecstasy, opening them to see his grey ones crinkling up with his smile.

He and the boys had carried their cases upstairs, and the

bags of provisions to the kitchen. The boys enthusiastically showed them all over the cottage, assuming Annie had forgotten where the bedrooms were, or how to connect to the Wi-Fi.

'Expecting snow?' he said as he put coats and boots to the boot room. 'You're going to need sun cream and swimsuits first.'

'We've brought them too,' Annie said. 'I remembered your dire warnings about how quickly the weather changes.' She grinned at him, recalling the blizzard in January.

* * *

While Annie unpacked their supplies in the kitchen, helped by the boys, David poured Charlotte a glass of wine and tentatively began exploring their new relationship.

'How do you feel about meeting Mhairi?' he asked. 'I hope it's not too upsetting for you.'

Charlotte looked thoughtful. 'I think it may be more upsetting for her, don't you think? I really don't want to distress her, but I would love to hear what sort of person John was. My mother hardly spoke about him. It was as if she cut herself off from everything that happened before or during the war. I always found it puzzling, but perhaps that's what happens with depression. Your grandmother had no obligation to share those personal letters with me, but they were so revealing, weren't they, those two from Christmas 1942? I could hardly believe what my mother did—or rather, what she didn't do. Do you think Mhairi wanted John's point of view to be heard by me?'

'By us all, perhaps. Yes, I think she assumed you would only have heard Elspeth's side of the story.'

Charlotte's face folded into sadness. 'Whereas in truth, there was no story told to me at all. My poor father, it must have been agonising for him. And for Mhairi, if they were lovers then.'

David was startled that she could voice the possibility. What a surprisingly unjudgemental woman she was.

'I think she'll tell you lots about him. Since we got Rhionna and her talking—did Annie tell you about the video calls?' Charlotte nodded, smiling. 'She's told my father much about the past, about the war, and John staying here at the croft, and great-grandfather Mackenzie's return, and her flit to Edinburgh. Things none of us knew till now. It's been like taking the cork out of a soda bottle.'

'Is it a happy fizz?' Charlotte asked thoughtfully. 'I mean sometimes everything pours out because it's been bottled up for so long, and it can be bitter rather than happy.'

That was quite insightful for an unknown aunt. 'I don't know that it was a happy fizz, but I think it was a relief. Rhionna is quite bracing and I think told her to get a life!' He grinned. 'You'll have to ask my—ask your brother.'

He heard the sudden intake of breath. 'I'm sorry. I shouldn't have said that.' His fingers tensed with embarrassment.

'No! No! Don't be sorry! It's just that—it's still coming home to me that I do have a brother, and I've never had one before. It's a peculiar feeling, having been an only child, to have a brother and a family!' Charlotte sounded newly astonished, although he knew from Annie that she had had this reaction several times before.

The boys joined them noisily, followed by Annie, carrying a depleted wine glass.

'They've got a ready-made fish pie!' Christopher exclaimed to his father with a hoot of laughter.

Annie blushed. 'You must have had the occasional ready meal, Christopher! I simply don't believe your father cooks everything from scratch!'

'Granny does,' Seamus said. 'We cook, too, don't we, Dad?'

'We live exclusively on millionaire shortbread, flapjacks and lemon drizzle cake,' said their father, 'and we are now going home, leaving Annie and—' he hesitated '—Lady Meredith not to Mr Tesco's fish pie, but to Granny's lasagne and a good night's sleep.'

'David,' Charlotte said firmly. 'I am Charlotte. To you, to the boys and to the rest of the family. Is that clear? I think I'm other things, too, but definitely not Lady Meredith.'

He had needed the permission for informality and was relieved that she had given it.

'OK. Thank you.' He kissed her cheek. 'We'll see you tomorrow about ten? For a family gathering. My grandmother is thoroughly nervous, but Dad can't wait to meet his big sister.' He laughed at Charlotte's apprehensive face. 'It'll be fine. Really. Later on, we can go to the school to check on the piano and you can have a practice session if you want. Be prepared for much cake.'

'Coffee and cake,' Charlotte said. 'Annie told me that it is an important part of life here.'

'Indeed it is,' he said, and Annie could sense his relief that she could joke when relationships hung in the balance. 'Coffee and cake. What would we do without it?' He rounded up the boys and gave Annie a parting wink, which made her stomach turn over with conspiratorial happiness.

* * *

David felt restless and unsettled as he drove back down the loch. Annie had stirred his senses again, his desire for her melting Shona's image in his mind. She was becoming indistinct, like a breath of wind on still water; he could hear the words she used to say, but not the intonation. He was losing her, as a lover, a wife, a mother. Like a dream, the harder he tried to hold her image, hear her voice, the more she blurred into non-memory. Sometimes at night, he laid the tips of his own fingers on his nose, letting them slide, feather light, from between the eyes to the tip. Shona would do that as he lay, eyes shut after the morning alarm had gone off. Her gentle awakening. Even that could not always evoke her, and instead Annie's face would drift on to the retina of remembrance. It was possible this melting away of Shona was happening to the boys, too, but he could not find the courage or even the sense of rightness to talk to either of them about it, fearful that he might make wrong and harmful inroads into their memories.

Sometimes he pulled out one of the photograph albums which she had so carefully made and sat at the kitchen table with the boys. They talked about the particular holiday or occasion, visually buttressing her memory. Each picture was meticulously captioned with names and ages and dates, the clear rounded lettering so indicative of her uncomplicated and open personality. For David, this was like picking scabs off half-healed wounds: painful but ir-resistible, but he could seldom see disturbance in the boys.

Other unwanted memories hovered, midges in his mind that he tried to bat away: the unspoken sympathy of his siblings, Seamus's cry of anger when he realised she was no longer there, Christopher's frozen silence, Annie Devereux's shocked and frightened face in the light of her headlights as he knocked her to the ground. Her tense misery in the kitchen at Inveruidh, the feel of her body against his as he comforted her. Their weekend in the New Forest. Skin on skin. His own desire.

Although their friendship had deepened, he had seen Annie only once since May. He sensed her sadness—hurt was too strong a concept— that he didn't take their re-lationship deeper, but he still experienced shame about allowing another woman into Shona's place. She had died almost two years ago, but it still felt too soon. It still felt like rebound. The boys' aversion to Isla Thompson, so obvious when she had been prone to dropping in, seemed a strong indication that they were not ready for their mother's place to be taken.

However, the moment he saw Annie again, swinging her long legs out of a rather smarter hire car than her previous one, the magnetism pulled again. As their eyes met, Annie's huge smile warmed him, and although it was outwardly only a social kiss on the cheek, the touch and smell of her skin swamped his senses. Some very light fresh scent, herby, summer petals.

He thought back to the obvious moves that Isla had made after Shona's death, bringing meals, offering washing, ironing and a listening ear. Isla was admirable in so many ways, from her supreme self-confidence and singular and beautiful voice to her extremely sharp mind, and love of finance in all its varied forms. He had no illusions about her intentions, the planned conquest of his bed being only the first step towards membership of the Mackenzie clan and all that it represented. She was good-looking, an excellent cook, and highly efficient. And she didn't come with any baggage like a previous husband or a desire to have children when she couldn't. She didn't seem to want children of her own. Isla had eventually taken, with offence, the hint that he didn't want any romantic relationship. He sighed. He almost wished he could have loved her. Isla would be less of a complication in his life than Annie would, but it was Annie who scratched at his mind and filled his thoughts.

* * *

David was with his parents on the doorstep when Charlotte and Annie arrived and David knew from his father's body language that he was nervous, in spite of having talked to Charlotte on the phone on several occasions. Charlotte took Jem's outstretched hand, but then threw polite greetings to the wind by kissing him firmly on the cheek before doing the same to Fiona. David smiled at Annie. He wanted to kiss her again. To run his fingers through the thick chestnut hair and touch her skin and breathe her scent.

'Welcome to the Mackenzie house and clan,' Jem said, ushering them in. Charlotte looked round at the comfortable sitting room, cups and cake already on the coffee table, Fiona chatting easily, dissipating any awkwardness.

'This is *lovely*,' Charlotte said. 'What a momentous occasion, to meet the brother I never knew I had, plus an enormous family.'

'And what momentous discoveries from your idea to find out about your father's history.' Jem handed out coffee and plates. 'David and Annie's researches have unearthed more than either of us ever bargained on. Although I'd have been very pleased to have had the information sooner.' His ironic smile made everyone laugh. 'My mother, even at ninety, is acutely nervous about meeting you, but the rest of the family can't wait. The first batch is coming for tea. We thought you might sink under the weight of Mackenzies if they all appeared at once.'

50

August 2012

Mhairi looked up at the woman Jem ushered into her sitting room. Tall, slim, elegant. Green eyes, dark brown hair—at her age? Surely coloured?—swept up into a soft shining chignon. They shook hands, Charlotte bending to her level, their eyes locking, taking in the unknown person. John's daughter. John's lover.

Charlotte smiled. 'I'm so glad to meet you,' she said. 'Are you as nervous as I am?'

Mhairi felt her mouth quirking up. 'I thought I'd given up being nervous at my age, but apparently not. I thought I'd given up being surprised, but this year has produced plenty of them.' She indicated the two armchairs and waited while Jem and Charlotte settled, coffee poured. Looking again at Charlotte, there was a long-forgotten echo of John's mouth, a memory of the tilt of his head.

'I have to thank you,' she said, needing to say it now, before anything else was said.

Charlotte's head tipped in query.

'For proof. For Jem.'

'Ah,' Charlotte said. 'The DNA? I did wonder if it was the right thing to do.'

'Of course, I'd heard of DNA tests, but it's a modern thing and I never quite understood what it was. In any case, until Annie came, I'd had no knowledge or connection with John's wife, and no idea that John had a daughter. Annie then told me she wasn't John's grand-daughter at all, so there was no blood connection.'

'So David's suggestion of Charlotte and I doing a DNA test came as a shock, didn't it?' Jem said. 'You were in two minds about it, which made me really worried.'

'All your life, Jem, I've looked at you and wondered whether nature or nurture had formed you and your character. A good son, husband and father. But you don't look like John, you look more like me—or Archie, who was brown-eyed and good-looking too. You're a musician, but for all I knew there could have been that ability in Archie's blood as well. There was a huge risk in taking that test. While I didn't know for sure who your father was, I could go on believing it was John. I didn't want the proof that it was Archie. That's why I was reluctant. It was a risk I wasn't sure I had the courage for.'

There was a silence and Jem turned to Charlotte. Turned to his sister. It was such a strange concept, Mhairi thought, the two of them, almost twins, growing up in the same world with nothing to connect them. Until Annie came. Annie, whose mother died in childbirth, just as her own mother had. Two generations and a world apart and yet this curious connection.

Jem's face was sombre. 'Before I knew Mother's story, I was curious. More than curious. I desperately wanted to know my roots. But after I heard her story, I was terrified. But I simply had to know one way or the other.'

Charlotte looked from Jem to Mhairi. 'Yes—it was a huge risk for you both, wasn't it? I think it was very courageous.' She hesitated. 'It's lonely being an only, I found. Did you feel that, too, before you married and had your huge family?' He nodded sombrely. 'I can't tell you how—' she searched for the word '—warming it was to discover that I wasn't an only. That I had a family.'

That was generous, Mhairi thought. Not everyone would have welcomed the connection to an illegitimate brother.

'I need to tell you something else, Charlotte.' Mhairi was surprised that her voice was even and steady. She held her hands rather tightly on her lap and took a moment to compose herself. 'Your father never betrayed your mother. And though I would like to think that he loved me as I loved him, I don't think he did. He loved Elspeth and he loved his little boys, and he never betrayed them, not really.' The sadness seeped into her again, as fresh as it had ever been. 'I was the betrayer.'

Both Charlotte and Jem looked mystified. They can't get their heads round that one, she thought. They can't imagine how that can be.

'If he'd come back from that convoy, he wouldn't have stayed with me, even though he might have wanted to. He would have gone back to Elspeth. John Elliott was the most honourable man I ever knew, and he would have agonised over having wrecked two women's lives. He would never have kept me a secret from Elspeth—he wasn't a man for secrets—and he would have supported me and Jem with Elspeth's full knowledge, even at the risk of his marriage.' She took a breath, a tremor running through her now. 'Years later, I was able to be glad that he never came back.'

She looked at Charlotte. 'All the fault was mine, not his. But I have never regretted what happened.'

Charlotte leant forward and took her hands. Her expression somehow washed out Mhairi's anxiety and nervousness and she could return to the pragmatic present.

'Now, my dear, Jem will get us more coffee and cake, and then I am going to tell you both more about your father.'

51

August 2012

'Don't you laugh at them,' Fiona said quasi-repressively to a grinning David as the connecting door closed behind Charlotte and Jem. 'It's no small matter to take on board when you've lived all your life as a single child. You wouldn't know how that feels.' She ineffectively cuffed his head and departed to the kitchen.

David turned Annie in his arms and tilted her head up to his. His hands spread through the thick hair, lightened with red lights by infrequent summer sun.

'Hello,' he said softly. 'I've missed you.'

'Mmm. Me too.' She smiled. Her arms went around his neck as his mouth touched hers, lips exploring, his thumbs running over her eyebrows, eyelids, cheekbones, and then he was kissing her; deeply, hungrily, and she was kissing him back.

A little later they walked down to the sea, fingers surreptitiously linked, and watched Christopher and Seamus playing with three friends amongst the boulders and seaweed, competing to hurl stones the furthest into the sea.

'Will Charlotte want to practise later?' he asked, finding a dry boulder large enough for them both, his hand round her waist and resting comfortably on her hip.

'She won't want to, but she will. She must. She's at the

Wigmore Hall next week. It's amazing that the school have such a good piano. I hope they have a good piano teacher to go with it.'

He glanced at her ruefully. 'There isn't even a music department, and the piano teacher survived one winter and left for sunnier pastures. There's a piper in Aultbea who gives bagpipe lessons and odd bods who come to teach various instruments. It's a shame, really. There isn't even a choir, but I suppose a remote corner of Scotland isn't much of a draw.'

The children were now finding small jellyfish on the sandy patches and in the pools and hurling them too. Annie shuddered.

'All squidgy and slimy! Don't they sting?'

'Only in the water, for some reason.'

He called to them. 'Do you want to swim?'

All five immediately shed clothes down to swimsuits and hurled themselves into the water. Annie put her head on one side.

'They don't swim without your say-so?'

'They don't swim without an adult around. I'm slightly paranoid, I suppose.' He hesitated, a little embarrassed. 'The thought of an accident. After Shona. The guilt. I get enough nightmares as it is. They swim like fishes, but still. Being a single parent is so different—suddenly you're totally responsible for their lives, when before I thought it was Shona's responsibility. I couldn't go through all that again, them falling off beds and tables, the time the child seat came unclipped when I braked to avoid a dog. Seamus nearly went through the windscreen.' He shivered, not altogether jokingly. 'It's a miracle anyone survives childhood, let alone babyhood. Small children are a nightmare. So are older ones sometimes.'

'So two is sufficient?'

He grinned. 'Two is plenty. No more babies, thank you! There comes a time when you'd give pure gold to get a full night's sleep, and even at their age—' he waved a hand towards the shrieking group of children '—they have nightmares, they get ill and throw up all over the bedclothes. Exhausting.'

Annie was silent for a time and he wished he hadn't reminded her, yet again, of her childlessness.

'Well, I'm impressed by their obedience.'

He changed the subject. 'Did you want to be a concert pianist, too, or did you think one in the family was enough?'

She laughed. 'The sheer hard work was rather off-putting. Being up close to someone who never lets a day go by without practising is a sharp reminder that there is little romance and a great deal of hard graft in achieving her level of brilliance. She loves it. She loves the music and she loves the performances, but she is well aware that the single-mindedness required can be destructive. She put my father, who she absolutely adores, and me, also ditto, as lower priorities than her career once it was back on track after Rebecca, and I know that often she regrets that. They would have liked another child, but she miscarried once, and they didn't try again.' Annie didn't sound at all resentful. Her lack of offence was curiously soothing.

'Were you—are you— sometimes regretful that you didn't try it as a career?'

'No, I never really wanted it,' she said thoughtfully. 'I guess I'm not ambitious enough. I wanted to be married and have a house, and children, and ponies in a field, and dogs and cats and learn how to garden and to teach—' She broke off briefly. 'I like children and I like all sorts of music. I wanted to teach music, to teach children how to enjoy it, and I'm quite good at doing that, or I was until I blew it.' There was only a faint tinge of bitterness under the light tone. He allowed the silence to lengthen.

'And have you inherited your father's talents for finance and figures as well?'

She shrugged. 'A bit, I think. But I've never really used it. He's someone who sees the big picture; he can paint a huge world of trends and fashions and morality and education and civilisation.' Her smile was tender. 'I just love listening to him and asking him questions. He's great. You'll like him. I wish he hadn't been away when you came to London, and he hates having to be in Brussels now instead of here.'

How endearing it was to hear the open affection in her voice. 'One of these days we'll coincide, but it's a shame he couldn't come this time.'

It was a day he knew he would remember, even without the photographs they took, when a strong sense of happiness and contentment pervaded him. The boys' acceptance of Annie's presence, treating her more like an older sister than another adult, was relaxing, and Annie's pleasure in their company seemed unforced and genuine.

Fiona's huge cottage pie was golden-topped, and there was celebration in the air. Mhairi joined the family for lunch and a smile lurked amongst the wrinkles as she raised a celebratory glass of wine to Jem's toast of 'Family'. There obviously hadn't been a dog fight, David thought.

He lifted his own glass to a beaming Charlotte. 'To my new aunt!'

'Oh!' she exclaimed. 'Fancy being an aunt! And a sister! And a great aunt too!' She turned to Christopher and Seamus. 'And there are lots more of you—I can't wait. You've no idea how exciting it is to suddenly find all these relations, because, you see, we don't have any. It's just been the three of us, me, my husband and Annie.'

'Only three!' said Christopher. 'We've got lots and lots, and then there's all Mum's family too. I don't know how many of them there are.'

'Talking of relations,' Fiona said, 'Uncle Hugh asked if you'd like to go kayaking with the girls this afternoon?

Then they are all coming for a late tea to meet Charlotte.'

'Wicked!' they said, and buzzed with anticipation all through lunch.

Mhairi retreated for a rest and Charlotte, Jem and Fiona settled down with coffee on the terrace, to continue catching up with two lifetimes while David drove the rest of them to meet Hugh. He was desperate to be alone with Annie. He supervised life jackets and helped launch the kayaks and they waved goodbye to the little flotilla under Hugh and Catherine's command. Then he turned to her.

'It seems we have the afternoon to ourselves.' He looked at her intently, willing her to feel like him. 'Shall we go home?'

'To your place?' Her voice was croaky, and her cheeks flushed.

'To my place,' he agreed. Perhaps the suggestion was too hasty, but her reaction to his kiss earlier had been eager and passionate and he thought she had been as aroused as he had. Taking her hand, he led her back to the car and kissed her again, her thumping pulse and shortened breath confirming that her desire was as great as his.

Flicking the snib down on the kitchen door, he led her upstairs to his room. As he kissed her, his mouth following his fingers down her shirt buttons, he was aware of her unease. He made himself stop, sliding his hands back to her shoulders.

'Do you want me to stop? Is it too fast? Too soon?'

He heard her indrawn breath and low laugh.

'No, I don't want you to stop, and yes, it's much too fast and much too soon. What on earth must you think of me? Leaping into bed with you virtually the moment we've arrived?'

'Well, it's not the first time we've made love, and I have to say that this may be our only opportunity.' He was laughing a bit ruefully. 'With the boys on holiday, privacy is at a premium.' He put his forehead against hers. 'I've been thinking of you, and missing you, and wanting you, but if this isn't what you want, you'd better tell me now.' He tipped his head back and blew out a long breath. 'Please don't tell me.' He pushed a strand of the red-tinted hair behind her ear and ran his thumbs along her cheekbones. 'I was so sure you felt the same as me.'

'You know I do,' she said, a tremor in her voice. 'I do feel like that, but I don't know that I can cope with an occasional, just when it's convenient, long-distance relationship. I don't think I'm made like that. I don't want it to be just sex, glorious though it is. Coming into your house is different somehow. It feels secretive. It *is* secretive. A bit underhand.' She flashed a sheepish smile. 'We are perhaps going too fast, too soon. Is it too soon for the boys to cope with a girlfriend; a lover? And would it seem like a betrayal to Shona's parents? Have you finished grieving for Shona? You see, I have been thinking about it from your point of view, not just mine.'

A shaft of anger speared through him. Her correct hypothesis. Her perception, her righteousness.

'You want a marriage proposal?' He heard the harshness in his own voice and sensed Annie shrinking, not physically, but emotionally.

'No! Of course not!' She shook her head uncertainly and he was immediately ashamed.

'I'm sorry. I'm really sorry. Of course you're right—I just didn't want you to be right.' He took another deep breath. 'I want to make love to you right now, but I also want it to be more than that. It's just that—' Words failed him because her perception had got there before him.

'It's too soon?' She sounded a little sad.

He hesitated. 'We can build on our beginnings—we've already started, haven't we?' He slid his hands down her arms and linked his fingers into hers, opening her mouth gently with his, pressing his body into hers, and then he knew she was equally as urgent as he was. Thin summer clothes took only seconds to fall away, and bare skin seethed in awareness as their hands explored each other. He buried his face between her breasts, inhaling the smell of her, resonant with that elusive fragrance. He tried to slow down, to control himself, to allow her time, but with a laugh she pushed him on to his back and straddled him, and their mutual release was joyful and fulfilling.

Later they lay side by side, touching the whole length of their bodies, toes to shoulders, fingers linked again on hips, idle, sleepy, complete. Later still he slowly woke her desire again, giving and receiving pleasure, discovering where his fingers caused her to arch and purr like a cat, behind the shoulder blades, the space between armpit and breast, the convex curve below her belly button. And her mouth and tongue, tracing the line of his rib, finding the nipple and causing giggling mayhem. He sighed when his mobile signalled the text from Hugh to say they were turning for home, and they both reluctantly came back to earth and showered together before going to help the tired and salty children pull the kayaks up above the tideline.

It occurred to him, as they returned to his parents' house, that both children and parents assumed that he and Annie had been with the other lot for the afternoon. Secretive was correct, but their assumptions were just as well, he thought.

Later, after tea, he took Charlotte and Annie to the school to try the piano. Charlotte ran her chords and arpeggios for some time and professed herself satisfied before settling down to an hour's practice. The tide was out, and David and Annie took their shoes off and walked on the almost empty beach.

'Is your mum really all right with the piano?' he said. 'Though I'm not sure what we could do if she wasn't. The tuner thought it was OK and Dad played on it, too, and thought the same.'

He linked his fingers into hers and a happy warmth spread through him as his thumb stroked rhythmically down hers.

'It's really fine.' The feel of her fingers, the abrasive sand under his insteps and the warm wind on his skin made him acutely aware of happiness in a way he couldn't remember. Was it different to the happiness he'd felt with Shona? Did each person produce different happiness vibes?

'She probably wouldn't want to play an important concert on it, but for practice purposes, it's absolutely fine. He's a natural musician, isn't he, your dad? I didn't realise he could play the piano. He's not just a violinist.'

'He can turn his hand to a lot of instruments. We all can.' What was his father going to do about his violin?

She looked at him with that little sideways tilt of her head. 'Really, did we need the DNA tests at all? It must have been obvious to Mhairi that John was Jem's father, mustn't it?'

He stopped to look westwards towards the dropping sun, his fingers linking more deeply between hers. 'What looks obvious to us may not have been so obvious to her. A love of music, musical ability, is not necessarily genetic. Archie Mackinnon was clearly an evil man and he raped her, so she was intensely relieved about the DNA results. And I never realised how much Dad minded not knowing who his father was. After hearing her story, he really did not want to think he had Archie's blood in him. He was extraordinarily pleased that John proved to be his father.' He turned towards her, bringing their linked hands up to his shoulder, his other hand cupping her face towards him. 'And I am extraordinarily pleased that you are here.' And that she was Rebecca's daughter, not Charlotte's. It had taken him some time to understand his sense of relief on discovering she was not his first cousin.

His thumb touched a tiny white scar on the point of her chin, feather light. He was aware of each strand of the silky hair, each fine line in her skin, her eyes wide and bright, the sun reflected in them. The natural curve of the eyebrows above the deep sockets and dark lashes. Her mouth, wide and generous, the lips a little open, revealing a glimpse of teeth. His breath shortened, and he bent his head to hers. The memory of Shona's image faded into Annie's reality. He could not have stopped himself from kissing her even if he had wanted to.

* * *

'Happy Birthday!' Jem said as he laid the violin case on her lap. Charlotte looked at it in silence for a moment or two, then smiled up at him. 'Is this what I think it is? Our father's violin?'

'Yes.' He stepped back as if distancing himself from the instrument could lessen the pain of parting from it. 'I'm really sorry that she never returned it. It was in the croft for twenty-five years while she was in Edinburgh, and when she came back, she gave it to me, and I've been playing it ever since. I never knew it was John's.'

Charlotte blinked. 'Did you start learning then—so late?'

'No.' With a jolt of tardy surprise he realised that Mhairi must have planned it. 'I started violin lessons when I was about six, with a cheap instrument. It was OK for dance music and such, but this one of John's is a lovely one.'

He took a breath. He was saying a very final goodbye. 'Anyway, it's yours, and I'm just sorry it's taken so long to get back to you.'

Charlotte opened the case, and lifted out the violin and bow, running her finger down the instrument from the scroll, round the curves of the waist and lower bout. She looked up at him and said, 'Odd to think that our father touched every part of it. Will you play it for us now?'

He considered for a moment and then took the instrument from her and began to play. Singing in harmony with his mother, David saw that both Charlotte and Annie were blinking back tears by the end.

> Farewell my love,
> The time has come for you to say,
> "Farewell" to me.
> You leave me now in this fair land,
> Where first we met so tenderly.
> I bless the days we were together,
> I know that parting is forever.
> Remember me when you recall
> The hills of Caledonia.
> My dearest heart, we always knew,
> Before I held you close to me,
> That stolen moments in your arms
> Must end in tears of destiny.
> So fare you well, my gentle lover.
> I know you're promised to another.
> We'll meet again in dreams, my love,
> In dreams of Caledonia.

Charlotte blew her nose and gave Jem an enormous hug.

'Thank you. Hearing you play was the best birthday present ever. But I am expecting many more birthdays, and how can I hear that violin again if you aren't playing it? We already have Becky's violin. However, I will hold you to giving me a birthday concert every year.' She gave him another hug. 'I hope you will leave John's violin to whichever of your grandsons learns to play.'

David could see that the surprise of Charlotte's dec-laration completely silenced his father. Fiona came to his rescue.

'That's a lovely bargain!' She raised her glass. 'Let's drink to an annual concert on Charlotte's birthday, and could we exchange the compliment and have a piano recital every year in October for Jem's birthday?'

52

September 2012

She left the doctor's surgery in a state of bemusement; a state of denial. Part of her wanted to shout to the world that she was not dying, she was living, and giving life; the other part of her was panic-stricken in an incomprehensible way. It could not be. It was impossible. Keep quiet and the whole idea, the whole situation, would go away. It was all a dream—or a nightmare—a swirling confusion of triumph and terror, of total loss of control over her life. How could she have been so stupid, so blind, so assenting of other people's assumptions?

She walked; the length of Queensgate, the Albert Hall, the Albert Memorial, Kensington Gardens, the Serpentine, Peter Pan. At the Diana Memorial she stood and watched the mothers and children clambering over the pirate ship. She was entirely unable to place herself here; she was a thing apart. It was all a huge mistake.

She walked on, down the wide stretch of tarmac, the skateboarders and Segway riders rolling past her like ball bearings on glass. At the Round Pond, the boats either floated out of reach or bumped the banks refusing to go adventuring. *Which am I? Can I set my sails well enough to go where I want to, where I need to?* She wrapped her arms over her stomach, over the swelling and strange sensations that had so frightened her, over the idiocy of not grasping a fact of life that every teenager in the country knew. For four months she had drunk wine, eaten unpasteurised cheese and chicken liver pâté. She had had early menopause and ovarian cancer. The only thing she hadn't had, she thought balefully, was the wit to take a pregnancy test.

She could not imagine what her parents would say or think. Would they be horrified, angry, pleased that they would be grandparents? When he heard the news, as was inevitable, Justin would accuse her of taking the pill or using an IUD to prevent herself from conceiving his child. Her friends would shriek with laughter at her stupidity, her naïveté.

And David, assured that there was no danger of conception, had accepted her word. Her mind flooded with his words.

'Small children are a nightmare—two is plenty.'

'No more babies, thank you!'

'Exhausting—those sleepless nights, dirty nappies and porridge-encrusted surfaces—we needed every bit of that youthful energy—I'd die of exhaustion now.'

' I couldn't go through all that again.'

She clutched her arms, hands to elbows, in a physical grip across her stomach, in that plunging horror that had assailed her since she'd left the surgery. David, who had adored his dead wife; David who had two sons already, sons who didn't want a sibling, a child not their mother's, or a substitute mother. A father who didn't want another child, who didn't want her as another wife. Oh God! She realised she had said it out loud, and that the two words were not just the blasphemy her father disliked, but two words which held all the desperation of a scream for help.

Quite without volition, through the fog of terror and triumph, came the tears at last, pouring out of her eyes, streaming down her face to drip wetly on the front of her sweatshirt. Strangers glanced at her curiously, sympathetically, embarrassed for her, distressed for her distress. She found a tissue, terrified that some kind person was going to touch her arm and ask her what the matter was and how could they help. And to her horror, that is what happened, except that the Indian woman in a sari said nothing whatever. She appeared out of nowhere, enveloped Annie in a billow of yellow silk, and held her in a grip that said not much of sympathy, but a great deal of strength and female solidarity. Just a few seconds and then she released her grasp, smiled at Annie and passed on. Annie was so startled by this evidence of sisterhood that the tears ceased to flow and with a final thorough nose-blowing she found she could walk forwards, through the park gates, and back into the world. Now the horror and terror evaporated into the amazement, the triumph, the excitement of a new existence and a new life.

The nine days before her mother returned from an American concert tour drifted past in an agony of slow motion, which quickened as the time shortened and became a roller coaster of equal dread and anticipation. Will got home from Brussels before Charlotte and came for supper and Annie's intention of pinning them both down to a date to tell them her news evaporated on seeing her father. She blurted it out along with claret from the bottle, her eyes on the glasses, her voice and hands trembling. Will took the glasses out of her hands.

'Don't let's spill it on the carpet,' he said calmly. 'I always thought white was an unwise option.' He put the wine on the coffee table and sat back in an armchair. 'Well, that's a surprise, considering Justin's complaints. Mud in his eye, and all that.' Annie glanced up at him, feeling a wavery half smile flickering on her mouth. His eyes were smiling. 'Don't look so hangdog, darling. People do get pregnant, even though with you it's a bit unexpected. Is it good news for you?'

'Oh, Daddy! How can you be so calm! I don't know! I don't know what to do. I feel such a fool—it never occurred to me—how could I have been so stupid? All those years of trying, and then just once, bang—Oh!' The word bang set them both off in unexpected laughter, and Annie found she was crying at the same time. 'No—it's not good news, for all sorts of reasons.'

Will waited, and she took a deep breath. 'I'm not married; the baby will be without a father. I can't think of anything more awful than not to have a father.'

'Well, perhaps not to have a mother. But there is a father. Is he married?' She recognised the slightly steely tone he used to use when she threw a teenage tantrum. An affair with a married man would come low down on Will's register of decent behaviour.

She took a deep breath. 'No. He was married. His wife died. He's got children, and he doesn't want any more, and he doesn't want another wife either. I told him I couldn't have children, so he didn't—' She inhaled a sob.

'—take any precautions.' Will's tone was dry. 'Nevertheless, he could take responsibility for a child. Have you thought about your options?'

'Options?' Annie looked and felt blank. 'No. What options?'

Will gave her a straight look. 'Option One: have the baby and bring it up, with or without the father's help. Option Two: have the baby and have it adopted. Option Three: an abortion.'

Annie stared at him open-mouthed; appalled, silenced. Her father looked back at her, level-eyed, expressionless, hard. Was this what he looked like in the city, dealing with dishonest bankers, greedy fund managers, foolish finance ministers? It was an aspect of her father which she had read about but seldom seen.

'There aren't any options,' she said, her hands clenching.

'I will have the baby and bring it up. It's not ideal, I know, but I've longed for a child and now I'm going to do my very best for it. I couldn't have it adopted—you have to sign away all rights to it, never see it, never know whether it's happy or sad, in a good home or a bad one. I know, I looked into it when Justin and I were trying.'

'And Option Three?' Will's face was still stern and unreadable.

'Daddy! That's just awful to suggest! No! Not in a million years would I do that, even if I could. How could you even think it was an option?' She was furious now, unconsciously folding her arms protectively over her body.

Will's expression changed to one of satisfied relief. 'My darling, your reaction is all I wanted. I had to know, that's all. Sometimes the options serve to clarify your feelings. You were in a muddle at the beginning and you're in less of a muddle now. I'm delighted you want the baby, and we will be thrilled to be grandparents, which we never thought would happen. Of course, it's not a perfect situation and we would love to see you happily married, but life is never perfect and we all have to make the most of what we've got.'

She breathed in deeply. 'You're an OK father, do you know that? Just in case I never get around to telling you, I'm telling you now. You have no idea what the last few days have been like, dreading this moment, and then you appear, and everything's cut down to size. Put into perspective.'

Putting her glass on the table, she went across to Will and hugged him. His arms around her were intensely comforting and she put her head on his shoulder and wept tears of pure relief.

After she'd mopped up yet again, Will asked, 'When are you due?'

She sighed, her shoulders dropping. 'February.'

Numbers were Will's forte. Nevertheless, he did the calculation twice.

'February? In five months?' He sounded incredulous. She nodded.

'You didn't tell us! Annie, have you been keeping this secret from us all this time?'

'No! I didn't tell you because I didn't know.' She shut her eyes tightly. 'I thought of every other possibility, but not that. Eventually, I went to the doctor. I was frightened—I thought I might have some—illness. It never occurred to me I could be pregnant. He took a test and confirmed it.' The tears were squeezing out from under her lids again and she gasped, 'I am so sorry. I am so stupid.'

'You don't have to be sorry, and I don't think you were stupid. I know that Justin's new wife of only two months has had a baby, and it makes me wonder whether it is, in fact, Justin's child. It makes me wonder whether it was Justin who was infertile. You seem to have proved the point that it wasn't you.'

She was stunned into silence, her Kleenex disintegrating into damp shreds between tense fingers.

'What sort of illness did you think you might have?' Will's brows met across his forehead. 'Cancer?'

She nodded. 'I felt—odd. Occasionally I felt sick in the evenings—it never occurred to me that morning sickness could be at night! And I remembered that old lady who lived in the flat below you. She was sick—I remember her being sick into a cardboard bowl when Mum and I went down with a meal for her. She died of cancer, and I thought perhaps I had the same thing.'

'But you didn't tell us!' he said, aghast. 'You went through four months of thinking you had cancer and you didn't tell us!'

She shook her head. 'No, I didn't, honestly. It wasn't four months. It was about July when I started to feel nauseous. But it was in the evenings, not the mornings. I was never sick, but it went on so long I eventually began to wonder. Then I realised I'd missed my periods—when I eventually noticed I thought it was either cancer or stress. I couldn't tell you—you had those awful IMF meetings, and so much work and worry, and Mum was preparing for America. I thought if I had cancer, I just couldn't tell you then.'

Will ran his fingers through his hair, still thick but steely grey now. 'My darling, that's what parents are for—to be there for you. How do you think your mother will feel to know you've kept that from her?'

Some of the tension drained out of her. 'I know, I'm sorry I messed up again.'

'Again?' His eyebrows lifted.

'You know. After that fiasco over the piano. It was dreadful publicity for you both, and I felt so bad about it. I let you both down.'

He smiled. 'I was quite proud of you, really, at the time. I know it was all horrible and it's had nasty repercussions for your job and I wish I'd been there for you and Mum, but honestly, darling, we all need to learn from our mistakes and to take it on the chin.' He shifted mental gears again, like an agenda item, Annie thought in wry affection. 'And now you will have to manage your present situation. It will require a considerable rethink of your life and responsibil-ities: finance, housing, work, to name but a few. How has the baby's father reacted?'

After a small silence, she said, 'I haven't told him.' Will said nothing, but his eyes widened. 'I don't know how to tell him—he'll think I deceived him, that I'm trying to trick him into marriage—into responsibilities he never asked for or wanted. I think it may be better not to tell him, but—Oh, it's awful—complicated. I need to think.'

'You do indeed,' Will said dryly. 'Do you love him?'

She stared past Will, her expression serious. 'Yes, I do. Yes. It's just—too soon.'

'My darling, if you love him, you need to tell him. Do you want to tell me about him?'

She shook her head slowly. 'No. No, I can't. Not yet.'

53

September 15th 2012

It was a nothing day. No sun, dirty wisps of slow-moving grey cloud above a chill autumn breeze. Tom and Tilly in sombre grey, Christopher and Seamus in grey school trousers hunched into black and grey windcheaters, and he, also subdued in dark grey, out of respect. Respect for who? Not for Shona, who had loathed grey. For Tom and Tilly, he supposed, who would have been startled and possibly upset had he appeared in bright red. Like last year, her gravestone was still polished, the etched letters clear of lichen or moss. He wondered again if they came regularly to clean it.

SHONA MARY BELL

BELOVED DAUGHTER, WIFE AND MOTHER

5th August 1977 – 15th September 2010

Forever remembered. Forever loved.

David stared glassily, resentfully, at the headstone. It may have been the custom for maiden names to be used, but it was as if she had been disconnected from him as a wife and reconnected to her parents. They hadn't even suggested the addition of 'wife of David Mackenzie'. His fault, he knew. He had let them make the arrangements, had not argued about the wording because he really hadn't taken it in at the time. Her absence had been so huge, the headstone was an irrelevance. But now, he felt it mattered.

He felt different, though. Last year he had been angry. Angry that she had left him, angry that medical science had not saved her, angry that the boys had no mother, angry that Tom and Tilly's grief was so raw, angry that he was on his own, wholly responsible for the boys' lives. Sheer self-pity, that had been.

His phone vibrated as Tom and Tilly laid their flowers, white lilies, at the base of the slab. He slid his hand into his pocket to silence it as Christopher clutched his own flowers and looked at him uncertainly. He smiled and nodded, gripping his shoulder encouragingly.

'Go ahead. And you, too, Seamus.'

The boys had chosen pink and orange roses respectively, not a brilliant colour combination, he thought with an inward smile. He had offended the florist by declining the paper and crackly, single-use cellophane and wriggly ribbons, reminding the boys that Shona had been an adamant eco-warrior. The flower petals would all be brown-tipped by morning and thoroughly dead by tomorrow evening. Like Shona. What a waste all round. Tilly's face was running with tears.

This year was different. The anger was gone, leaving a rather frightening feeling of being separated from the rest of them. Emotionally apart. What the hell is wrong with me? I should feel regret and sadness, not this impatient frustration. This inner shout of 'Let's move on!'

He laid his own flowers, deep red roses, beside the others and stood back, feeling his phone vibrate again.

He walked behind the others back to the car park, Tilly holding Seamus's hand and Christopher, he noticed, holding Tom's in a protective, grown-up, comforting way. He glanced down at Annie's text. 'Can we talk?' The desire to talk to her and not to think about Shona was immense and immediately the familiar tide of guilt enveloped him.

'No. Not today,' he texted back. 'Shona's anniversary. At the graveside.'

He wanted someone else to share his guilt.

54

February 2013

She had no expectation of surprise when the doorbell rang, thinking it was an Amazon delivery, and was stunned into silence at the sight of David, tidy but as always somehow constrained, in slacks and sports jacket, shabby briefcase in hand. An immediate stomach-lurching delight instantly turned to miserable terror. He looked at her face and then his eyes dropped down to rest on the straining T-shirt over her enormous belly. Shock held them both briefly speechless.

'Come in.' Her voice was just a croak. She pulled the door wider and closed her eyes briefly as he squeezed past her stomach into the sitting room, the scores piled abnormally tidily on the piano, in preparation for a new kid on the block. Her head spun and she held on to the doorpost to keep upright, her heart thumping noisily in her ears.

Her inability to decide when and what to tell him had come home to roost and now here he was, not at the end of a telephone or email inbox, but physically, actually, solidly, present.

She gave him the coffee he asked for, though he looked so traumatised she wondered if a strong whisky would be more appropriate. Her hand was shaking so much it made a puddle on the table and she had to fetch a cloth to mop it up. He was still mesmerised by her bulk.

'Can we talk about the elephant in the room, which looks as if it might arrive tomorrow, but on my understanding shouldn't exist at all?' His voice had thickened, and he cleared it. 'It can't be an immaculate conception, so are congratulations or commiserations in order?'

Annie gulped, held in a dreadful uncertainty. 'I didn't know. It shouldn't have happened – I don't know how it happened. Justin—'

'Justin?' he said sharply. 'This is Justin's child? After you divorced?'

'No!' It came out as a shout of frustration. 'Of course it isn't Justin's!' The room was slowly spinning and she took a deep breath, praying that she wouldn't faint. 'I meant Justin divorced me because I couldn't get pregnant, and then his wife had a new baby so I assumed—I couldn't. And then I was.' She tailed off into a silence which he was slow to break.

'So when is this baby due?'

She was dismayed by the hardness of his tone. 'Now. Last week actually.'

'I see.' Like Will, he could do the calculations. 'Am I the father?' She was held again in that paralysis of indecision, an enormous stone sitting on her chest. His eyes narrowed. 'Or aren't you sure?'

Oh! That hurt. Was he remembering Mhairi? 'Of course I'm sure.' She realised that her words were ambiguous.

His cold expression cut her. 'I'm not stupid, Annie. It is more than possible that I am the baby's father.' He took a deep breath. 'Can I ask you again, just for clarity's sake. Am I the father of this baby?'

She knew her answer would have long-term consequences, not just for the baby or for her and David, but for a host of others. In her mind's eye, she could see a long queue of people, like the political billboard 'Labour Isn't Working', with Mhairi at the head of her huge family, followed by her own parents, with Justin's family at the tail. She could not, at this moment, foresee the results on all these people if she told a lie now, to David's face.

'Yes.' Her voice was just a whisper. 'I'm so sorry.' The stupidity and cowardice of not telling him engulfed her.

He looked stunned. 'You're really sure?'

The skin of her face was suddenly too tight for the bones. 'I haven't slept with anyone other than you since the divorce.'

He was astounded. 'And you weren't going to tell me!' His fists clenched. 'Your emails tail off and then virtually stop, your phone goes to voicemail. You're away when I come to London. It made me assume you'd found someone more to your taste and that you didn't have the decency to tell me I was just a passing fancy. Why on earth didn't you tell me you were pregnant?'

Annie briefly closed her eyes. 'I did try. I did. And you were angry and I hadn't the guts to try again. I'd told you I couldn't get pregnant. I told you precautions weren't necessary. I thought it would look like I was trying to trick you. To manipulate you into a relationship. Or to get money off you for maintenance when I am one of the idle rich.' It was sarcasm directed at herself. 'You had lost your wife who you adored, you didn't want to marry again or start a relationship.' She ignored his protest. 'You said you would hate to embark on having a baby at your age with two quite grown-up boys who don't want a new sibling or a replacement mother. And I am an unsuitable Londoner, with a rather public and unsavoury divorce behind me. I just didn't know how to tell you something that would be so unwelcome.' She found she had wrapped her arms around her bulk in protective misery.

After a moment he got up and went to the window, staring at the cobbled mews and bright painted conversions opposite.

'Some of what you've said is true,' he acknowledged tightly. 'I certainly hadn't thought of another relationship so soon after Shona's death.'

It's two and a half years since your wife died, Annie thought, anger seeping into the self- censure. How long does one mourn for? How long can you make it an excuse for having an affair without any commitment?

He turned back to her. 'But most of your thinking is pretty flawed.' There was another silence in which she reviewed which bits of her thinking were flawed. 'What about your parents?'

'What about them?' She hadn't meant it to sound so aggressive.

'I suppose they know I'm the father?' She shook her head and his brows twitched together in astonishment. 'You haven't told them? Were you going to?' The astonishment was giving way to cold anger. 'But we're family! How could you possibly think you could keep this secret?'

How *had* she thought she could keep it a secret?

'Oh David! I'm so sorry!' As the words came out, she wished she had stood up for herself a bit more.

'Did you really think I wouldn't find out? Are you expecting me not to tell my family I have another child?' She tried to break in, but he ignored her. 'With all that we've found, our mutual family, it surely wasn't going to be a one-night stand, a spur of the moment, let's move on sort of relationship, was it? Was it? Didn't we talk about this in Scotland? Did you really think that our two families wouldn't be in contact? In close touch? How could you possibly have thought we wouldn't find out you had a baby?'

How indeed. There was no explanation for her cowardice. No justification for her silence which had become more and more difficult to break as the weeks had passed. 'I don't know,' she said miserably. 'But it was so complicated. It wasn't a relationship that could easily develop with you up north and me in London. Even if you'd wanted it, which I knew you didn't, I couldn't just move in. You've got two young sons, a business, a reputation, a whole family on your doorstep—the boys still miss their mother. But most of all, I'd told you I couldn't have children.'

He wasn't really listening. 'You must have been three months pregnant when you came up in August. Why didn't you tell me then?'

'I didn't know!' she cried. 'I didn't know I was pregnant.'

He was disbelieving. 'What on earth do you mean "you didn't know you were pregnant"? How could you not know?' He paused, with the final bitter misunderstanding. 'But of course, how slow of me. An adoption, the baby that never was, the pregnancy that didn't happen. How very inconvenient of me to have turned up at this moment. A few more days and I would never have known.'

She shook her head frantically. 'No! That's not true! I never even considered adoption.'

She simply could not explain the impossibility of what had happened. In her efforts not to cry her throat had swollen up so that she couldn't speak. She spread her hands hopelessly.

His anger was overlaid with distress. 'If you weren't intending an adoption, *why didn't you tell me?*'

She flinched and forced herself to speak, her voice cracking.

'I was four months when the doctor said it was a baby. I didn't believe it—until I had the test result—I thought I had something—' The tears were pouring down her face, her nose leaking like a burst pipe. She burrowed for a hanky.

'You thought you had something?' His brows drew together in incomprehension. 'What do you mean?'

'I thought I was ill. I never thought it was a baby.' She breathed in hard, her stomach contracting as if it had been punched.

'But that doesn't excuse your—your lack of information, your non-communication. Why didn't you tell me you thought you were ill?' His cold anger was like a slap in the face.

She straightened, hurt. 'After Shona? Oddly enough, I was reluctant to do that.'

He stared at her, taken aback. 'You thought you had cancer?'

'Eventually I went for tests. And when they said it was a baby, I couldn't believe it. After my parents came back, I told them I was pregnant, but not that you were the father. I couldn't tell them before I'd told you. It took me ages to have the courage, but I did try to tell you.'

She remembered feeling crassly insensitive having texted him in the middle of their visit to Shona's grave to tell him she was pregnant, and the fact that he hadn't called her back had added to her embarrassment. Even now, her skin prickled hot with mortification and her stomach cramped again in sudden pain.

'I didn't mean to make you pay for something that was my fault, not yours. I was thinking of you, and your sons and your family. I didn't want to ruin all your lives.' To her dismay, she found her face was running with tears again. Another sudden pain in her lower belly took her by surprise and she pressed her hands against it.

'Ruin?' he said, 'Where are you coming from? We're living in the twenty-first century, not the Victorian age, or even post-war Scotland! Having a child outside marriage is par for the course. Nobody's life is going to be ruined by you having a baby, except possibly the life of a child without a father.'

'I know.' She found herself almost shouting. 'But you didn't *want* another child.' She swiped at her wet face. 'I knew you'd do the right thing, take responsibility, all that. But you'd have resented the baby. Resented me. I didn't want you to resent me, to blame me, to put up with the situation. I wanted you to—' Her voice cracked and stopped. Warm liquid seeped down her thighs. Oh please! Not now.

'What?'

She heaved in a breath. Justin had resented her inability to conceive, and David would resent the fact that she had. Why was it always the woman's fault? And why must she always fall for the wrong bloody man?

'What?' he said again. 'You wanted me to what?' His voice was gentler, but the pain had come again, the muscles in her belly progressively cramping and hardening.

'Oh. *Ow!*'

He gave her jeans a serious stare, took out his mobile and punched in a number. She was coping with the pain and didn't hear the conversation. When it passed, she saw that he had shrugged on his coat.

'Where are you going?' She was suddenly terrified that he was walking out and leaving her forever.

He sighed. 'Your waters have broken. I'm taking you to hospital. Taxi's on its way.'

55

February 2013

He sat next to Annie's head in a state of battered disbelief. This cannot be happening. He had only been in London twenty-four hours.

Now, ridiculously, he was at the sharp end of a birth he hadn't foreseen and the totally unexpected weight of responsibility for a baby which was apparently his and a woman who was at this moment crushing both his hands to pulp when she wasn't trying to sink her teeth into them.

Shona had produced both his boys with no fuss and little noise within an hour of entering hospital. Annie had been in labour for fourteen hours and her language was blue and loud.

The midwife was loudly encouraging from the very sharp end and suddenly addressed him rather than Annie.

'Now then, David. Gloves on, and up here. At the double.'

And unbelievably, the small bundle of pink and purple humanity slid into his hands, black hair plastered to the tiny skull, wrinkled face screwed up in grave and almost immediate vocal disapproval of the clinical white world.

'Congratulations. You have a beautiful daughter.'

The midwife swooped, the scrap was blanketed,

swaddled, placed into Annie's exhausted and triumphant arms. The miracle, third time around.

He leant his head against mother and daughter, enclosed them in a gentle embrace, thankful that he was a man.

In due course, he was swept out while the two heroines were cleaned up. Will and Charlotte leapt to their feet in the waiting room and he could see the long hours of worry etched into their eyes. Not for the first time he thought of Will going through this with Rebecca, and now with their daughter, with the possibility, no matter how remote, that Annie might die as well.

'We're told it's a girl!' Charlotte gasped, throwing her arms round his neck and kissing him on both cheeks. 'Congratulations! Are they all right?'

'I think so. It was quite awful for Annie.' He turned to shake Will's hand, meeting his drained, but relieved eyes. 'Congratulations to you too. Your granddaughter took one appalled look at me and yelled.' He sat heavily in one of the easy chairs. 'I do feel rather pole-axed.'

'You've had quite a dramatic day,' Will said dryly. 'We, at least, had some warning.' He pulled a silver hip flask from his coat pocket and gave it to David. 'I think you need some of that, even if it is breakfast time.'

David took it gratefully and the whisky burned down into his exhaustion. He put his head back and shut his eyes. His lover of only a few nights had given birth to his daughter with no warning and apparently no intention of telling him. Or living with him or sharing responsibility or love for this child. Not for him the pram under the trees or walks in the park; no swinging on swings, no buying of dresses, no ice-cream disasters on carpets. No sister for brothers, no paternal grandparents, aunts, uncles, cousins. Tears pricked behind his eyelids and immediately he summoned anger to deal with that indignity. What would

Shona have said? No. Shona would not have said. The situation would not have arisen. The question was, what would Shona say now? Now that she was dead. What would Christopher and Seamus say, think, do? His thoughts fluttered like leaves in a winter's wind, piling into untidy heaps only to be blown in a thousand different directions.

He was pulled back into reality by Will.

'Stiffen the backbone, boy, and make no decisions. They'll turf her out tomorrow morning, and she'll be home, never having changed a nappy or fed a baby in her life. Charlotte will be fairly useless, as will I, and the mother will cope. We've done it all before and Annie is still with us. Decisions need to be taken when all parties have put their brains together and not before. Do you hear me?'

David stared at him wordlessly. Annie's birth and Rebecca's death must have been a hundred times worse. He nodded, took a mouthful of whisky and rose to his feet. 'Thank you,' was all he could muster.

* * *

Annie was exhausted and moving like a crab, but she and the baby had been sent home. In spite of himself, he was amused by her inept nappy changing and found in himself a forgotten aptitude for baby-handling. Various professionals came in and out to check on the baby and help Annie start on breastfeeding while his own thoughts were like moths, hurling themselves at lamps, singeing and burning, heedless of rational processes. Only the Merediths were remotely prepared for this situation, and then only for a baby, not for the unexpected addition to the Mackenzie family.

His anger at Annie's deception and secrecy had drained away, to be replaced by a deep sadness and shame about his own thoughtless assumptions. He remembered her text in the cemetery, 'Can we talk?'

He remembered his reply. Annie had not known it was the anniversary of Shona's death, or that he would be visiting her grave. How could he have been so unkind? His later communications had been about his travel plans and getting the boys back to school and he had not referred to her message, nor had he apologised, ashamed by his texted response. He could hardly blame her for not having had the courage to try again.

His parents were away in Morocco and his heart sank at the thought of communicating this news to them while they were having their first decent holiday in years. Could he leave it another week? And how long could he leave Christopher and Seamus in ignorance of a new baby sister? He'd have to go back home before any plans could be made about the future.

He rang Hugh and Catherine, who were looking after the boys in his absence.

'How the hell am I going to tell them? And what do I do when I have? Bring Annie and the baby north? Where will she live if the boys don't want her in the house?' He was bordering on panic. 'And if she stays in London, how can I be a father to a child who lives six hundred miles away?'

Hugh was calm. 'Stop freaking out. The first thing you need to get straight is whether you love her or not. Do you?'

He squeezed his eyes shut. 'Yes. No. I don't know—Shona.'

Hugh's calmness tilted towards brisk pragmatism. 'Shona is not here. But Shona would not have wanted you to be mourning her death for ever. She'd want you to be happy. Would Annie make you happy?' David couldn't respond. 'It is allowed, you know, to fall in love again. Shona's been gone over two years. Do you love Annie, or was she just a one-night stand?'

'God. No. I mean it wasn't just one night. But she promised she couldn't have children. I thought—I do love her—I just wasn't letting myself get that far—'

'Far enough to bring another child into the world,' Hugh said dryly. 'Would she make you happy or would you always be comparing her to Shona? That wouldn't be very healthy.' He waited through another silence. 'Is Annie kind? Would she be good to the boys? If not, then you have to take responsibility for the baby financially and let them go.' He waited again, and David found himself hating the thought of letting Annie go. Of letting the baby go.

'I need to think.' He slumped on to the hotel bed. 'In the meantime, what do I tell the boys?'

'You come home and tell them what you've told me. And you tell Mum and Dad when they get back. I think you'll find the reaction is not quite so Victorian as you expect. Granny had a child out of wedlock, and Dad has been OK with that and so have all of us. It's hardly unusual these days. For what it's worth, everybody likes Annie, and the new aunt, and you seem to like the new uncle too. One step at a time.' David could hear the affection in his brother's voice. 'Come north as soon as you can and tell the boys. After that, you can make decisions about what sort of living arrangements are going to be best.'

David choked on a half laugh. 'What it is to have a sensible older brother! Thanks for calming me down.'

He had fended off, as gracefully as he could manage, Charlotte and Will's persuasive invitation to stay with them, preferring to go back to his hotel and his own stressful phone calls. Already he had been away from the boys for more than a week and knew he had to go back. Somehow explain to them what had happened. Explain that he had betrayed their mother, that a sister had made her way on to the family platform, that a baby was already encroaching on the hard-won even keel they had attained after Shona's death. That an almost unknown woman was now at the heart of their privacy, at the heart of their life. Guilt and anger churned through him, like a washing machine gone mad. And he acknowledged another complication—his ridiculous, incomprehensible, protective love for this baby.

* * *

'Her eyes are the colour of the sky in summer,' Annie murmured, gazing at the unfocused orbs in question. She glanced up at David. 'I suppose they will change. Perhaps they'll be grey like yours. Like John Elliott's.' He knew she was aware of his turmoil, however hard he tried to conceal it. 'What are we going to call her? We could ask the boys to suggest names, couldn't we? So long as you kept the right of veto, in case they choose Wilhelmina.'

'Summer Sky?' he said, smiling faintly.

'Skye is nice. After the island? Suitably Scottish.'

'I'll suggest it to the boys.'

'There's your taxi.' She gathered the shawls around the now sleeping baby before handing her to David and painfully getting to her feet. 'Yes, you really do need to go home and face the music. I'll come with her as soon as you want me to and as soon as the hospital gives me the go-ahead.'

He was noncommittal rather than encouraging. 'We can work out the details later.'

He put his lips briefly to the baby's head, breathing in the warm milky fragrance of her skin before handing her back to Annie. Turning at the door he saw her lift the baby to her shoulder and wipe something shiny off the dark, spiky hair. As the taxi turned out of the mews, he deeply regretted that he had not kissed her goodbye.

56

March 2013

'So, your parents want me to take Skye up to Scotland to meet the family?' Annie said. 'How very welcoming. And how long are they expecting me to stay? A weekend? And where?' She was on the cusp of aggression and the ravages of too little sleep and being a single-handed parent were not making her more diplomatic. Skye wriggled in David's lap and Annie saw the tenderness as he bent to kiss her, smiling into her startlingly blue month-old eyes.

'You should stay for as long as you want,' he said cautiously. 'Mum and Dad have lots of space.'

She thought of the vast amount of equipment that seemed to be essential to the modern baby that would require to be carried, transported and housed and noted that she was not invited to stay in David's house, nor had he expressed a wish for her to stay longer than a weekend. It was a toss-up between aggression or tears, and she was not going to cry.

'So you're suggesting a weekend—perhaps we could stretch to a long weekend—and Skye and I would stay with your parents. Are you expecting me to fly up on my own? Or come by train? Or perhaps it would be better if I drove up?'

She was glad to see that he looked upset.

'Of course you can't drive up. I'd have to come down here and help with the journey.' She noted the 'have to'.

Irritability got the better of her. 'You're not being very specific. I think I understand that you don't want me and Skye permanently in Scotland and that we're not welcome in your house. A weekend to meet the family and then, job done, she can go back to London and get on with it. Correct?'

He looked more than upset now. 'It's not that you're not welcome in the house, but I just don't know how the boys will react to you being there. And you might hate it too. I don't want to tie you down without—' He swallowed.

'Without trying it out?' She smiled grimly over her rising temper. 'But do you want me and Skye in Scotland at all? You can't have one without the other, I'm afraid. Wouldn't you prefer us here? So you could just visit when convenient?'

He closed his eyes. 'Annie—I don't know what to think. I don't know what's best for any of us and you may remember that I haven't had much time to think clearly about how anything would work.' They were both about to lose their tempers, Annie realised. 'I would like you and Skye to be living near us, but I must put Christopher and Seamus first.' She wondered what reaction the boys had had to make David so wary, and the sense of rejection hit her almost physically. Why must he put the boys first? Why not her and Skye? Why couldn't they all find a middle way?

'Right. You want us to be living near you, but you don't want us in your house and the boys don't want us in the house either, so where would you suggest we live? I can't stay with your parents for more than a few days.'

'Inveruidh?' he said hesitantly. 'Just to start with. I'll see if I can rent somewhere closer.'

No mention of living together, being partners, let alone getting married. A single mother living in a closed Scottish community? It was Mhairi all over again. Who was the loser in this game? Her temper boiled over.

'OK. You can organise it— decide how we'll travel and everything. By the time you have transported me, Skye, and Skye's clobber, you may wish you'd flown every member of your family south and booked them into a hotel instead.' He looked shocked by her obvious anger. 'And I will have a lot to do before coming to live permanently—' she imbued the word with heavy irony '—in Wester Ross. Like terminating the rental here and packing up my life. I doubt I'll manage it before the spring, as looking after a baby is fairly time-consuming, I've discovered.'

Not until she was sure he had really gone did she allow herself the luxury of howling.

* * *

He had been highly efficient, she had to admit, and their journey north by air was, if not simple, at least reasonably stress-free. He had flown down twice since Skye's birth and Annie could see his love and tenderness towards his unexpected daughter. Now it was David who held the baby when she cried during take-off and landing, and who carried her on and off the aircraft. He had reduced her equipment by about eighty per cent, assuring Annie that most of her requirements had been in Jem and Fiona's loft and were now ready and waiting. But she was tense and tired and when he briefly comforted her with a hug, she shrugged him off, confused by wanting the hug to be longer.

'She's got her own private bar,' he said, rocking his daughter expertly on his shoulder, 'and Mr Tesco has delivered everything else.'

Their visit was to be for a week and Annie found herself

a bag of nerves, visualising disapproving relatives and a series of cold shoulders, despite David's assurances to the contrary.

'The boys told schoolfriends and teachers the news as soon as they heard, so the whole community was informed within a day. We've been deluged with cards, emails and telephone calls ever since.'

Annie was cautious about believing it and was taken aback by the warm welcome as she was embraced, and the baby held and rocked and cooed over.

Christopher and Seamus appeared to be unworried by the arrival of a baby sister and were keen to become acquainted as soon as possible. They observed Skye curiously, proffering cautious fingers which she obligingly gripped. Nobody had any illusions that Christopher, at any rate, was unaware of the facts of life.

'Nine months pregnancy is just boring when you're used to instant gratification.' Fiona shook her head in mock despair. 'It's like waiting for Christmas. Everyone else requires months to get used to the idea, but kids just want the end result.'

Yes, thought Annie. The boys clearly have no problem with the situation, and nor do Jem and Fiona and the rest of the family.

Which meant, she thought with a heavy sadness that settled in the pit of her stomach, that David's problem wasn't with his sons' reaction. It was with her.

57

September 2013

'Why can't Annie come fishing too?' Seamus sounded sulky.

'She'd have to bring Skye and you can't take babies fishing.'

'Why not? Annie takes her everywhere in the backpack.'

He swallowed his guilt. Annie and Skye had been staying at Inveruidh since May, and he guessed that the isolation she had so adored on her first visit must have morphed into pure loneliness now. 'I know, but it's not very safe with hooks flying about. And it's too far. By the time she could get here the overcast will have gone and the fish won't take.'

'I wish Annie could stay at our house. Then she wouldn't have to drive to see us.'

Seamus's wish disturbed him. He glanced at Christopher in the rear-view mirror, but he had his earphones in, his thoughts miles away. 'I thought you wouldn't like her to be in the house. Taking the place of Mum.'

The annual pilgrimage to Edinburgh had been the previous week. Exactly a year since Annie had tried to tell him she was pregnant. Exactly three years since Shona died. The memories of Shona had been miserably revived not only by the graveside visit but also by Tilly inviting some of their old friends to tea afterwards. He wondered if she had done it to make him feel ashamed about Annie and Skye. If so, she had been quite successful.

Seamus almost snorted. 'She wouldn't take the place of Mum. Mum is Mum and Annie is Annie.'

Mum *is* Mum? How weird is that? Does Christopher think Mum is Mum? Did he, David, think Shona *is* Shona, or was Shona? He didn't know how to express the question to Seamus, so didn't attempt to. He parked the car, detached Christopher from his wires, smeared them all with Smidge and got them into gumboots for the trek across the soggy ground to the loch.

During the holidays the boys had semi-absorbed Annie and Skye into their friendship group of cousins and schoolmates, and both Charlotte and Will had visited, as had Tom and Tilly, although not together. David's nervousness and discomfort had been unnecessary, he realised, due to the innate good manners of all these adults, including his own family, and their genuine desire to make the best of an imperfect situation.

His and Annie's relationship still veered towards the polite end of normal, with a gradual lessening of tension as Skye bridged the parental differences with seven-month-old charm, her now grey eyes sombre and grave until she worked out that funny faces made her chuckle.

After half an hour they had all caught fish. 'Shall we ask Annie and Skye to join us?' David said as casually as he could manage. 'Or we could go to Inveruidh and cook them there?'

'Let's go to Inveruidh.' Seamus was enthusiastic. 'Annie needs to practice cooking trout. And cleaning them.' He sploshed along the bank to a fresh spot and David watched him cast with a surge of pride.

'We need two or three more fish for supper. Seamus has caught the most on a Butcher. Do you want to change your fly?' he asked Christopher.

'It's OK. I like my Peter Ross.' There was a little pause. 'Do you want to go to Inveruidh, Dad?'

David turned to look at him, his antennae standing on end. Christopher was intent on grooming his fly and checking the cast.

'I don't mind. We won't if you'd rather not, and we don't need to ask Annie and Skye to come to us either. We can just have a boys' fish supper—and there's cheesecake too.'

'I didn't mean I didn't want to. I just thought—you don't always like going there.'

David was aware that if he closed this window of conversational opportunity, it might never open again. He took a careful breath.

'I just don't want you to feel that Annie and Skye are intruding on your lives. You never asked for them and I'm not going to force them on you. We'll all have to accommodate them a certain amount, but it doesn't have to be for everything. And certainly not for fish suppers if you'd rather not. Us three are us three, OK?'

Christopher nodded. 'OK. I don't mind though. I like going to Inveruidh. Annie's nice, not like Isla. I didn't like Isla.'

Bang. Just like that. *I didn't like Isla.* 'Oh!' He had to laugh. 'OK. Well, Isla isn't a particular friend. I'm glad you like Annie, though. How do you like Skye?'

'Skye's OK. I like it when she laughs. She'll be more fun when she's older. Do you want to go to Inveruidh? It doesn't matter if you don't, we can entertain ourselves.'

How adult was that. He thought he heard a note of sighing weariness and took a gamble.

'I'd like to go. I expect Annie is a bit fed up with just Skye to talk to and would like to play a game with you two. I'll ring her later when we get network cover. We'd better get on with catching more fish.'

They had a row of seven half-pounders, and one of

nearly a pound, caught by Seamus, and David rang Annie to suggest a trout tea.

'You could come to us if you'd like an outing, but the boys are keen to come up to the cottage.'

She sounded a little edgy. 'If you don't mind coming here, I think it would be better. Skye seems very unsettled. Perhaps she's teething.' David could hear shrill crying in the background and itched under the familiar guilt that Annie had to cope with all the normal ups and downs of babyhood while he avoided them.

'OK. We're going home to change first. We all smell of bog and fish.'

It was nearly an hour later when they reached the cottage. Annie came out to meet them looking tense and a little frightened.

'I'm sorry, but Skye doesn't seem well at all. She's never made a noise like this before. Something's really wrong.' Her voice was wobbly.

David saw her fists were clenched with anxiety and took her hands in his, wanting to calm her. He could hear Skye long before they got inside.

He ran upstairs, dread filling his chest. The crying was shrill and gasping and the baby was thrashing about in her cot. He picked her up and immediately she arched her body and screamed even louder. He put her down again, sensing she was in severe pain.

'She doesn't like to be touched,' Annie said desperately. 'She's much worse than when you first called, but I don't know what's wrong. That's not teething. Do you think she has a twisted gut?'

'I don't know.' Anxiety filled him. 'Her breathing is odd, too, but that may be because she's screaming so hard. You should have called the medical centre. The number's in the information file.' Annie sobbed in panic and he wished he hadn't said 'should have'. As she ran downstairs to get the number, Skye vomited. David turned her quickly on her side, wiping it away with a Kleenex.

The duty doctor knew the Mackenzie family well and had met Annie and a sunny chirpy Skye the week before. She didn't need to ask about the screaming. David put the phone on loudspeaker. The questions were quick and to the point.

'Has she vomited?'

'Just this second. Yes.' He pushed down the terror. What was happening to this baby?

'Very gently put two fingers over the top of her head and feel if there is any swelling at the fontanelle.'

Annie did so, her fingers trembling as David tried to hold the shrieking baby steady. She shouted to the phone, 'Yes, I think so. Normally it's a sort of dent, and now it isn't.' Her voice cracked on a sob.

'Strip her down and tell me if you can see a rash anywhere on her body. Look under her nappy as well.' Between them he and Annie stripped the babygro and nappy off the writhing body, the crescendo of screams terrifying them both.

'No spots,' Annie's breath was coming in sharp gasps. 'but her skin looks patchy—pale in places and reddish in places.'

'Blotchy. OK. I'm calling the helicopter to take her and Mum to Raigmore. It is possible it's meningitis, but if so it's almost certainly viral—the least serious. Get her down to the medical centre at Gairloch immediately. We'll give her a shot of antibiotic just in case and then she'll be safe in hospital. The chopper will be here in fifteen or twenty minutes, but drive carefully. A screaming baby can make you panic. So don't. See you in a while.' She hung up.

Annie's eyes were enormous and frightened and full of tears as they got the flailing, screaming baby dressed again and buckled into her car seat. On David's instructions, she threw a toothbrush and some spare clothes into a bag and he tossed it into the boot as everyone scrambled into the car.

'I put the fish in the freezer,' Christopher said, his voice tremulous over Skye's screams. He and Seamus had come upstairs and had heard the phone call. 'What's menging—mengingthingy?'

'Brilliant boy!' David said, trying to reassure them. 'Otherwise we'd have had rotten fish to deal with on top of everything else.' He was driving fast and had to almost shout over the noise. 'Annie, ring my parents and tell them what's happening.' He suddenly remembered with a sinking heart that his parents had gone to Ullapool for the day. 'Then ring Hugh and Catherine. They'll take the boys home.'

'Where are you going? You can't leave us!' Seamus was sobbing.

'What's mengingtitus?' Christopher said, his voice high and frightened. 'Is it the same as Mum?' He clutched himself round his tummy.

David saw a flash of Annie's pallid face in the rear-view mirror. Her fear reflected his own.

'No!' she said urgently. 'It is not the same as your mum. Meningitis can be treated and hopefully Skye will be absolutely fine. It's just important that it's quick. She may not even have it—they just need to make sure.' She steadied the baby seat as the car rocked round a bend. 'You're going to see a helicopter up close. That'll be exciting.' Skye's screaming was ear-splitting and he could see frightened tears pouring down her face even as she tried to make her voice calm for the boys.

He wanted to tell her he wouldn't leave her and Skye, but the boys needed him too. He had no idea what his priority should be. Swinging on to the main road at Poolewe, he let the car rip, and they saw the helicopter power over them on its way to Gairloch.

Annie was shaking all over, but managed to ring Fiona and found them nearly back from Ullapool. Her disjointed explanations were fortified by the noise until suddenly Skye stopped screaming and Annie was shouting in a sudden silence.

'Oh God!' she said, horrified. The baby's eyes were open but glazed, and her flailing body suddenly floppy.

'We'll come to Gairloch,' he heard his mother say calmly over the loudspeaker. 'The doctor will look after the boys until we get there and we'll ring Hugh and Catherine. Concentrate on Skye.'

Seamus was hysterical. 'You can't go, Daddy. You can't leave us.'

His throat closed. He had had nightmares in the past about the boys drowning and having to choose one of his children to save because he could not save them both. This was the same nightmare of choice, but it was real this time. Huge racking sobs tore out of Christopher's chest every few seconds.

The silence was, if anything, more frightening than the screaming, but they were speeding down the steep hill into Gairloch and the helicopter was there in the middle of the field by the Medical Centre, its blades slowly turning.

The moment they were out of the car, the doctor gave Skye a rapid examination. As she straightened up, her syringe now empty, she smiled tautly at a shaking Annie.

'There! Pretty fast service, don't you think?' The doctor's outward calm belied the concern in her face and fear surged through him once more. She dealt with the needle and oversaw Skye and Annie installed safely with the para-medics. 'You'll be there very quickly, and they're all ready for you. A lumbar puncture looks horrible, but the baby won't notice. Try not to worry—this couldn't have been dealt with more quickly. You can go with them, David.' But both boys had a death grip on his trouser belt and Seamus was screaming in panic.

'Don't go, Daddy. Don't leave us. You can't go. Don't go.'

The doctor ducked away and he made his decision. Replacing the doctor briefly, he stretched out a hand to touch Skye's unresisting face. What if this was the last time he saw his daughter alive? His throat closed and tears pricked at his lids.

'Please come with us.' Fear had drained Annie's face of colour.

'I can't leave the boys in this state, but I'll be there as soon as I can. Be brave.' He choked on the words and as plainly as if he had hit her, he saw the pain of his choice in her eyes.

'Of course you can't leave them,' she said, and her voice steadied. 'They need you. We'll be fine.'

He kissed Annie's forehead hard, holding her face tightly between his palms, and backed away. She hadn't clung to him or asked him again. She had retreated behind some gracious, well-bred stiff upper lip, even if her daughter was dying.

The boys were inconsolable, both of them shaken with racking sobs by the terror and the speed of the drive and the screaming and then the chilling silence. The doctor gave David something to calm them and the sobs gradually abated as they clung to him and the tablets took effect. Fiona and Jem arrived with Hugh and Catherine and he was immensely grateful that the hysteria had passed and that they were eventually persuaded to go home with their grandparents.

Fiona was grimly calm. 'We'll phone Louise to make sure beds are ready, and Hugh is driving you to Inverness.'

On the way, the doctor rang with news that the lumbar puncture tested for viral meningitis, not bacterial, and that the prognosis was hopeful, even though Skye was still unconscious. There was no news from Annie, and her phone went to voicemail. David found himself unable to think.

He put his head in his hands and prayed incoherently, helplessly.

Hugh overtook an oil tanker at speed on a long straight. 'The doctor said Skye would be all right—she's in the right place and she'll get the right treatment.' David thought he sounded helpless too.

They drove in silence for a few miles and then Hugh said, as if he'd come to some conclusion after much thought, 'You know all the family really like Annie, don't you? I know she made a bad call, but don't we all, at one time or another? And I think she meant well, even if she didn't think it through.'

And I made a bad call. I made the call to stay with the boys and not go with Annie. I had to, but it was still a bad call. I turned away her effort to tell me she was pregnant. I had to, but it was still a bad call. I never apologised for that text from the cemetery or explained later. That was a bad call too.

He rolled his head towards his brother. 'You think she *meant* well? Not telling me she was pregnant with my child?'

He shut his eyes.

Hypocrite. I had more than a partial responsibility for Skye's existence, and for Annie's failure to tell me she was pregnant.

Seamus and Christopher's comments about Annie re-verberated round his skull, and he wondered how he could possibly reverse the tsunami of hurt that had engulfed them both.

'Why do I get the feeling that the entire family are on Annie's side, not mine?'

'We're not on anyone's *side*. We want the best for you and Skye and Annie.'

'Well, that's a big ask and not an easy one. My priority must be for Christopher and Seamus.' He was ashamed of his petulance, and his priority was not just for the boys, he realised. Annie and Skye had become equally important, and Skye being in such danger made him sick with desperation. What if she never recovered consciousness and died? What would that do to Annie and himself?

* * *

'Skye is stable,' Annie said exhaustedly when Charlotte phoned her, 'but they don't know if there has been any damage.' It was her turn to sleep at Louise's house while David stayed at the hospital. Louise dosed her with sleeping pills every other night.

'Both of us will come as soon as we possibly can.' Annie was aware that the reverberations of Rebecca's death were echoing in both Charlotte's and Will's heads.

'Mum, she's stable. You can't break your tour, I know you can't.'

'My darling, I can always break a wrist, then I'd have to.'

'Don't even go there.'

Will extracted himself from his meetings before Charlotte could, and he arrived first. Annie let herself be enveloped in his expansive, calm embrace, closing out the sight of David's tense, shuttered face, his palpable fear for Skye's life. The tension between them was like a rubber band at full stretch, and she was intensely relieved when he reluctantly left the ward to get them all a coffee. He hardly left Skye's side, sitting as close to her as he could, his finger lying in her tiny palm.

Will gazed down at his comatose granddaughter in her intensive care plastic box, tubes and cannulas sprouting from the little body.

'When will they know anything?'

Annie shrugged helplessly. 'I don't know. I don't know

what to do. Whatever the outcome, I can't live at Inveruidh, it's too remote.' And, she acknowledged, she had come
to hate and fear the remoteness she had once so loved.
'And David doesn't want me living in his house.' Putting
that bitter fact into words hurt almost physically. 'Even if
he changed his mind, I wouldn't. He loves Skye, but he
doesn't love me.' How was it possible to feel so rejected?
First Justin, and now David.

Will just held her.

'Jem and Fiona adore her, but obviously they have their
own lives to live. I think I'm going to come back to London.
Find somewhere to live. Find a job.' She turned towards
him, her shoulders sagging. 'Skye may be damaged, and
need to be near a hospital, doctors. I don't know.'

* * *

He and Annie had communicated for the past days purely
on practical subjects; who would stay with Skye when,
who would sleep at Louise's flat. She held herself in a taut
coolness, as if she might disintegrate if she conveyed any
emotion to him. He had watched her finding reassurance
in her father's arms and was consumed by jealousy and
regret, unable to comfort her even while he longed to do so.
She had retreated to some unreachable cold pinnacle, and
he knew that it was up to him to bring her down. Did she
think he blamed her for Skye's illness? He was fearful that
she would reject any apology or plea for understanding, so
he did not offer either.

Skye was out of danger, out of the Special Care Baby
Unit and back into the children's ward, her more frequent
wakeful moments alternating between bouts of crying—
which the staff said were caused by headaches—and
occasional grins, two pearly teeth gleaming in her lower

jaw, and one serrated edge pushing out from the top. The extraordinary love he had for this so-nearly-lost daughter sometimes choked him, and he spent as much time as he was allowed holding her in his arms.

At the weekend, Jem and Fiona brought the boys over to Inverness. Tom and Tilly came up from Edinburgh and took them Loch Ness Monster hunting.

He tackled the boys first. 'What would you think about Annie and Skye coming to live with us? I want to know what you really think, not what you think I want to hear.'

'I'd like it.' Seamus was definite. Christopher said nothing.

'Chris?' His heart sank, which was odd, as he hadn't realised what it was that he himself wanted. 'Do you think I'd forget about Mum? I wouldn't, you know.'

Surprisingly, Christopher shook his head. 'It's not that. I don't want you to be sad and if you don't like Annie and Annie doesn't like you, you will be, even if Skye's with us. We can't have Skye without Annie.'

David took a breath. 'No, Annie wouldn't leave her. I do like Annie, anyway.'

Christopher looked straight at him, grey eyes fierce. 'You don't show it. You make her cry sometimes. She doesn't know I know, but I do.'

David didn't ask how. Horrified, he heard the force of the accusation. 'And therefore Annie doesn't like me, is that it?'

Christopher's eyes slipped from his. 'I don't know.'

David rubbed his face with both hands. 'I didn't want a baby to change your life. You can't take a much younger child to football, or go fishing, or kayaking, or climbing.'

And Annie isn't Shona. Annie doesn't look like Shona, or speak like Shona, or dress like Shona or cook like Shona. Annie comes from a different planet, a planet of wealth and influence. Annie rubs shoulders with the rich and famous. He couldn't say any of that, but he also couldn't say that Shona was still uppermost in his mind, however hard he tried to make her so, because she wasn't. She had faded into fondness, into somewhere it didn't hurt so much not having her.

Seamus had lost interest in the conversation and Christopher kicked Louise's kitchen table leg with a sullen rhythm of trainer on wood. David got up and stared out at the River Ness flowing out on a full tide. When he turned back, both boys had gone, and the television blared from the sitting room.

He stared blankly at Louise's fridge, and thought about how Annie had been since coming to Inverasdale. How she seemed to have grown a hard shell, which he couldn't penetrate. She would smile with her mouth, but not with her eyes, and speak to him politely. When David and the boys visited, she would leave him with Skye while she played games with the boys or did household chores. Sometimes David took Skye for a walk, but in his heart, he knew she thought it was to make the point that he didn't want her company, not to give her respite from baby care. And in a way it was true. Her company was not the easy conversations and comfortable silences of their friendship before Skye's birth. It was forced conversations and awkward silences. He knew that she used to take Skye to Jem and Fiona's on mornings when he would be at work. He knew she used to walk the beaches, the empty roads and sometimes parts of the moorland, the baby snug in her backpack, either sleeping or thumping her fists on Annie's head. To all intents and purposes, a contented existence. But David could not shake his son's words from his head. 'You don't show that you like her.' Had he made Annie truly unhappy? Did she hate him? And if so, how could he change that?

As David stood at the ward door the next day, he looked

at Annie with Christopher's eyes as she sang nursery rhymes and made silly faces, making the baby squeak with laughter.

She looked up as he came in, removing a chunk of her hair from Skye's fingers.

'She's definitely better. Every hour she seems more alert.'

He nodded. 'I've just spoken to the Ward Sister. They seem to be happy with her progress and said she could probably be discharged tomorrow. She can go home, so long as she's checked regularly by the doctor.'

'Yes. Home. I've been thinking, and I've come to some conclusions.' She sounded firm and decisive and David's stomach lurched in sudden apprehension. She turned towards him, cradling Skye against her breast. 'I'm going to go back to London. I want to be within easy reach of a good hospital and I'll get a small house near a big park and a good school. Clapham Common, or Hampton maybe. Somewhere we can call home.'

Somewhere we can call home. It was a terrible and valid accusation. He had put her in rented accommodation, not in his home, even though his children would like them all to be together. That excuse, that the boys would mind, had been born of anger and pique. It was a bucket with no bottom.

'You can't leave! You can't take her!' The thought of them leaving caused an acute desolation.

'Why not?' She sounded polite, as if it was a general enquiry.

'But why?' he said. 'I thought you liked it here!' What a fatuously stupid remark that was.

'Did you?' Again, she was so polite. 'What did you think I liked? The single mother with the occasional visit from Dad bit? The remote location with a small baby bit? The opportunities for work bit? The fishing, the football, the really amazing supportive social network bit? The father who may love his daughter but has not an iota of affection for the mother.' She tilted her head questioningly. 'What's not to like?'

He stared at her wordlessly, the accusations like flung grit. His parents' unheeded warnings, his siblings' perplexity. Mhairi's silent disapproval, a disapproval not of Annie, he acknowledged now, but of him. Christopher's stern admonition. All ignored, all smothered, to protect him from the guilt of disloyalty to a dead wife. He had sown his anger with unforgiveness and knew he was about to reap the harvest.

After a few seconds she continued. 'I suppose it just hasn't crossed your mind, has it, that there was anything not to like? Well, I've done my best. Mhairi and your parents and Hugh and Catherine have been wonderful, and I like them a lot. Kate and Iain Mackinley ditto. And I love Christopher and Seamus. But I'm sorry, it simply isn't enough. I thought I could—what's the word—expiate my sins, but you've made it quite clear that I can't, and therefore I see no point in going on trying.' She straightened up in front of him and he had the impression of bare steel. 'You can come and see her, but it will be on my terms, not yours, and at my convenience, though I will do my best to accommodate you.' She handed Skye over to him gently. 'My reasons for not telling you I was pregnant were right, even if I handled it badly.'

Picking up her handbag and a pile of baby clothes for washing, she turned at the door and looked back at him. 'I wish I had told you a lie. Told you that you weren't the father. We'd both have been happier.'

When she had gone, he looked down at his daughter and knew that he had been the architect of a disaster that would haunt him for ever. The punishment he had meted out to Annie was about to be visited on him. Sitting in the ubiquitous hospital chair he sat Skye on his knees facing him and touched his forehead to hers. She grabbed at his hair before toppling in slow motion into his hands.

'What have I done?' he said to her. 'What the hell have I done?'

58

March 2014

Annie had never felt loneliness as she felt it these days. Hollow and floppy, as if all the stuffing had been pulled out of her. The house on the edge of Richmond Park was comfortable and had plenty of room, but she was restlessly incomplete. When her parents were in London it was a little better, but not much.

David came regularly to see them, but he didn't stay in the house, and she didn't ask him to. He had seemed preoccupied and sombre on his last few visits; she found him watching her, rather than watching or playing with Skye. She was always nervous before he arrived, tense while he was there, and miserably lonely the moment he left. She found the loneliness confusing because, with Skye, she wasn't alone and she was seemingly occupied twenty-four hours a day with many good friends. She made sure, with a fierce determination, that even through the permanent exhaustion from lack of sleep, she didn't drift into not bothering to put make-up on her now thin face or wear nice clothes on her now thin body or go out with friends. How did any mother cope with more than one child? Perhaps because there was a father to share the load. The hospital aftercare had been regular and re-assuring and although they had warned of the possibility of neurological problems later in Skye's life, the specialist had been comforting. 'Keep her head warm,' he had said, smiling, on discharging her.

Lifting a noisy Skye, she strapped her, fleece-cocooned, into the buggy. Outside, where the tree roots lifted the paving stones, the naked branches bent and clattered in a damp and bitter March wind, the dead leaves skittering and whirling across the street. She shivered at the thought of going into it, but it was no colder than the chill in her soul.

Leaning down she kissed Skye on the nose, through the furry hood of the coat that David had bought, before wrapping a scarf round her own neck. The baby beamed and whacked her legs up and down inside her footmuff bag.

'Right. We're off to have coffee with all your friends unless we get blown away before we get there.' She snuggled a blanket round Skye's face until just her grey eyes were showing. David's eyes. Everything about Skye reminded her of David, from the straight dark hair to her surprisingly long toes, and every time she was reminded, she missed him with a twisting pain deep inside. Stupidity and cowardice coupled with a foolish and imprudent decision had combined to destroy not just her future, but Skye's too.

The Toddler Café was their favourite destination. The mums had barista coffees and home-made cupcakes while automatically preventing children from pushing their peers off plastic rocking horses or hitting each other with toy saucepans. The babies crawled about on rugs and didn't seem to mind being tripped over by the older toddlers. The conversation was loud, frequently lewd, and always spiced with bad jokes and noisy laughter. It was Annie's favourite part of the day, with women who had become good and supportive friends. The part of the day without loneliness.

Annie had her back to the door when one of the mothers tapped her on the wrist.

'Annie, if I'm not mistaken, I think that's your guy at the door looking for you.'

'What!' She spun round in shock and lurched to her feet. 'David!' Turning back, she mumbled, 'Can you watch Skye a few minutes?'

'Sure. Don't worry about her. Keep calm, girl!'

It was ridiculous, the effect of seeing him unexpectedly. His next visit wasn't due for three weeks. Her mouth dried.

'David! Are you all right? Is something wrong? Is it Mhairi?'

'No, no. Everything's OK. When you weren't at home, I guessed you'd be here. I'm sorry I didn't ring, I forgot to charge my phone.' He looked nervous.

She wanted to put her arms round him but managed not to.

His eyes flicked to the noisy group of babies and he smiled when he saw Skye. 'Can we talk somewhere? A bit quieter?'

'Of course. Give me a minute to organise it.'

He knelt beside Skye, who regarded him solemnly for a moment before producing a toothy smile. Annie saw her curl her fingers around his forefingers and was assailed by a sudden cramping desire to be gripped by those same strong hands. She was comforted by assurances of childcare for the entire morning if necessary and tried to control her thumping heart.

'Mummies to the rescue,' he said as he helped her into her coat. 'I only met that one once and she recognised me immediately. Seared into her memory, obviously.'

Annie had recovered from the shock of his sudden appearance. 'Shall we go to the coffee shop next door where it's child-free? You won't miss out on Skye—unless you have to rush?'

'Child-free would be good. I need my head screwed on.'
He didn't look happy.

She frowned. 'That sounds ominous. Something is wrong, isn't it?' Cappuccinos poured, and a corner table procured, she waited apprehensively.

He put cold fingers round his hot cup, collecting his thoughts.

'There's lots wrong, Annie. But only with me.' She was horrified. Cancer. Motor Neurone Disease. Terminal—anything. He wasn't looking at her, and once again she wanted to touch him. To hold him. To be held.

Looking up, he saw her face. 'Sorry. I didn't mean anything physical.' There was a little pool of silence and then he drew a deep breath.

'I thought—I wondered if we could try a fresh start. Together.' He took another deep breath. 'Living as a family.' He raised his eyes to hers. 'Every time I see you—you have no idea how much I regret—I don't just miss Skye.' There was a sudden rush of words as if he'd pulled a plug out. 'I miss you. I miss everything about you. I miss loving you. It's you I want to share things with—thoughts and ideas and where to live and what to do and Skye's future, and how to handle teenage boys. All the things that need to be talked about and needs two people. When it's only me, I get it all wrong.' His mouth compressed. 'I got it all wrong.' He looked at her directly and she saw the pain in his eyes. 'And I was unbelievably stupid. I hurt you and need your forgiveness for what I said and did. Leaving you all alone to look after Skye, in a strange, unfriendly place, when we could all have been together as a family.' He closed his eyes briefly as if to shut out the past. 'I'm sorry. I'm really, really sorry.' He looked desolate. 'Could you think about a fresh start?'

A fresh start! As if she hadn't fantasised about a fresh start. She fantasised about never having made that enormous, terrible, stupid, life-changing bad decision not to tell him she was pregnant. Not to tell him that she loved him. She swallowed, her mouth dry again. He was hunting for the right words.

'When you left Scotland, I realised what I'd done. How unkind. How hostile. I've missed you. I see your face in windows, hear your voice in the silences, smell your scent on the wind.' He looked up, searching her face. 'You haunt me.'

He put his elbows on the table, his hands heeled over his eyes, the thick dark hair flopping over his fingers. She wondered if he was crying underneath them and touched his arm involuntarily. He put one hand over hers and lifted his head.

'I love you. I think I began loving you the night you tried to break into the cottage.' He smiled at the memory, and then sobered. 'But I never gave myself permission to love you. How could I be so attracted to someone when I was grieving for Shona, the mother of my children? It didn't make sense, and it didn't seem right.' He shook his head in bewilderment. 'And then I thought about your parents. I went to see your father a few weeks ago—' Annie straightened in surprise. Will had never mentioned it.

'We talked. When your mother died, it wasn't your father's fault and he didn't wallow in guilt. He married again, and within eighteen months. He loved Rebecca and he loved you, but it didn't stop him loving Charlotte and you love her too. He asked me what made my situation so different that I shouldn't fall in love again and have a whole family? He made me question all my thinking. All my guilt. Why should it be wrong to move on from Shona's death? Her cancer wasn't my fault. It wasn't anybody's fault, and I know she'd want me and the boys to be happy. And I'm not. I feel absolutely desperate without you. I've been utterly miserable.'

There was a huge lump in her throat threatening to choke her. She tried to swallow it away.

'Me too. I've been miserable too. All my stupid decisions, the mess I made of everything.' She blinked away tears, embarrassed to lose control in a public place, and gulped coffee, trying for a less emotional topic, wondering whether the sadness she had sensed on his last visits had been the precursor to this unexpected one.

'Have you talked to Christopher and Seamus?'

'Yes. I said I was coming to talk to you and they were pleased. They obviously know I'm thinking of moving— getting a proper job, finding a new school. But—' he lifted his eyes to hers again, his face sombre, 'I didn't think you felt anything for me any more, and I didn't want to raise their hopes.'

Astonishment made her blink.

'Raise their hopes? Hopes of what?'

He rubbed his fingertips up his cheeks. 'They've always wanted you and Skye to live with us. When you were at Inveruidh they couldn't understand why we couldn't all be together. And I couldn't explain that I'd fallen in love with you—I couldn't explain how disloyal I felt about Shona. How I'd let someone else take the place of their mother so quickly.' He hesitated. 'It felt as if I was rubbing Shona out of our lives. But Seamus said, 'Mum is Mum and Annie is Annie.' Oh God! I should have listened. The boys are miserable and difficult because—' He frowned, searching for the reason.

'—because you are?'

He glanced at her with a glimmering smile. 'Yes, I think so. I certainly hope it's not just bloody-mindedness. If it is, they may be hell for the next ten years.'

'And the job?'

'I've been looking. After Shona died, I left my job and went to Wester Ross because everything in Edinburgh had her in it. Everything I touched, she'd touched. The kitchen was how she organised it, she'd chosen everything in the flat. I just couldn't bear it. You asked me once if I was running away, and I suppose I was. But you can't run away from memories. Or responsibilities.' He glanced at her sideways, seeming a little ashamed. 'I told myself I needed to distance myself from the stress of her illness and how it had affected us. I told myself that less pressure, jobs without the management hassle, would be good for all of us, with my parents taking some of the strain.' His shoulders dropped. 'I told myself Tom and Tilly needed to grieve in peace, without having to support me and the boys.' His hands opened in a gesture of defeat. Or perhaps an admission of failure, Annie thought.

'Were you wrong?'

'Maybe. I don't know. Probably.' He straightened his back. 'I think I was deluding myself. I need to stop running away, to focus on the future, start a new life. I'm not using my brain, but even if I was—' he gave a harsh little laugh '—I wouldn't be happy, not even content. And that's because you aren't there.' His hand tightened on hers. 'I've had an offer from a company based in Wimbledon which sounds genuinely interesting. I wasn't going to accept it until I'd talked to you.' He held her eyes. 'You aren't turning down the idea—of us? Being together?'

She looked at him for a long moment.

'No. I'm not turning it down. Not at all. But this is pretty sudden, for me anyway. I'd been so stupid. And such a coward. I didn't think you could possibly forgive me. Or love me.'

The self-reproach that had been with her from the moment of discovering she was pregnant, through her miserable time in Scotland and Skye's illness, almost overwhelmed her. After all this time, was it possible that his anger and hurt could have turned to loving her again?

I need time to think this through—time to work out how it could be put together. No, you don't. You don't need any time at all. This is what you've been wishing for. Praying for. Longing for. Dreaming of. How can this have suddenly all happened? She studied his face carefully, seeing, as if for the first time, the anxious grey eyes under the dark, rather badly cut, hair. The presently unused laughter lines, the straight flared nose, the firm mouth in the clean-shaven jaw. The lips that had given her such delight, such bliss.

He looked devastated by her hesitation. 'Annie, it's not just me that loves you. Well, I'm the only one that loves you in that particular way—but the whole family love you, and they love Skye. We could make this work—we could try to make it work—for everyone's sake. You, me, the kids, past generations and present, and future.' The apprehension was clear in his expression. 'The big if is whether you can forgive me after how I've behaved, or whether you could even try. Whether you can love me again, after all that's happened.'

She sniffed. The lump had moved to her chest and threatened to burst out of it.

'You seem to have forgiven me for all my bad judgements. I do love you. I loved you from the beginning—well, not the burglary bit—it was because I loved you I made that stupid decision.'

She gripped her coffee cup hard enough to shatter it and heaved in a choked breath.

'I've missed you every day. I've been miserable and lonely. I think of you all the time. Skye reminds me of you every day. I think about her not having a dad around. Not having all her family around.' She put the cup carefully back in the saucer, trying not to rattle it. 'We can't just brush all the past under the carpet and pretend it never happened. We'd have to sort it out.'

He glanced at her slantwise, his smile crooked. 'I believe

we've already started to lift the carpet and chuck out the debris.'

She looked back at him uncertainly. 'I'm quite tidy too. A spring clean is quite cathartic I think.' She rubbed her face again. 'Loving someone is quite complicated, isn't it? And I suppose making mistakes is part of being human. The trick is to learn from them, I guess.' She brought herself back down to earth. 'I should go and retrieve Skye. She gets tetchy when she's tired and she still has a mid-morning nap. Can you come back with us?'

David put his hand in hers between the coffee shop and the Toddlers Café and a warm sense of happiness began to flood into her heart, washing out the lump. Her own hand tightened on his.

As David pushed the buggy, the wind blew stronger and colder in their faces, icy rain beginning to patter from the lead-grey sky. Under the rain cover, the child slept in her sleeping bag.

Closing the front door, they dropped their wet coats on the hall chair, and he took Annie in his arms and let her rest against him. After the clamour of the chilly wind, the silence of the house was soothing. The warmth of his body enclosed her as she lifted her face to his.

She was coming in from a long time in the cold.

E N D

Sources and Bibliography

The Road to Russia: Arctic Convoys 1942-45
Bernard Edwards

My Sea Lady: an epic account of the Arctic convoys
Graeme Ogden

Loch Ewe during World War 2
Steve Chadwick

Most of the place names in Wester Ross are actual, but I have tended to simplify locations i.e. I have written Cove where locals would expect Rubha nan Sasan, or Gairloch where they would know it is Strath I mean! This is in the interests of those who do not know the area and might become confused by too many place names. The school references are also fictitious and comments about it from book characters serve only the plot. I have also taken licence with the actual location of the Indian camp near Inverasdale, and some of the military checkpoints, again for plot purposes. The convoy dates are correct, but it is unlikely that Lt. John Elliott would have been in the same ship for so many convoys, so please forgive this 'bending' of naval postings.

Thank You

Thank you for reading *Come In From The Cold* and I hope you enjoyed it. If you did, please do post a review on Amazon or Goodreads or share any enthusiasm on your Facebook page. That would be wonderful as reviews as very valuable to authors!

I write because I love writing, but my reason for publishing this story, as it was for my previous novel, Dolphin Days, is to raise funds for a charity called 'An African Dream'.

In 1997 Mark Wynter felt a call from God to go to work in Western Uganda. In 1998 he married our daughter Sophie and while in the UK for the birth of their first son, Mark was re-diagnosed with cancer. He died aged 31 in 2005 just after their second son was born. Sophie set up 'An African Dream' in his memory and although she now lives in the UK, she is still much involved with the charity and visits Uganda regularly.

'An African Dream' built St Mark's primary school and provides education for about 400 children, mainly orphans, and also funds the teachers' salaries. It supports health days for the community, sponsors a huge teen development ministry, and provides training and micro-enterprise opportunities for widows. It also funds training for Christian pastors, all in partnership with the local church in East Kasese.

If you would like further information, (or if you'd like to sponsor one of the gorgeous children!), please contact

Mrs Sophie Campbell-Wynter
Email: info@aaduganda.org
www.aaduganda.org
Registered Charity No: 1123231
Twitter and Facebook @aaduganda

Acknowledgements

Above all, my thanks go to my editor Kia Thomas, for her patience and wide angled vision in restructuring the timelines of the story. It had become as complicated as a wind-knotted salmon cast and I could never have untangled it alone. And to Hilary Johnson, who proofread, copy edited and line edited amongst the greyhounds.

To Jane Dixon Smith of JD Smith Design, who created the lovely cover and formatted the book content.

To Alex Gray of Wordworks, Gairloch for the reproduction of his map of Loch Ewe and to Steve Chadwick for his kind permission to reproduce it from his book *Loch Ewe during World War 2.*

To the members of my writing groups, Write On Hants and We Write Stuff for listening patiently and for their constructive criticism. To my Romantic Novelists Association readers for their advice and encouragement.

My thanks go to Helena Bowie in Wester Ross for her sharp proof-reading eyes and encouraging enthusiasm.

And finally, to my patient husband who never complains about being left to fend for himself when I am writing. And quite often cooks.

About the Author

I grew up in lots of places, being a naval daughter, but home was always a fabulous house buried in the woods above the Tweed valley in the Borders of Scotland. It seemed to be a childhood of summer sun and winter snow and ice, of rough ponies, cats, dogs, the river and in hindsight, huge amounts of risk and freedom for me and my three older brothers.

I trained as a secretary at The House of Citizenship and worked for a software house (early days of computers!) before going, in 1966, to live in Kampala, Uganda for two years, as PA to the Dean of Makerere University.

Forty years later my daughter went to Uganda with her husband Mark and 'An African Dream' was born. Any royalties from the sale of Come In From the Cold are going to that charity.

I now live with my patient, supportive husband in a retirement village near Southampton, about half-way between our son and daughter and seven grandchildren. We travel mainly in Europe now, due to age and balance, our favourite places being an island in Greece (where my first novel, *Dolphin Days*, is set) and a cottage near Loch Ewe in Wester Ross, Scotland where *Come In From The Cold* was conceived.

Also by Charlotte Milne

Dolphin Days

Lightning Source UK Ltd.
Milton Keynes UK
UKHW010918310120
357948UK00001B/91